SMOKE GHOST

AND OTHER APPARITIONS

SMOKE GHOST
AND OTHER APPARITIONS

FRITZ LEIBER

OPEN ROAD
INTEGRATED MEDIA
NEW YORK

Copyright © 2001 by The Estate of Fritz Leiber,
2001 by John Pelan, 2001 by Steve Savile, 2001 Ramsey Campbell

ISBN 978-1-4976-4219-5

This edition published in 2014 by Open Road Integrated Media, Inc.
345 Hudson Street
New York, NY 10014
www.openroadmedia.com

SMOKE GHOST

AND OTHER APPARITIONS

ACKNOWLEDGMENTS

The editors would like to acknowledge the invaluable assistance of Susan Chernauskas, David Read, Stefan Dziemianowicz, Darrell Schweitzer, Allen Koszowski, Jim Rockhill, Peter Enfantino, Brian Metz of Green Rhino Graphics, and most especially Julie Grob of the Special Collections Department at the University of Houston for their help in the preparation of this volume.

CONTENTS

INTRODUCTION

"NOR WILL SCIENCE ever be able to kill the feelings of wonder in the human spirit. The mystery of the black outer gulfs, and of the deepest cognitive processes within us, must always remain unplumbed—and against these imagination must always frantically pound..."

So wrote H. P. Lovecraft to his young correspondent Fritz Leiber on 19 December 1936, somewhat less than three months before his own death. Lovecraft had sought to educate his new friend in the classics of the various imaginative genres, from M. R. James through Lord Dunsany all the way to Olaf Stapledon. Like Lovecraft, Leiber would base his writing on this study and use the knowledge to unite British and American methods in developing—what exactly? Quite a few of his tales seem to occupy a territory that is purely his. We shall encounter some in the present collection, though it's devoted to the supernatural and macabre.

It takes its title from one of his radical tales, in which the modern urban environment is the source of the supernatural rather than being invaded. Here and in "The Hill and the Hole" there's more than a touch of M. R. James at his most reticent, but nobody could mistake the tales for imitations. They first saw pulp publication, as did "The Power of the Puppets". Here one may detect a yellowing smell, but the blend of *noir* fiction and the supernatural has life in it yet, and deserves its resurrection. By contrast, the later "Cry Witch!" feels based on folklore, though its haunting eroticism is typical of Fritz. The erotic is more openly expressed in "The Enormous Bedroom", which progresses in a series of tableaux reminiscent of a perverse MGM musical.

I like to think that "Black Glass" may have derived from Fritz's stay in New York around the 1976 World Fantasy Convention, after which occasion he delighted a party at Jack Sullivan's apartment with a reading of "Little Old Miss Macbeth". When we walked him to the subway the notion of his travelling alone worried my wife, but he was forever adventurous. The setting of the climax of "Black Glass" at the top of the World Trade Center above a devastated city is far too poignant now. Nevertheless the tale was one of his most evocative transformations of an urban landscape into a vista of fantastic menace, though let me hear no talk of prescience.

"I'm Looking for Jeff" mates *noir* and supernatural to create an apparition as lyrically sexual as it is eerie: M. R. James wouldn't have cared for it at all. "The Eeriest Ruined Dawn World" is a post-apocalyptic elegy; perhaps a distant echo of Donald Wandrei may be heard. Like "Jeff", "The Winter Flies" is an alcoholic's tale, though I hesitate to suggest how much of its unique Leiberesque surrealism may derive from that state. "Replacement for Wilmer" seems to reminisce about the condition too, with an affection that doesn't preclude criticism, while it subtly evokes the spectral.

"The House of Mrs. Delgato" is ingenious and, as you'll see when you finish it, very Fritz, if minor. I imagine Jeffrey Archer would like it. "The Black Ewe", on the other hand, takes on the future as an unknowable nightmare. Although it was published in *Startling Stories*, it can be seen as anti-science, though perhaps that isn't singular in that magazine. It demonstrates how Fritz was as much at home with science fiction as fantasy and horror, not a common range. "Richmond, Late September, 1849" is equally at ease with the past, and offers an ingeniously visionary interpretation both of Poe's tales and of his fascination with the mysterious feminine, one of the threads of the present book and indeed of Fritz's career.

Two stories venture onto Robert Bloch's psychological territory, though "MS. Found in a Maelstrom" is even darker and more tortured—not least in its prose—than Bob generally got, while "Do You Know Dave Wenzel?" is surely seminal in showing an everyday marriage psychotically invaded from within. "A Visitor from Back East" might have been written to demonstrate Lovecraft's contention that if "atmosphere is genuine while it lasts", a final rationalisation need not rob apparently supernatural images of their power. "Dark Wings" is an unqualified fantasy, but rooted in Jung. When I bought it for my first anthology, Fritz mentioned that he hoped to see it produced as a play; alas, I'm not aware that it was. As for "The Button Molder", which I take out of sequence in order to end with it, it represents Fritz's relaxed later mode. A story both discursive and precise, it deals with a ghost but touches on science fiction too, and is one of his most openly autobiographical tales.

On with the feast! This book demonstrates not only Fritz's scope but also that of horror fiction at its best, to the development of which he was crucial. I was privileged to meet the man, but those who know only the work may learn a good deal about him—a gentle and generous spirit, and a great dreamer. He left us much to build upon.

Ramsey Campbell
Wallasey, Merseyside
1 October 2001

SMOKE GHOST

MISS MILLICK WONDERED just what had happened to Mr. Wran. He kept making the strangest remarks when she took dictation. Just this morning he had quickly turned around and asked, "Have you ever seen a ghost, Miss Millick?" And she had tittered nervously and replied, "When I was a girl there was a thing in white that used to come out of the closet in the attic bedroom when I slept there, and moan. Of course it was just my imagination. I was frightened of lots of things." And he had said, "I don't mean that kind of ghost. I mean a ghost from the world today, with the soot of the factories on its face and the pounding of machinery in its soul. The kind that would haunt coal yards and slip around at night through deserted office buildings like this one. A real ghost. Not something out of books." And she hadn't known what to say.

He'd never been like this before. Of course he might be joking, but it didn't sound that way. Vaguely Miss Millick wondered whether he mightn't be seeking some sort of sympathy from her. Of course, Mr. Wran was married and had a little child, but that didn't prevent her from having daydreams. The daydreams were not very exciting, still they helped fill up her mind. But now he was asking her another of those unprecedented questions.

"Have you ever thought what a ghost of our times would look like, Miss Millick? Just picture it. A smoky composite face with the hungry anxiety of the unemployed, the neurotic restlessness of the person without purpose, the jerky tension of the high-pressure metropolitan worker, the uneasy resentment of the striker, the callous opportunism of the scab, the aggressive whine of the panhandler, the inhibited terror of the bombed civilian, and a thousand other twisted emotional patterns. Each one overlying and yet blending with the other, like a pile of semi-transparent masks?"

Miss Millick gave a little self-conscious shiver and said, "That would be terrible. What an awful thing to think of."

She peered furtively across the desk. Was he going crazy? She remembered having heard that there had been something impressively abnormal about Mr. Wran's childhood, but she couldn't recall what it was. If only she could do something—laugh at his mood or ask him what was really wrong. She shifted the extra pencils in her left hand and mechanically traced over some of the shorthand curlicues in her notebook.

"Yet, that's just what such a ghost or vitalized projection would look like, Miss Millick," he continued, smiling in a tight way. "It would grow out of the real world. It would reflect all the tangled, sordid, vicious, things. All the loose ends. And it would be very grimy. I don't think it would seem white or wispy or favour graveyards. It wouldn't moan. But it would mutter unintelligibly, and twitch at your sleeve. Like a sick, surly ape. What would such a thing want from a person, Miss Millick? Sacrifice? Worship? Or just fear? What could you do to stop it from troubling you?"

Miss Millick giggled nervously. There was an expression beyond her powers of definition in Mr. Wran's ordinary, flat-cheeked, thirtyish face, silhouetted against the dusty window. He turned away and stared out into the grey downtown atmosphere that rolled in from the railroad yards and the mills. When he spoke again his voice sounded far away.

"Of course, being immaterial, it couldn't hurt you physically—at first. You'd have to be peculiarly sensitive even to see it, or be aware of it at all. But it would begin to influence your actions. Make you do this. Stop you from doing that. Although only a projection, it would gradually get its hooks into the world of things as they are. Might even get control of suitably vacuous minds. Then it could hurt whomever it wanted."

Miss Millick squirmed and read back her shorthand, like the books said you should do when there was a pause. She became aware of the failing light and wished Mr. Wran would ask her to turn on the overhead. She felt scratchy, as if soot were sifting down on to her skin.

"It's a rotten world, Miss Millick," said Mr. Wran, talking at the window. "Fit for another morbid growth of superstition. It's time the ghosts, or whatever you call them, took over and began a rule of fear. They'd be no worse than men."

"But"—Miss Millick's diaphragm jerked, making her titter inanely—"of course there aren't any such things as ghosts."

Mr. Wran turned around.

"Of course there aren't Miss Millick," he said in a loud, patronizing voice, as if she had been doing the talking rather than he. "Science and common sense and psychiatry all go to prove it."

She hung her head and might even have blushed if she hadn't felt so all at sea. Her leg muscles twitched, making her stand up, although she hadn't intended to. She aimlessly rubbed her hand back and forth along the edge of the desk.

"Why, Mr. Wran, look what I got off your desk," she said, showing him a heavy smudge. There was a note of clumsily playful reproof in her voice. "No wonder the copy I bring you always gets so black. Somebody ought to talk to those scrubwomen. They're skimping on your room."

She wished he would make some normal joking reply. But instead he drew back and his face hardened.

"Well, to get back to that business of the second class mailing privileges," he rapped out harshly, and began to dictate.

When she was gone he jumped up, dabbed his finger experimentally at the smudged part of the desk, frowned worriedly at the almost inky smears. He jerked open a drawer, snatched out a rag, hastily swabbed off the desk, crumpled the rag into a ball and tossed it back. There were three or four other rags in the drawer, each impregnated with soot.

Then he strode over to the window and peered out anxiously through the gathering dusk, his eyes searching the panorama of roofs, fixing on each chimney and water tank.

"It's a neurosis. Must be compulsions. Hallucinations," he muttered to himself in a tired, distraught voice that would have made Miss Millick gasp. "It's that damned mental abnormality cropping up in a new form. Can't be any other explanation. But it's so damned real. Even the soot. Good thing I'm seeing the psychiatrist. I don't think I could force myself to get on the elevated tonight -" His voice trailed off, he rubbed his eyes, and his memory automatically started to grind.

It had all begun on the elevated. There was a particular little sea of roofs he had grown into the habit of glancing at just as the packed car carrying him homeward lurched around a turn. A dingy, melancholy little world of tar-paper, tarred gravel, and smoky brick. Rusty tin chimneys with odd conical hats suggested abandoned listening posts. There was a washed-out advertisement of some ancient patent medicine on the nearest wall. Superficially it was like ten thousand other drab city roofs. But he always saw it around dusk, either in the smoky half-light, or tinged with red by the flat rays of a dirty sunset, or covered by ghostly wind-blown white sheets of rain-splash, or patched with blackish snow; and it seemed unusually bleak and suggestive, almost beautifully ugly, though in no sense picturesque; dreary, but meaningful. Unconsciously it came to symbolize for Catesby Wran certain disagreeable aspects of the frustrated, frightened century in which he lived, the jangled century of hate and heavy industry and total wars. The quick, daily glance into the half darkness became an integral part of his life. Oddly, he never saw it in the morning, for it was then his habit to sit on the other side of the car, his head buried in the paper.

One evening toward winter he noticed what seemed to be a shapeless black sack lying on the third roof from the tracks. He did not think about it. It merely registered as an addition to the well-known scene and his memory stored away the impression for further reference. Next evening, however, he decided he had been mistaken in one detail. The object was a roof nearer than he had thought. Its colour and texture, and the grimy stains around it, suggested that it was filled with coal dust, which was hardly reasonable. Then, too, the following evening it seemed to have been blown against a rusty ventilator by the wind—which could hardly have happened if it were at all heavy. Perhaps it was filled with leaves. Catesby was surprised to find himself anticipating his next daily glance with a minor note of apprehension. There was something unwholesome in the posture of the thing that stuck in his mind—a bulge in the sacking that suggested a misshapen head peering around the ventilator. And his apprehension was justified, for that evening the thing was on the nearest roof, though on the farther side, looking as if it had just flopped down over the low brick parapet.

Next evening the sack was gone. Catesby was annoyed at the momentary feeling of relief that went through him, because the whole matter seemed too unimportant to warrant feelings of any sort. What difference did it make if his imagination had played tricks on him, and he'd fancied that the object was crawling and hitching itself slowly closer across the roofs? That was the way any normal imagination worked. He deliberately chose to disregard the fact that there were reasons for thinking his imagination was by no means a normal one. As he walked home from the elevated, however, he found himself wondering whether the sack was really gone. He seemed to recall a vague, smudgy trail leading across the gravel to the nearer side of the roof, which was marked by a parapet. For an instant an unpleasant picture formed in his mind—that of an inky humped creature crouched behind the parapet, waiting. Then he dismissed the whole subject.

The next time he felt the familiar grating lurch of the car, he caught himself trying not to look out. That angered him. He turned his head quickly. When he turned it back his compact face was definitely pale. There had only been time for a fleeting rearward glance at the escaping roof. Had he actually seen in silhouette the upper part of a head of some sort peering over the parapet? Nonsense, he told himself. And even if he had seen something, there were a thousand explanations which did not involve the supernatural or even true hallucination. Tomorrow he would take a good look and clear up the whole matter. If necessary, he would visit the roof personally, though he hardly knew where to find it and disliked in any case the idea of pampering a silly fear.

He did not relish the walk home from the elevated that evening, and visions of the thing disturbed his dreams and were in and out of his mind all next day at the office. It was then that he first began to relieve his nerves by making jokingly serious remarks about the supernatural to Miss Millick, who seemed properly mystified. It was on the same day, too, that he became aware of a growing antipathy to grime and soot. Everything he touched seemed gritty, and he found himself mopping and wiping at his desk like an old lady with a morbid fear of germs. He reasoned that there was no real change in his office, and that he'd just now become sensitive to the dirt that had always been there, but there was no denying an increasing nervousness. Long before the car reached the curve, he was straining his eyes through the murky twilight, determined to take in every detail.

Afterward he realized that he must have given a muffled cry of some sort, for the man beside him looked at him curiously, and the woman ahead gave him an unfavorable stare. Conscious of his own pallor and uncontrollable trembling, he stared back at them hungrily, trying to regain the feeling of security he had completely lost. They were the usual reassuringly wooden-faced people everyone rides home with on the elevated. But suppose he had pointed out to one of them what he had seen—that sodden, distorted face of sacking and coal dust, that boneless paw which waved back and forth, unmistakably in his direction, as if reminding him of a future appointment—he involuntarily shut his eyes tight. His thoughts were racing ahead to tomorrow evening. He pictured this same windowed oblong of light and packed humanity surging around the curve— then an opaque monstrous form leaping out from the roof in a parabolic swoop—an unmentionable face pressed close against the window, smearing it with wet coal dust -huge paws fumbling sloppily at the glass -

Somehow he managed to turn off his wife's anxious inquiries. Next morning he reached a decision and made an appointment for that evening with a psychiatrist a friend had told him about. It cost him a considerable effort, for Catesby had a well-grounded distaste for anything dealing with psychological abnormality. Visiting a psychiatrist meant raking up an episode in his past which he had never fully described even to his wife. Once he had made the decision, however, he felt considerably relieved. The psychiatrist, he told himself, would clear everything up. He could almost fancy him saying, "Merely a bad case of nerves. However, you must consult the oculist whose name I'm writing down for you, and you must take two of these pills in water every four hours," and so on. It was almost comforting, and made the coming revelation he would have to make seem less painful.

But as the smoky dust rolled in, his nervousness returned and he let his joking mystification of Miss Millick run away with him until he realized that he wasn't frightening anyone but himself.

He would have to keep his imagination under better control, he told himself, as he continued to peer out restlessly at the massive, murky shapes of the downtown office buildings. Why, he had spent the whole afternoon building up a kind of neo-medieval cosmology of superstition. It wouldn't do. He realized then that he had been standing at the window much longer than he'd thought, for the glass panel in the door was dark and there was no noise coming from the outer office. Miss Millick and the rest must have gone home.

It was then he made the discovery that there would have been no special reason for dreading the swing around the curve that night. It was, as it happened, a horrible discovery. For, on the shadowed roof across the street and four stories below, he saw the thing huddle and roll across the gravel and, after one upward look of recognition, merge into the blackness beneath the water tank.

As he hurriedly collected his things and made for the elevator, fighting the panicky impulse to run, he began to think of hallucination and mild psychosis as very desirable conditions. For better or for worse, he pinned all his hopes on the psychiatrist.

* * * *

"So you find yourself growing nervous and ... er ... jumpy, as you put it," said Dr. Trevethick, smiling with dignified geniality. "Do you notice any more definite physical symptoms? Pain? Headache? Indigestion?"

Catesby shook his head and wet his lips. "I'm especially nervous while riding in the elevated," he murmured swiftly.

"I see. We'll discuss that more fully. But I'd like you first to tell me something you mentioned earlier. You said there was something about your childhood that might predispose you to nervous ailments. As you know, the early years are critical ones in the development of an individual's behaviour pattern."

Catesby studied the yellow reflections of frosted globes in the dark surface of the desk. The palm of his left hand aimlessly rubbed the thick nap of the armchair. After a while he raised his head and looked straight into the doctor's small brown eyes.

"From perhaps my third to my ninth year," he began choosing the words with care, "I was what you might call a sensory prodigy."

The doctor's expression did not change. "Yes?" he inquired politely.

"What I mean is that I was supposed to be able to see through walls, read letters through envelopes and books through their covers, fence and play ping-pong blindfolded, find things that were buried, read thoughts." The words tumbled out.

"And could you?" The doctor's expression was toneless.

"I don't know. I don't suppose so," answered Catesby, long-lost emotions flooding back into his voice. "It's all confused now. I thought I could, but then they were always encouraging me. My mother ... was ... well ... interested in psychic phenomena. I was ... exhibited. I seem to remember seeing things other people couldn't. As if most opaque objects were transparent. But I was very young. I didn't have any scientific criteria for judgment."

He was reliving it now. The darkened rooms. The earnest assemblages of gawking, prying adults. Himself sitting alone on a little platform, lost in a straight-backed wooden chair. The black silk handkerchief over his eyes. His mother's coaxing, insistent questions. The whispers. The gasps. His own hate of the whole business, mixed with hunger for the adulation of adults. Then the scientists from the university, the experiments, the big test. The reality of those memories engulfed him and momentarily made him forget the reason why he was disclosing them to a stranger.

"Do I understand that your mother tried to make use of you as a medium for communicating with the ... er ... other world?"

Catesby nodded eagerly.

"She tried to, but she couldn't. When it came to getting in touch with the dead, I was a complete failure. All I could do—or thought I could do—was see real, existing, three-dimensional objects beyond the vision of normal people. Objects anyone could have seen except for distance, obstruction, or darkness. It was always a disappointment to mother."

He could hear her sweetish patient voice saying, "Try

again, dear, just this once. Katie was your aunt. She loved
you. Try to hear what she's saying." And he had answered,
"I can see a woman in a blue dress standing on the other side
of Dick's house." And she replied, "Yes, I know, dear. But
that's not Katie. Katie's a spirit. Try again. Just this once,
dear." The doctor's voice gently jarred him back into the
softly gleaming office.

"You mentioned scientific criteria for judgement, Mr.
Wran. As far as you know, did anyone ever try to apply them
to you?"

Catesby's nod was emphatic.

"They did. When I was eight, two young psychologists
from the university got interested in me. I guess they did it
for a joke at first, and I remember being very determined
to show them I amounted to something. Even now I seem
to recall how the note of polite superiority and amused
sarcasm drained out of their voices. I suppose they decided
at first that it was very clever trickery, but somehow they
persuaded mother to let them try me out under controlled
conditions. There were lots of tests that seemed very
businesslike after mother's slipshod little exhibitions. They
found I was clairvoyant—or so they thought. I got worked
up and on edge. They were going to demonstrate my super-
normal sensory powers to the university psychology faculty.
For the first time I began to worry about whether I'd come
through. Perhaps they kept me going at too hard a pace, I
don't know. At any rate, when the test came, I couldn't do a
thing. Everything became opaque. I got desperate and made
things up out of my imagination. I lied. In the end I failed
utterly, and I believe the two young psychologists got into a
lot of hot water as a result."

He could hear the brusque, bearded man saying, "You've
been taken in by a child, Flaxman, a mere child. I'm
greatly disturbed. You've put yourself on the same plane
as common charlatans. Gentlemen, I ask you to banish
from your minds this whole sorry episode. It must never
be referred to." He winced at the recollection of his feeling
of guilt. But at the same time he was beginning to feel

exhilarated and almost light-hearted. Unburdening his long-repressed memories had altered his whole viewpoint. The episodes on the elevated began to take on what seemed their proper proportions as merely the bizarre workings of overwrought nerves and an overly suggestible mind. The doctor, he anticipated confidently, would disentangle the obscure subconscious causes, whatever they might be. And the whole business would be finished off quickly, just as his childhood experience—which was beginning to seem a little ridiculous now—had been finished off.

"From that day on," he continued, "I never exhibited a trace of my supposed powers. My mother was frantic and tried to sue the university. I had something like a nervous breakdown. Then the divorce was granted, and my father got custody of me. He did his best to make me forget it. We went on long outdoor vacations and did a lot of athletics, associated with normal, matter-of-fact people. I went to business college eventually. I'm in advertising now. But," Catesby paused, "now that I'm having nervous symptoms, I've wondered if there mightn't be a connection. It's not a question of whether I really was clairvoyant or not. Very likely my mother taught me a lot of unconscious deceptions, good enough to fool even young psychology instructors. But don't you think it may have some important bearing on my present condition?"

For several moments the doctor regarded him with a slightly embarrassing professional frown. Then he said quietly, "And is there some ... er ... more specific connection between your experiences then and now? Do you by any chance find that you are once again beginning to ... er ... see things?"

Catesby swallowed. He had felt an increasing eagerness to unburden himself of his fears, but it was not easy to make a beginning, and the doctor's shrewd question rattled him. He forced himself to concentrate. The thing he thought he had seen on the roof loomed up before his inner eye with unexpected vividness. Yet it did not frighten him. He groped for words.

Then he saw that the doctor was not looking at him but over his shoulder. Colour was draining out of the doctor's face and his eyes did not seem so small. Then the doctor sprang to his feet, walked past Catesby, threw open the window and peered into the darkness.

As Catesby rose, the doctor slammed down the window and said in a voice whose smoothness was marred by a slight, persistent gasping, "I hope I haven't alarmed you. I must have frightened him, for he seems to have gotten out of sight in a hurry. Don't give it another thought. Doctors are frequently bothered by *voyeurs* ... er ... Peeping Toms."

"A Negro?" asked Catesby, moistening his lips.

The doctor laughed nervously. "I imagine so, though my first odd impression was that it was a white man in blackface. You see, the colour didn't seem to have any brown in it. It was dead-black."

Catesby moved toward the window. There were smudges on the glass. "It's quite all right, Mr. Wran." The doctor's voice had acquired a sharp note of impatience, as if he were trying hard to reassume his professional authority. "Let's continue our conversation. I was asking you if you were"— he made a face—"seeing things."

Catesby's whirling thoughts slowed down and locked into place. "No, I'm not seeing anything that other people don't see, too. And I think I'd better go now. I've been keeping you too long." He disregarded the doctor's half-hearted gesture of denial. "I'll phone you about the physical examination. In a way you've already taken a big load off my mind." He smiled woodenly. "Good night, Dr. Trevethick."

* * * *

Catesby Wran's mental state was a peculiar one. His eyes searched every angular shadow, he glanced sideways down each chasm-like alley and barren basement passageway, and kept stealing looks at the irregular line of the roofs, yet he was hardly conscious of where he was going. He pushed away the thoughts that came into his mind, and kept moving. He became aware of a slight sense of security as he turned into a lighted street where there were people and high buildings and blinking signs. After a while he found himself in the dim lobby of the structure that housed his office. Then he realized why he couldn't go home—because he might cause his wife and baby to see it, just as the doctor had seen it.

"Hello, Mr. Wran," said the night elevator man, a burly figure in blue overalls, sliding open the grillwork door to the old-fashioned cage. "I didn't know you were working nights now."

Catesby stepped in automatically. "Sudden rush of orders," he murmured inanely. "Some stuff that has to be gotten out."

The cage creaked to a stop at the top floor. "Be working very late, Mr. Wran?"

He nodded vaguely, watched the car slide out of sight, found his keys, swiftly crossed the outer office, and entered his own. His hand went out to the light switch, but then the thought occurred to him that the two lighted windows, standing out against the dark bulk of the building, would indicate his whereabouts and serve as a goal toward which something could crawl and climb. He moved his chair so that the back was against the wall and sat down in the semi-darkness. He did not remove his overcoat.

For a long time he sat there motionless, listening to his own breathing and the faraway sounds from the streets below: the thin metallic surge of the crosstown streetcar, the farther one of the elevated, faint lonely cries and honkings, indistinct rumblings. Words he had spoken to Miss Millick in nervous jest came back to him with the bitter taste of truth. He found himself unable to reason critically or connectedly, but by their own volition thoughts rose up into his mind and gyrated slowly and rearranged themselves, with the inevitable movement of planets.

Gradually his mental picture of the world was transformed. No longer a world of material atoms and empty space, but a world in which the bodiless existed and moved according to its own obscure laws or unpredictable impulses. The new picture illumined with dreadful clarity certain general facts which had always bewildered and troubled him and from which he had tried to hide: the inevitability of hate and war, the diabolically timed machines which wrecked the best of human intentions, the walls of willful misunderstanding that divided one man from another, the eternal vitality of cruelty and ignorance and greed. They seemed appropriate now, necessary parts of the picture. And superstition only a kind of wisdom.

Then his thoughts returned to himself, and the question he had asked Miss Millick came back, "What would such a thing want from a person? Sacrifices? Worship? Or just fear? What could you do to stop it from troubling you?" It had become a practical question.

With an explosive jangle, the phone began to ring. "Cate, I've been trying everywhere to get you," said his wife. "I never thought you'd be at the office. What are you doing? I've been worried."

He said something about work.

"You'll be home right away?" came the faint anxious question. "I'm a little frightened. Ronny just had a scare. It woke him up. He kept pointing to the window saying 'Black man, black man.' Of course it's something he dreamed. But I'm frightened. You will be home? What's that, dear? Can't you hear me?"

"I will. Right away," he said. Then he was out of the office, buzzing the night bell and peering down the shaft.

He saw it peering up the shaft at him from the deep shadows three floors below, the sacking face pressed against the iron grillwork. It started up the stair at a shockingly swift, shambling gait, vanishing temporarily from sight as it swung into the second corridor below.

Catesby clawed at the door to the office, realized he had not locked it, pushed it in, slammed and locked it behind him, retreated to the other side of the room, cowered between the filing cases and the wall. His teeth were clicking. He heard the groan of the rising cage. A silhouette darkened the frosted glass of the door, blotting out part of the grotesque reverse of the company name. After a little the door opened. The big-globed overhead light flared on and, standing just inside the door, her hand on the switch, he saw Miss Millick.

"Why, Mr. Wran," she stammered vacuously, "I didn't know you were here. I'd just come in to do some extra typing after the movie. I didn't ... but the lights weren't on. What were you -"

He stared at her. He wanted to shout in relief, grab hold of her, talk rapidly. He realized he was grinning hysterically.

"Why, Mr. Wran, what's happened to you?" she asked embarrassedly, ending with a stupid titter. "Are you feeling sick? Isn't there something I can do for you?"

He shook his head jerkily, and managed to say, "No, I'm just leaving. I was doing some extra work myself."

"But you *look* sick," she insisted, and walked over toward him. He inconsequentially realized she must have stepped in mud, for her high-heeled shoes left neat black prints.

"Yes, I'm sure you must be sick. You're so terribly pale." She sounded like an enthusiastic, incompetent nurse. Her face brightened with a sudden inspiration. "I've got something in my bag that'll fix you up right away," she said. "It's for indigestion."

She fumbled at her stuffed oblong purse. He noticed that she was absent-mindedly holding it shut with one hand while she tried to open it with the other. Then, under his very eyes, he saw her bend back the thick prongs of metal locking the purse as if they were tinfoil, or as if her fingers had become a pair of steel pliers.

Instantly his memory recited the words he had spoken to Miss Millick that afternoon. "It couldn't hurt you physically—at first ... gradually get its hooks into the world ... might even get control of suitably vacuous minds. Then it could hurt whomever it wanted." A sickish, cold feeling came to a focus inside him. He began to edge toward the door.

But Miss Millick hurried ahead of him.

"You don't have to wait, Fred," she called. "Mr. Wran's decided to stay a while longer."

The door to the cage shut with a mechanical rattle. The cage creaked. Then she turned around in the door.

"Why, Mr. Wran," she gurgled reproachfully, "I just couldn't think of letting you go home now. I'm sure you're terribly unwell. Why, you might collapse in the street. You've just got to stay here until you feel different."

The creaking died away. He stood in the centre of the office motionless. His eyes traced the course of Miss Millick's footprints to where she stood blocking the door. A sound that was almost a scream was wrenched out of him.

"Why, Mr. Wran," she said, "you're acting as if you were crazy. You must lie down for a little while. Here, I'll help you off with your coat."

The nauseously idiotic and rasping note was the same; only it had been intensified. As she came toward him he turned and ran through the storeroom, clattered a key desperately at the lock of the second door to the corridor.

"Why, Mr. Wran," he heard her call, "are you having some kind of fit? You must let me help you."

The door came open and he plunged out into the corridor and up the stairs immediately ahead. It was only when he reached the top that he realized the heavy steel door in front of him led to the roof. He jerked up the catch.

"Why, Mr. Wran, you mustn't run away. I'm coming after you."

Then he was out on the gritty gravel of the roof, the night sky was clouded and murky, with a faint pinkish glow from the neon signs. Form the distant mills rose a ghostly spurt of flame. He ran to the edge. The street lights glared dizzily upward. Two men walking along were round blobs of hat and shoulders. He swung around.

The thing was in the doorway. The voice was no longer solicitous but moronically playful, each sentence ending in a titter.

"Why, Mr. Wran, why have you come up here? We're all alone. Just think, I might push you off."

The thing came slowly toward him. He moved backward until his heels touched the low parapet. Without knowing why or what he was going to do, he dropped to his knees. The face he dared not look at came nearer, a focus for the worst in the world, a gathering point for poisons from everywhere. Then the lucidity of terror took possession of his mind, and words formed on his lips.

"I will obey you. You are my god," he said. "You have supreme power over man and his animals and his machines. You rule this city and all others. I recognize that."

Again the titter, closer. "Why, Mr. Wran, you never talked like this before. Do you mean it?"

"The world is yours to do with as you will, save or tear to pieces." He answered fawningly, as the words automatically fitted themselves together into vaguely liturgical patterns. "I recognize that. I will praise, I will sacrifice. In smoke and soot and flame I will worship you for ever."

The voice did not answer. He looked up. There was only Miss Millick, deathly pale and swaying drunkenly. Her eyes were closed. He caught her as she wobbled toward him. His knees gave way under the added weight and they sank down together on the edge of the roof.

After a while she began to twitch. Small noises came from her throat, and her eyelids edged open.

"Come on, we'll go downstairs," he murmured jerkily, trying to draw her up. "You're feeling bad."

"I'm terribly dizzy," she whispered. "I must have fainted. I didn't eat enough. And then I'm so nervous lately, about the war and everything, I guess. Why, we're on the roof! Did you bring me up here to get some air? Or did I come up without knowing it? I'm awfully foolish. I used to walk in my sleep, my mother said."

As he helped her down the stairs, she turned and looked at him. "Why, Mr. Wran," she said, faintly, "you've got a big black smudge on your forehead. Here, let me get it of for you." Weakly she rubbed at it with her handkerchief. She started to sway again and he steadied her.

"No, I'll be all right," she said. "Only I feel cold. What happened, Mr. Wran? Did I have some sort of fainting spell?"

He told her it was something like that.

Later, riding home in an empty elevated car, he wondered how long he would be safe from the thing. It was a purely practical problem. He had no way of knowing, but instinct told him he had satisfied the brute for some time. Would it want more when it came again? Time enough to answer that question when it arose. It might be hard, he realized, to keep out of an insane asylum. With Helen and Ronny to protect, as well as himself, he would have to be careful and tight-lipped. He began to speculate as to how many other men and women had seen the thing or things like it.

The elevated slowed and lurched in a familiar fashion. He looked at the roofs again, near the curve. They seemed very ordinary, as if what made them impressive had gone away for a while.

THE POWER OF THE PUPPETS

I

A Plot Afoot?

"LOOK AT THE UGLY little thing for yourself then, and tell me if it's an ordinary puppet!" said Delia, her voice rising.

Curiously I examined the limp figure she had jerked out of her handbag and tossed on my desk. The blue-white doll-face grinned at me, revealing yellowish fangs. A tiny wig of black horse hair hung down as far as the empty eye-sockets. The cheeks were sunken. It was a gruesome piece of workmanship, with a strong flavor of the Middle Ages. The maker had evidently made a close study of stone gargoyles and stained-glass devils.

Attached to the hollow papier-mâché head was the black garment that gave the figure its appearance of limpness. Something after the fashion of a monk's robe, it had a little cowl that could be tucked over the head, but now hung down in back.

I know something about puppets, even though my line is a far cry from puppeteering. I am a private detective. But I knew that this was not a marionette, controlled by strings, but a hand puppet. It was made so that the operator's hand could be slipped up through the empty garment until his fingers were in a position to animate the head and arms. During an exhibition the operator would be concealed beneath the stage, which had no floor, and only the puppet would be visible above the footlights.

I drew the robe over my hand and fitted my index finger up into the head, my second finger into the right sleeve, and my thumb into the left sleeve of the puppet. That, as I recalled, was the usual technique. Now the figure was no longer limp. My wrist and forearm filled out the robe.

I wiggled finger and thumb, and the manikin waved his arms wildly, though somewhat awkwardly, for I have seldom manipulated a puppet. I crooked my first finger and the little head gave a vigorous nod.

"Good morning, Jack Ketch," I said, making the manikin bow, as if acknowledging my salutation.

"Don't!" cried Delia, and turned her head away.

Delia was puzzling me. I had always thought her a particularly level-headed woman and, up to three years ago, I had seen a great deal of her and had had a chance to judge.

Three years ago she had married the distinguished puppeteer, Jock Lathrop, with whom I was also acquainted. Then our paths had separated. But I'd had no inkling of anything being amiss until she had appeared this morning in my New York office and poured out a series of vague hints and incredible suspicions so strange that anything resembling them did not often come a private detective's way, though I hear many odd and bizarre stories during the course of a year's work.

I looked at her closely. She was, if anything, more beautiful than ever, and considerably more exotic, as might be expected now that she was moving in artistic circles. Her thick, golden hair fell straight to her shoulders, where it was waved under. Her gray suit was smartly tailored, and her gray suede shoes trim. At her throat was a barbaric-looking brooch of hammered gold. A long golden pin kept a sketchy little hat and a handful of veil in place.

But she was still the old Delia, still the "softie Viking," as we sometimes used to call her. Except that anxiety was twisting her lips, and fear showed in her big gray eyes.

"What really is the matter, Delia?" I said, sitting down beside her. "Has Jock been getting out of hand?"

"Oh, don't be foolish, George!" she replied sharply. "It's nothing like that. I'm not afraid of Jock, and I'm not looking for a detective to get any evidence for me. I've come to you because I'm afraid for him. It's those horrible puppets. They're trying ... Oh, how can I explain it! Everything was all right until he accepted that engagement in London you must remember about, and began prying into his family history, his genealogy. Now there are things he won't discuss with me, things he won't let me see. He avoids me. And, George, I'm certain that, deep in his heart, he's afraid too. Terribly afraid."

"Listen, Delia," I said. "I don't know what you mean by all this talk about the puppets, but I do know one thing. You're married to a genius. And geniuses, Delia, are sometimes hard to live with. They're notoriously inconsiderate, without meaning to be. Just read their biographies! Half the time they go around in a state of abstraction, in love with their latest ideas, and fly off the handle at the slightest provocation. Jock's fanatically devoted to his puppets, and he should be! All the critics who know anything about the subject say he's the best in the world, better even than Franetti. And they're raving about his new show as the best of his career!"

Delia's gray suede fist beat her knee.

"I know, George. I know all about that! But it has nothing to do with what I'm trying to tell you. You don't suppose I'm the sort of wife who would whine just because her husband is wrapped up in his work? Why, for a year I was his assistant, helped him make the costumes, even operated some of the less important puppets. Now he won't even let me in his workshop. He won't let me come back-stage. He does everything himself. But I wouldn't mind even that, if it weren't that I'm afraid. It's the puppets themselves, George! They—they're trying to hurt him. They're trying to hurt me too."

I searched for a reply. I felt thoroughly uncomfortable. It is not pleasant to hear an old friend talking like a lunatic. I lifted my head and frowned at the malevolent doll-face of Jack Ketch, blue as that of a drowned man. Jack Ketch is the hangman in the traditional puppet play, *"Punch and Judy."* He takes his name from a Seventeenth Century executioner who officiated with rope and red-hot irons at Tyburn in London.

"But Delia," I said, "I don't see what you're driving at. How can an ordinary puppet -."

"But it isn't an ordinary puppet!" Delia broke in vehemently. "That's why I brought it for you to see. Look at it closely. Look at the details. *Is* it an ordinary puppet?"

Then I saw what she meant.

"There are some superficial differences," I admitted.

"What are they?" she pressed.

"Well, this puppet has no hands. Puppets usually have papier-mâché or stuffed hands attached to the ends of their sleeves."

"That's right. Go on."

"Then the head," I continued unwillingly. "There are no eyes painted on it—just eyeholes. And it's much thinner than most I've seen. More like a—a mask."

Delia gripped my arm, dug her fingers in.

"You've said the word, George!" she cried. "Like a mask! Now do you see what I mean? He has some horrible little creatures like rats that do it for him. They wear the puppets' robes and heads. That's why he won't allow me or anyone else to come backstage during a performance. And they're trying to hurt him, kill him! I know. I've heard them threaten him."

"Delia," I said, gently taking hold of her arms, "you don't know what you're saying. You're nervous, over-wrought. Just because your husband invents a new type of puppet—

why, it explains itself. It's because of his work on these new-type puppets that he's become secretive."

She jerked away from me.

"Won't you try to understand, George? I know how mad it sounds, but I'm *not* mad. At night, when Jock has thought I was asleep I've heard them threaten him with their high little voices like whistles. 'Let us go—let us go or we'll kill you!' they cry, and I'm so weak with fear I can't move. They're so tiny they can creep about everywhere."

"Have you seen them?" I asked quickly.

"No, but I *know* they're real! Last night one of them tried to scratch my eyes out while I was asleep. Look!"

She swept back the thick hair from her temple, and at that moment I also felt as if the needle-touch of fear had been transmitted to me. There in the creamy skin, an inch from the eye, were five little scratches that looked as if they might have been made by a miniature human hand. For a moment I could almost see the ratlike little creature Delia had described, its clawed hand upraised...

Then the image faded and I was realizing that such grotesque happenings were impossible. But oddly I felt as if I no longer could attribute everything Delia had told me to her neurotic fancies. *I* feared, also—but my fear was that there was a plot afoot, one meant to terrify her, to work on her superstitious fears, and delude her.

"Would you like me to visit Jock?" I asked quietly.

Some of the weight seemed to drop from her shoulders. "I was hoping you'd say that," she said, with relief...

The exquisitely lettered sign read:

LATHROP'S PUPPETS-2ND FLOOR

Outside, Forty-second Street muttered and mumbled. Inside, a wooden stair with worn brass fittings led up into a realm of dimness and comparative silence.

"Wait a minute, Delia," I said. "There are a couple of

questions I'd like you to answer. I want to get this whole thing straight before I see Jock."

She stopped and nodded, but before I could speak again our attention was attracted by a strange series of sounds from the second floor. Heavy stamping, then what seemed to be an explosion of curses in a foreign language, then rapid pacing up and down, another explosion of curses, and more pacing. It sounded as if a high-class tantrum were in progress.

Suddenly the noises ceased. I could visualize a person "pausing and swelling up in silent rage." With equal suddenness they recommenced, this time ending in a swift and jarring *clump-clump* of footsteps down the stairs. Delia shrank back against the railing as a fattish man with gray eyebrows, glaring eyes, and a mouth that was going through wordless but vituperative contortions neared us. He was wearing an expensive checked suit and a white silk shirt open at the neck. He was crumpling a soft felt hat.

He paused a few steps above us and pointed at Delia dramatically. His other hand was crumpling a soft felt hat.

"You, madam, are the wife of that lunatic, are you not?" he demanded accusingly.

"I'm Jock Lathrop's wife, if that's what you mean, Mr. Franetti," Delia said cooly. "What's the matter?"

I recognized Luigi Franetti then. He was often referred to by the press as the "Dean of Puppeteers." I remembered that Jock had been in his workshop and studied under him several years ago.

"You ask me what is the matter with me?" Franetti ranted. "You ask me that, Madam Lathrop? Bah!" Here he crumpled his hat again. "Very well—I will tell you! Your husband is not only a lunatic. He is also an ingrate! I come here to congratulate him on his recent success, to take him to my arms. After all, he is my pupil. Everything he learned from me. And what is his gratitude? What, I ask you? He will not let me touch him? He will not even shake hands! He will not let me into his workshop! Me! Franetti, who taught him everything!"

He swelled up with silent rage, just as I'd visualized it. But only for a moment. Then he was off again.

"But I tell you he is a madman!" he shouted, shaking his finger at Delia. "Last night I attended, unannounced and uninvited, a performance of his puppets. They do things that are impossible—impossible without Black Magic. I am Luigi Franetti, and I know! Nevertheless, I thought he might be able to explain it to me today. But no, he shuts me out! He has the evil eye and the devil's fingers, I tell you. In Sicily people would understand such things. In Sicily he would be shot! Bah! Never will I so much as touch him with my eyes again. Let me pass!"

He hurried down the rest of the stairs, Delia squeezing back and turning her head. In the doorway he turned for a parting shot.

"And tell me, Madam Lathrop," he cried, "what a puppeteer wants with rats!"

With a final "Bah!" he rushed out.

II

Strange Actions

I DIDN'T STOP LAUGHING until I saw Delia's face. Then it occurred to me that Franetti's accusations, ludicrous as they were, might seem to her to fit with her own suspicions.

"You can't take seriously what a man like Franetti says," I remonstrated. "He's jealous because Jock won't bow down to him and make a complete revelation of all his new technical discoveries and inventions."

Delia did not reply. She was staring after Franetti, absentmindedly pulling at the corner of a tiny handkerchief with her teeth. Watching her, I knew again the fear she felt, as if again she were feeling a little creature gouging at her temple.

"Anything to that last remark of Franetti's?" I asked lightly. "Jock doesn't keep white rats for pets by any chance?"

"I don't know," Delia said abstractedly. "I told you he never lets me in his workroom." Then she looked at me. "You said you wanted to ask me some more questions?"

I nodded. On the way here I had been revolving in my mind an unpleasant hypothesis. If Jock no longer loved Delia and had some reason for wanting to be rid of her he might be responsible for her suspicions. He had every chance to trick her.

"You said the change in Jock began to show while you were in London," I said. "Tell me the precise circumstances."

"He'd always been interested in old books and in genealogy, you see, but never to the same extent," she said, after a thoughtful pause. "In a way it was chance that began it. An accident to his hands. A rather serious one, too. A window fell on them, mashing the fingers badly. Of course a puppeteer's no good without hands, and so Jock had to lay off for three weeks. To help pass the time, he took to visiting the British Museum and the library there. Later he made many visits to other libraries to occupy his time, since he's apt to be very nervous when anything prevents him from working. When the war started we came back, and the London dates were abandoned. He did not work here, either, for quite a long time, but kept up his studies.

"Then when he was finally ready to start work again he told me he'd decided to work the puppets alone. I pointed out that one man couldn't give a puppet show, since he could only manage two characters at a time. He told me that he was going to confine himself to puppet plays like *Punch and Judy*, in which there are almost never more than two characters in sight at one time.

"That was three months ago. From that day he's avoided me. George—" her voice broke "—it's almost driven me crazy. I've had the craziest suspicions. I've even thought that he lost both his hands in the accident and refused to tell!"

"What?" I shouted. "Do you mean to tell me you don't know?"

"No. Seems strange, doesn't it? But I can't swear even to that. He never lets me come near, and he wears gloves, except in the dark."

"But the puppet shows—"

"That's just it. That's the question I keep asking myself when I sit in the audience and watch the puppets. *Who* is manipulating them? What's inside them?"

At that moment I determined to do everything I could to battle Delia's fear.

"You're not crazy," I said harshly. "But Jock is!"

She rubbed her hand across her forehead, as it if itched.

"No," she said softly, "it's the puppets. Just as I told you."

As we went on upstairs then I could tell that Delia was anxious to get my interview with Jock started. She had had to nerve herself up to it, and delays were not improving her state of mind. But apparently we were fated to have a hard time getting up that flight of stairs.

This time the interruption came when a slim man in a blue business suit tried to slip in the semi-darkness unnoticed. But Delia recognized him.

"Why, hello, Dick!" she said. "Don't you know old friends?"

I made out prim, regular features and a head of thinning neutral-colored hair.

"Dick, this is George Clayton," Delia was saying. "George, this is Dick Wilkinson. Dick handles my husband's insurance."

Wilkinson's "Howdya do?" sounded embarrassed and constrained. He wanted to get away.

"What did Jock want to see you about?" asked Delia, and Wilkinson's apparent embarrassment increased. He coughed, then seemed to make a sudden decision.

"Jock's been pretty temperamental lately, hasn't he?" he asked Delia.

She nodded slowly.

"I thought so," he said. "Frankly, I don't know why he wanted to see me this morning. I thought perhaps it was something in connection with the accident to his hands.

He has never done anything about collecting any of the
five-thousand-dollar insurance he took out on them two
years ago. But whether that was it or not I can't tell you.
He kept me waiting the best part of half an hour. I could
not help hearing Mr. Franetti's display of temper. Perhaps
that upset Jock. Anyhow when Franetti went away, fuming,
five minutes later Jock leaned out of his workshop door
and curtly informed me that he had changed his mind—he
didn't say about what -and told me to leave."

"I'm so sorry, Dick," murmured Delia. "That was rude of
him." Then her voice took on a strangely eager note. "Did
he leave the door of his workshop open?"

Dick Wilkinson wrinkled his brow. "Why yes, I—I believe
he did. At least, that was my impression. But, Delia—"

Delia had already slipped on ahead, running swiftly up
the steps. Hastily I said good-by to the perplexed insurance
agent and I followed her.

When I reached the second floor I went into a short hall.
Through an open door I glimpsed the closely-ranked seats
of the puppet theater. Delia was vanishing through another
door down the hall. I followed her.

Just as I came into a small reception room, I heard her
scream.

"George! George! He's whipping the puppet!"

With that bewildering statement ringing in my ears, I
darted into what I took to be Jock Lathrop's workshop,
then pulled up short. It too was dim, but not as dim as the
hall. I could see tables and racks of various kinds, and other
paraphernalia.

Delia was cowering back against a wall, stark fear in
her eyes. But my attention was riveted on the small, stocky
man in the center of the room—Delia's husband. On, or
in, his left hand was a puppet. His gloved right hand held
a miniature cat-o'-nine-tails and he was lashing the puppet.
And the little manikin was writhing and flailing its arms
protectively in a manner so realistic that it took my breath
away. In that strange setting I could almost imagine I heard
a squeaking, protesting voice. Indeed, the realism was such

and the grin on Lathrop's face so malign that I heard myself saying:

"Stop it, Jock! Stop it!"

He looked up, saw me, and burst into peals of laughter. His snub-nosed, sallow face was contorted into a mask of comedy. I had expected anything but that.

"So even the skeptical George Clayton, hard-boiled sleuth, is taken in by my cheap illusions!" he finally managed to say.

Then he stopped chuckling and drew himself up nonchalantly, like a magician about to perform a feat of sleight-of-hand. He tossed the whip onto a nearby table, seized the puppet with his right hand and, to all appearances, wiggled his left hand out of it. Then he quickly flipped me the limp form, thrust both hands into his pockets, and began to whistle.

Delia gave a low, whimpering cry and ran out of the room. If it had been easy for me to imagine a tiny, nude creature scuttling away behind Jock, half concealed by his left hand, what must it have been for her, in her tortured, superstitious state?

"Examine the thing, George," Lathrop directed coolly. "Is it a puppet, or isn't it?"

I looked down at the bundle of cloth and papier-mâché I had caught instinctively. It was a puppet all right, and in general workmanship precisely similar to the one Delia had shown me at my office. Its garments, however, were a gay, motley patchwork. I recognized the long nose and sardonic, impudent features of Punch.

I was fascinated by the delicate craftsmanship. The face lacked the brutishness of Jack Ketch, but it had a cunning, hair-trigger villainy all its own. Somehow it looked like a composite of all the famous criminals and murderers I had ever read about. As the murderous hero of *Punch and Judy*, it was magnificent.

But I had not come here to admire puppets.

"Look here, Jock," I said, "what the devil have you been doing to Delia? The poor girl's frightened to death."

He regarded me quizzically.

"You're taking a lot for granted, aren't you?" he said quietly. "I imagine she hunted you up as a friend, not in your capacity as a detective, but don't you think it would have been wiser to hear both sides of the case before forming judgment? I can imagine what sort of wild stories Delia's been telling you. She says I'm avoiding her, doesn't she? She says there's something queer about the puppets. In fact, she says they're alive, doesn't she?"

I heard a furtive scuffling under the work table, and was startled in spite of myself. Jock Lathrop grinned, then whistled shrilly between his teeth. A white rat crept hesitatingly into view from behind a pile of odds and ends.

"A pet," he announced mockingly. "Is it Delia's belief that I have trained rats to animate my puppets?"

"Forget Delia's beliefs for the present!" I said angrily. "Whatever they are, you're responsible for them! You've no excuse in the world for mystifying her, terrifying her."

"Are you so sure I haven't?" he said enigmatically.

"Good Lord, she's your wife, Jock!" I flung at him.

His face became serious and his words took on a deeper quality.

"I know she's my wife," he said, "and I love her dearly. But George, hasn't the obvious explanation of all this occurred to you? I hate to say it, but the truth is that Delia is bothered by—er—neurotic fancies. For some crazy reason, without the slightest foundation she has become obsessed with some sort of deep-seated—and thoroughly unreasonable—jealousy, and she's directing it at the puppets. I can't tell you why. I wish I knew."

"Even admitting that," I countered quickly, "why do you persist in mystifying her?"

"I don't," he flatly denied. "If sometimes I keep her out of the workshop, it's for her own good."

His argument was beginning to make sense. Jock Lathrop's voice had a compelling matter-of-fact quality. I was beginning to feel slightly ridiculous. Then I remembered something.

"Those scratches on her face—" I began.

"I've seen them," said Jock. "Again I hate to say it, but the only rational explanation I can see is that they were self-inflicted with the idea of bolstering up her accusations, or perhaps she scratched herself in her sleep. At any rate, people with delusions have been known to do drastic things. They'll go to any lengths rather than discard their queer beliefs. That's honestly what I think."

Pondering this quiet statement, I was looking around. Here were all the tools of the expert puppet-maker. Molds, paints, varnishes, clay models of heads, unformed papier-mâché, paper clippings, and glue. A sewing machine littered with odds and ends of gay-colored cloth.

Tacked above a desk were a number of sketches of puppets, some in pencil, some in colors. On a table were two half-painted heads, each atop a stick so that the brush could get at them more easily. Along the opposite wall hung a long array of puppets -princesses and Cinderellas, witches and wizards, peasants, oafs, bearded old men, devils, priests, doctors, kings. It almost made me feel as if a whole doll-world was staring at me and choking back raucous laughter.

"Why haven't you sent Delia to a doctor?" I asked suddenly.

"Because she refuses to go. For some time I've been trying to persuade her to consult a psychoanalyst."

I didn't know what to say. The white rat moved into my line of vision. It occurred to me that a rat could be used to explain the scuffling sounds made by anything else, but I put such an irrational thought out of my mind. More and more I found myself being forced into complete agreement with Lathrop. Delia's suspicions were preposterous. Lathrop must be right.

"Look here," I continued feebly, "Delia keeps talking about something that happened to you in London. A change. A sudden interest in genealogy."

"I'm afraid the change was in Delia," he said bitterly. "As for the genealogy business, that's quite correct. I did find out some startling things about a man whom I believe to be an ancestor of mine."

As he spoke, eagerly now, I was surprised to note how

his features lost their tight, hard appearance. The look of impudence was gone.

"I *do* love Delia very much," he said, his voice vibrant, low. "What would she think of me, George, if it turned out that her accusations were partly true? Of course, that's nonsense. But you can see that we are in trouble, George—bad trouble, that is considerably out of the line of work a private detective follows. Your work is concrete, though in your criminal investigations you must have learned that the mind and body of a man are sometimes subject to brutal powers. Not supernatural—no. But things—hard to talk about.

"George, would you do something for me? Come to the performance tonight. Afterward we can discuss this whole matter more fully. And another thing. See that old pamphlet over there? I have good reason for thinking it concerns an ancestor of mine. Take it with you. Read it. But for heaven's sake don't let Delia see it. You see, George—"

He broke off uncertainly. He seemed about to take me into his confidence about something, but then the hard, self-contained look returned to his face.

"Leave me now," he said abruptly. "This talk, and that business with the old fool, Franetti, has made me nervous."

I walked over to the table, carefully laid down Punch, and picked up the yellow-paged, ancient pamphlet he had indicated.

"I'll see you tonight after the show," I said.

III

Punch and Judy

AS I CLOSED THE DOOR behind me, I thought I saw in Lathrop's eyes that same look of fear I had seen in Delia's. But it was deeper, much deeper. And only then did I remember that not once during our interview had Jock Lathrop taken his hands out of his pockets.

Delia rushed up to me. I could tell she had been crying.

"What will we do, George—what will we do? What did he say to you? What did he tell you?"

I had to admit that her hectic manner was consistent with Jock's theory of neurotic fancies.

"Is it true, Delia," I asked abruptly, "that he's been urging you to see a psychoanalyst?"

"Why, yes." Then I saw her stiffen. "Jock's been telling you it's only my imagination, and you've been believing him," she accused.

"No, that's not it," I lied, "but I want to have time to think it all over. I'm coming to the performance tonight. I'll talk with you then."

"He *has* persuaded you!" she insisted, clinging to my sleeve. "But you mustn't believe him, George. He's afraid of them! He's in worse trouble than I am."

"I agree with you partly," I said, not knowing this time whether I was lying or not, "and after the performance we'll talk it over."

She suddenly drew away. Her face had lost something of its helpless look.

"If you won't help me," she said, breathing heavily, "I know a way of finding out whether I'm right or wrong. A sure way."

"What do you mean, Delia?"

"Tonight," she said huskily, "you may find out."

More than that she wouldn't say, although I pressed her. I took away with me a vision of her distraught gray eyes, contrasted oddly with the thick sweep of golden hair. I hurried through the hall, down the stairs. The measured pandemonium of Forty-second Street was welcome. It was good to see so many people, walk with them, be jostled by them and forget the fantastic fears of Delia and Jock Lathrop.

I glanced at the pamphlet in my hand. The type was

ancient and irregular. The paper was crumbly at the edges. I read the lengthy title:

> A TRUE ACCOUNT, as related by a Notable Personage to a Trustworthy Gentleman, of the CIRCUMSTANCES attending the Life and DEATH of JOCKEY LOWTHROPE, an Englishman who gave PUPPET SHEWS; telling how many surmised that his Death was encompassed by these same PUPPETS.

Night was sliding in over New York. My office was a mass of shadows. From where I was sitting I could see the mammoth Empire State Building topping the irregular skyline.

I rubbed my eyes wearily. But that did not keep my thoughts from their endless circling. Who was I to believe? Delia or Jock? Was there a disordered mind at work, fabricating monstrous suspicions? And if so, whose mind was it? They were questions outside the usual province of a private detective.

I tilted the pamphlet to catch the failing light and re-read two passages that had particularly impressed me.

> At this Time it was rumored that Jockey Lowthrope had made a Pact with the Devil, with a view to acquiring a greater Skill in his Trade. There were many who testified privately that his Puppets acted and moved with a Cunningbeyond the ability of Christian Man to accomplish. For Jockey took no assistants and would explain to no one how his Manikins were activated...
>
> Some say that Moll Squires and the French Doctor did not tell all they saw when they first viewed Jockey's Corpse. Certain it was that a long, thin Needle pierced his Heart and that both Hands were hacked

off at the Wrists. Jockey's wife, Lucy, would have been held for Trial for Murder at the Assizes, only that she was never seen afterwards. Moll Squires averred that the Devil had come to fetch Jockey's hands, to which he had previous granted an unholy Skill. But many maintain that he was slain by his own Puppets, who chose the Needle as being a Weapon suitable to their Size and Dexterity. These recall how the Clergyman Penrose inveighed against Jockey, saying, "Those are not Puppets, but Imps of Satan, and whosoever views them is in Danger of Damnation."

I pushed the pamphlet to one side. What could one make of events that had happened one hundred and fifty years ago—faint reverberations from the Eighteenth Century fear-world that had underlaid the proud Age of Reason? Especially when one read of them in an account obviously written for the sake of sensation-mongering?

True, the names were oddly similar. Lowthrope and Lathrop were undoubtedly alternate spellings. And from what Jock had said he had further evidence of a blood relationship.

The pamphlet angered me, made me feel as if someone were trying to frighten me with nursery tales of ghosts and goblins.

I switched on the light and blinked at the electric clock. It was seven-forty-five ...

When I reached the puppet theater it was buzzing with conversation and the hall outside was already blue with cigarette smoke. Just as I was getting my ticket from the sad-eyed girl at the door, someone called my name. I looked up and saw Dr. Grendal. I could tell that the garrulous old man had something on his mind besides his shiny, bald pate. After a few aimless remarks he asked his question.

"Seen Jock since he got back from London?"

"Just to say hello to," I answered cautiously.

"How'd he impress you, hey?" The doctor's eyes glanced sharply from behind their silver-rimmed spectacles.

"A little uneasy," I admitted. "Temperamental."

"I thought you might say something like that," he commented, as he led me over to an empty corner. "Fact is," he continued, "I think he's definitely queer. Between ourselves, of course. He called me in. I thought he needed me in a professional capacity. But it turned out he wanted to talk about pygmies."

He couldn't have surprised me more.

"Pygmies?" I repeated.

"Just so. Pygmies. Surprised you, didn't it? Did me, too. Well, Jock was especially curious about the lower limits of possible size of mature human beings. Kept asking if there were any cases in which they were as small as puppets. I told him it was impossible, except for infants and embryos.

"Then he began shifting the conversation. Wanted to know a lot about blood relationship and the inheritance of certain traits. Wanted to know all about identical twins and triplets and so on. Evidently thought I'd be a mine of data because of the monographs I've scribbled about medical oddities. I answered as best I could, but some of his questions were queer. Power of mind over matter, and that sort of stuff. I got the impression his nerves were about to crack. Told him as much. Whereupon he told me to get out. Peculiar, hey?"

I could not answer. Dr. Grendal's information put new life into the disturbing notions I had been trying to get out of my mind. I wondered how much I dared tell the old physician, or whether it would be unwise to confide in him at all.

The people in the hall were moving into the theater. I made a noncommittal remark to Grendal and we followed. A rotund figure pushed in ahead of us, muttering -Luigi Franetti. Evidently he had not been able to resist the temptation presented by his former student's puppets. He threw down the price of the ticket contemptuously, as if it were the thirty pieces of silver due Judas Iscariot. Then he stamped in, sat down, folded his arms, and glared at the curtain.

There must have been two hundred people present, almost a full house. I noticed quite a splash of evening dresses and dress suits. I didn't see Delia, but I noted the prim features of Dick Wilkinson, the insurance agent.

From behind the curtain came the reedy tinkle of a music box—tones suggestive of a doll orchestra. The seats Grendal and I had were near the front, but considerably to one side.

The little theater grew dim. A soft illumination flowed up the square of red silk curtain. The melody from the music box ended on a note so high it sounded as though something in the mechanism had snapped. A pause. The deep, somber reverberation of a gong. Another pause. Then a voice, which I recognized as Lathrop's pitched in falsetto.

"Ladies and gentlemen, for your entertainment Lathrop's Puppets present—*Punch and Judy!*"

From behind me I heard Franetti's "Bah!"

Then the curtain parted and slid rustling to the sides. Punch popped up like a jack-in-the-box, chuckled throatily, and began to antic around the stage and make bitingly witty remarks, some of them at the expense of the spectators.

It was the same puppet Jock had let me examine in the workshop. But was Jock's hand inside? After a few seconds I quit worrying about that. This, I told myself, was only an ordinary puppet show, as clever as the manipulations were. The voice was Jock Lathrop's, pitched in puppeteer's falsetto.

It is ironic that *Punch and Judy* is associated with children and the nursery, for few plays are more fundamentally sordid. Modern child educators are apt to fling up their hands at mention of it. It is unlike any fairy tale or phantasy, but springs from forthright, realistic crime.

Punch is the prototype of the egotistical, brutish criminal—the type who today figures as an axefiend or sashweight slayer. He kills his squalling baby and nagging wife, Judy, merely because they annoy him. He kills the doctor because he doesn't like the medicine. He kills the policeman who comes to arrest him. Finally, after he is thrown into jail and sentenced to death, he manages to outwit and murder the fearsome executioner Jack Ketch.

Only in the end does the devil come to fetch him, and in some versions Punch kills the devil. During all these crimes Punch seldom loses his grim and trenchant sense of humor.

Punch and Judy has long been one of the most popular puppet plays. Perhaps the reason children like it is that they have fewer moral inhibitions than grown-ups to prevent them from openly sympathizing with Punch's primal selfishness. For Punch is as thoughtlessly selfish and cruel as a spoiled child.

These thoughts passed rapidly through my mind, as they always do when I see or think of *Punch and Judy*. This time they brought with them a vivid memory of Jock Lathrop whipping the puppet.

I have said that the beginning of the play reassured me. But as it progressed, my thoughts crept back. The movements of the puppets were too smooth and clever for my liking. They handled things too naturally.

There is a great deal of clubbing in *Punch and Judy,* and the puppets always hold on to their clubs by hugging them between their arms—the thumb and second finger of the puppeteer. But Jock Lathrop had made a startling innovation. His puppets held their weapons as a man normally does. I wondered if this could be due to some special device.

Hurriedly I got out my opera glasses and turned them on the stage. It was some time before I could focus on one of the puppets; they jerked about too much. Finally I got a clear view of Punch's arms. As far as I could make out, they ended in tiny hands -hands that could shift on the club, clenching and unclenching in an uncannily natural way.

Grendal mistook my smothered exclamation for one of admiration.

"Pretty clever," he said, nodding.

After that I sat still. Of course the tiny hands were only some sort of mechanical attachment to Lathrop's fingertips. And here, I thought, was the reason for Delia's fears. She had been taken in by the astonishing realism of the puppets.

But then how to explain Jock's actions, the strange questions he had put to Dr. Grendal? Merely an attempt to create publicity?

It was hard for a "hard-boiled sleuth" to admit, even to himself, that he did have an odd feeling that those manikins were alive. But I did, and I fought against this feeling, turning my eyes from the stage.

Then I saw Delia. She was sitting in the row behind and two chairs further to the side. There was nothing of the "softie Viking" about her now, despite the glimmering, curving lines of her silver lamé evening dress. In the ghostly illumination from the stage, her lovely face was cold, stony, with a set determination that made me apprehensive.

I heard a familiar mutter and turned to see Franetti moving down the far aisle as if the stage were drawing him like a magnet. He was glaring at the puppets and talking to himself.

Twice I heard him mutter, "Impossible!" Patrons gave him irritated looks as he passed or murmured complainingly. He took no notice. He reached the end of the aisle and disappeared through the black curtained doorway that led backstage.

IV

Dark Heritage

RAPIDLY THE PLAY was drawing towards its climax. Punch, in a dark and dismal prison, was whining and wailing in self-pity. Jack Ketch was approaching from one side, his face and black hair hideous in the dim light. In one hand he carried a noose; in the other, a needlelike sword about five inches long. He brandished both dexterously.

I could no longer view the scene in a matter-of-fact way. This was a doll-world, where all the dolls were brutes and murderers. The stage was reality, viewed through the wrong end of a telescope.

Then came an ominous rustle behind me. I turned. Delia had risen to her feet. Something was gleaming in her upraised hand. There was a sharp crack, like a whip. Before anyone could stop her she emptied the chambers of a small revolver at the stage.

On the fourth shot I saw a black hole appear in Punch's mask.

Delia did not struggle against the bewildered men who had risen to pinion her hands. She was staring fixedly at the stage. So was I. For I knew what she hoped to prove by those shots.

Punch had disappeared, but not Jack Ketch. He seemed to be staring back at Delia, as if the shots had been an expected part of the performance. Then the high tuning voice screamed, a reedy scream of hate. And it was not Jock Lathrop's falsetto voice that screamed. Then Jack Ketch raised his needlelike sword and plunged down out of sight.

The scream that followed was a full-voiced cry of desperate agony that silenced and froze the milling audience. And this time it was Jock's voice.

Hurriedly I pushed my way toward the curtained door. Old Grendal was close behind me. The first thing that caught my eye in the backstage confusion was the trembling form of Luigi Franetti. His face was like wax. He was on his knees, murmuring garbled prayers.

Then, sprawled on his back beneath the puppet-stage, I saw Lathrop.

Hysterical questions gave way to shocked whispers, which mounted to a chorus as others swarmed backstage.

"Look! He's dead—the man that works the puppets!"

"She got him all right! Fired through the curtains underneath!"

"I saw her do it myself. She shot him a dozen times."

"Somebody said she's his wife."

"She got him on the last shot. I heard him scream. She's crazy."

I understood the mistake they were making, for I knew that everyone of Delia's shots had hit above stage level. I walked over to Jock Lathrop's body. And it was with the shock of my life that I saw that Jack Ketch's pygmy sword had been driven to the hilt in Lathrop's right eyeball. And on Jock Lathrop's right and left hands were the garments and papier-mâché heads of Punch and Jack Ketch.

Grendal hastened forward and knelt at Lathrop's side. The chorus of frightened whispers behind us kept rising and falling in a kind of mob rhythm. The drab insurance agent Wilkinson stepped up and peered over Grendal's shoulders. Indrawn breath whistled between his teeth. He turned around slowly and pointed at Franetti.

"Mr. Lathrop was not shot, but stabbed," he said in a curiously calm voice that caught the crowd's ear. "I saw that man sneak back here. He murdered Mr. Lathrop. He was the only one who could have done it. Get hold of him, some of you, and take him out front."

Franetti offered no resistance. He looked utterly dazed and helpless.

"The rest of you had better wait out front too," Wilkinson continued. "I shall telephone the police. See to it that Mrs. Lathrop is not troubled or annoyed. She is hysterical. Do not allow her to come back here."

There was a rustle of hushed interjections and questions, but the crowd flowed back into the theater. Wilkinson, Grendal, and myself were left alone.

"There's no hope, is there?" I managed to say.

Grendal shook his head.

"He's dead as a nail. The tiny instrument penetrated the eyesocket and deep into the brain. Happened to be driven in exactly the proper direction."

I looked down at Lathrop's twisted body. Even now I could hardly repress a shudder at the sight of the puppets. The vindictive expressions on their masks looked so purposeful. I regarded the bullet hole in Punch's mask. A little blood was welling from it. The bullet must have nicked Lathrop's finger.

At that moment I became aware of a confused surge of footsteps outside, and of the crowd's whispering, muffled by the intervening hangings, rising to a new crescendo.

"Look out, she's getting away!"

"She's running! Stop her!"

"Has she still got the gun?"

"She's going back there. Grab her, somebody!"

The black draperies eddied wildly as Delia spun through the door, jerking loose from a hand that had sought to restrain her. In a swirl of golden hair and shimmering silver lamé she came in. I glimpsed her wild gray eyes, white-circled.

"*They* killed him, I tell you, *they* killed him!" she screamed, "Not me. Not Franetti. *They*! I killed one. Oh, Jock, Jock, are you dead?"

She ran toward the corpse. Then came the final nightmare.

The arms of blue-faced Jack Ketch began to writhe, and from the puppet-mask came squealing, malevolent laughter.

Delia, about to fling her arms around her dead husband, slid to the floor on her knees. A sigh of horror issued from her throat. The silver lamé billowed down around her. And still the puppet tittered and squealed, as if mocking her and triumphing over her.

"Pull those blasted things off his hands!" I heard myself crying. "Pull them off!"

It was Wilkinson who did it, not the feebly pawing Dr. Grendal. Wilkinson didn't realize what was happening.

He was still convinced that Franetti was the murderer. He obeyed automatically. He seized the papier-mâché heads roughly, and jerked.

Then I knew how Jock Lathrop had died. I knew why he had been so secretive, why the ancient pamphlet had affected him so profoundly. I realized that Delia's suspicions had been correct, though not what she had believed. I knew why Jock Lathrop had asked Grendal those peculiar questions. I knew why the puppets had been so realistic. I knew why Jockey Lowthrope had had his hands hacked off. I knew why Jock

Lathrop had never let anyone see his own ungloved hands, after that "change" had begun in London.

The little finger and ring finger on each of his hands were normal. The others—the ones used in motivating a puppet—were not. Replacing the thumb and second finger were tiny muscular arms. The first finger was in each case a tiny, wormlike body, of the general shape of a finger, but with a tiny sphincterlike mouth and two diminutive, malformed eyes that were all black pupil. One was dead by Delia's bullet. The other was not. I crushed it under my heel...

Among Jock Lathrop's papers was found the following note, penned in longhand, and evidently written within a few days of the end:

If I die, *they* have killed me. For I am sure they hate me.

I have tried to confide in various people, but have been unable to go through with it. I feel compelled to secrecy. Perhaps that is *their* desire, for *their* power over my actions is growing greater every day. Delia would loathe me if she knew. And she suspects.

I thought I would go mad in London, when my injured fingers began to heal with a *new* growth. A monstrous growth—that where my brothers who were engulfed in my flesh at the time of my birth and did not begin to develop until now! Had they been developed and born at the proper time, we would have been triplets. But the *mode* of that development now!

Human flesh is subject to horrible perversions. Can my thoughts and activities as a puppeteer have had a determining influence? Have I influenced their minds until those minds are really those of Punch and Jack Ketch?

And what I read in that old pamphlet. Hands hacked off ... Could my ancestor's pact with the devil have given him his fiendish skill? Given him the monstrous growth which led to his ruin? Could this physical characteristic have been inherited, lying dormant until such time as another Lathrop, another puppeteer, summoned it forth by his ambitious desires?

I don't know. What I do know is that as long as I live I

am the world's greatest puppeteer—but at what cost! I hate *them* and *they* hate me. I can hardly control them. Last night one of them clawed Delia while I slept. Even now, when my mind wandered for a moment, the *one* turned the pen and tried to drive it into my wrist...

I did not scoff at the questions that Jock Lathrop had asked himself. I might have at one time. But I had seen *them*, and I had seen the tiny sword driven into Lathrop's eye. No, I'm not going to spend any more time trying to figure out the black mystery behind the amazing skill of Jock Lathrop. I'm going to spend it trying to make Delia forget.

CRY WITCH!

THE GIRL WAS very beautiful and she came into the café on the arm of a young writer whose fearless idealism has made him one of the most talked of figures of today. Still, it seemed odd to me that old Nemecek should ignore my question in order to eye her. Old Nemecek loves to argue better than to eat or drink, or, I had thought, to love, and in any case he is very old.

Indeed, old Nemecek is almost incredibly old. He came to New York when the homeland of the Czechs was still called Bohemia, and he was old then. Now his face is like a richly tooled brown leather mask and his hands are those of a dapperly gloved skeleton and his voice, though mellow, is whispery. His figure is crooked and small and limping, and I sometimes feel that he came from a land of ancient myth. Yet there are times when a certain fiery youthfulness flashes from his eyes.

The girl looked our way and her glance stopped at Nemecek. For a moment I thought they had recognized each other. A cryptic look passed between them, a guardedly smiling, coolly curious, rapid, reminiscent look as if they had been lovers long ago, incredible as that might be. Then the girl and her escort went on to the bar and old Nemecek turned back to me.

"Idealism?" he queried, showing that he had not forgotten my question. "It is strange you should ask that now. Yes, I certainly am an idealist and have always been one, though I have been deserted and betrayed by my ideals often enough, and seen them exploited in the market place and turned to swords and instruments of torture in the hands of my enemies."

The tone of his voice, at once bitter and tender, was the same as a man might use in talking of a woman he had known and lost long ago and still loved deeply.

"Ideals," he said softly and fingered the glass of brandy before him and looked at me through the eyeholes of his Spanish leather mask. "I will tell you a story about them. It happened to a very close friend of mine in old Bohemia. It is a very old story, and like all the best old stories, a love story."

SHE WAS NOT like the other village girls, this girl my friend fell in love with (said Nemecek). With the other village girls he was awkward, shy, and too inclined to nurse impossible desires. He walked past their houses late at night, hoping they would be looking out of a darkened window, warm white ghosts in their cotton gowns. Or wandering along the forest path he imagined that they would be waiting alone for him just around the next turn, the sunlight dappling their gay skirts and their smiles. But they never were.

With her it worked out more happily. Sometimes it seemed that my friend had always known her, back even to that time when a jolly Old Man in Black had made noises at him in his crib and tickled his ribs; and always their meetings had the same magical conformity to his moods. He would be trudging up the lane, where the trees bend close and the ivy clings to the cool gray wall, thinking of nothing, when suddenly he would feel a hand at his elbow and turn and see her grave, mysterious, sweet face, a little ruffled from having run to overtake him.

When there was dancing in the square and the fiddlers squealed and the boards thundered and the bonfires splashed ruddy gilt, she would slip out of the weaving crowd and they would whirl and stamp together. And at night he would hear her scratching softly at his bedroom window like a cat almost before he realized what it was he had been listening for.

My friend did not know her name or where she lived. He did not ask her. With regard to that he was conscious of an unspoken agreement between them. But she always turned up when he wanted her and she was very artful in her choice of the moment to slip away.

More and more he came to live for the hours they spent together. He became contemptuous of the village and its ways. He recognized, with the clarity of anger, the village's shams and meannesses and half-masked brutalities. His parents noticed this and upbraided him. He no longer went to church, they complained. He sneered at the schoolmaster. He was disrespectful to the mayor. He played outrageous tricks on the shopkeepers. He was not interested in work or in getting ahead. He had become a good-for-nothing.

When this happened he always expected them to accuse him of wasting his time on a strange girl, and to put the blame on her. Their failure to do this puzzled him. His curiosity as to her identity was reawakened.

She was not a village girl, she was not a gypsy, and she certainly was not the daughter of the nobleman whose castle stood at the head of the valley. She seemed to exist for him alone. Yet, if experience had taught him anything, it had taught him that nothing existed for him alone. Everything in the village had its use, even the beggar who was pitied and the dog who was kicked. He racked his brains as to what hers might be. He tried to get her to tell him without asking a direct question, but she refused to be drawn. Several times he planned to follow her home. When that happened she merely stayed with him until he had forgotten his plan, and by the time he remembered it she was gone.

But he was growing more and more dissatisfied with the conditions of their relationship. No matter how delightful, this meet-at-the-corner, kiss-in-the-dark business could not go on forever. They really ought to get married.

My friend began to wonder if she could be concealing something shameful about her background. Now when he walked arm-in-arm around the square with her, he fancied that people were smirking at him and whispering behind his back. And when he happened on a group of the other young men of the village, the talk would break off suddenly and there would be knowing winks. He decided that, whatever the cost, he must know.

IT WAS NEAR May Eve. They had met in the orchard opposite the old stone wall, and she was leaning against a bough crusted with white blossoms. Now that the moment had come, he was trembling. He knew that she would tell the truth and it frightened him.

She smiled a little ruefully, but answered without hesitation.

"What do I do in the village? Why, I sleep with all of them—the farmers, the preacher, the schoolmaster, the mayor..."

There was a stinging pain in the palm of his hand. He had slapped her face and turned his back on her, and he was striding up the lane, toward the hills. And beside him was striding an Old Man in Black, not nearly so jolly as he had remembered him, cadaverous in fact and with high forehead deeply furrowed and eyes frosty as the stars.

For a long way they went in silence, as old comrades might. Over the stone bridge, where once he and she had dropped a silver coin into the stream, past the roadside shrine with its withered flowers and faded saint, through the thin forest, where a lock of his hair and hers were clipped together in a split tree, and across the upland pasture. Finally he found words for his anger.

"If only she hadn't said it with that hangdog air, and yet as if expecting to be praised! And if it had happened only with some of the young fellows! But those old hypocrites!"

He paused, but the Old Man in Black said nothing, only a certain cold merriment was apparent in his eyes.

"How can she do it and still stay so lovely?" my friend continued. "And how can they know her and not be changed by it? I tell you I gave up a great deal for her! But they can enjoy her and still stick like leeches to the same old lies. It's unfair. If they don't believe in her, why do they want her?"

The Old Man laughed shortly and spoke, and the laugh and the words were like a wind high above the earth.

"She is a harlot, yet whosoever possesses her becomes highly respectable thereby. That is a riddle."

"*I* have not become respectable."

The Old Man showed his teeth in a wintry smile. "You really love her. Like old King David, *they* desire only to be warm."

"And she really sleeps with them all? Just as she said?"

The Old Man shook his head. "Not all. There are a few who turn her away. The philosopher who stays in the little cottage down the road and scowls at the religious processions and tells the children there is no god. The nobleman whose castle stands at the head of the valley. The bandit who lives in the cave on the hill. But even they cannot always endure life without her, and then they get up in the chilly night and go to the window and open it, and the bandit goes to the frost-rimmed mouth of his cave, and they call brokenly in the moonlight, hating themselves for it, and she comes, or her ghost."

The Old Man turned his head and his sunken eyes were very bright.

"They are weak," he said, "but you may be stronger. It's a gay life in the crags."

"Old Man," my friend answered, "you've shown me two paths and I'll take neither. I won't leave her and freeze to death in the crags, no matter how gaily. And I won't share her with those fat hypocrites. I have a plan."

And he turned and went whistling down the hill, his hands in his pockets.

WHEN HE HAD almost come to the village, he saw a tall hay-wagon coming up the lane. There were two rich farmers on the seat, with still collars and thick vests and fat gold watchchains, and she was sitting between them and their arms were around her shoulders. The schoolmaster had begged a ride and was lying on the hay behind the seat, and he had slyly managed to slide his arm around her waist.

Watching them from the middle of the road as the wagon slowly creaked nearer, my friend chuckled and shook his head, wondering how he could ever have been so blind as not to realize that she was the town harlot. Why, he had seen her a hundred times, drunken, clinging to some man's arm, hitching at her skirt, singing some maudlin song. Once she had beckoned to him. And it had never occurred to him that they were the same woman.

He laughed again, out loud this time, and stepped forward boldly and stopped the horses.

The farmer who was driving got up unsteadily, jerking at the reins, and roared in a thick, tavern voice, "Loafer! Good-for-nothing! Get out of our way!" And the whip came whistling down.

But my friend ducked and the lead horse reared. Then he grabbed the whip and pulled himself up onto the wagon with it, and the tipsy farmer down. The other farmer had found the bottle from which they had been swigging and was fetching it up for a blow, when he snatched it away from him and broke it over his head, so that the brandy drenched his pomaded hair and ran into his eyes. Then he tumbled him off into the road and laid the whip onto the horses until they broke into an awkward gallop which made up in jouncing what it otherwise lacked in speed.

When the fight started, the schoolmaster had tried to slip off the back of the wagon. Now he tried to hang on. But hay is not easy stuff to cling to. First his books went, then his tall hat, then he. There was a great brown splash. The last they saw of him, he was sitting in the puddle, his long legs spread.

By the time they reached the bridge, the horses were winded. My friend jumped nimbly out and swung her down. She seemed to be amused and perhaps even delighted at what was happening. Without any explanation, he took her firmly by the wrist and headed for the hills.

Every now and then he stole a glance at her. He began to marvel that he had ever thought her perfect. The dearest thing in the world, of course, but perfect?—why, she was much too cream-and-sugary, too sit-by-the-fire, too cozy and stodgy-respectable, almost plump. Well, he'd see to that, all right.

And he did. All through the long summer and into the tingling fall their life went like what he had always imagined must come after the happy endings of the fairy tales his grandmother had told him. He repaired the little old cabin in the hills beyond the upland pasture, and stuffed the old mattress with fresh green grass, and carved wooden dishes and goblets and spoons, and made her a pail out of bark to fetch water. Sometimes he managed to filch from the outlying farms a loaf of new-made bread, sometimes some flour, sometimes only the grain, which she ground between stones and baked unleavened on another stone over the fire. He hunted rabbits and squirrels with his revolver, but occasionally he stole chickens and once he killed a sheep.

She went with him on his hunting expeditions, and once or twice they climbed into the crags, which seemed not at all cold and forbidding, as on that afternoon when he had walked with the Old Man. He made slim flutes out of willow wands, and they piped together in the evenings or out in the sunny forest. Sometimes, as a solemn jest, they wove twigs and flowers into wreaths as an offering to fancied forest gods. They played games with each other and with their pets—a squirrel who had escaped the pot and a brave young cat who had come adventuring from the village.

True to my friend's expectations, his beloved grew brown, lithe, and quick. She went barefoot and tucked up her skirt. All signs of the village faded from her, and her grave, mysterious, sweet expression grew sparklingly alive, so that he sometimes shivered with pride when he looked at her. All day long she was with him, and he went to sleep holding her hand and in the morning it was always there.

He had only one worry, a trifling and indeed unreasonable one, since it was concerned with the absence rather than the presence of ill fortune, yet there it was. He could not understand why the farmers did not try to track him down for his thefts, and why the village folk had not done anything to him for taking their harlot.

He knew the people of the valley. He was not so credulous as to believe he had fooled them by hiding in the hills. Any poacher or thief who tried that had the dogs baying at his heels before morning. They were tight-fisted, those valley people. They never let anything out of their hands unless they made a profit. But what the profit could be in this case, he could not for the life of him determine.

In a small way it bothered him, and one night just before Hallowmas he woke with a start, all full of fear. Moonlight was streaming through the doorway. He felt her hand in his and for a moment that reassured him. But the hand felt cold and dry and when he tugged at it to waken her, it seemed weightless. He sprang out of bed and to the doorway and the hand came with him. In the moonlight he saw that it was a dead hand, severed at the wrist, well preserved, smelling faintly of spices.

He kicked the fire aflame and lit a candle from it. The cat was pacing uneasily. Every now and then it would look toward the doorway and its fur would rise. The squirrel was huddled in a corner of its cage, trembling. My friend called his beloved's name, very softly at first, then more loudly. Then he shouted it with all the power of his lungs and plunged outside.

All night he searched and shouted in vain through the forest, striking at the inky branches as if they were in league with her captors. But when he returned at dawn, scratched and bruised, his clothes all smeared and torn, she was busy cooking breakfast. Her face, as she raised to greet him, was tranquil and guiltless, and he found that he could not bring himself to question her or to refer in any way to the night's happenings. She bathed his cuts and dried his sweat and made him rest a little before eating, but only as if he had gone out for an early ramble and had had the misfortune to fall and hurt himself.

The cat was contentedly gnawing a bit of bacon rind and the squirrel was briskly chattering as it nibbled a large crumb. My friend searched surreptitiously for the dead hand where he had dropped it but it was gone.

All that day the sky was cloudless, but there was a blackness in the sunlight, as if he were dizzy and about to faint. He could not tire himself of looking at her. In the afternoon they made an expedition to the hilltop, but as he clasped her in his arms he saw, over her shoulder and framed by rich autumnal leaves, tinied by the distance, the figure of a man in a long black cloak and a broad-brimmed hat, standing high in the crags and seeming to observe them. And he wondered why the Old Man had stayed away from them so long.

That night she was very tender, as if she too knew that this night was the last, and it was hard for my friend to keep from speaking out. He lay with his eyes open the barest slit, feigning sleep. For a long time there was no movement in the cabin, only the comfortable sounds of night and her breathing. Then, very slowly, she sat up, and keeping hold of his hand, drew from under the bed a box. From this she took a small flute, which seemed, by the moon and flickering firelight, to be made not of willow but of a human bone. On this, stopping it only with three fingers, still keeping hold of his hand, she played a doleful and drowsy melody.

He felt a weight of sleep descend on him, but he had chewed a bitter leaf which induces wakefulness. After the tune was done, she held the flute over his heart and gently shook it. He knew that a little grave-yard dust must have fallen from the stops, for he felt a second compelling urge of sleepiness.

Then she took from the box the severed hand and warmed it in her bosom. All this while he had the feeling that she suspected, was perhaps certain, that he was not asleep, but still carried out faithfully her ritual of precaution. After a long time, she gently eased her hand from his and placed the

dead hand there and slipped out of bed and silently crossed
to the doorway and went out.

HE FOLLOWED HER. The whiteness of her smock in the
moonlight made it easy. She went down the hill and across
the upland pasture. It became apparent to him that she was
heading for the village. She never once looked back. On
the edge of the village she turned into a dark and narrow
lane. He followed closer, stopping to avoid the shrubs that
sometimes overhung the walls.

After circling halfway round the village, she opened a
wicket and went through. Watching from the wicket, he
could see that she was standing before a dark window in a
low-roofed house. Faintly there came the sound of rapping.
After a long time the window was opened. As she climbed
over the sill she turned so that in the clear moonlight he
caught a glimpse of her face. It was not the frozen and
unearthly expression of a sleep-walker or one enchanted,
not even the too gentle, too submissive expression of old
days, but the new, sparklingly alive look that had only come
with their summer together.

He recognized the house. It was the schoolmaster's.

Next morning the church bells were ringing as he strode
back to the village, his revolver in his pocket. His steps were
too long, and he held himself stiffly, like a drunkard. He did
not turn into the circling lane, but went straight across the
square. As he passed the open doors of the church, the bells
had stopped and he could hear the voice of the preacher.
Something about the tone of the voice made him climb the
steps and peer in.

There was the smell of old woodwork and musty hangings,
week-long imprisoned air. After the glaring sunlight, the
piously inclined heads of the congregation seemed blurred
and indistinct, sunk in stuffy gloom. But a shaft of rich
amber fell full upon the pulpit and on her.

She was squeezed between the preacher and the carved
front of the pulpit—rather tightly, for he could see how the

wood, somewhat worn and whitened at that point by the repeated impress of fervent hands, indented her thigh under the skirts. The preacher's thin, long-chinned face, convulsed with oratory, was thrust over her shoulder, his blown spittle making a little cloud. With one hand the preacher pointed toward heaven, and with the other he was fondling her.

And on her face was that same shining, clear-eyed expression that he had seen there last night and that had seemed in the green forest caverns like the glance of some nymph new-released from evil enchantment, and that he knew his love alone had brought. With the amber light gilding her, he thought of how Aaron had made a Golden Calf for the Israelites to worship.

But had Aaron really made the Golden Calf, or had he stolen it? For the old words that the preacher mouthed had a new and thrilling ring to them, which could only come from her.

My friend groped sideways blindly, touched the back of a pew, steadied himself and screamed her name.

The floor of the church seemed to tilt and rock, and a great shadow swooped down, almost blotting out the frightened, backward turning faces of the congregation. She had slipped from the pulpit and was coming down the center aisle toward him. He was holding out his hand to fend her off and dragging at his pocket for the revolver. The preacher had ducked out of sight.

She was very close to him now and her hands were lovingly outstretched and her expression was unchanged. He brought up the revolver, stumbling back, frantically motioning her to keep away. But she kept on coming and he fired all six charges into her body.

As the smarting gray smoke cleared, he saw her standing there unharmed. Someone was screaming "Witch! Witch!" and he realized it was himself and that he was running across the square and out of the village.

* * *

NOT UNTIL HE ran himself out and the shock of terror passed, did the Old Man in Black fall into step with him. My friend was glad of the Old Man's presence, but he did not look too closely, for sidewise glances warned him that the cadaverousness had become extreme indeed, and that the cheeks were white as bone, and that for good reason there were no longer any wrinkles in the domelike forehead.

The Old Man did not speak, which was a kindness, and showed no signs of elation at his victory. Together they paced towards the distant crags. Down the road they passed the little cottage in which the philosopher lived, and the philosopher came out and stood watching them go by. He looked very shriveled and dry and his hair was dusty, his clothes were old-fashioned and very tight. When they were almost past he raised his hand in a jerky salute and went inside and shut the door.

After a while they left the road and cut across the hills past the castle that stands at the head of the valley. On the battlements was a tiny man who waved at them once with his cloak, very solemnly it seemed. At the foot of the crags they passed the cave where the bandit lived, and the bandit stood in the stony mouth and raised his gaudy cap to them in a grave, ironic greeting.

They were all day climbing the crags. By the time they reached the top, night had come. While his companion waited for him, my friend walked back to the crag's edge for a last look at the valley.

It was very dark. The moon had not yet risen. Beyond the village there was a great circle of tiny fires. He puzzled dully as to what caused them.

He felt thin hard fingers touch his shoulder and he heard the Old Man say, "She isn't in the village any more, if that's what you're wondering. An army passed through the valley today. Those are the campfires you see in the distance. She's left the preacher, and the schoolmaster, as much as she ever leaves anyone. She's gone off with the soldiers."

Then the Old Man sighed faintly and my friend felt a

sudden chill, as if he had strayed to the margin of oblivion, and it seemed to him that a coldness had gone out from the Old Man and flowed across the whole valley and lapped up into the sky and made the very stars glittering points of ice. He knew that there was only one creature in the whole world immune to that coldness.

So he lifted his hand to his shoulder and laid it on the smooth finger-bones there and said, "I'm going back to her, Old Man. I know she'll never be true to me, and that she'll always yield herself eagerly to any mind with wit enough to imagine or learn a lie, and that whatever I give her she'll hurry to give to them, as a street woman to her bully. And I'm not doing this because I think she's carrying my child, for I believe she's sterile. And I know that while I grow old, she'll always stay young, and so I'm sure to lose her in the end. But that's just it, Old Man—you can't touch her. And besides, I've given myself to her, and she's beautiful, and however false, she's all there is in the world to be faithful to."

And he started down the crags.

OLD NEMECEK LEANED back and fingered his brandy glass, which he had not yet raised to his lips, and looked at me smilingly. I blinked at him dully. Then, as if finishing the story had been a signal, the beautiful girl came out of the bar, still on the arm of the young writer. She hesitated by our table and it seemed to me that the same cryptic look passed between her and old Nemecek as when she had come in. And because she was very beautiful and very young, and because the young writer was famous for his idealism, I found myself shivering uncontrollably as I watched her walk toward the door.

"Here, drink your brandy," said Nemecek, eyeing me solicitously.

"The girl," I managed to say, "the girl in the story—did she come to the New World?" I was still under the spell of the fairy tale to which I had been listening.

"Drink your brandy," said Nemecek.

"And her lover," I went on. She was gone now. "That very close friend of yours. Was he really—?"

"The closest," said Nemecek.

THE HILL AND
THE HOLE

TOM DIGBY SWABBED his face against the rolled-up sleeve of his drill shirt, and good-naturedly damned the whole practice of measuring altitudes with barometric instruments. Now that he was back at the bench mark, which was five hundred eleven feet above sea level, he could see that his reading for the height of the hill was ridiculously off. It figured out to about four hundred forty-seven feet, whereas the hill, in plain view hardly a quarter of a mile away, was obviously somewhere around five hundred seventy or even five hundred eighty. The discrepancy made it a pit instead of a hill. Evidently either he or the altimeter had been cock-eyed when he had taken the readings at the hilltop. And since the altimeter was working well enough now, it looked as if he had been the one.

He would have liked to get away early for lunch with Ben Shelley at Beltonville, but he needed this reading to finish off the oil survey. He had not been able to spot the sandstone-limestone contact he was looking for anywhere but near the top of this particular hill. So he picked up the altimeter, stepped out of the cool shadow of the barn behind which the bench mark was located, and trudged off. He figured he would be able to finish this little job properly and still be in time for Ben. A grin came to his big, square, youthful face as he thought of how they would chew the fat and josh each other. Ben, like himself, was on the State Geologic Survey.

Fields of shoulder-high corn, dazzlingly green under the broiling Midwestern sun, stretched away from the hill to the flat horizon. The noonday hush was beginning. Blue-bottle flies droned around him as he skirted a manure heap and slid between the weather-gray rails of an old fence. There was no movement, except a vague breeze rippling the corn a couple of fields away and a farmer's car raising a lazy trail of dust far off in the opposite direction. The chunky, competent-looking figure of Tom Digby was the only thing with purpose in the whole landscape.

When he had pushed through the fringe of tall, dry-stalked weeds at the base of the hill, he glanced back at the shabby one-horse farm where the bench mark was located. It looked deserted. Then he made out a little tow-headed girl watching him around the corner of the barn, and he remembered having noticed her earlier. He waved, and chuckled when she dodged back out of sight. Sometimes these farmer's kids were mighty shy. Then he started up the hill at a brisker pace, toward where the bit of strata was so invitingly exposed.

When he reached the top, he did not get the breeze he expected. It seemed, if anything, more stiflingly hot than it had been down below, and there was a feeling of dustiness. He swabbed at his face again, set down the altimeter on a level spot, carefully twisted the dial until the needle stood directly over the middle line of the scale, and started to take the reading from the pointer below.

Then his face clouded. He felt compelled to joggle the instrument, although he knew it was no use. Forcing himself to work very slowly and methodically, he took a second reading. The result was the same as the first. Then he stood up and relieved his feelings with a fancy bit of swearing, more vigorous, but just as good-natured as the blast he had let off at the bench mark.

Allowing for any possible change in barometric pressure during the short period of his climb up from the bench mark, the altimeter still gave the height of the hill as under four hundred fifty. Even a tornado of fantastic severity could not account for such a difference in pressure.

It would not have been so bad, he told himself disgustedly, if he had been using an old-fashioned aneroid. But a five-hundred dollar altimeter of the latest design is not supposed to be temperamental. However, there was nothing to do about it now. The altimeter had evidently given its last accurate gasp at the bench mark and gone blooey for good. It would have to be shipped back east to be fixed. And he would have to get along without this particular reading.

He flopped down for a breather before starting back. As he looked out over the checkerboard of fields and the larger checkerboard of sections bounded by dirt roads, it occurred to him how little most people knew about the actual dimensions and boundaries of the world they lived in. They looked at straight lines on a map, and innocently supposed they were straight in reality. They might live all their lives believing their homes were in one county, when accurate surveying would show them to be in another. They were genuinely startled if you explained that the Mason-Dixon line had more jags in it than a rail fence, or if you told them that it was next to impossible to find an accurate and up-to-date detail map of any given district. They did not know how rivers jumped back and forth, putting bits of land first in one state and then in another. They had never followed fine-looking, reassuring roads that disappeared into a weedy nowhere. They went along believing that they lived in a world as neat as a geometry-book diagram, while chaps like himself and Ben went around patching the edges together and seeing to it that one mile plus one mile equaled at least something like two miles. Or proving that hills were really hills and not pits in disguise.

It suddenly seemed devilishly hot and close and the bare ground unpleasantly gritty. He tugged at his collar, unbuttoned it further. Time to be getting on to Beltonville. Couple glasses of iced coffee would go good. He hitched himself up, and noticed that the little girl had come out from behind the barn again. She seemed to be waving at him now, with a queer, jerky, beckoning movement; but that was probably just the effect of the heat-shimmer rising from the fields. He waved too, and the movement brought on an abrupt spell of dizziness. A shadow seemed to surge across the landscape, and he had difficulty in breathing. Then he started down the hill, and pretty soon he was feeling all right again.

"I was a fool to come this far without a hat," he told himself. "This sun will get you, even if you're as healthy as a horse."

Something was nagging at his mind, however, as he realized when he got down in the corn again. It was that he did not like the idea of letting the hill lick him. It occurred to him that he might persuade Ben to come over this afternoon, if he had nothing else to do, and get a precise measurement with alidade and plane table.

When he neared the farm, he saw that the little girl had retreated again to the corner of the barn. He gave her a friendly, "Hello." She did not answer but she did not run away, either. He became aware that she was staring at him in an intent, appraising way.

"You live here?" he asked.

She did not answer. After a while, she said, "What did you want to go down there for?"

"The State hires me to measure land," he replied. He had reached the bench mark and was automatically starting to take a reading, before he remembered that the altimeter was useless. "This your father's farm?" he asked.

Again she did not answer. She was barefooted, and wore a cotton dress of washed-out blue. The sun had bleached her hair and eyebrows several degrees lighter than her skin, giving something of the effect of a photographic negative. Her mouth hung open. Her whole face had a vacuous, yet not exactly stupid expression.

Finally she shook her head solemnly, and said, "You shouldn't of gone down there. You might not have been able to get out again."

"Say, just what are you talking about?" he inquired, humorously, but keeping his voice gentle so she would not run away.

"The hole," she answered.

Tom Digby felt a shiver run over him. "Sun must have hit me harder than I thought," he told himself.

"You mean there's some sort of pit down that way?" he asked quickly. "Maybe an old well or cesspool hidden in the weeds? Well, I didn't fall in. Is it on this side of the hill?" He was still on his knees beside the bench mark.

A look of understanding, mixed with a slight disappointment, came over her face. She nodded wisely and observed, "You're just like Papa. He's always telling me there's a hill there, so I won't be scared of the hole. But he doesn't need to. I know all about it, and I wouldn't go near it again for anything."

"Say, what the dickens are you talking about?" His voice got out of control, and he rather boomed the question at her. But she did not dart away, only continued to stare at him thoughtfully.

"Maybe I've been wrong," she observed finally. "Maybe Papa and you and other people really do see a hill there. Maybe *They* make you see a hill there, so you won't know about *Them* being there. *They* don't like to be bothered. I know. There was a man come up here about two years ago, trying to find out about *Them*. He had a kind of spyglass on sticks. *They* made him dead. That was why I didn't want you to go down there. I was afraid *They* would do the same thing to you."

He disregarded the shiver that was creeping persistently along his spine, just as he had disregarded from the very beginning with automatic scientific distaste for eeriness, the coincidence between the girl's fancy and the inaccurate altimeter readings.

"Who are *They*?" he asked cheerfully.

The little girl's blank, watery blue eyes stared past him, as if she were looking at nothing—or everything.

"*They* are dead. Bones. Just bones. But *They* move around.

They live at the bottom of the hole, and *They* do things there."

"Yes?" he prompted, feeling a trifle guilty at encouraging her. From the corner of his eye he could see an old Model-T chugging up the rutted drive, raising clouds of dust.

"When I was little," she continued in a low voice, so he had to listen hard to catch the words, "I used to go right up to the edge and look down at *Them*. There's a way to climb down in, but I never did. Then one day *They* looked up and caught me spying. Just white bone faces; everything else black. I knew *They* were thinking of making me dead. So I ran away and never went back."

The Model-T rattled to a stop beside the barn, and a tall man in old blue overalls swung out and strode swiftly toward them.

"School Board sent you over?" he shot accusingly at Tom. "You from the County Hospital?"

He clamped his big paw around the girl's hand. He had the same bleached hair and eyebrows, but his face was burnt to a brick red. There was a strong facial resemblance.

"I want to tell you something," he went on, his voice heavy with anger but under control. "My little girl's all right in the head. It's up to me to judge, isn't it? What if she don't always give the answers the teachers expect. She's got a mind of her own, hasn't she? And I'm perfectly fit to take care of her. I don't like the idea of your sneaking around to put a lot of questions to her while I'm gone."

Then his eye fell on the altimeter. He glanced at Tom sharply, especially at the riding breeches and high, laced boots.

"I guess I went and made a damn fool of myself," he said swiftly. "You an oil man?"

Tom got to his feet. "I'm on the State Geologic Survey," he said.

The farmer's manner changed completely. He stepped forward, his voice was confidential. "But you saw signs of oil here, didn't you?"

Tom shrugged his shoulders and grinned pleasantly. He

had heard a hundred farmers ask that same question in the same way. "I couldn't say anything about that. I'd have to finish my mapping before I could make any guesses."

The farmer smiled back, knowingly but not unfriendly. "I know what you mean," he said. "I know you fellows got orders not to talk. So long, mister."

Tom said, "So long," nodded good-bye to the little girl, who was still gazing at him steadily, and walked around the barn to his own car. As he plumped the altimeter down on the front seat beside him, he yielded to the impulse to take another reading. Once more he swore, this time under his breath.

The altimeter seemed to be working properly again.

"Well," he told himself, "that settles it. I'll come back and get a reliable alidade reading, if not with Ben, then with somebody else. I'll nail that hill down before I do anything."

BEN SHELLEY SLUPPED down the last drops of coffee, pushed back from the table, and thumbed tobacco into his battered brier. Tom explained his proposition.

A wooden-bladed fan was wheezing ponderously overhead, causing pendant stripes of fly paper to sway and tremble.

"Hold on a minute," Ben interrupted near the end. "That reminds me of something I was bringing over for you. May save us the trouble." And he fished in his briefcase.

"You don't mean to tell me there's some map for this region I didn't know about?" The tragic disgust in Tom's voice was only half jocular. "They swore up and down to me at the office there wasn't."

"Yeah, I'm afraid I mean just that," Ben confirmed. "Here she is. A special topographic job. Only issued yesterday."

Tom snatched the folded sheet.

"You're right," he proclaimed, a few moments later. "This might have been some help to me." His voice became sarcastic. "I wonder what they wanted to keep it a mystery for?"

"Oh, you know how it is," said Ben easily. "They take

a long time getting maps out. The work for this was done two years ago, before you were on the Survey. It's rather an unusual map, and the person you talked to at the office probably didn't connect it up with your structural job. And there's a yarn about it, which might explain why there was some confusion."

Tom had pushed the dishes away and was studying the map intently. Now he gave a muffled exclamation which made Ben look up. Then he hurriedly reinspected the whole map and the printed material in the corner. Then he stared at one spot for so long that Ben chuckled and said, "What have you found? A gold mine?"

Tom turned a serious face on him. "Look, Ben," he said slowly, "This map is no good. There's a terrible mistake in it." Then he added, "It looks as if they did some of the readings by sighting through a rolled-up newspaper at a yardstick."

"I knew you wouldn't be happy until you found something wrong with it," said Ben. "Can't say I blame you. What is it?"

Tom slid the map across to him, indicating one spot with his thumbnail. "Just read that off to me," he directed. "What do you see there?"

Ben paused while he lit his pipe, eyeing the map. Then he answered promptly, "An elevation of four hundred forty-one feet. And it's got a name lettered in—'The Hole.' Poetic, aren't we? Well, what is it? A stone quarry?"

"Ben, I was out at that very spot this morning," said Tom, "and there isn't any depression there at all, but a hill. This reading is merely off some trifle of a hundred and forty feet!"

"Go on," countered Ben. "You were somewhere else this morning. Got mixed up. I've done it myself."

Tom shook his head. "There's a five-hundred-eleven-foot bench mark right next door to it."

"Then you got an old bench mark." Ben was amusedly skeptical. "You know, one of the pre-Columbus ones."

"Oh, rot. Look, Ben, how about coming out with me this afternoon and we'll shoot it with your alidade? I've got to do it some time or other, anyway, now that my altimeter's out of whack. And I'll prove to you this map is chuck-full of errors. How about it?"

Ben applied another match to his pipe. He nodded. "All right, I'm game. But don't be angry when you find you turned in at the wrong farm."

It was not until they were rolling along the highway, with Ben's equipment in the back seat, that Tom remembered something. "Say, Ben, didn't you start to tell me about a yarn connected with this map?"

"It doesn't amount to much really. Just that the surveyor—an old chap named Wolcraftson—died of heart failure while he was still in the field. At first they thought someone would have to re-do the job, but later, when they went over his papers, they found he had completed it. Maybe that explains why some of the people at the office were in doubt as to whether there was such a map."

Tom was concentrating on the road ahead. They were getting near the turn-off. "That would have been about two years ago?" he asked. "I mean, when he died?"

"Uh-huh. Or two and a half. It happened somewhere around here and there was some kind of stupid mess about it. I seem to remember that a fool country coroner—a local Sherlock Holmes—said there were signs of strangulation, or suffocation, or some other awful nonsense, and wanted to hold Wolcraftson's rodman. Of course, we put a stop to that."

Tom did not answer. Certain words he had heard a couple of hours earlier were coming back to him, just as if a phonograph had been turned on: "Two years ago there was a man come up here, trying to find out about *Them*. He had a kind of spyglass on sticks. *They* made him dead. That's why I didn't want you to go down there. I was afraid *They* would do the same thing to you."

He angrily shut his mind to those words. If there was anything he detested, it was admitting the possibility of supernatural agencies, even in jest. Anyway, what difference did her words make? After all, a man had really died, and it was only natural that her defective imagination should cook up some wild fancy.

Of course, as he had to admit, the screwy entry on the map made one more coincidence, counting the girl's story and the cockeyed altimeter readings as the first. But was it so much of a coincidence? Perhaps Wolcraftson had listened to the girl's prattling and noted down "The Hole" and the reading for it as a kind of private joke, intending to erase it later. Besides, what difference did it make if there had been two genuine coincidences? The universe was full of them. Every molecular collision was a coincidence. You could pile a thousand coincidences on top of another, he averred, and not get Tom Digby one step nearer to believing in the supernatural. Oh, he knew intelligent people enough, all right, who coddled such beliefs. Some of his best friends liked to relate "yarns" and toy with eerie possibilities for the sake of a thrill. But the only emotion Tom ever got out of such stuff was a nauseating disgust. It cut too deep for joking. It was a reversion to that primitive, fear-bound ignorance from which science had slowly lifted man, inch by inch, against the most bitter opposition. Take this silly matter about the hill. Once admit that the dimensions of a thing might not be real, down to the last fraction of an inch, and you cut the foundations from under the world.

He'd be damned, he told himself, if he ever told anyone the whole story of the altimeter readings. It was just the silly sort of "yarn" that Ben, for instance, would like to play around with. Well, he'd have to do without it.

With a feeling of relief he turned off for the farm. He had worked himself up into quite an angry state of mind, and part of the anger was at himself, for even bothering to think about such matters. Now they would finish it off neatly, as scientists should, without leaving any loose ends around for morbid imaginations to knit together.

He led Ben back to the barn, and indicated the bench mark and the hill. Ben got his bearings, studied the map, inspected the bench mark closely, then studied the map again.

Finally he turned with an apologetic grin. "You're

absolutely right. This map is as screwy as a surrealist painting, at least as far as that hill is concerned. I'll go around to the car and get my stuff. We can shoot its altitude right off the bench mark." He paused, frowning. "Gosh, though, I can't understand how Wolcraftson ever got it so screwed up."

"Probably they misinterpreted something on his original manuscript map."

"I suppose that must have been it."

After they had set up the plane table and telescope-like alidade directly over the bench mark, Tom shouldered the rod, with its inset level and conspicuous markings.

"I'll go up there and be rodman for you," he said. "I'd like you to shoot this yourself. Then they won't have any comeback when you walk into the office and blow them up for issuing such a map."

"Okay," Ben answered, laughingly. "I'll look forward to doing that."

Tom noticed the farmer coming toward them from the field ahead. He was relieved to see that the little girl was not with him. As they passed one another, the farmer winked triumphantly at him. "Found something worth coming back for, eh?" Tom did not answer. But the farmer's manner tickled his sense of humor, and he found himself feeling pretty good, all irritation gone, as he stepped along toward the hill.

The farmer introduced himself to Ben by saying, "Found signs of a pretty big gusher, eh?" His pretense at being matter-of-fact was not convincing.

"I don't know anything about it," Ben answered cheerfully. "He just roped me in to help him take a reading."

The farmer cocked his big head and looked sideways at Ben. "My, you State fellows are pretty close-mouthed aren't you? Well, you needn't worry, because I *know* there's oil under here. Five years ago a fellow took a drilling lease on all my land at a dollar a year. But then he never showed up again. Course, I know what happened. The big companies bought him out. They know there's oil under here, but they won't drill. Want to keep the price of gasoline up."

Ben made a noncommittal sound, and busied himself loading his pipe. Then he sighted through the alidade at Tom's back, for no particular reason. The farmer's gaze swung out in the same direction.

"Well, that's a funny thing now, come to think of it," he said. "Right out where he's going, is where that other chap keeled over a couple of years ago."

Ben's interest quickened. "A surveyor named Wolcraftson?"

"Something like that. It happened right on top of that hill. They'd been fooling around here all day—something gone wrong with the instruments, the other chap said. Course I knew they'd found signs of oil and didn't want to let on. Along toward evening the old chap—Wolcraftson, like you said—took the pole out there himself—the other chap had done it twice before—and stood atop the hill. It was right then he keeled over. We run out there, but it was too late. Heart got him. He must of thrashed around a lot before he died, though, because he was all covered with dust."

Ben grunted appreciatively. "Wasn't there some question about it afterward?"

"Oh, our coroner made a fool of himself, as he generally does. But I stepped in and told exactly what happened, and that settled it. Say, mister, why don't you break down and tell me what you know about the oil under here?"

Ben's protestations of total ignorance on the subject were cut short by the sudden appearance of a little tow-headed girl from the direction of the road. She had been running. She gasped. "Papa!" and grabbed the farmer's hand. Ben walked over toward the alidade. He could see the figure of Tom emerging from the tall weeds and starting up the hill. Then his attention was caught by what the girl was saying.

"You've got to stop him, Papa!" She was dragging at her father's wrist. "You can't let him go down in the hole. *They* got it fixed to make him dead this time."

"Shut your mouth, Sue!" the farmer shouted down at her, his voice more anxious than angry. "You'll get me into trouble with the School Board, the queer things you say.

That man's just going out there to find out how high the hill is."

"But, Papa, can't you see?" She twisted away and pointed at Tom's steadily mounting figure. "He's already started down in. *They're* set to trap him. Squattin' down there in the dark, all quiet so he won't hear their bones scrapin' together—stop him, Papa!"

With an apprehensive look at Ben, the farmer got down on his knees beside the little girl and put his arms around her. "Look, Sue, you're a big girl now," he argued. "It don't do for you to talk that way. I know you're just playing, but other people don't know you so well. They might get to thinking things. You wouldn't want them to take you away from me, would you?"

She was twisting from side to side in his arms trying to catch a glimpse of Tom over his shoulder. Suddenly, with an unexpected backward lunge, she jerked loose and ran off toward the hill. The farmer got to his feet and lumbered after her, calling, "Stop, Sue! Stop!"

Crazy as a couple of hoot owls, Ben decided, watching them go. Both of them think there's something under the ground. One says oil, the other says ghosts. You pay your money and you take your choice.

Then he noticed that during the excitement Tom had gotten to the top of the hill and had the rod up. He hurriedly sighted through the alidade, which was in the direction of the hilltop. For some reason he could not see anything through it—just blackness. He felt forward to make sure the lens cover was off. He swung it around a little, hoping something had not dropped out of place inside the tube. Then abruptly, through it, he caught sight of Tom, and involuntarily he uttered a short, frightened cry and jumped away.

On the hilltop, Tom was no longer in sight. Ben stood still for a moment. Then he raced for the hill at top speed.

He found the farmer looking around perplexedly near the far fence. "Come on," Ben gasped out, "there's trouble," and vaulted over.

When they reached the hilltop, Ben stooped to the sprawling body, then recoiled with a convulsive movement and for a second time uttered a smothered cry. For every square inch of skin and clothes was smeared with a fine, dark-gray dust. And close beside one gray hand was a tiny white bone.

Because a certain hideous vision still dominated his memory, Ben needed no one to tell him that it was a bone from a human finger. He buried his face in his hands, fighting that vision.

For what he had seen, or thought he had seen, through the alidade, had been a tiny struggling figure of Tom, buried in darkness, with dim, skeletal figures clutching him all around and dragging him down into a thicker blackness.

The farmer kneeled by the body. "Dead as dead," he muttered in a hushed voice. "Just like the other. He's got the stuff fairly rubbed into him. It's even in his mouth and nose. Like he'd been buried in ashes and then dug up."

From between the rails of the fence, the little girl stared up at them, terrified, but avid.

THE ENORMOUS BEDROOM

HEAVEN HAS JUST one set of Pearly Gates, but Hell has a variety of entrances to suit its various guests. Some of the gates of Hell are jumping with red devils against a background of yellow flames, some are lined by languorous catlike women who look very seductive in their nakedness until they grow green or orange-and-black fur and unsheathe their dagger-claws, some have warders as emaciated and grim as the inmates of a Nazi death-camp— which they may very well have been in real life.

But no one ever found a door to Hell quite so peculiar and deceptive as the one discovered by the late playboy and racing car driver Nicholas Teufler.

It began with a tiny silver bell ringing inside his head, it felt. Very fast, very shrill, worse than a fire siren. And why did that particular comparison come into his mind, he wondered?

Nevertheless he ordered the tinkling to fade away and for a wonder it did. Then he cautiously worked open his eyes, which felt glued by hangover.

He was in a strange bedroom and it certainly wasn't a man's. That was not altogether unusual on mornings when he woke with bells ringing in his head—though never wedding bells as yet, by a stipend due stroke of good fortune for which Nicholas had never been properly grateful.

But this time he wondered if his run of luck hadn't come to an end.

He was looking at a vanity table cluttered with perfume bottles. He was sitting on the edge of a fully made-up bed topped with a fluffy-stuffed white satin coverlet dimpled with tiny gold buttons and he was wearing black pajamas with red piping. These details bothered him. They were ominous, in fact—the mingled aromas added up to lilies with the rotten-sweet under-scent of gardenias, while the white satin coverlet reminded him of the inside of a coffin. He shuddered. Nicholas had often said that marriage was a prison, but he hadn't had quite that tight a cell in mind. Well, this room seemed spacious enough at the moment, at any rate, to his still-blurry eyes.

His left wrist felt hot and a little painful, as if he had tried to punch someone in the snoot last night and missed and scraped a door-post. He pulled back the sleeve of his pajamas and saw a gunmetal wristwatch with a red face and black numerals and with thin black hands pointing at eighteen minutes to four. He'd never seen it before in his life. It felt almost hot to the touch.

As he started to unbuckle the black band, which felt like reptile hide, he blinked his eyes to clear them and looked at the wall behind the vanity.

There was no wall. For a moment he thought that he had wandered into a department-store window display, but there were no peering faces of mothers and kiddies, or scornful teenagers, or anyone at all. Then he saw that there was no plate of glass and that the room simply went on and on, with clusters of furniture and soft lights here and there, as far as he could see.

Maybe he was in a department-store furniture section. Where *had* last night's party ended. He remembered driving on a freeway ... and a lot of noise ... including sirens?

He looked up. There was a ceiling at least. Not more than eight feet above his head, for he could touch it. A gray slick ceiling like the screen of a dead television set.

Very slowly he turned around. In every direction the room

stretched endlessly, furnished at about thirty-foot intervals with easy chairs, sofas, studio couches, beds -Hollywood beds, oval beds, round beds, contour beds, beds with canopies and curtains -and each lit by lamps that glowed in pastel shades of blue, violet, pink, topaz, green -every color imaginable except red. The lamps farthest away clustered and ran together like distant nebulas in a giant telescope.

Overhead and underfoot, the slick gray ceiling and thick gray carpeting stretched off toward infinity. He felt like a bug in a crack. What if the crack should snap shut? What if the room did go on forever? What mightn't be hiding behind the furniture? For a moment he knew fear.

He asked himself what kind of engineering could hold up a ceiling that stretched without visible support for ... miles? Even in Texas -

Suddenly he noticed that he was no longer alone. Beside a long gray velvet sofa about ten yards away stood a girl in a low-cut red velvet evening sheath. A golden zipper ran down the front of her dress, glinting here and there in the rich scarlet. She was blonde, looked about twenty-one, and was smiling at him. It was a warm inviting smile, hinting at secrets—not the sort of smile you'd expect on even a perfectly built shop-window mannequin, though that had been his first thought on seeing her.

But then she leaned forward to pick up something from a low table which held a rose-glowing lamp. Nicholas Teufler didn't see what the something was, for he was looking down the front of her dress at two firm ivory breasts with nipples like coral lipstick ends. She seemed to be offering them for his inspection on a red satin tray, the material lining her dress.

He was moving toward her. His whole attitude toward his weird surroundings had brightened greatly. He and this wonder-girl would try out every piece of furniture in the place, he told himself enthusiastically. From sofa to couch to bed they would flit like butterflies—well, walk light-footedly at any rate. What did it matter if it took an eternity? And surely places that could materialize girls like this one could produce fresh-popped bottles of blonde champagne in golden ice-buckets with corded scarlet handles—it had to be, by the Law of Similars.

He was close to her now. She straightened up and reached out a slim arm toward him. He saw what she'd picked up—a tiny silver bell with an ebony handle she held between scarlet-nailed finger and thumb. With her other hand she began slowly to draw down the tag of her golden zipper. He reached out a hand toward hers.

The bell tinkled. At this frosty sound Nicholas felt a wave of dizziness. He exerted his will to banish the sound, as he had the first time, but it grew louder. Streaks of blackness swam in front of his eyes with narrowing streaks of crimson, girl, and gold. Then he was staggering and veering in darkness.

When his vision cleared, he was looking across ten yards of gray carpeting at a girl in a black lace negligee sprawled like a cat on a bed with green sheets and high old-fashioned head and foot made of silvery rods screwed together by silvery knobs large and small into rectangles of unequal size in which silver ornaments hung. Her shining black hair was tousled and one hand propped her chin as she gazed at him with a sultry dreaminess. A green-shaded lamp beside the bed intensified the green of the sheets and her eyes. It was clear that she was wearing nothing but girl under the black negligee.

Nevertheless it took Nicholas a moment to redirect his desires. He was angry with the girl in red for having thwarted him. Not "Ring Bell and Wait," but "Ring Bell and Vanish!" Most annoying. He would like to spank her.

He was still standing near the rose-lit gray velvet sofa. A quick, stooping look around it, a quick scan around the everyway-endless-room—no sign of the blonde in red, no sign of anyone at all except the new dark-haired charmer.

She was still watching him, her lips now fixed in an enigmatic catlike smile. Very well, thought Nicholas, if you're a cat, I'm a panther. No more of this vanish stuff. He strode toward her purposefully.

He wondered, though it didn't slow him, why the green light made him think of corpses; the short silver bed-rods, of coffin handles; the musky perfume of dead meat.

Still smiling, she rolled over quickly, her negligee falling open to show a perfect narrow black-haired triangle and the larger long one made by that and the coppery nipples of her firm breasts. At the same time she reached out a sun-tanned arm and, just as he dived at her wrist to stop her, flicked with a black fingernail one of the ornaments hanging in the squares—a tiny silver bell.

He hit carpet rather than bed. The dizzying tingle died away as swiftly as the highest notes of a piano, yet in the interval Nicholas blacked out to find himself looking up from the floor at a barefoot platinum-haired girl in a gunmetal mink coat beside a black davenport and a small black table on which stood a half empty bottle of scotch and a silver lamp casting a blue glow. She was staring at him haughtily, but a little unsteadily, and as she swayed, shifting gleams of a pale dress or pale flesh winked at him from the half-clutched front of her smokily gleaming fur coat.

Well, he thought, at least this one looks a little too drunk to play tricks with bells or anything like that. If only he could lay his hands on those other two tricksters, he'd ...! But he'd better concentrate on this one. A girl in the hand ... He warily got to his feet.

The blue light made Nicholas think of midnight and of impulsive sweet young lushes too eager to take a walk—and too adventurous—to bother to dress. It also made him think of drowned people—though this girl looked drowned in nothing but scotch. While the gunmetal shade of the mink reminded him of his strange new steam-heated wrist watch. He glanced at the latter. The hands still stood at eighteen minutes to four. And this time he also noticed a hair-thin sweep second hand standing still against the red face. The damned thing wasn't even running.

He started to rip it off, but at that instant there was a giggle. The mink coast had fallen open. It had hid flesh, not dress, all right—flesh formed in a torso like that of a slimmer Venus de Medici—and either her hair was naturally platinum or she was a completist. Her haughty lips had softened into a welcoming smile.

He lunged toward her, noting with approval that the streamlined silver lamp had no trace of dangling ornaments. The girl leaned eagerly forward and nodded encouragingly— which shook the two silver bells which were her earrings and which her platinum hair had camouflaged.

A blacked-out second later Nicholas was standing on black-morticed flagstones of black shale. A dozen steps away there was the yellow dancing of a wood fire crackling gayly on ornate silver andirons. Its shimmering fumes and faint smoke were drawn up into a hood of silver jutting down from the slick gray ceiling like the mouth of a giant trumpet.

He was still in the enormous bedroom, however. Everywhere else the gray carpeting with its clusters of furniture and lamps still stretched off toward infinity—a gray desert with furniture oases.

On a polar-bear rug by the fire lay a cream-skinned freckled redhead in a white sharkskin bikini fastened with white bow knots on her left hip and under her right arm. She was eyeing him measuringly, challengingly.

Nicholas accepted the challenge. He couldn't punish those three other teasers -not at the moment, at any rate— so he would wreak his wrath on this one. They all must be in cahoots, anyway.

What was that old sign?—In Case of Fire, Walk, Do Not Run, Toward ... Well, he was afire right now, and the sign had it just backwards.

He ran, rather than walked, toward the redhead.

She snatched a silver poker from the set beside the fire, losing her bikini top in the act, drew the poker back in mock threat—and hit the andirons, from which silver bells hung.

As Nicholas slid to a stop, sight blacked-out and skull tormented by tinkling, the floor under his bare feet turned from warm flagstones to something cold, wet, and squishy. Instantly he was thinking of mold and ooze and snakes and other crawlers—all the death-thoughts that had been haunting him from the dark side of his mind, while these infuriating girls tormented and obsessed the bright side.

But then the tinkling in his ears was replaced by a curiously familiar roaring. His eyes cleared and he saw it was that of a shower cascading down fiercely from a nickel fixture in the ceiling toward a slotted nickel drain met below in a floor of hexagonal white tiles. The gray carpeting was wet for yards around from the splashing and he was standing on the edge of the wet area.

A pink ghost was in the shower. Emerging, it became a curvy strawberry blonde who instantly snatched from the standing rack and clutched around her a brown bath towel. Orange light from heat lamps set in the ceiling did charming things to her skin. She looked at Nicholas with an expression of intense but not unhappy and very special surprise—the sort of look a woman seldom wastes on husbands and wandering electricians, but reserves for handsome secret agents on the prowl and—at a pinch—racing car drivers. Then came the familiar inviting smile.

But Nicholas had become extremely suspicious of inviting smiles. He wondered why none of these frustrating girls ever spoke to him—or he to them for that matter. Because they'd all been expecting him?

He didn't make a move. He felt very much four times bitten, five times shy. He also began to wonder if he'd just missed touching not four, but, say, four hundred girls—and consciously, but not subconsciously, forgotten the rest. He *felt* that frustrated and, looking back, there'd been a silver bell dinning in his ears when he first woke sitting on the white satin coverlet.

What the Devil was behind these peculiar frustrations?—he asked himself, deliberately keeping his attention off the strawberry blonde with the towel. He'd offended some girls in his life, hurt the feelings of others, perhaps even slightly cracked a heart or two—but surely these things didn't amount to enough to get a whole team of girls plotting to drive him mad. Besides, practical jokers didn't build rooms the area of cities—not even if they had the bankrolls of international financiers or last-century kings. A dream?—but he'd never had a dream with one-hundredth the Technicolor, definition, and sound-fidelity. Had his psychiatrist been feeding him LSD or mescalin? That seemed a better bet, but he hadn't seen Dr. Obermann for more than a year, if he could trust his memory. Besides, Dr. Obermann was -

He didn't complete that thought. Once again, sudden rage had filled him. Some day, he told himself, he would catch these devilish girls, preferably all five together, and then ...

With an effort he made himself think rationally again. How the Hell long would these peculiar and painful frustrations go on? Gazing around the enormous bedroom with its Milky Way of distant lamps, he seemed to glimpse the faint spectral forms of innumerable girls—blondes, brunettes, redheads, oddballs with blue and greenish locks, girls in sables and girls in shirts, girls stepping out of skirts or unbuttoning blouses or pulling sweaters over their heads, girls cross-legged on rumpled beds, sprawled on overstuffed furniture, straddling wire-backed with their forearms resting on the topmost loop of wire—there was no numbering the variety of their poses and stages of undress. Was he doomed to be frustrated by all of them? Until girls meant no more to him than grasshoppers? A voyeur's paradise—but Nicholas was discovering that unrelieved voyeurism can become more tiring than making love.

The ghost girls dimmed and faded entirely—if they had ever been anything more than imagination—leaving the infinite gray surround bare except for the strawberry blonde in front of the shower.

Nicholas tried furiously to resist—these frustrations were enragingly humiliating -but her smile became super-inviting, she kept almost losing her brown towel, and finally he yielded to the irresistible—though this time he moved forward without a grain of hope, despite the great seeming hope in the water-dewed girl's eyes.

He rationalized it by telling himself that it was interesting and even educational to see, even if very briefly, some of the intimate construction—details of such a variety of young females. Besides, he was curious as to where the devilish bell was hidden this time.

It was hanging, of course, from the shower head, previously hidden (and its tinkling muted) by the sizzling water. The blackout and skull-scream that seized him when she flicked it with her towel were quite as black and tormenting as any that had gone before.

Then he was moving slowly but compulsively toward a slim coffee-and-cream girl whose large brown eyes stared at him with a mysterious impassiveness. To one side of her was a cluster of bright violet globes, to the other a four-foot bronze arch supporting a yard-wide dark bronze gong with black leather-padded striker hanging beside it. The gong had enameled on it a curious design of red flames.

The girl stood absolutely motionless, her legs straddled and her arms zigzagged in a pose from a Siamese dance. She wore a silver girdle and breast cups of silver filigree, a silver turban was wound round her head, silver slave bracelets weighted her wrists, while from her ankles dangled clusters of tiny silver bells.

Why, this time the plotters weren't even taking the trouble to hide them! The girl had only to shake a foot and he'd be off again into blackout and pain and the next frustration.

Nicholas suddenly sat down on the gray carpeting and locked his hands around his knees. He'd be damned if he'd let himself be tricked again.

Damned?

He looked at his queer wrist watch. It was still stuck at eighteen to four, with the sweep second hand motionless and the two other downward-beating black hands looking like the wings of a bat coming out of Hell.

Hell?

What was his mind trying to tell him?

The brown eyes of the girl in the silver-filigree bikini brightened. She began to dance languorously with the upper half of her body. Momently Nicholas expected her legs to move, just a little, and the ankle-bell to tinkle, but her control was perfect. Grimly Nicholas held still himself, refusing to budge from his spot. To keep himself from going batty, he imagined in great detail what he could do to these six girls when he caught them without their bells. There was one fantasy in which, dressed as little girls, they sat obediently at desks too small for them, while he, with a supply of willow switches and other academic instruments of correction at hand, lectured them interminably on all topics from human anatomy to the Spanish Inquisition.

Nicholas' control was not perfect. The physical effects of such imaginings, added to the posturings of the coffee-and-cream girl, were slow in coming, but they came. His desire slowly rekindled, became overpowering. In an effort to surprise the silent danger, he tried to spring up swiftly, but his legs had become stiff and kinky and he stumbled.

The dancer's brown eyes grew very bright. Still without stirring her ankles, she reached out and lifted the leather-padded striker and struck the fire-emblazoned gong on its very center.

The gong's note was deep as the grave and its vibrations bone-shaking. Nicholas felt them battering him into insensibility. His fury fought back at this clubbing with sound waves, but that only made the pain worse. And this time his blackout was twice as black.

When he came to, limp as his black pajamas and aching everywhere, he was sitting in front of a large, gleamingly surfaced black desk in a very large black windowless room lined with black filing cabinets with numbering in red and labeled with a large red script that looked halfway between Arabic and Runic. Behind the desk was a most comfortable looking black swivel chair, empty. To the right of the chair, within easy reaching distance, was a great silver console covered with pushbuttons of an infinitude of pastel shades. He noted a line of them colored rose, green, blue, yellow, orange, and violet in that order and it made him remember the soft-lit six girls and his fury was re-fired so far as his debilitated state would permit.

To the left of the swivel chair and almost equally accessible, sat a girl in a high-necked black suit with red piping along the seams and pockets. Around her slim waist was a wide shining black leather belt with two red buttons. Her gleaming black pumps were edged with the same fiery vermilion and he could glimpse red clocks on her black stockings. She held a black notebook poised on her knee with a black pencil lightly held between her slim fingers and she sat very straight, like the properest of proper secretaries.

Her black hair was fixed in bangs, like Cleopatra's. Her black eyebrows were arched, her eyes were greenish-yellow, her face was slim, her mouth wide and painted with lipstick red as fire.

And she was grinning at him—quite nastily, Nicholas had to admit. Her eyes weren't at all like those of the other girls. They were *alive*—as a tiger's.

In addition to all this, she looked vaguely yet unpleasantly familiar to him. She was associated with some painful period in his life that he didn't want to bring to mind -and at the moment couldn't.

And he didn't for an instant associate her with the other six girls. They had all had, despite their abominable teasing, something of the mindless quality of houris or odalisques. This one looked like a very beautiful murderess about to defend herself from the witness stand, her every sense alert, her wits crackling, her dagger-claws barely sheathed.

To tell the truth, she frightened Nicholas a little. Her silent grinning seemed to hold a peculiar sort of menace. He blamed this uneasiness on his debilitated state and looked back from her to the desk.

There were only two objects on it: a tiny silver bell with a tiny red handle—he looked away from *that* quickly—and a large hour-glass with about as much white sand in its top as in its bottom.

Then he noticed a strange thing. He could see the white sand very sharply against the black background and there wasn't any dropping down from the top half of the hour-glass into the bottom. The hour-glass was stuck. He stared at it fascinatedly.

The silence of the room was profound, yet not complete. After a bit Nicholas identified a tiny sound breaking it—a soft ticking. He glanced down at his wrist watch. The hour-thin sweep second hand was moving around purposefully and the others already stood at sixteen to four—the longer wing of the bat was slowly rising.

The hour-glass was stuck, but the wrist watch was running—a highly suggestive but baffling circumstance.

Then he distinguished a second sound—a soft wispy snoring—and started with surprise. In the big black swivel chair behind the desk slumped a fat man. How the Devil had he missed him before? Impossible! Yet it seemed almost equally impossible that anyone could have crept into the chair without him noticing.

The fat man was wearing a strangely familiar gray suit. A dark pearl pin, also familiar, was affixed to his deep red silk necktie. His bald head was slumped forward on a cushion of chins and around it a dozen or so flies circled. Their lazy buzzing made a third small sound.

Nicholas Teufler recognized the man. He had sat on the opposite side of a desk from him often enough.

He was about to call, "Dr. Obermann," when he caught the girl in black with a vermilion fingernail quickly raised to her lips. Her grin had changed from nasty to something more like mischievous.

And now he realized why she looked familiar: although there were several differences, she made him think of Dr. Obermann's last secretary, a Miss Ferenzi.

He thought furiously. Had Dr. Obermann been giving him electroshock treatments? That would account for the blackouts and his muddled memory—including his memory of how long since he had seen the doctor.

Or dosing him with LSD or mescalin? More likely still. Those drugs also gave colorful and exciting hallucinations—visions which *could* turn nasty.

But this wasn't remotely like Dr. Obermann's office. Ten

times as big, for one thing. Also, while the new girl resembled Miss Ferenzi a bit, the latter had been a slim graying woman of forty with silver-rimmed glasses and a Viennese accent.

Besides, Dr. Obermann couldn't be treating him in any case, because Dr. Obermann was -

Again he almost shouted awake the snoring man. Again the girl's quick authoritative gesture stopped him. Now he could *feel* the aliveness in her eyes, as if they sent out invisible stinging rays. Besides "Be quiet!" what was she trying to tell him? Something she couldn't, daren't say out loud?

He stood up, noting that on the dark round seat of his chair was a red design exactly like that of the flames enameled on the gong which the girl in the silver bikini had struck.

He glanced behind him and involuntarily retreated toward the desk.

Only a few inches behind the back legs of his chair was the edge of a rectangular depression in the floor—a depression big as a tennis court which occupied all but a narrow border of the three-quarters of the room behind his chair.

Down inside it was a picture or expanse dotted with thousands of tiny points of light of all colors except bright red.

He couldn't tell if it was a dark picture or screen a few inches down or a great field of lights hundreds of feet below. Or even the star-fields of another, more colorful universe more than light-years away—except that some of the light moved. Still, there was the feeling that if he stepped off the edge, he might fall out of the world.

He sprawled down on the thickly carpeted, red-figured black floor and reached down his arm full length without feeling anything.

From this position it seemed to him that the strange pastel star-fields extended under the floor, beyond the bounds of the rectangle.

Was it a reality or was it a map?

Then his eyes fixed on a particular zig-zag of stars colored in this order: rose, green, blue, yellow, orange and violet.

They matched the lamps of the girls who had teased him. His anger flamed again. But—had he been *down there?*

He glanced at his watch. Still ticking. The black hands stood at ten to four—one straight line against the red face.

He got to his feet and turned around. The scene hadn't changed. Dr. Obermann still snored, but the smile of the girl in black seemed to have become conspiratorial. She wet the smile with the tip of her tongue. And now he saw that she was beckoning to him by curling the vermilion-tipped forefinger of the hand that held the black notebook.

He was passing the corner of the desk when he heard another sound—a very faint pattering.

The hour-glass had come unstuck. White sand was falling in a tiny stream.

And Dr. Obermann's snore had stopped, his bald head was upright, the flies still circling it, and his big hypnotic eyes, which Nicholas remembered without pleasure, were open.

"Hello, Teufler," he grunted, as if this were just another of their old sessions. "Take a pew."

Nicholas hesitated. The girl in black gave him one quick anxious nod. Dr. Obermann glanced toward her, but by then she was only smiling again—nastily. Nicholas sat down on the fire-stamped chair on which he had awakened and wondered why the doctor didn't bat at the flies, why he accepted this dark noisy coronet.

Dr. Obermann studied him with a little bored smirk. "Well, my boy," he asked, "how are your symptoms? Any interesting dreams to report?"

Nicholas snapped his fingers and said, "I know why this can't be happening—why I must be imagining it. You're dead! You died of fatty blockage of the blood vessels almost a year ago."

Dr. Obermann leaned forward, put his fat elbows on the desk, supported his chin-pillows with his pudgy fists. His smirk became a grin.

"On the contrary, my boy," he said, "that's exactly *why* this can be happening."

Nicholas swallowed. "You mean," he said, "I'm dead too?"

Dr. Obermann nodded beatifically. Nicholas thought: pain, glaring lights, a car hurtling out of the freeway exit he was headed toward ... No! Or rather, most regrettably, yes.

He said, "So that's why I kept smelling mold and decay and thinking of coffins."

Dr. Obermann nodded. "Yes, the shock of death is great and creates some vibrations that are a long time damping out."

"But you haven't changed a bit," Nicholas observed. "You're your ugly old self. While Miss Ferenzi has become an exceedingly beautiful young woman."

The psychiatrist scowled. "Miss Ferenzi didn't die with me. What gave you such a stupid idea? She's disorganizing some other doctor's files up above. This is my new secretary, Miss Diable."

Nicholas bowed to her. She nodded, murmuring in a husky contralto, "You're looking quite handsome yourself."

Dr. Obermann shot her a suspicious glance, than reached out a fat hand and laid it on her black-stockinged knee in a manner Nicholas found most offensive.

"But then where the Hell am I?" he demanded loudly. "Or," he added, "have I answered my own question?'"

"You have, my boy," the other told him in the sugary pat-on-the-shoulder tones which he'd used in the old days to inform Nicholas that he'd had a valid insight into his problems.

"But what the Devil then is a newcomer like you doing running Hell?" Nicholas demanded.

Dr. Obermann finally swiped negligently at the flies circling his shining cranium. Nicholas remembered that Beelzebub was called the Lord of the Flies. Then the psychiatrist said, "Not quite *the* Devil, my boy, though given a couple of years more..." His voice trailed off meaningly, then he went on briskly, "You forget that I arrived ten months ahead of you. And it turns out that Hell had become a typical big modern organization, my boy, in fact the biggest in the known universe. And you know how fast a man can get ahead in a big organization if he can discover the ropes and find where the bodies—so many of them here!—are buried—or burning! And who would be better than an ... ahem! ... unscrupulous psychiatrist ...?" He gave the black-stockinged knee a peculiarly intimate squeeze.

"—to discover the ropes of Hell!" Nicholas finished for him. "That I'll agree to." He shook his head. "But that Hell should actually exist when even ministers have given up pretending to believe in it—that's fantastic!"

Dr. Obermann shrugged. "But true. Like atom bombs in China, euphorics in glue, brassieres on Bali, light-rays that kill, and craters on Mars."

Nicholas hesitated. "But I always thought that Hell would be..." He grimaced distastefully.

"Full of pitchforks and flaming pitch and tortures and torments and all those other medieval curiosa?" Dr. Obermann finished for him. "My dear boy, you haven't visited all our departments, at least as yet. In some of them—" He shrugged and made a little grimace. "But although it has its secret concentration camps, Hell on the whole has become as progressive as the world—managerial, self-governing, democratic, with advancement open to anyone who keeps his wits about him." He smiled complacently. "Also, Hell has become highly competitive, just as our own culture—competition inside one big happy organization. You study the man above you for weaknesses, find the means to topple him, seize your opportunity and—presto!—you've advanced to the next power-level, whether it be assistant department manager or senior executive.

"Moreover," he went on, "Hell has become a welfare state, with rehabilitation rather than punishment its aim, especially when it comes to Vice rather than Violence."

"What's the exact difference?" Nicholas wanted to know.

"Violence is what harms another person, whether it injures them only a little or hurts them to the point of death," Dr. Obermann dogmatized. "While Vice is what harms the doer alone. In fact, anything done compulsively or to the point of boredom—to the point where it unbalances your life and makes it less rich—is vice! In your own case, my dear boy, the pursuit of girls. Especially the pursuit of girls unnecessarily prolonged. Your dossier shows that you have a bit of the voyeur in you. It's even been suggested that you'd rather chase girls than get them—Don't fume, Teufler! It never helps—that you'd rather watch girls do things than do things to them yourself.

"Of course, this again is characteristic of our culture with its increasing use of sex stimulation for purposes properly called perverse, such as money-making, and with so many more exciting desirable girls in advertisements, on billboards, in movies, TV and books than there are in the flesh."

Nicholas squeezed in, "It seems unfair that I should be punished—"

"Oh, you consider what's been happening to you punishment?" Dr. Obermann interrupted. "Some philosophers affirm that anticipation is far more delightful than fulfillment. In which case you've been in paradise, my boy."

"I didn't find it that way," Nicholas said gruffly, again battling down his rage at the six girls. "The old Chinese used uninterrupted sex as a torture. I think that in your intolerable anticipation indefinitely prolonged you've gone them one better. But what I was trying to say was that it's unfair that I should be punished for a fault of my own culture."

Dr. Obermann yawned. "War does exactly the same thing to the individual. It's the rule in this neck of the cosmos. A man has to be able to outthink his culture or else suffer the consequences. Vice is vice and must be given the treatment it deserves. Hence your frustrations, which I trust will now at least be more intelligible to you when I return you to them."

By chance or design, his hand moved toward the silver bell. Nicholas measured the distances—he had no chance of reaching it first. And if by some miracle he won the grab, he'd be sure to ring the thing. He looked around desperately. For an instant Miss Diable narrowed her eyes at him and tapped her left wrist with her right forefinger. The gesture meant nothing to him.

"I'd like to know one thing," he burst out hurriedly. "Is that map behind me—" He indicated the rectangle in the floor, "—an actual map of the place where I was, or a televised projection of it, or the thing itself, far below, and seen through its transparent gray roof?"

"Suppose you figure that out for yourself," the doctor retorted coldly. "But do consider the possibility that I can bring any part of it close by television, so that Miss Diable and I—if I wish—can amuse ourselves by watching your antics." His pudgy hand now moved definitely toward the bell.

"But why's the place down there so huge?" Nicholas demanded hurriedly.

The doctor halted his hand. "My dear boy," he grinned savoringly, "do you imagine you're the only man damned to that department of Hell, that it was constructed solely for you? No, there are thousands, millions of men going through it all the time, invisible to each other. Your vice is an extremely common one, as I explained. These days it takes a trained—and unscrupulous—psychiatrist to think of anything really new or interesting in the way of sexual deviations. Which reminds me, Miss Diable..."

He picked up the bell, but so delicately it didn't tinkle once.

Nicholas froze. Throat dry, he asked, "Does that mean you have millions of beautiful ... well ... she-devils working down there all the time?"

The doctor set down the bell with equal care. Apparently he thought such a rare bit of naiveté as Nicholas' could not be allowed to go unsquelched, for he said with a pitying smile, "My boy, Hell is above everything else efficient. If I may refresh a stale euphemism, we use even the squeal of the damned. The only she-devil you have viewed thus far is my charming Miss Diable. No, all the girls you encounter down there are bona fide female human beings damned for the vices of self-adoration and teasing, though some of our moralists consider the latter sin a mild violence. Their dossiers are there—" He indicated the nearest tier of filing cabinets, "—and they make quite interesting reading. A few of the naughty little lambs were murdered. Others grew into embittered old maids—though in Hell they're all young again so that they can practice their vice to the point of extreme frustration. You see, in almost every case they think it is *you* who jingles the silver bell to dismiss them. The one with the gong—a sadly superstitious little Hindu—had been led to believe that its sound would enchant you and keep you from escaping."

He continued, "They get pretty depressed with this constant rejection, as you can imagine, though they keep on smiling. When the suffering of one of them becomes simply too great, I summon her here and give her consolation. They're very grateful, the poor dears."

"How do you summon them?" Nicholas asked, still playing for time.

"Simply by pressing the appropriate one of these buttons," the other replied, turning toward the silver panel with great satisfaction. "You'll notice their interestingly large number, like the stars or the sands of the desert—if a psychiatrist may be permitted to wax poetic."

Nicholas looked toward Miss Diable. Now that her employer was turned away she quickly made a face of disgust, then for an instant pursed her vermilion lips at Nicholas. It was exactly the morale-restorer he needed.

Turning back, Dr. Obermann sighed, "I truly wish you too were a button-pusher, Nicholas, instead of the one for whom the bell is rung," and once again he reached toward the tiny red-handled instrument.

Nicholas fixed his features in a sneer. "Oh, I'd take it for granted that you could have your will of any of those poor little damned girls. After all, you're the great psychiatrist, you're the boss. But such easy conquests must be small satisfaction to you, I'm sure. Just as I'm sure you have no power over any of the girls with *status* in Hell, any of the really interesting ones, such as Miss Diable."

"Is that so?" Dr. Obermann asked harshly, drawing back his hands. "You really have the nerve to think that and tell me that to my face? Miss Diable! Come here and take some dictation!"

Rather ostentatiously he sat forward in his chair and thrust out a pillowy knee. He tossed his head, saying, "Off with you now," and the circling flies vanished.

Miss Diable stood up. While she was still turned away from the doctor, she stared intently again at Nicholas and again tapped her left wrist. Then, her eyes obediently downcast, with only the faintest professional smirk on her lips, she went over and sat down. Dr. Obermann at once clasped her with a gesture so intimate that Nicholas felt that any fiendess of good breeding should show strong signs of distaste and begin to struggle violently, perhaps employing a discrete judo chop. But Miss Diable merely poised her notebook and pencil, taking no notice of the hand crawling like a fat pink spider near her waist, except that her fiery nails thinned a little and her nostrils flared.

"You don't like this, Miss Diable, do you?" Dr. Obermann asked benevolently.

"I detest it," she replied cooly.

"And *this* even less?"

"You fill me with disgust and loathing."

"Yet you endure my attentions because you are my secretary and because this is Hell?"

"Yes, Dr. Obermann," she replied meekly.

Dr. Obermann turned his head to sneer at Nicholas. "Perhaps Teufler, you'll soon be begging me to ring the silver bell, eh?"

"Just two more questions, sir," Nicholas replied brightly, doing his best to hide his chivalrous anger. The hint of a master stratagem had come to his mind, but he could not quite bring it into focus. "Why did my wrist watch stop while I was having those ... well ... experiences *down there*— and then start up when I arrived here? And why was your hour-glass stuck when I arrived?—and then start to trickle when you woke and noticed me? Perhaps these are mysteries beyond my limited understanding, but—"

"Indeed they are, except in their simplest manifestations," Dr. Obermann said with happy contempt, meanwhile running his hand over Miss Diable's in a series of caresses which Nicholas found highly offensive. "Suffice it for you, Teufler, that time is not the tyrant here it is in the mortal world. By use of various clever gadgets we can start, stop, advance and reverse it. The mighty hour-glass is *my* gadget, the humble wrist watch yours. Your experiences, as you refer to them take place in the timelessness of eternity. As for myself, I sometimes travel from this workaday desk to seek refreshment in worlds of mystic enjoyment beyond your ken—secret realms of wonder known only to the upper executive echelons of Hades.

"But now I have various pressing matters to attend to, and I do not desire to bore you and perhaps pain you to excess by forcing you to witness them. So it is time I returned you to your ... ah ... experiences. I believe your next ... er ... receptionist is a professional stripper with lifelong mysophobia. Or is it a debutante accident prone as to scams and shoulder straps but unshakably credulous of the horrid picture of sex her mother painted her? No matter. Now, Miss Diable, prepare yourself to endure—"

With his free hand he snatched at the silver bell.

At that instant Nicholas seized the tiny milled knob of his wristwatch and set the time back from ten minutes past four to fifteen to.

The effect was all that could have been desired. Dr. Obermann's hand stopped an inch from the bell, his other paw dropped away from Miss Diable's person, and his hypnotic eyes closed. His pillow of chins received his bald head, while a dozen flies appeared from nowhere and began to circle it, and he began gently to snore.

Miss Diable sprang from his knee. With equal alacrity Nicholas came around the desk, carrying the flame-emblemmed chair, and set it down beside Dr. Obermann. With Miss Diable eagerly assisting, he transferred the gross bulk of the psychiatrist from one chair to the other. The dozing man did not wake, though the flies buzzed for a moment angrily. Nicholas took off his watch and strapped it on the doctor's wrist. Then he confidently seated himself in the swivel chair and tinkled the silver bell sharply.

Air whispered as it rushed in to occupy the space where Dr. Obermann had been. A clot of colliding flies buzzed frantically, then flew off like bullets.

Miss Diable set her fists on her black sheathed hips and said with great satisfaction, "Well, that takes care of *him*!"

Nicholas reached out a gentle but authoritative hand and gathered her onto his knee. She shivered delightfully—it gave his knee gooseflesh—and sighed, "Oh, Nick!" He repeated the claspings and caresses he had watched Dr. Obermann apply and discovered that there was not anything offensive about them at all—in fact, that they were the height of friendly courtesy. Miss Diable snuggled closer to him. He remarked on the similar colors of their costumes and she explained to him that she had planned it that way, after falling in love with his picture in the files. Thereafter she had guided Dr. Obermann's every step leading to his downfall.

Nicholas proceeded to demonstrate his gratitude. In putting his arm around her waist, he touched one of the red buttons on her belt. To his considerable interest, her skirt began slowly to shorten, though it was impossible to see where the material was disappearing to. Not that that problem concerned his mind greatly, he was more interested in discovering where her stockings ended. She looked down too, her cheek against his, as if she were as mystified as he—but after a bit she pressed the other button. Her skirt crawled down an inch, to mid-thigh, and stopped.

"For now," she said softly, adding, "Hell has some extremely clever couturiers, don't you think? And they're not one-idea men either."

He explored her jacket. A glint of silver at the end of the red piping of one of her pockets intrigued him. He delicately pinched the zipper-tag between finger and thumb and pulled it four inches sideways. There popped out a breast that would have fitted a champagne glass, but now rested in a half-cup red silk brassiere. Feeling that symmetry must always be maintained, he repeated the action with the other pocket, with the same result. Miss Diable luxuriated against him like a cat, looked up at him innocent-eyed and asked, "Didn't you ever know why they were called breast pockets? There are at least six other stimulating gadgets on this wardrobe. I think it would be nice, Nick, if in the spirit of a treasure hunt—"

But by then the word "six" had registered on Nicholas' mind. He suddenly sat up straight, almost dumping Miss Diable on the floor.

"This is all very well," he said in tones of fury, "but—"

"I should think it's all very well," Miss Diable countered indignantly, glaring at him. "I've often been told it's the greatest."

"Oh, all very, *very* well," he placated her. "You have opened up to me lines of exploration which I have no doubt I will spend intoxicated hours investigating. But—" (Again his voice became furious) "—there are a certain six girls who have frustrated me abominably. I assure you I cannot concentrate on anything else until I have admonished each of them severely. So please explain to me the system of the buttons on this silver panel, so we can have them up in sequence, beginning with one particular slim blonde wearing a red velvet evening sheath with a red zipper."

Miss Diable stood up, quivering with suppressed anger, yet looking most engaging in her short-short skirt and with her pocketless breast pockets filled.

"Mr. Teufler," she said evenly, "I cannot accede to this humiliating request. That you should prefer any or all of six damned little minxes to *me*, one of the upper crust of Hell, one of the status figures, as you yourself said—"

"I infinitely prefer you to any one or all six of them together, Miss Diable," he assured her. "In fact, I detest them to the point of obsession—but that's just the point! Until I have rebuked each of them *very* severely, I cannot possibly think of anything, or even *anyone* else."

"Do you think you have the strength to rebuke all six?" she sneered.

"Do not increase my anger, dear divine—I mean devilish Miss Diable," he told her, "but obey my orders. Oh, and while you're at it, please fetch me from the files the dossiers of each of the girls, so that I will be able to interrogate them searchingly before I rebuke them. I intend to reduce each one of them to a quivering—"

"Can't you at least get it through your thick head," she shouted, "that they weren't trying to frustrate but hold onto you? That they were suffering in their schoolgirl way as much as you?'

Nicholas frowned. "I hadn't thought of that," he admitted, smiling. "Perhaps I'll give them medals after admonishing them. Kindly scout up for me a half dozen silver pitchfork brooches or whatever else seems appropriate."

"Mr. Teufler!" Miss Diable asserted ringingly, the contents of her breast pockets quivering. "You are on the way to making me as angry with you as I was with Dr. Obermann. Do you see that tiny red light moving about down there?" She pointed beyond the desk to where a tiny bright point of red light was indeed moving among the pastel ones. "*That* is Dr. Obermann, who is even now suffering the tantalizations and torments you were going through with the same six damned little demi-virgins. Do you want to put yourself on his level? Do you expect me to sit quietly by, taking notes, while—"

The vision enchanted Nicholas. "Miss Diable, I will tolerate no further delay!" he said incisively. "You are *my* secretary now and must obey all my orders, just as you did those of Dr. Obermann. And I want you to understand—in fact, I order you to understand—that what I am doing is only to rid my emotions of an intolerable burden. So explain to me at once the system of the buttons and also teach me the appropriate dossiers and medals!"

"I won't," she said, folding her arms at waist height, which made a frame for her breast pockets.

"Very well!" he blustered, well aware that he knew

nothing whatever of the system whereby Dr. Obermann had enforced the obedience of Miss Diable, or if there had been such a system. "Very well, then I'll do it for myself. Don't think I can't; the colors are seared on my memory: rose, green, blue, yellow, orange, violet. And I earlier noted a line of buttons of those hues." He studied the panel briefly. "Ah, here they are! Now, Miss Diable," he said, turning to her triumphantly, "are you going to fetch me the dossiers—and medals!—and explain to me customary procedures, or am I simply going to press this rose button?"

She stood straight no longer, but crouched like a cat, her green eyes glaring. "So you insist," she hissed, "that I demonstrate to you that you are not all-powerful. Very well, be it on your own head—or tail, if that's the way you happen to land!"

In one blur of movement, she seized the hour-glass on the desk and tipped it almost on its side, so that the trickle of sand nearly stopped, became the barest sliding of one or two grains at a time.

Nicholas was instantly paralyzed. His right forefinger, already touching the rose button, could not exert an atom of force against it.

At the same time the room around him grew dim, so that he saw it only as a shadow, while at the same time he found himself in another room, lit with burningly hot white lights. Here he was one of a considerable group of men and a few women crouched around a very large circular table. Each of them had the look of a high executive, a master of men, yet each was obviously in a state of pitiable shock, apprehension, and terror. In the center of the table squatted an obscene monster, half man, half dragon, with a barbed black tail and burningly red eyes. It was the size of a medium tank. It was clearly giving all the upper-crust underlings, all the presumable department heads, a dreadful tongue-lashing— both figuratively (in a voice like an orchestra of drums, sirens, machine-guns, and cannon) and literally (with a very long barbed black tongue that snaked out from between slabby lips and yellowed fangs to flog the backs of super-folk screeching out pain and promises.)

Through this tumult Nicholas could still hear the voice of Miss Diable saying meaningfully, "Now you understand that Dr. Obermann was in somewhat the same position as you were down below. A considerably worse position, in fact. You are witnessing one of the 'worlds of mystic enjoyment in which he refreshed himself,' as Dr. Obermann somewhat falsely described it. Now, will you return and behave like a sensible executive, running your department under my guidance in such a way as to avoid such rebukes and admonitions as you are now witnessing?—*and will you stop nattering about those six girls?*—or would you rather I turned the hour-glass fully on its side for a period of, say—"

The very long, very barbed black tongue was already lashing the man beside Nicholas—an executive giant with the build of a football guard, who cowered weeping and bleating.

"I promise!" Nicholas called loudly. "I promise, dear Miss Diable! I'll never mention those six girls again. All my animosities have vanished, I assure you. It's quite impossible to maintain them in this atmosphere. Just be quick! I promise ... on my hour-glass!"

The hateful bright room vanished. The black room returned. Nicholas collapsed into the black swivel chair. Miss Diable smiled at him in gentle triumph until his shaking had abated, then seated herself again upon his knee.

Interweaving her fingers behind his neck, she said softly, "My dear Nick, I knew you'd be sensible when you understood the realities of the situation."

Yielding gracefully to the inevitable, Nicholas embraced her in turn. "I am sure you are quite the loveliest fiend in all Hell," he murmured. "Quite the most charming she-devil in all Gehenna. I cannot imagine how I could ever, while looking at you, have had a single thought of any of those miserable little damned girls down there."

"They are miserable, aren't they?" she agreed, yawning. "So miserable, in fact, that I feel no jealousy of them at all. In fact, if you're especially nice to me, over an extended period, I might let you look at one or two of their dossiers and even experiment with the buttons a bit, on long boresome afternoons."

"Darling," he said, embracing her with renewed enthusiasm and adding with almost complete sincerity, "The only buttons I am remotely interested in are yours. If I should press the one on your belt again and at the same time the one I can feel through your skirt at the base of your spine—"

Her lips burned, her tongue was a flame, her slim body through the unthreading seams of her black suit was like fire—almost.

BLACK GLASS

ON A CHILLY SATURDAY in late autumn last year I was walking slowly east on Forty-second Street in New York, threading my way through the somewhat raunchy throngs and noting with some wonder and more depression the changes a quarter-century had made in the super-metropolis (I'd visited the city several times recently, staying in Greenwich Village and Chelsea, but this was the first time in more than twenty years that I'd walked any distance across midtown Manhattan), when there was borne in on me the preponderance of black glass as a facing material in the newer skyscrapers, as though they were glisteningly robing themselves for an urban funeral -perhaps their own.

Well, there was justification enough for that, I told myself with a bitter smile, what with the grime, the smog, the general filth and pollution, garbage strikes, teachers' strikes, the municipal universities retrenching desperately, municipal financing tottering near bankruptcy, crime in the growling, snarling streets where the taxi drivers, once famed for their wise-guy loquacity, were silent now, each in his front-seat fort, communicating with his passenger only by voice tube and payment slit. For two blocks now I'd been passing nothing but narrow houses showing X-rated films with an emphasis on torture, interspersed with pornographic bookstores, leather shops, hardware stores displaying racks of knives, a few seedy drug and cigar stores, and garish junk-food bars.

Did my gloomy disapproval of all this reflect nothing but my piled-up years? I asked myself. (Those around me were mostly young, though with knowing eyes and used-looking flesh.) I'd reached the age where the rest of life is mostly downhill and more and more alone, when you know that what you haven't gotten already you most likely will never get—or be able to enjoy if you do, and when your greatest insights are apt to transform next moment into the most banal clichés, and then back again and forth still once more, bewildering. And just lately I'd tried and failed to write a book of memoirs and personal philosophy—I'd set out to make a net to capture the universe and ended by creating a cage for my solitary self. Had New York City really changed at all? For example, hadn't Times Square, across which I was now pressing, been for the last seventy-five years a mass of gigantic trick advertisements flaring aloft—monstrous ruby lips that puffed real smoke, brown bottles big as tank cars pouring unending streams of grainy electric whisky? Yes, but then they had evoked wonder and amusement; the illusions had been fun; now they got only a bored acceptance and a dark resentment at the establishment power they represented; the violence seething just below the surface in the city was as real as the filth upon that surface, and the skyscrapers had reason to foresee doom and robe themselves in black.

Of course the glass wasn't really black—an opaque black—although it looked like that from the outside. But when you went inside (as I now did, through revolving doors, into the spacious lobby of the Telephone Building at Forty-second and Sixth Avenue), you saw at once it was only somewhat dusky, as if a swift-traveling storm cloud had blotted out the sun while you were going in. Or as if (it occurred to me with a twinge of fear) the small gray churning edged shadow in my left eye were expanding out to cover the whole visual field—and invading my right eye also. (I'd discovered that evidence of retinal degeneration a year ago, and the optical surgeon had treated it with skillfully aimed bursts of laser light, whose pinpoint cautery had scarred the diseased

tissue, arresting the shadow's spread—but for dreary weeks
I'd anticipated going blind and practiced for that by feeling
my way around my room for an hour each day with my eyes
shut tight.)

Now through the dusky glass I saw a young woman in a
dark green cloak and gloves and jaunty visored cap pulled
down—it was a chilly day, foreshadowing winter -striding
along purposefully in the direction I'd been going, and her
example inspired me to shake off my dismal thoughts, push
out through the dizzying doors, and follow after. I enjoyed
passing iron-fenced Bryant Park with its winter-dark bushes
and grass, although the wind bit keenly—at least there
were no neon promises of sick thrills, no violet-glowing
mercury-vapor commands to buy. And then I came to the
great Public Library at Fifth Avenue, which always gives me
a lift with its semblance of being an island of disinterested
intelligence in a dingy, commercial sea—although today,
in tune with the times, a small scattered crowd encircled
a swarthy man juggling flaming torches on the library's
broad steps (encourage local street artists!—it promotes
integration) while the two proud stone lions flanking the
wide entry seemed to look away disdainfully. Some skinny
children ran around the northern one, two rangy blacks
conversing earnestly rested themselves against its side, and
then my striding young woman in green, coming suddenly
out of a crowd, passed in front of the lion, but as she did so,
she briefly paused with face averted and laid her hand upon
its mane in a gesture that was at once compassionate and
commanding and even had an odd and faintly sinister note
of ritual. I knew I was being imaginative to read so much
into a stranger's gesture seen at a distance, but it nevertheless
struck me as being somehow *important*.

She had reversed directions on me, going back toward
Sixth, and once more I took my cue from her for my own
strolling. I wasn't following her with any real intentness, or
at least that's what I told myself then—why, I hadn't even
glimpsed her face either time—but I did want to see more of
those black glass buildings, and they had seemed to cluster

most thickly north on Sixth. At any rate, by the time I'd reached Sixth again, I'd lost sight of her, though I somehow had the impression she'd turned north there.

I reminded myself it isn't called Sixth any more, but been rather grandiosely renamed the Avenue of the Americas. Though really it's the same old knock-about Sixth that once had an elevated and then was forever being dug up. And it's still Sixth underground—the Sixth Avenue IND subway.

I found enough black glass as I wended north, peering upward like a hick, to delight my sense of the grotesque. After New York Telephone there was RCA Corporation and Bankers Trust and West Side Federal Savings and W.R. Grace and Company, where the dark glass sloped, and the Stevens Tower, where the black facings were separated by gravestone pale verticals. And at 1166 they had black glass with *stars*, by God (but why were green faceless people painted on the wooden facing masking the lobby they were rebuilding there? Here be mysteries, I thought.)

But all the time that I was playing my game with the buildings, I was aware of a not altogether pleasant change that had begun to take place in the scene around me after I'd looked out of the lobby of the Telephone Building and seen the day suddenly darken. That darkening effect had kept up after I'd got outside, as if the afternoon were drawing to an end sooner than it should, or as if—melodramatic fantasy!— an inky infection were spreading from the pernicious black glass to the air and space around it. The farther north I pressed, block by block, the more I noticed it, as though I were penetrating deeper and deeper into some realm of not altogether unfrightening mystery.

As for the girl in green, although I once or twice thought I'd caught sight of her a block or so ahead, I made no effort to catch up with her and verify my guess (or see her face.) So she could hardly be responsible for the darkly romantic element (the feeling of playing with mysterious dangers) that had entered my fantasies. Or so I believed at the time.

And then I found I'd arrived at Rockefeller Plaza, where the black tried to disguise itself with dim silvery verticals, and the game became by degrees a little more somber and frightening. I think the transition occurred at the Pool of the Planets. I noted that oddly but not unpleasantly jarring feature (in the midst of the metropolitan commercial, the cosmic) down in a sunken court. I was instantly attracted and descended by means of broad gray granite steps. Nearby were chaste advertisements for a municipal theater offering something called "The New York Experience," which somehow struck me a bit comically, as though London should announce it was going to impersonate London. And there were other features which I have forgotten.

The pool itself was dark and very shallow, perfectly circular and quite wide, and from it rose on slender metal stems, all at their proper distances from the center and in their proper sizes, amazingly, as far as I could determine, the spheres of the planets done in some darkened silver metal and blackish brass. Simple inset plates of the same metals gave the names, symbols, dimensions, and distances. Truly, a charming conceit, but with sinister touches (the theme of darkening, the idea of the planets emerging from, or menaced by, a great unknown sea in space), so that when I finally turned away from it and especially when I'd mounted the stairs again to the sidewalk, I was not altogether surprised to find the scene around me altered still further. The people seemed to have grown fewer and I was unaccountably hesitant to look at their faces, and it had grown much, much darker—a sort of grainy blackness sprinkled everywhere—so that for the first time in months I felt for a moment in sharpest intensity the fear I'd had a year ago of going blind, while in my mind, succeeding each other rapidly, there unrolled a series of very brief darting visions: of New York and its high-rises drowned in a black sea, of the girl in green whirling on me and showing under her cap's visor no face at all, of the northern library lion coming suddenly awake at memory of the girl's touch (post-hypnotic command?) and shaking his pale mane and suppling his stony flanks and setting out after us, the pads of his paws grating on the steps and sidewalk, like giant's chalk—those fugitive visions and a dozen like them, such as the mind only gets when it's absorbing presentations from inner space at top speed, too many to remember.

At the first break in those visions, I wrenched my attention away from inner space to the sidewalk just ahead of me and I moved away from the sunken court. It worked. My surroundings didn't darken any further (that change was arrested) and the people grew no fewer, though I didn't yet risk looking at their faces. After a space I found myself grasping a thick brass railing and gazing down into a larger and—thank God! -more familiar sunken area. It was the skating rink, and there, one more figure among the graceful circlers in the white-floored gloom (a couple of them in rather flamboyant costumes, a couple of them suggesting animals), was my girl in green with cap pulled down and cloak swinging behind her, taking the long strokes you'd have expected from her striding.

I was entranced. I remember telling myself that she'd had just enough time, while I'd paused at the Pool of the Planets, to put on her skates and join the others. It was a delight to watch her moving swiftly without having to chase after her. I kept wishing she'd look up and I'd see her face and she'd wave. I concentrated so on her that I hardly noticed the gloom once more on the increase, and the other skaters growing fewer as they broke away to glide from the rink, and the low murmur of comment growing around me. It was as if there were an invisible spotlight on her.

And then there entered the rink with a rush, skidding to a near stop at its center, an amazing figure of clownish comedy, so that the murmur around me changed to laughter. It was that of a man in a wonderfully authentic tawny-pale lion's costume with more of a real lion's mask than a man's face, as with the Cowardly Lion in *The Wizard of Oz*, so that for a moment (but a moment only) I recalled my fantasy of the library lion coming to life. The girl in green came smoothly gliding toward him, as if they were supposed to waltz together, and he moved to meet her but then skidded off at an unlikely angle, fighting to keep his balance, and the laughter rose obediently.

It went on like that for a while, the lion proceeding around the rink in a series of staggering rushes and skids, flailing his front paws (his arms) in every direction, the girl circling him solicitously and invitingly, dipping in toward him and out, to the accompaniment of the laughter.

But then the scene grew darker still, as if the invisible spotlights were failing, and the grating of the lion's skates against the ice louder as he skidded (so that my library-lion fantasy came uneasily back to my mind), and he moved more slowly and drooped his great maned mask as if he were sick, so that his efforts to keep balance became more pathetic than comical, and the laughter, and then all the other sounds too, died away as though someone had turned on a tap marked "Silence."

And then he collapsed in a sprawling heap on the ice and the girl reached him in one long glide and knelt low over him, and the darkness became so great that I could no longer see the green in her visored cap or in her cloak trailed on the ice behind her, or in the gloves on her hands cupping his huge jowls, and the gloom closed in completely.

It was then that my trick of concentrating on the pavement just ahead of me (there was light enough for that, it was lighter up here) and not looking at faces (there were people crowding around me now, though they made no noise) stood me in good stead, so that I was able to get away, step by step, from the sunken court of the skating rink drowned in inky darkness.

I don't know with certainty what my intentions were then. I think they were to get down to her somehow and help her with her unfortunate partner. At any rate, one way or another, letting myself move with the crowd here, clutching along a stair rail there, I did manage to descend several levels, one of them by escalator, until I finally emerged into that brightly lit, somewhat low-ceilinged world of dingy white tile which underlies so much of New York.

There was one difference, however. Although the place

was lined with colorful busy storefronts, and marked with arrow-trails leading to various street exits and subways, and although there were throngs and scatters of people following along them, everything went silently, or at most with a seashell-roaring suggestion of muted noise, as if I had actually gone temporarily deaf from a great but unremembered sound, or else descended rapidly from a very great height and my ears not yet adjusted to it.

Just then I was caught up in a hurrying crowd of people coming from one of the subway entrances, so thick a crowd that I was forced to move with it for a ways while I edged sideways to get free. And then this crowd was in turn further constrained by another crowd pushing in the opposite direction—into the subway—so that my efforts to extricate myself were further hampered. And then, while I was in that situation, just being hemmed in and carried along, I saw my young woman in green in the same predicament as myself, apparently, but in the other crowd, so that she was being carried toward and then past me. I saw her face at last: It was rather narrow and somehow knifelike with glowing hazel eyes, and I got the instant impression of invincible youth strangely matured before its time. She looked angry and somewhat disheveled, her green cap pushed back with visor askew and brown hair foaming out from under it. She didn't have her lion man being crowded along with her (*that* would have been a sight, I told myself—and might have gained her some space, too) but she *was* carrying, clutched to her chest, a pale-tan long-haired cat. And then, just when she'd been carried opposite me and I unable for the moment to move a step closer to her—there must have been a dozen people between us; we could only see each other clearly because we were both quite tall -why, just then she looked straight at me and her hazel eyes widened and her brown eyebrows went up, and lifting one cupped hand alongside her lips while she clutched her cat more closely with the other, she twice called something to me, working her lips and face as though she were trying to enunciate very clearly, before she was rapidly carried out of my sight—and all the lights around me dimmed a little. I made a real effort to get free and follow her then, but it only resulted in a minor altercation that further delayed me—a woman I was squeezing past snarled at me, and as I begged her pardon while still trying to get past, a man beside her grabbed me and told me to quit shoving and I grabbed his elbows and shook him a bit in turn, while still apologizing. By that time the crowd had started to melt away, but it seemed too late now to go tearing after the girl into the subway. Besides, I was still trying to make sure of and puzzle out the cryptic message I thought she'd called to me—actually I was pretty sure of it, what with my hearing having gotten somewhat better and a bit of reading her lips as they carefully shaped the few words. Twice.

Spoken in the manner of someone who announces a change of rendezvous or a place to get together in case of separation, the repeated message was simply: "Cortlandt Street. Tower Two. The Deck."

Now that wasn't cryptic at all, I told myself, now that I'd hopefully got it down straight. Cortlandt Street was simply a subway address of the World Trade Center, Tower Two was the southern-most of the lofty twins, and the 107th floor was the observation deck with the open-air promenade on the 110th, the roof, to which you could go by a long three-story escalator—I knew all about that. I'd been up there myself only two days ago to enjoy the magnificent view of Manhattan, Queens, Brooklyn, the East River and the Hudson, Staten Island, the Jersey shore. It lay on the same subway line (only a few stations farther along) I'd be taking myself in a bit to get back to where I was visiting with my son in Greenwich Village.

For I wasn't going aboveground in this locality again today—that much I was sure of. I was no longer so sure of exactly what had happened up there, how much had been due to a weird weather change or a confusion about time (though a wall clock told me just then that it was still more than an hour until sunset) and how much had been subjective, a matter of my mood and the strange directions my imagination had taken. There are people who get panicky in crowds and narrow places, such as big city streets, they actually go crazy. I'd never had any trouble that way that I knew of, but there's always a first time. In fact, there are all sorts of strange things that happen to you and you find out about yourself as you grow older. Such as playing a game with yourself or pretending to be attracted to younger and younger women and following them in the street. All sorts of nonsense. (Another part of my mind was reminding me that her message to me had been real and that she had touched the library lion and skated with a sick lion-man and been carrying a long-haired cat of the same color when last seen. What was to be made of that?) But however much nonsense or no, nonsense and vivid daydreams, I wasn't going to go up to Rockefeller Plaza again today and look down into the Pool of Planets or the skating rink. No, I wasn't going to do that.

As my thoughts reached that point, the underground lights flickered again, shadows racing across the white tile, and dimmed down another notch. "What's the matter with the lights?" I involuntarily demanded aloud, fighting to keep the note of panic out of my voice.

The man who happened to be shuffling past me at that moment was quite short. He was wearing a black overcoat worn smooth in spots with a dusty-looking astrakhan collar. His head was bowed under the weight of a black derby, also worn shiny in spots, and he had it pulled down to his jutting ears, making them jut out still farther.

He halted and lifted his face toward mine (it took quite a swing of his head) and I got a considerable minor shock, for covering his entire face below his eyes was a white gauze mask such as the Japanese favor during cold epidemics. But it wasn't altogether white by any means. Centered on it were two coal-black spots where his nostrils would be underneath. Each was surrounded by a wide grey border fading up to white at a distance of about two inches from the dull jet centers. They overlapped, of course. While below them was a horizontal grey-bordered line only less black marking his mouth. I wondered in what atmosphere he could have been all day to have accumulated so much pollution. Or had he worn the same mask for several days?

Then, keeping his fierce dark eyes fixed on mine, he growled somewhat muffledly (the mask) but in the measured tones of an originally mild man grown truculent, even recklessly so, with the years and repeated disillusion, "So what's the matter with the lights? Nothing's the matter with the lights. They're always like that—only sometimes worse. This is a little above average. Where have you been all your life?"

"I'm just visiting New York," I told him. "My son."

"So who visits New York?" he demanded, continuing to eye me suspiciously. "We should be so lucky as to be somewhere else. Your son hasn't gotten away yet? That's terrible. My condolences."

I didn't quite know how to answer that one, so I just continued to look at him sideways. Somehow while talking we'd begun to walk on slowly together toward the subway.

"So what's with *this*, you're asking maybe?" he said challengingly, indicating his mask. "The old schmuck has got the crazies about germs, they're trying to assassinate him? That's what my wife thought, and my brother-in-law the druggist, when I started to wear it." He shook his head slowly and emphatically. "No, my friend, I'm not afraid of germs. Germs and me, we get on all right, we got an understanding, things in common. Because germs are alive. No, it's the dead Dreck I don't want none of, the Guck (that's the goyish word for it), the black foam."

His muffled, muttering voice was indescribably odd. There was nothing wrong about my hearing now, incidentally. I searched for a relationship between the visual and auditory dimmings I'd been experiencing, but there didn't seem to be any, their cycles didn't jibe.

I was going to ask him what industry or business the black foam figured in, though it didn't sound like a very specific thing, but by then we were at the subway. I half expected him to head uptown for the Bronx, but he stuck with me and changed with me a station or two later to the IRT.

"I'm getting off at Fourteenth Street," I volunteered, adding after a moment, "Or maybe I'll go on to the Cortlandt. You were saying something about black—"

"So why shouldn't you?" he demanded, interrupting. "Or change your mind as much as you want? Myself, I change at Chambers and keep on to Brooklyn. You're thinking it's maybe queer I live in Brooklyn? That's where my brother-in-law's got his drugstore. He's very ambitious—wants to be a chemist. Now about the black foam, the Dreck, I'm the expert on that, believe me, I'm your rabbi there, because I foresaw its coming before anyone else." And he turned toward me and laid a hand on my forearm and gripped it, and he fixed on me his dark eyes above the filthy mask.

We were sitting side by side on one of the long seats in a car that was more than three-quarters empty, the windows and walls crawling with graffiti that were hard to read because the lights were dimming and flickering so. The other passengers paid us no heed, locked in their thoughts or stupefactions. As the train set off with a lurch and a low screech, he began.

"You remember when detergents first started getting in sewage and mounding up in rivers and lakes, killing the fishes—mountains of white foam that wouldn't go away? The Guck, the Dreck began like that, only black, and it came from the air and crawling along the ground and working up from under the ground. The street-washing trucks couldn't pick it up, not all of it, brooms and hoses couldn't move it, it built up in corners and cracks and angles. And people ignored it, pretended it wasn't there, like they always do at first with muggings and thrashings and riots and war and death. But I could see it. Sometimes I was sure I was the only one, but sometimes I thought my niece Chana could see it too and admit it to herself—Chana, a very nice, delicate girl, refined and plays the piano—from the way she looked quick out the window and then away and washed her hands over and over. Chana and her cat, who stopped going out. I watched the Dreck getting thicker and thicker, building up higher and higher, blacker and blacker—the black foam."

"But why a foam?" I asked him. "Why not just dirt or dust?"

"Because it clings and smears and creeps, don't blow like dust. Comes through the air, but once it lands, don't blow no more. You know those foams the firemen got that shut in fire, strangle it to death? The Guck works the same with life, you should believe me.

"When I started wearing this mask and making my wife stop opening windows ever and never open an inside door without shutting the outside one, she decides I'm getting sensitive (her nice word for the crazies, maybe) and wants her brother recommend a doctor should give me shots. 'So now I'm sensitive, am I?' I say to her." (He lifted a finger to his mask's center.) "Then what's this?" I ask her. 'Poppy seeds? You maybe want to try filling a blintz with it?'"

We ground to a stop at the Fourteenth Street platform and after a while the doors slid shut with hollow thuds and we humped out of it, and I'd had no thought of getting off. I was spellbound by the way this man's grotesque tale of his paranoia, or whatever, fitted with my own experiences and fantasies this afternoon, as if it were the same story (a black story!) told in a different language or as if it were perhaps a contagious insanity manifesting itself differently, but with one basic theme, in each victim.

My Ancient Mariner of the Subway continued, still fixing me with his glittering dark eye. "When the Dreck got so bad everyone had to admit it, then my brother-in-law was the first comes to me, you should expect it, with all sorts of explanations of what it was and why it wasn't so bad as it looked, we should love it maybe.

"'The scientists understand it and are learning to control it,' he tells me, like we should celebrate.

"'Which means they can't do anything about it right now?' I say. 'Is that news?'

"'It is the ultimate para-terminal waste product,' he says, holding up a finger like a professor (the words he's got! like he's a Doctor of Dreck! and he repeats himself until I've learned them by heart, *Zeeser Gottenyu!*), 'created by a catalytic action of various industrial wastes on each other under conditions of extreme congestion. As a result it has maximum stasis—'

"'It stays, all right,' I say, 'if that's what you're getting at.'

"'—and is the ultimate in unbiodegradable paraplastics,' he keeps on with.

"'It's degrading to us,' I agree. 'And it's making us all into paraplegics, *nu?*'

"He tries again with, 'In a very general way, simplifying it for the layman, it is as if the organic, under unprecedented pressures, were trying to return to the inorganic, and succeeding only too well.'

"'If you mean it's black death spreading itself like sour cream, covering everything, I knew it already. Tell me, was it invented at Dachau or Belsen?'"

Christopher Street went by, Houston, Canal. Sluggish passengers braved the dim stations. The car emptied. The masked man kept on, quoting his brother-in-law.

"'In structure,' he says, making with the finger again, 'it is a congeries'—*Oy, Gottenyu*, his words!—'of microscopic bubbles that are monomolecular, hence black—'

"'Ah-ha! Like poppy seeds! I was just telling Rivke',' I say.

"'—and in many ways it behaves like a para-liquid, a gas of fixed volume—'

"'It's fixes us,' I tell him, 'and it's keeping on fixing.' "'—but it has been proven by scientists,' he keeps up, so I can't get a word in, 'to be absolutely noncarcinogenic, completely inert, and therefore utterly harmless!'

"'So why won't Chana's cat go out in it?' I ask him."

The train slowed. My companion stood up. "Chambers Street, I should change," he explained. He placed his hands on my shoulders. "You should stay on. Your stop is next, Cortlandt. But, pardon me, you should get yourself a mask if you don't mind me telling you. They've started to carry them at cigar stores, so you shouldn't get Dreck in your tobacco smoke. Goodbye, it's been a pleasure listening to you."

I heard the sliding doors thud shut. I looked around. The car was empty. I wasn't exactly frightened, but I stood up and continued to look around as we surged along, and when the doors opened at the next stop, after having seemed to hesitate deliberately for a long moment, I felt a gust of relief and I slid out quickly.

As I did so, a somewhat silly mood of nervous, high-spirited excitement boiled up in me without warning. The afternoon's happenings would make a great vaudeville act, I told myself, for the young woman in green to tour in—and I'd tell her so if I ever caught up with her, and maybe be her manager. She'd have herself—a graceful girl's always an attraction—and her clumsy lion man, and the little Jewish comedian from the bad old days of broad racial humor. We'd put him on skates too. Would he be afraid of the lion? Of course. But his dirty mask would have to go. On him it might make people think of concentration camps and suffocation. We'd have to do something about that.

The white tile underworld was loftier and cleaner here and brighter too (no dimming or muting, at least at the moment—my eyes and ears seemed working okay.) The only thing I wondered about was the absence of hurrying crowds at rush hour—until I remembered it was Saturday.

I wandered with the other solitary movers across those fantastically large underground pleasances, not hurrying particularly but taking long strides, relishing the exercise. We were like ants in a giant's bathroom, each on our separate linear course.

My companions grew fewer as I progressed, and by the time I had purchased my ticket and reached the massive underpinnings of Tower Two, unobtrusive in a vast gleaming, science-fictional, multi-storied hall hung with great panels of aluminum and plates of glass, I was alone. And I alone was lofted on the endlessly mounting steps of the silvery escalator to the high mezzanine, so that I had a comically grandiose vision of myself as Ludwig the Mad King of

Bavaria on my way to a performance at the royal theatre that had only one seat in it. On the mezzanine I quickened my stride, thinking of how frustrating it would be to move more slowly and just miss a trip and have to wait, so that by the time I rounded a corner into the alcove of the express elevator I was almost running.

The elevator was in, but its big silvery doors had just begun to close.

I am a man who almost never acts on impulse, but this time I did. I sprinted forward and managed to get aboard, encountering at the last moment an odd physical resistance I had to force my way through, with an extra effort, though I was in the clear and didn't have to squeeze past persons or the closing doors—it was something invisible, more like a science-fictional field.

Then the doors closed and the car began to mount and I realized that it was completely dark inside and that I couldn't remember seeing any people in it; my eyes had been only on the closing doors.

No, not completely dark. High on the back wall a small ghostly white light was moving from left to right behind the numbers of the floors. But it wasn't enough light to show anything else, at least not to my unadjusted vision.

I asked myself what the devil could have happened. Was I the only passenger, going up on automatic? But this express elevator always carried an operator, didn't it? Also I recalled there had been a spiel (live or recorded?) about the more-than-quarter-mile nonstop vertical trip lasting less than a minute, the more-than-twenty-mile-per-hour vertical speed, and so on. There wasn't now.

I listened intently. After a bit I began to hear, from the point to my left where I'd recalled the operator standing, a very faint strange croaking and breathy whining, the sort of sound a deaf-and-dumb person makes when he's trying hard to communicate—perhaps as if such a person were thinking hard to himself.

I moved involuntarily to my right and forward without encountering anyone—or thing. I remembered the door at the top was the back of the elevator, opposite to what it was at the bottom. Was the trip going to last forever? The ghost light was hardly halfway across the wall. Would the door at the top open?

I could no longer hear the "deaf-and-dumb" breathing. Was that because of the distance I'd moved or the blood pounding in my ears? Or had the breather stopped thinking and begun to take action? How did one pass time like this while holding still? Playing a routine chess opening in one's head? Reciting the prime numbers under one hundred? Counting the coins in one's pocket by feel? No, they might chink.

The cage stopped. A vertical crack of dull light appeared ahead of me and I squeezed through as soon as it was wide enough. I took a dozen forward steps measuredly, started to turn around, but didn't. I listened uneasily for footsteps behind me.

There was a sound. I turned. The silver doors had closed and the space between me and them was empty.

Then I noticed that the doors themselves were blotched and corroded, the floor under my shoes was faintly gritty, there was an oily, coaly stench in my nostrils, though the air felt dry as a desert's and was *blowing* (indoors!), the place was unnaturally silent except for the air's windy sighing, and there was something very strange about the light.

I turned again and moved cautiously out of the elevator's alcove.

The layout of the enclosed observation deck is very simple. A broad corridor made up of continuous windows on the outside runs all the way around, making a great square. Along the inner wall are murals, displays, booths for attendants, that sort of thing. I was in the corridor on the building's east side.

I looked both ways and didn't see a soul, neither visitors nor the deck's personnel. But I did see trails of footprints and of at least one wheeled vehicle in the dull dust coating the floor.

I couldn't see much of anything out of the windows, at

least from where I stood back from them in the middle of the corridor. They seemed to be very dusty, too, and through the dust there wasn't anything visible outside but a dark expanse lightening toward the top and streaked with a dull sunset red. There were no inside lights on.

I didn't approach the windows any closer but walked quietly north in search of an explanation for the incredible transformation that had occurred—or the weird hallucination from which I was suffering. Can one walk through a hallucination one is having? For some reason that question didn't seem nonsensical to me then. Exactly how are inner and outer space related?

The dry, insect-wailing wind brushed my face with its feathery touch. It seemed icy now on my forehead and cheeks because of its rapid evaporation of my sweat of fear. And now, through it, I could hear other noises from ahead: faint rutchings, creakings, and gratings, as if some heavy object were with difficulty being moved. I myself moved more slowly then, in the end hardly at all as, holding my breath, I peered sidewise down the north corridor.

This one wasn't empty. Halfway along it a dozen black-clad figures, black-hooded and black-trousered, were at work where two of the observation windows had been jaggedly smashed open to the dark, reddening sky. Through that large gap came the dry wind that now blew against me more strongly. About half the black figures were busy manhandling a gun (from the first I knew it was a gun) so that it pointed north out the gap. The weapon, formed of a grayish metal, resembled a field piece of the world wars, but there were perplexing differences. The barrel was pointed sharply upward like a mortar's but was longer, more like that of a recoilless rifle. The breech bulged unnaturally— too big. It was mounted on a carriage with small wheels that seemed to turn with difficulty, judging from the way the black figures strained at it, while beside it on a squat tripod was a steaming cauldron heated by a small fire built on the floor.

The other six or seven figures were closely grouped

around the edges of the gap and peering out of it intently and restlessly, as though on watch and guard for something in the sky. Each held ready, close against him, a small missile weapon of some sort.

All the figures were silent, appearing to communicate by some sort of sign language that involved twitchings of the head and grippings of one another's upper arms and legs—perhaps a language more of touch than visual signs.

Despite their silence, there was such a venom and hatred, such a killer's eagerness, about the way the gunhandlers heaved at their cranky weapons, strained and touch-talked, and in the window guards the same, though in them mixed more with dread, that my genitals contracted and my stomach fluttered and I wanted to retch.

Inch by inch I withdrew, thankful for their single-minded intentness on the gap and for the crepe soles of my shoes. I retraced my path past the elevator, its blotched doors still shut at the back of the shadowy recess, and peered with circumspection into the southern corridor. It seemed as empty as the one I was in. The windows at its far end glowed red with sunset light. A short distance along it, the escalator to the open observation deck on the roof three stories above began its straight-line ascent. Its treads weren't moving (I hardly needed visual confirmation of that), but up through it the dry wind, now on my neck, seemed to be blowing out, escaping from this floor.

I had no desire to explore the red-lit west corridor, the only one I hadn't peered along, or to wait by the stained doors of the elevator. The oily, coaly stench was sickening me. I began the long ascent of the stalled escalator.

At first I went slowly, to avoid noise, then I speeded up nervously from the dry wind's pressure on my back and its faint whistlings, and in my feelings a queer mixture of claustrophobia and fear of exposure—the feeling of being in a long, narrow opening. Then I slowed down to avoid getting winded. And the last few steps I took very slowly, for fear of running into a guard (or whatever) at the top—that and a certain hesitation to see what I would see.

Spying from the entry, I first closely surveyed the open observation deck—really just a wide, railed, rectangular catwalk, supported by a minimum of metal framework, about fifteen feet above and twenty feet back from the edges of the flat roof of the building proper, those edges having a stout high mesh fence, the top wires of which were electrified to further discourage would-be suicide jumpers and such. (I knew these details from my earlier visit.)

I didn't spot anyone or anything in the twilight (anyone standing or crouching, at least), though there was the opposite exit structure matching mine, around which it would be possible to hide, and at one point the railing was gone and a slanting ladder led down to the roof—a crude stairs. Also a good deal of the outer fence appeared to have been torn away, though I didn't try to check that very closely.

Thus reassured (if you can call it that), I straightened up, walked out, and looked around. First to the west where a flattened sun, deep red and muted enough to look at without hurt, was about to go beneath the Jersey horizon. Its horizontal rays gave the low heavens a furnace glow that made "the roof of Hell" a cliché no longer, though lower down the sky was dark.

The horizon all around looked *higher* than it ought to be. From it in toward me stretched an absolutely flat black plain, unbroken save for several towers, mostly toward the north, their western walls uniformly red-lit by the sunset, their long shadows stretching endlessly to the east, a few of the towers rather tall but some quite squat.

I looked in vain for the streets of New York, for the lights that should be coming on (and becoming more apparent) by now, for the Hudson and East rivers, for the bay with its islands and for the Narrows.

None of those things were there, only the dull ebon plain, across which the dry north wind blew ceaselessly. Oh, the utter flatness of that plain! It was like the waters of an absolutely still great lake, not a quiver in it, thickly filmed with coal dust and across which spiders might run.

And then I began to recognized the towers by their tops.

That one to the north, the tallest in that direction except for one at almost twice the distance, its somewhat rounded stepbacks were unmistakable—Kong-unmistakable. It was the Empire State shrunken to less than half its height without a corresponding diminishment in breadth. And that still slender spire was the top quarter of the graceful Chrysler Building, its bottom three quarters chopped off by (were they beneath?) the plain. And there was the RCA Building at Rockefeller Center where I'd just been—the top hundred feet of it.

But what were those two structures rather taller (allowing for differences in distance) than the Empire State? One mostly truncated pyramid, the most distant northern one; the other to the northeast, about where the United Nations enclave would be. Were they buildings built after my ... well, I had to face up to the possibility of time travel, didn't I?

And there were lights, I began to see now, as the red western walls started to darken—a very few windows scattered here and there among the towers. One of them was in a most modest structure nearby—hardly four stories with a pyramidal roof. I knew it from boyhood, the Woolworth Building, New York's tallest in 1920 and for some years after, which the black plain had almost inundated.

Yes, the black plain, which lay only some five or six hundred feet beneath me, not the thirteen hundred and fifty it ought to be.

And then I knew with an intuitive, insane certainty the black plain's nature. It was the final development of the Guck, the Dreck, the sinister, static, ineradicable foam, the coming of which the old Jew had described to me.

But how in hell could there be *this* much accumulation of waste of whatever sort, seven or eight hundred feet of it? Unless one imagined the whole process as being catalytic in some way and reaching and overpassing some critical value (analogous to fission and fusion temperatures in atomics), after which the process became self-perpetuating and self-devouring—"Death taking over," as he'd said.

And how far, in God's name, did the black plain extend?

To the ends of the Earth? It would take more than the melting of a couple of black icecaps to do that to the planet. Oh, I was beginning to think in a crazy way, I told myself...

At the same time a line from the cauldron scene in *Macbeth* joggled its way to the surface of my mind: "Make the gruel thick and slab..."

But the gruel wouldn't have to be thick, I reminded myself with insane cunning, because it was composed of microscopic *bubbles*. That would stretch the Guck, make it seem that there was much more Dreck than there really was. And it wouldn't be solid and massy like liquids are, but feathery and soft as finest soot or new-fallen snow, hundreds of feet of it...

New-fallen black snow...

But if the stuff were foam, why didn't it mound up in hillocks and humps, like the life-choking detergent foams the old Jew had talked about? What force, what unnatural surface tension, constrained it to lie flat as a stagnant pond?

And why did I keep coming back to *his* ideas, monotonously? My intuition was insane, all right, as insane as what was happening to me, or as his own paranoid ideas—or mine. I shook my head to clear it of them all and to stir myself to action, and I began to move around the catwalk, studying my closer surroundings. The first thing to catch my eye and almost stop me was the wire-hung narrow suspension bridge connecting the northwest corner of this roof with the nearest corner of the roof of Tower One. It was a primitive affair, the junkyard equivalent of a jungle structure of bamboo and braided vines. The two main wires or thin cables, guyed through holes driven in the roof edges, also served as its rails, from which was flimsily suspended the narrow footway made of sections of thin aluminum sheeting of varying lengths. It swayed a little and creaked and sang in the dry wind from the north.

I could see no figures or movement on the roof of Tower One, though another of its corners was simply gone for twenty feet or so, as if gigantically chopped or bitten off.

I came to the first right-angle turn (to the east) in the

catwalk and (just beyond it) the gap in the rail where the ladder went down.

Scanning north again, I saw the last red highlights on the scanty cluster of towers fade as the crouched-down scarlet sun flattened itself completely behind the western horizon, but the hell glow lingered on the low, cramping sky, under which that dry wind from the pole blew on and blew. Squinting my eyes against it, I thought I saw shapes in movement, soaring and flapping, around the most distant northern tower, the tall, unfamiliar, mysterious one. If they were fliers and were really there, they were gigantic, I told myself uneasily.

My gaze dropped down to the lowly pale Woolworth tower with its single dim light and I noticed that its roof edge was damaged somewhat like that of Tower One, and I had a vision (the soaring shaped had paved the way for it) of a vast dragon's head with jaws agape (and mounted on a long neck like that of a plesiosaur) emerging from the black plain and menacing the structure, while great dull black ripples spread out from it in ever-widening circles. Another scrap of poetry came to my mind, Lanier's "But who will reveal to our waking ken/The forms that swim and the shapes that creep/Under the waters of sleep?"

As I mused on that, I heard a not very loud but nevertheless arresting sound, a gasp of indrawn breath. Glancing sharply ahead along the catwalk, I saw, near the exit structure, something that may or may not have been there before (I could have missed it in my survey): a body sprawled flat with that attitude of finality about it which indicates utter exhaustion, unconsciousness, or death. It was clad in what looked in the dusk dark green—cloak, cap, gloves ... and trousers.

Before I could begin to sort out my reactions to that sight (although I instantly moved softfootedly toward it), another dark-green-clad figure emerged swiftly from the exit-structure and swiftly knelt to the sprawled form in a way that was complete identification for me. I had seen that identical movement earlier today, though then it had been on skates.

When I was less than a dozen feet away, I said, clearing my throat, "Excuse me, but can I be of any help to you?"

She writhed to her feet with the sinuous swiftness of a cobra rearing and faced me tensely across the dead or insensate form, her eyes blazing with danger and menace in the last light from the west. I almost cringed from her. Then there was added a look of tentative recognition, of counting up.

"You're the man in the subway," she said rapidly. "Neutral, possibly favorable, at least not actively hostile—I took a chance on you and that's how I still read you. The man from Elsewhen."

"The subway, yes," I said. "I don't know about the Elsewhen part. I presume from what I see I've time-traveled, but I've always thought that time travel, if such a thing could possibly be, would be instantaneous, not by a weird, crooked series of transformations and transitions."

"Then you were wrong," she said, rather impatiently. "You don't do *anything* all at once in the universe. To get from here to there you traverse a space-time between. Even light moves a step at a time. There are no instantaneous transitions, though there are short cuts, no actions at a distance. There are no miracles."

"And as for being possibly favorable," I went on, "I've already asked if I could help you."

"You say that as lightly as if it meant tipping your hat or holding a door open. You don't know what you're getting into," she assured me. "You saw the men on the lower deck?"

"The men in black with the gun, yes."

"You mention the gun. That's good," she commented quickly, and for the first time there was a hint in her voice and look that I might be accepted. She went on, "That's the gun my brother and I were going to knock out, when ... when..." Her gaze flickered down toward the flattened form, dark green, death pale, between us, and her voice stumbled.

"I'm terribly sorry—" I began.

"Please!—no sympathy," she interrupted. "We haven't time and I haven't the strength. Now listen to me. In this age the blackness has almost buried New York. We are the sole survivors, we in these two towers and like lonely groups on those out there, a desolate few." She indicated the scattered tops to the north and around. "We should be brothers in adversity. Yet all that those men on the lower deck can feel is hate, hate for all men in other towers than their own, hate and the fears from which their hatred grew -dread of the blackness and of other things. They dress in black because they fear it so and hope so to gain for themselves all the cruel power and exulting evil they read in it, while their avoidance of spoken language is another tribute to their fear—in point, the Guck's their god, their devil-god."

She paused, then commented, "Man lacks imagination, doesn't he? Or even a mere talent for variety in his reactions. Sometimes it seems appropriate he should drown squealing in the dark."

I said, uneasy at this chilly philosophizing, "I'd think you'd be afraid they'd come up here and find us. I wonder that they haven't posted guards."

She shook her head. "They never come out under the sky unless they have to. They fear the birds—the birds and other things."

Before I could ask her another question she resumed the main thread of her talk. "And so all that those men on the lower deck can think to do is to destroy all other towers save their own. That is the business they're about just now (the business of the gun) and one on which they concentrate ferociously—another reason we needn't fear them surprising us here.

"Someday," she said, and for a moment her voice grew wistful, "someday we may be able to change their hearts and minds. But now all we can do is take away their tools, remove their weapon, the gun that's capable of killing buildings.

"And so now, sir," she said briskly, looking toward me, "will you aid me in this venture, knowing the risks? Will you play the part my brother would have played -receive my fire? For I must tell you that *my* weapon requires both a firer and a receiver. One soul can't work it. Also it works only against their weapon, not against them (I would not wish it otherwise), and so it cannot save us from their aftermath. Escaping will be your own business, with my help. How say you, sir?"

It sounded crazy, but I was in a crazy situation and my feelings fitted themselves to it—and I remembered the sickening venomousness I had sensed in the black-clad men below.

"I'll help you," I told her in a low, choked voice, swallowing hard and nodding sharply.

She laughed, and with a curtsy to her brother's corpse, knelt by it again and from a pouch at the belt removed something which she held out to me.

"Your receiver, sir," she said gaily, smiling over it. "Your far-focus, yin to the yang of mine. I believe you have seen something like it earlier today. Here, take it, sir."

It was a pale brown cube with rounded corners, about as big as a golf ball and surprisingly heavy. When I looked at it close up I saw that it was the figure of a lioness crouching, quite stylized, the body all drawn together to fit the cubic form—one face of the cube, for instance, was all proud, glaring head and forepaws. It was a remarkable piece, so far as I could make out in the dusk. The eyes appeared to flash, though it seemed all of one material.

"Here is its mate," she said, "my near-focus, my firer," and she held close to my eyes for a long moment a like figure of a maned lion. "And now the plan. It is only necessary that we be on opposite sides of our target, in this case the gun, so that I may weave the web and you anchor it. When we get to the foot of the long stair, you go to the left, I'll go to the right. Walk rapidly but quietly as you can to the end corridor they're in. Stand in the middle of it facing them and holding the receiver in front of you. It doesn't matter if it's hidden in your fist, only don't stir then and whatever happens, don't drop it." She chuckled. "You won't have to wait long for me once you get there. Oh, and one other thing. Although your receiver is no weapon against them afterwards, except to weight your fist—no weapon at all without the aid of mine— it has one virtue: If you lack for air (as, *viz.*, they use the Guck on you) hold it close to your nostrils or your lips. That, I believe, is all." She gently clapped her left arm around the back of my waist from where she was standing close beside me and looked up a bit at me and said, "So, sir, let's go.

"But first," she added somewhat comically, "my thanks for your companioning in this venture. Ill met and worse to follow!" And she leaned around laughingly and rather quickly kissed me.

As our lips were pressed together there came a jarringly loud sound from close below. It sounded like a giant cough from very deep in a dark throat. As we pulled apart, turning each toward the north, we saw an incandescent scarlet line rapidly mounting out from the tower beneath, belched from the midst of a spreading smoke puff. It soared across the last darkening carmine streaks of sunset in the top of the sky, seemed to hang there, then fell more and more rapidly through the last of its parabolic course and was extinguished (it seemed) in the black plain short of the Empire State. But then began a churning and a mounding and a glowing in the Guck, ending in a tumultuous eruption of blackness and flame. I was vividly reminded of depth-charging at night, only this glare was redder. And the flash seemed to last longer too, for by its darkening red glow I saw the facade of the Empire State hugely splotched and pied with inky black—napalm that didn't burn.

I was losing my balance—it was by companion dragging my arm. "Come on," she yelled. "Same plan, only we run."

We ran. Halfway to the stalled escalator we were given an extra shove by the great muffled thunderclap of the explosion. I pounded down the dark silvery, gritty stairs, recklessly for me, watching her draw farther and farther ahead. And then, by God, I heard her *whistling* loud in a fast, rocking rhythm. It was the *cavalry charge*, so help me!

She waited at the bottom to point me left, make sure I got

it. And then as I was loping down the west corridor, nearing my goal, the windows ahead of me were painted with a bright red flash against which the small figure of the Empire State was silhouetted. This time they'd struck beyond her, had her bracketed. The third shell...

I shot into the north corridor and came to an arm-waving halt just as the dark glass ahead of me bent inward, but did not shatter, with the second muffled thunderclap. And then I faced myself at where the bent black figures were toiling exultantly in their reloading and I held my receiver out in front of me. I remember I held it gripped between right thumb and bent forefinger with the lioness' head looking at them (that seemed important, though the girl hadn't said so) and with my left hand gripped around my right. My legs were bent and spread wide too, so that I must have looked like some improbably elderly macho with a magnum straight out of TV.

I didn't see her arrive beyond them (she was probably there ahead of me) but suddenly my conjoined hands were tingling and there was a narrow sheaf of bright violet lines fanning out from that double fist to touch the extremities of the ugly gun and around it illumine staring ghost eyes and spectral mouths gaping with surprise within black hoods, before they drew together again (the violet lines) into a glowing point which showed me, just above it, very tiny— her face—for all the world as if she and I were playing cats' cradle together with the fluorescent violet string, the gun the figure we'd created.

The tingling spread to my arms and shoulders, but I didn't drop my receiver or writhe around very much.

Then the lines vanished (and my hands stopped tingling) but a swirled Kirlian aura of the same shade of violet hung around the gun, making it glow all over as though new-forged and highlighting the frozen figures around it. Then one of those figures reached out slowly and fearfully and touched the muzzle, and at that point a very fine iridescent violet snowfall began, the individual flakes winking out before they touched the deck, and the snowfall spreading rapidly, eating its way into the glowing metal, until the entire gun had trickled away into dust.

The frozen figures broke then into such a frenzy of arm-and-thigh-gripping, and head-twitching, that it was like a battle (or an orgy) in a soundless hell. Then most of them raced away from me, but two toward me, and I heard a high sweet whistling, three mounting notes. She was sounding taps, the *retreat*.

I was already in flight. The west corridor seemed longer than it had coming. She was waiting for me again at the foot of the escalator, but started up as soon as she saw me. I'd not mounted a dozen steps when the faint tattoo of our pursuers' footsteps was abruptly amplified as they poured into the south corridor. It didn't so much frighten me as make me feel wild—an unfamiliar sort of excitement.

I was panting before I was halfway up. I could hear her breathing hard too, though I think she deliberately slowed down so as not to get too far ahead. When I got to the top I did a foolish, show-off thing—I took the deepest gasping breath I could and then turned and bellowed inarticulately down the stairs—roared, you might say, perhaps in honor of the lioness clenched in my fist. And then I went dancing out onto the catwalk, not straight ahead following her, but around the opposite way, with some crazy idea of drawing the pursuit away from her, and pausing to turn and bellow nastily once or twice more.

My storybook ruse didn't work at all. The main body of our silent pursuers went racing after her without even hesitating, though a couple did come skulking after me. She paused at the railing gap to shake her fist at me, or wave me on, I don't know which, and then she ran down the slanting ladder, and across the roof to its northwest corner, and up and out onto the rickety suspension bridge. Two of her pursuers stopped and made hurling motions, there were sharp reports and then two bright white lights were floating above her head and then slowly past her—star-grenades, to give them a name.

She was halfway across the bridge when a swarm of

figures appeared at its other end. The glare showed them to be black-clad, black-hooded. She stopped. Then, pausing only for a sweeping gesture of defiance—or a wave of farewell—she ducked under one of the main wires and dove down head first, her green cloak trailing behind her. Almost at once the roof edge cut her off from my sight and there were only the eagerly bent, black-hooded heads peering down.

And then, without warning, there was clapped over my face from behind a double handful of fine-grained darkness that was soft as soot, intimate as cobweb, somehow oily and dry at the same time, and instantly cutting off all sight and breath. In my convulsive struggles, during which I was thrown down on my back, I lifted my hands to my face and though I did not manage to tear whatever it was away, I became able to see through it dimly and draw shallow breaths. I made a supreme effort and then -

Have you ever begun to wake up from a nightmare that's happening in the same room you're actually sleeping in, and for a while been able to see both rooms at the same time, the nightmare one and the real one, almost coinciding but not quite? It was that way with me. It was night and I was down on my back on the open observation deck of Tower Two at the World Trade Center and there were people bent over me and handling me. And sometimes the sky would be utterly black and the faces hooded ones and the hands gripping cruelly to hurt. And then the dark sky would have a pale cast with reflected light and the faces open and solicitous, and the hands gentle and trying to help. After a brief but dizzying alteration the second scene won out, you might say, and I was drawn to my feet and supported and patted and told that a doctor had been summoned. Apparently I'd been walking along quite normally, enjoying the view (though one person maintained I'd looked troubled), when I'd suddenly collapsed in a faint or a fit. I offered no explanations, suppressed my agitation and astonishment as well as I could, and waited. I remember looking down from time to time at the diamond pattern of New York's street lights (they looked *so very* far below!) and being greatly reassured by that, so much so that once or twice I almost forgot why I felt so bereaved and forlorn.

I let myself be taken to the hospital, where they couldn't find much of anything wrong with me (except that after a bit I felt very tired) and from which my son retrieved me the next day. After a while I told him the whole story, but he's professed himself no more able than I am to decide between what seem to be the two chief possible explanations: that I suffered an extremely vivid and protracted hallucination, during which I moved through the World Trade Center completely blacked out (and possibly through the subway and Rockefeller Plaza in the same state), or that I actually time-traveled.

And if it were a hallucination, when did it begin? (Or if the other, when did *that* begin?) At the Pool of the Planets? Or even earlier, with my first glimpse of the Girl in Green? Or when I dashed into the express elevator and found it dark (there had been my feeling of breaking through a barrier at that point)? There are endless possibilities.

Did I hallucinate the old Jew, was he completely fabricated from materials in my unconscious? Or was he an intermediate stage in my time travel, belonging to an era somewhere between today and that blackly overwhelmed New York of the future? Or was he completely real, just one more freak at large in today's city?

My tired feeling afterwards convinced me of one thing— that whether an experience is real or hallucinatory (or a dream, for that matter, or even something you write), you always have to put the same amount of work into it, it takes the same energy, it takes as much out of you. Does that say something about outer and inner space? (My son says, "Don't dream so strenuously next time," though of course he says that's entirely my choice.)

If it *was* a hallucination, one thing that has to be explained is when and where I acquired the small and very heavy stylized sculpture of a lioness I had tightly clenched in my left fist at the end of my experience. No one has been able to identify the tawny material composing it, or its style or school, though resemblances have been noted to Bufano's work and to the stitcheries of Martha McElroy. I've experimented with it a bit, I admit, but it appears to have no mystical or weird scientific properties, though I do think it helps my breathing. I carry it as a pocket piece now. Might come in handy some day -though I suppose that's a rather foolish thought.

As for the Young Woman in Green, I have a theory about her. I don't think she plunged to her death when she went off the suspension bridge between the two towers -she'd never have leaped off so lightheartedly unless she'd known she had a way of escape. No, I don't mean she sprouted wings or broke out a small jet or levitation unit after she'd fallen out of my sight. But from what the old Jew told me of the Dreck, and from my own observations of it I think it is like soft, powdery new-fallen snow, able to cushion any fall, from no matter how great a height. And I think there are ways of living in it, of moving and breathing, no matter how deeply one is buried. She implied as much when she told me about the additional value of my receiver. And she did have her firer with her at the end. I tell myself she survived.

In any case, my feelings about her are such that I would very much like to find her again, even if it were only to begin another hallucination.

I'M LOOKING
FOR JEFF

AT SIX-THIRTY THAT afternoon, Martin Bellows was sitting at the bar of the Tomtoms. In front of him was a tall glass of beer and behind the bar were two men in white aprons. The two men, one of them so old he was past caring about it, were discussing a matter—and while Martin wasn't really listening, much of the discussion seemed to be for his entertainment.

"If that girl comes in again I won't serve her. And if she starts to get funny I'll give her some real eye-shadow!"

"Regular fire eater, aren't you, Pops?"

"All this week, ever since she started to come in here, there's been trouble."

"Listen to him, will you? Aw, Pops, there's always trouble at a bar. Either somebody makes a play for somebody's girl, or else it's two life-long buddies—"

"I mean nasty trouble. What about those two girls Monday night? What about what the big guy did to Jack? What about Jake and Janice picking the Tomtoms to break up, and the way they did it? *She* was behind it every time. What about the broken glass in the cracked ice?"

"Shut up! Pops *is* nuts, friend. He gets wild ideas."

Martin Bellows looked up from his beer at Sol, the young working owner of the Tomtoms, and at the other man behind the bar. Then he glanced down the empty stretch of polished mahogany and over his shoulder at the dim, silent stretches of the booths, where the lights from behind the bar hardly picked up the silver and gilt. He grimaced faintly.

"Anything for a little life."

"Life!" Pops snorted. "That isn't what she'd give you, Mister."

There's no lonelier place in the world than a nightspot in the early hours of evening. It makes one think of all the guys who are alone—without a girl or a friend—restlessly searching. Its noiseless gloom is a sounding board for the faintest fears and aches of the heart. Its atmosphere, used to being pushed around by the loud mouths of happy drunks, is stagnant. The dark corners that should be filled with laughter and desire are ghostly. The bandstand, with the empty chairs sitting around in lifelike positions.

Martin felt it and hitched his stool an inch closer to the old man and the anxious, sharp-eyed Sol.

"Tell me about her, Pops," he said to the old man. "No, let him, Sol."

"All right, but I'm warning you it's a pipe dream."

Pops ignored his boss's remark. He spun the glass he was polishing in a slower rhythm. His face, puffed by beer and thumbed into odd hills and gullies by a lifetime of evanescent but illuminating experiences, grew thoughtful. Outside, traffic moaned and a distant train hooted. Pops pressed his lips together, bringing out a new set of hummocks in his cheeks.

"Name's Bobby," he began abruptly. "Blonde. About twenty. Always orders brandies. Smooth, kid face, except for the faintest scar that goes all the way across it. Black dress that splits down to her belly-button."

A car slammed to a stop outside. The three men looked up. But after a moment they heard the car go on.

"Never set eyes on her till last Sunday night," Pops continued. "Says she's from Michigan City. Always asking for a guy named Jeff. Always waiting to start her particular kind of hell."

"Who's this Jeff?" Martin asked.

Pops shrugged.

"And what's her particular kind of hell?"

Pops shrugged again, this time in Sol's direction. "He don't believe in her," he said gruffly.

"I'd like to meet her, Pops," Martin said smilingly. "Like some excitement. Beginning to feel a big evening coming on. And Bobby sounds like my kind of a girl."

"I wouldn't introduce her to my last year's best friend!"

Sol laughed lightly but conclusively. He leaned across the bar, confidentially, glancing back at the older man with secretive humor. He touched Martin's sleeve. "You've heard Pop's big story. Now get this: I've never been able to notice this girl, and I'm always here until I close. So far as I know, nobody's ever been able to notice her except Pops. I think she's just one of his pipe dreams. You know, the guy's a little weak in the head." He leaned a bit closer and spoke in a loud and mocking stage-whisper. "*Used weed when he was a boy.*"

Pop's face grew a bit red, and the new set of hummocks stood out more sharply. "All right, Mr. Wise," he said. "I got something for you."

He put the glass down in the shining ranks, hung up the towel, fished a cigar box from under the bar.

"Last night she forgot her lighter," he explained. "It's covered with a dull, shiny black stuff, same as her dress. Look!"

The other two men leaned forward, but when Pops flipped up the cover there was nothing inside but the white paper lining.

Sol looked around at Martin with a slow grin. "You see?"

Pops swore and ripped out the lining. "One of the band must have swiped it!"

Sol laid his hand gently on the older man's arm. "Our musicians are nice, honest boys, Pops."

"But I tell you I put it there last thing last night."

"No, Pops, you just thought you did." He turned to Martin. "Not that strange things don't sometimes happen in bars. Why, just these last few days—"

A door slammed. The three men looked around. But it must have been a car outside, for nothing came in.

"Just these last few days," Sol repeated, "I've been noticing the damnedest thing."

"What?" Martin asked.

Sol shot another of his secretively humorous glances toward Pops. "I'd like to tell you," he explained to Martin, "but I can't in front of Pops. He gets ideas."

Martin got off his stool, grinning. "I got to go anyhow. I'll see you later."

Not five minutes later, Pops smelled the perfume. A rotten, sickly smell. And his ears caught the mouse-faint creaking of the midmost barstool, and the tiny, ghostly sigh. And the awful feel of it went deep down inside him and grated on his bones like chalk. He began to tremble.

Then the creaking and the sigh came again through the gloom of the Tomtoms, a little impatiently, and he had to turn, although it was the last thing he wanted to do, and he had to look at the emptiness of the bar. And there, at the midmost stool, he saw it.

It was terribly indistinct, just a shadowy image superimposed on the silvers and gilts and midnight blues of the far wall, but he knew every part of it. The gleaming blackness of the dress, like the sheerest black silk stocking held up in the near darkness. The pale gold of the hair, like motes in the beam of an amber spotlight. The paleness of face and hands, like puffs of powder floating up from a spilled compact. The eyes, like two tiny dark moths, hovering.

"What's the matter, Pops?" Sol asked sharply.

He didn't hear the question. Although he'd have given anything not to have to do it, he was edging shakily down the bar, hand grasping the inner margin for support, until he stood before the midmost stool.

Then he heard it, the faint clear voice that seemed to ride a mosquito's whine, as they say the human voice rides a radio wave. The voice that knifed deep, deep into his head.

"Been talking about me, Pops?"

He just trembled.

"Seen Jeff tonight, Pops?'

He shook his head.

"What's the matter, Pops? What if I'm dead and rotting? Don't shake so, Pops. You should be complimented I show myself to you. You know, Pops, at heart every woman's a stripper. But most of them just show themselves to the guy they like, or need. I'm that way. I don't show myself to the bums. And now give me a drink."

His trembling only increased.

The twin moths veered toward him. "Got polio, Pops?"

In a spasm of haste he jerked around, stooping. By blind fumbling he found the brandy bottle under the ranked glasses, poured a shaky shot, set it down on the bar and stepped back.

"What the hell are you up to!"

He didn't even hear the angry question, or realize that Sol was moving toward him. Instead, he stood pressed back as far as he could, and watched the powdercloud fingers wind around the shot glass like tendrils of smoke, and heard the bat-shrill voice laugh ruefully and say, "Can't manage it that way, haven't got the strength enough yet," and watched the twin moths, and something red and white-edged just below them, dip toward the brandy.

Then for a moment a feeling reached out and touched Sol, for though no hand was on the bar, the shot glass shook, and a little rill of brandy snaked down its side and pooled on the mahogany.

"What the..." Sol began, and then finished, "those damn trucks, they shake the whole neighborhood."

And all the while Pops was listening to the bat-shrill voice: "That helped, Pops," and then, with a wheedling restlessness, "What's on tonight, Pops? Where can a girl get herself some fun? Who was the tall, dark and handsome that left a while ago? You called him Martin?"

Sol, finally fed up, came striding toward Pops. "And now you'll please explain just what the—"

"Wait!" Pops' hand snapped out and clamped on Sol's

arm so that the younger man winced. "She's getting up," he gasped. "She's going after him. We got to warn him."

Sol's sharp gaze quickly flashed where Pops was looking. Then, with a little snarl, he shook off Pops' hand and gripped him in turn. "Look here, Pops, are you really smoking weed?"

The older man struggled to free himself. "We got to warn him, I tell you, before she drinks herself strong enough to make him notice her, and starts butting her broken-bottle ideas into his head."

"Pops!" The shout in the ear stiffened the older man, so that he stood there quietly, though rigid, while Sol said, "They probably have some nut bars out on West Madison Street they don't mind having nuts behind. Probably. I don't know. But you're going to have to start looking for one of them if you pull any more of these goofy acts, or start talking about any Bobby and broken glass." His fingers kneaded the old man's biceps. "Get it?"

Pop's eyes were still wild. But he nodded twice, stiffly.

THE EVENING STARTED out feeling heavy and indigestible for Martin Bellows, but after a while it began to float like the diamond-dusted clouds of light around the street lamps. The session with Pops and Sol had given him a funny sort of edge, but he rode out the mood, drifting from tavern to tavern, occasionally treating a decent-looking guy to a drink and letting himself be treated in turn, sharing that courtesy silently, not talking very much, kidding a bit with the girls behind the bars while he covertly eyed the ones in front. After about five taverns and eight drinks he found he'd picked up one of them.

She was a small willowy girl with hair like a winter sunrise and a sleekly-fitting black dress, high-necked but occasionally revealing a narrow ribbon of sweet flesh. Her eyes were dark and friendly, and not exactly law-abiding, and her face had the smooth, matte quality of pale doeskin. He was aware of a faint gardenia perfume. He put his arm around her and kissed her lightly, under the street lamp, not closing his eyes, and as he did so he noticed that her face had a blemish. The tiniest line of paler flesh, like a single strand of spiderweb, began at her left temple and went straight across the lids of her left eye and the bridge of her nose and back across the right cheek. It enhanced her beauty, he thought.

"Where'll we go?" he asked.

"How about the Tomtoms?"

"A little too early." Then, "Say! Your name is Bobby. That's the name Pops ... I'll bet you're..."

She shrugged. "Pops likes to talk."

"Sure you are! Pops was spieling about you at a great rate." He smiled at her fondly. "Claims you're an evil influence."

"Yes?"

"But don't worry about that. Pops is stark, raving nuts. Why, only this evening—"

"Well, let's go some place else," she interrupted. "I need a drink, lover."

And they were off, Martin with his heart singing, because what you always look for and never find had actually happened to him: he had found a girl that set his imagination and his thirst aflame. Every minute made him more desirous and prouder of her. Bobby was the perfect girl, he decided. She didn't get loud, or quarrelsome, or complaining, or soul-baring, or full of supposedly cute, deliberately exasperating whims. Instead, she was gay and smooth and beautiful, fitting his mood like a glove, yet with that hint of danger and savagery that can never be divorced from the dizzy fumes of alcohol and the dark streets of cities. He found himself growing very foolish about her. He even came to dote on her spiderlike scar, as if it were an expert repair job done on an expensive French doll.

They went to three or four delightful taverns, one where a gray-haired woman sang meltingly, one that showed silent comedies on a small screen instead of television, one full of framed pencil portraits of unknown, unimportant people. Martin got through all the early stages of intoxication— the eager, the uneasy, the dreamily blissful—and emerged safely into that crystal world where time almost stands still, where nothing is surer than your movements and nothing realer than your feelings, where the tight shell of personality is shattered and even dark walls and smoky sky and gray cement underfoot are sentient parts of you.

But after a while he kissed Bobby again, in the street, holding her longer and closer this time, plunging his lips to her neck, drowning in the autumn-garden sweetness of gardenia perfume, murmuring unsteadily, "You've got a place around here?"

"Yes."

"Well..."

"Not now, lover," she breathed. "First let's go to the Tomtoms."

He nodded and drew a bit back from her, not angrily. "Who's Jeff?" he asked.

She looked up at him. "Do you want to know?"

"Yes."

"Look, lover," she said softly, "I don't think you'll ever meet Jeff. But if you do, I want you to promise me one thing—I won't ever ask for anything else." She paused, and all the latent savagery glowed in the pale mask of her features. "I want you to promise me that you'll break the bottom off a beer bottle and jam it into his fat face."

"What'd he do to you?"

The pale mask was enigmatic. "Something much worse than you're thinking," she told him.

Looking down at Bobby's still, expectant face, Martin felt a thrill of murderous excitement go through him.

"Promise?" she asked.

"Promise," he said huskily.

SOL WAS CONTENT only during the busy hours when life ran high in the Tomtoms. Lovers for an evening or forever, touching knees under the tables, meant money in the register.

Sol and Pops had had a busy two hours, but now there

was a lull between jazz sessions and Sol had time to chew the rag a bit with a burly and interesting-looking stranger.

"Talk about funny things, friend, here's one for you," he said, leaning across the bar with a confidential smile. "See that stool second on your left? Every night this week, after one a.m. nobody sits on it."

"It's empty now," the burly man told him.

"Sure, and the one next you. But I'm talking about after one a.m.—that's a couple of minutes yet—when our business hits its peak. No matter how big the crowd is—they could be standing two deep other places—nobody ever occupies that one stool. Why? I don't know. Maybe it's just chance. Maybe there's something funny I haven't figured out yet makes them sheer off from it."

"Just chance," the burly man opined stolidly. He had a fighter's jaw and a hooded gaze.

Sol smiled. Across the room the musicians were climbing back onto the bandstand, leisurely settling themselves. "Maybe, friend. But I got a feeling it's something else. Maybe something very obvious, like that it's got a leg that's a teensy bit loose. But I'm willing to bet it'll stay empty tonight. You watch. Six nights in a row is too good for just chance. And I'd swear on a stack of Bibles it's been empty six nights straight."

"That just ain't so, Sol."

Sol turned. Pops was standing behind him, eyes scared and angry like they'd been earlier, lips working a little.

"What do you mean, Pops?" Sol asked him, trying not to show irritation in front of his new customer.

Pops walked off muttering.

"Got to see that the girls are taking care of the tables," Sol excused himself to the burly man and went after Pops. When he caught up with him he said in an undertone, not looking at him, "Damn it, Pops, are you just trying to make yourself unpleasant?" Across the room the bandleader stood up and smiled around at his boys. "If you think I'm going to take that kind of stuff from you, you're crazy."

"But, Sol," Pops' voice was quavery now, almost as if he

were looking for protection, "there ain't ever been an empty place at the bar after one a.m. this week. And as for that particular stool—"

The humorous trumpet-bray opening the first number, spraying a ridicule of all pomp and circumstance across every square inch of the Tomtoms, cut him short.

"Yes?" Sol prompted.

But now Pops was no longer aware of him. It was one a.m. and across the smoky distance of the Tomtoms he was watching her come, materializing from the gloom of the entry, no longer a thing of smoke but strong with the night and the night's secret powers, solidly blocking off the first booths and the green of the dice-tables as she passed them.

He noted without surprise or regret that she'd caught the nice boy she'd gone after, as she caught everything she went after. And now nearer and nearer—the towel dropped from Pop's fingers—past the bandstand, past the short, chromium-fenced stretch of bar where the girls got the drinks for the tables, until she spun herself up onto the midmost barstool and smiled cruelly at him. "'Lo, Pops."

The nice boy sat down next to her and said, "Two brandies, Pops. Soda chasers." Then he took out a pack of cigarettes began to battle through his pockets for matches.

She touched his arm. "Get me my lighter, Pops," she said.

Pops shook.

She leaned forward a little. The smile left her face. "I said get me my lighter, Pops."

He ducked like a man being shot at. His numb hands found the cigar box under the bar. There was something small and black inside. He grabbed it up as if it were a spider and thrust it down blindly on the bar, jerked back his hand. Bobby picked it up and flicked her thumb and lifted a small yellow flame to the nice boy's cigarette. The nice boy smiled at her lovingly and then asked, "Hey, Pops, what about our drinks?"

For Martin, the crystal world was getting to be something of a china shop. Stronger and stronger, slowly and pleasurably working toward a climax like the jazz, he could feel the urge toward wild and happy action. Masculine action, straight-armed, knife-edged, dramatic, destroying or loving half to death everything around him. Waiting for the inevitable—whatever it was would be—he almost gloated.

The old man half spilled their drinks, he was in such a hurry setting them down. Pops really did seem a bit nuts, just like Sol had said, and Martin stopped the remark he'd half intended to make about finding Pops' girl. Instead, he looked at Bobby.

"You drink mine, lover," she said, leaning close to be heard over the loud music, and again he saw the scar. "I've had enough."

Martin didn't mind. The double brandy burned icily along his nerves, building higher the cool flame of savagery that was fanned by the band blaring derision at the haughty heads and high towers of civilization.

A burly man, who was taking up a little too much room beside Martin, caught Sol's attention as the latter passed inside the bar, and said, "So far you're winning, it's still empty." Sol nodded, smiled, and whispered some witticism. The burly man laughed, and in appreciation said a dirty word.

Martin tapped his shoulder. "I'll trouble you not to use that sort of language in front of my girl."

The burly man looked at him and beyond him, said, "You're drunk, Joe," and turned away.

Martin tapped his shoulder again. "I said I'd trouble you."

"You will, Joe, if you keep it up," the burly man told him, keeping a poker face. "Where is this girl you're talking about? In the washroom? I tell you, Joe, you're drunk."

"She's sitting right beside me," Martin said, enunciating each word with care and staring grimly into the eyes of the poker face.

The burly man smiled. He seemed suddenly amused. "Okay, Joe," he said, "let's investigate this girl of yours. What's she like? Describe her to me."

"Why, you—" Martin began, drawing back his arm.

Bobby caught hold of it. "No, lover," she said in a curiously intent voice. "Do as he says."

"Why the devil—"

"Please, lover," she told him. She was smiling tightly. Her eyes were gleaming. "Do just as he says."

Martin shrugged. His own smile was tight as he turned back to the burly man. "She's about twenty. She's got hair like pale gold. She looks a bit like Veronica Lake. She's dressed in black and she's got a black cigarette lighter."

Martin paused. Something in the poker face had changed. Perhaps it was a shade less ruddy. Bobby was tugging at his arm.

"You haven't told him about the scar," she said excitedly.

He looked at her, frowning.

"Tell him about the scar, too."

"Oh, yes," he said, "and she's got the faintest scar running down from her left temple over her left eyelid and the bridge of her nose, and across her right cheek to the lobe of her—"

He stopped abruptly. The poker face was ashen, its lips were working. Then a red tide started to flood up into it, the eyes began to look murder.

Martin could feel Bobby's warm breath in his ear, the flick of her wet tongue. "Now, lover. Get him now. That's Jeff."

Swiftly, yet very deliberately, Martin shattered the rim of his chaser glass against the shot glass and jammed it into the burly man's flushing face.

A shriek that wasn't in the score came out of the clarinet. Someone in the booths screamed hysterically. A barstool went over as someone else cringed away. Pops screamed. Then everything was whirling movement and yells, grabbing hands and hurtling shoulders, scrambles and sprawls, crashes and thumps, flashes of darkness and light, hot breaths and cold drafts, until Martin realized that he was running with Bobby beside him through gray pools of street light, around a corner into a darker street, around another corner ...

Martin stopped, dragging Bobby to a stop by her wrist. Her dress had fallen open. He could glimpse her small breasts. He grabbed her in his arms and buried his face in her warm neck, sucking in the sweet, heavy reek of gardenia. She pulled away from him convulsively. "Come on, lover," she gasped in an agony of impatience. "Hurry, lover, hurry."

And they were running again. Another block and she led him up some hollowed steps and past a glass door and tarnished brass mailboxes and up a worn-carpeted stair. She fumbled at a door in a frenzy of haste, threw it open. He followed her into darkness.

"Oh, lover, hurry," she threw to him.

He slammed the door.

Then it came to him, and it stopped him in his tracks. The awful stench. There was gardenia in it, but that was the smallest part. It was an elaboration of all that is decayed and rotten in gardenia, swollen to an unbearable putrescence.

"Come to me, lover," he heard her cry. "Hurry, hurry, lover, hurry—what's the matter?"

The light went on. The room was small and dingy with table and chairs in the center and dark, overstuffed things back against the walls. Bobby dropped to the sagging sofa. Her face was white, taut, apprehensive.

"What did you say?" she asked him.

"That awful stink," he told her, involuntarily grimacing his distaste. "There must be something dead in here."

Suddenly her face turned to hate. "Get out!"

"Bobby," he pleaded, shocked. "Don't get angry. It's not your fault."

"Get out!"

"Bobby, what's the matter? Are you sick? You look green."

"*Get out!*"

"Bobby, what are you doing to your face? What's happened to you? *Bobby! BOBBY!*"

POPS SPUN THE glass against the towel with practiced rhythm. He eyed the two girls on the opposite side of the bar with the fatherliness of an old and snub-nosed satyr. He drew out the moment as long as he could.

"Yep," he said finally, "it wasn't half an hour after he screwed the glass in that guy's face that the police picked him up in the street outside her apartment, screaming and gibbering like a baboon. At first they were sure he was the one who killed her, and I guess they gave him a real going-over. But then it turned out he had an iron-clad alibi for the time of the crime."

"Really?" the redhead asked.

Pops nodded. "Sure thing. Know who really did it? They found out."

"Who?" the cute little brunette prompted.

"The same guy that got the glass in the face," Pops announced triumphantly. "This Jeff Cooper fellow. Seems he was some sort of a racketeer. Got to know this Bobby in Michigan City. They had a fight up there, don't know what, guess maybe she was two-timing him. Anyway, she thought he was over being mad, and he let her think so. He brought her down to Chicago, took her to this apartment he had, and beat her to death.

"That's right," the old man affirmed, rubbing it in when the cute little brunette winced. "Beat her to death with a beer bottle."

The redhead inquired curiously. "Did she ever come here, Pops? Did you ever see her?"

For a moment the glass in Pops' towel stopped twirling. Then he pursed his lips. "Nope," he said emphatically, "I couldn't have. 'Cause he murdered her the night he brought her down to Chicago. And that was a week before they found her." He chuckled. "A few days more and it would have been the sanitary inspectors who discovered the body—or the garbage man."

He leaned forward, smiling, waiting until the cute brunette had lifted her unwilling fascinated eyes. "Incidentally, that's why they couldn't pin it on this Martin Bellows kid. A week before—at the time she was killed—he was hundreds of miles away."

He twirled the gleaming glass. He noticed that the cute brunette was still intently watching him. "Yep," he said reflectively, "it was quite a job that other guy did on her. Beat her to death with a beer bottle. Broke the bottle doing it. One of the last swipes he gave her laid her face open all the way from her left temple to her right ear."

THE EERIEST RUINED DAWN WORLD

THE ASTROGATOR'S DEAR Friend asked, "But of all the worlds you found where awareness had budded and then destroyed itself—and there were more of them than I had realized!—which was the most interesting?"

"I can't tell you that, you cold-blooded fish!" the Astrogator replied. "They were all equally interesting ... and equally sad." He paused. "But I can tell you which was the strangest—no, that's not the word."

"The eeriest," the Planetographer supplied.

"Yes, that describes it," the Robotist agreed, "provided you were both referring to the star we called Lonely and its planet Hope. I thought so! Yes, the eeriest!"

"Oh, good!" the Robotist's Fond Companion urged. "I love spooky stories."

"Tales of death and desolation—by all means!" the Planetographer's Sweet Love chimed, smacking her lips.

"Morbid monster!" he told her playfully.

"Prurient parasite!" she joked back.

"Which of us should begin?" the Astrogator asked.

"You!" they all chorused: his two fellow explorers and the stay-at-home mates of all three of them were gathered together in convivial and truly symbiotic friendship for the first time since the three explorers' great voyaging.

The Astrogator finished his drink, was poured another,

and began, "We surfaced from hyperspace out in the Arm. Our destination was a star in a tiny cluster, a star so small and somehow woebegone we called her Lonely."

"Out in the Arm!" his Dear Friend commented. "Then it was during the period when we were out of telepathic contact entirely. *Our* lonely time."

"That's right. As we approached her, we studied her planets. The Seventh was trebly ringed, quite a rarity. The Fifth was long since shattered, almost pulverized. An old deep nuclear suicide, or else a dual planet, inharmoniously paired. Analysis of data we recorded may still tell."

"Or perhaps (remotely possible) he encountered a small dark wanderer passing through Lonely's space," the Planetographer put in.

"What a way to go!" his Sweet Love said. "Serve him right for playing around."

"No fault of his—he'd be a sitting duck."

"Who's telling this?" the Astrogator complained. "Now moving in closer to Lonely, we found her Third altogether ideal for life, right in the middle of the viable volume. And he was paired, with tides to stir his atmosphere and waters—no chance of stagnation. The secondary was quite small, had long ago died a natural death—"

"Perhaps," the Planetographer interjected.

The other continued without comment, "—but the primary was the right size with a rich atmosphere, so we named him Hope. And there were radiations patterned by intelligence coming from him. That seemed conclusive, and yet"—he paused—"and yet almost from the start there was something about him that seemed wrong."

He paused again. The Planetographer nodded and said, "His atmosphere was rich, all right—too rich in hydrocarbons to my taste."

The Robotist observed, "And as for those radiations indicating intelligence, well, there began to be a sameness about them, a lack of interplay, a lack of the day-to-day dynamisms characteristic of mental life in ferment."

"A time of cultural calm?" his Fond Companion suggested. "A quiet period?"

"We thought so for a while, my dear."

The Astrogator went on, "I put *Quester* into a parking orbit inn Three's natural period of rotation so that our ship hung above one meridian, shuttling north and south through an arc of about one-fourth of a circle as Three spun."

He looked toward the Planetographer across the table floating between them.

"Three showed at least three times as much ocean as land," the latter took up. "Our daily swing took us across two continents joined by a serpentine isthmus, from the east coast of the northern continent to the west coast of the southern near its tip, and back again. Three was, or had been, inhabited all right, and by beings of considerable if strange mentation, for we passed over numerous cities—"

"Cities? What are those?" the Astrogator's Dear Friend wanted to know.

"Abnormal concentrations of dwellings and other structures. Inorganic cancers. As I was saying—over numerous cities and great wide roads and paved flat fields that might have been for the mass celebration of religious rites, or else for the launching and landing of large winged vehicles. In fact, the inhabitants of Three seemed to have had a passion for sealing in the surfaces of their continents with various inorganic materials."

"How very strange," the Robotist's Fond Companion observed.

"Yes, indeed. At the north end of our daily swing there was an especially large concentration of cities—a cluster of inorganic boils, you might say—beside and in the ocean's edge. The one of these containing the most monstrous structures was a long narrow island surrounded by a mighty dike at least one-fourth the height of the tallest structures it guarded—and they were tall!—and against the top of which, or near, the dark, restless oceanic waters ceaselessly lapped and crashed. This city stood just off the continent. A very deep river led down to it from the north, while farther to the northwest lay five great, swollen lakes, half run together."

"Did he have ice caps? I mean Three, of course," the Planetographer's Sweet Love inquired sharply.

"No."

"But had he formerly?"

"My love, you are intuitive. Yes, he'd had ice caps until very recently, and they had melted, raising the ocean's level, and the dike had been built against that, stage by stage.

"But oh, the monstrousness of those buildings the dike guarded!—especially toward the south end of the island. Their height, immensity, and blocky shapes! But most particularly the way they were crowded together stiflingly like giant columns of prismatic basalt. With your own eyes or by telepathy you've all seen monuments on other planets, built by races that favor such oddities. Well, imagine them *without vistas*, jammed side to side, literally wall against wall, hundreds and hundreds of them, thousands and thousands—and many scores of them tall enough to peer over the dike at the illimitable, wind-fretted sea. Or think of planets heavily overpopulated, so that two skyscrapers actually approach each other as closely as the sum of their heights, and then imagine *them* packed together with no room between, the windows of their eyes blinded, the doors of their mouths screaming against solidity—as if space herself had been conquered by matter, as threatens in the hearts of some dwarf stars. I tell you, as we stared down through our instruments at that monstrous city, we wondered only why it had not squeezed itself out of existence—popped like a pressured seed out of the space-time fabric into chaos!"

"But just how high, really, was the dike?" his Sweet Love asked.

"A hundred times my height."

"So, ten times my length. Yes, that's pretty tall," she allowed, smiling at him beside her. The other four around the floating table nodded or otherwise expressed agreement.

The Planetographer continued. "The walled and narrow off-shore island city, although spectacular and with a macabre fascination all its own, did not monopolize our attention. We studied other cities along our swing—in fact, all the sea and land we passed over. We set up two observation satellites in other orbits along other meridians. We sent down probes to sample the atmosphere and waters. We pinpointed the sources of Three's radiation and further analyzed it. By every means we knew, we looked for life.

"Gradually it was borne in on us (and to our considerable astonishment since we'd seen the cities) that our first horrible suspicion was correct. Hope (Three) was dead—as sterile as an asteroid in intergalactic space, or baking as it orbits a star just outside her corona. By their unbridled industrial and technological development, Three's inhabitants had doomed and destroyed all life there, even the monocellular and the viral. The atmosphere was lethal. The great oceans were poison."

"And the patterned radiations," the Robotist put in, "were being broadcast by automatic, self-repairing instruments that would continue to do so until their sun-power failed. Mere echoes of intelligence long since dead."

There was a general silence.

The Planetographer resumed, elegiacally, "The ruined dawn worlds are all sad, a hundred self-destroyed for every one that manages to cope with the first great crisis of intelligence: environment's control, ecology. Sad, sad to see a planet blasted by nuclear warfare, perhaps riven to its very core. But such deaths at least are swift and sudden. Saddest of all to see a planet like Hope, dead of slow poison, where even his intelligent inhabitants became, by overpopulation, only one more pollutant. To think of his vigorous peoples creating and building, entertaining all sorts of romantic and grandiose plans for the future, believing themselves in control of their lives, when all the while they were only quietly digging their own graves, planning their deaths, building their monstrous tombs, patiently elaborating the venoms that would carry them off—and all local life with them. For life was gone on Hope, totally gone."

There was, as it were, a collective sigh from the three stay-at-homes around the floating table.

"But then," the Planetographer said dramatically, "there came the event that appeared to refute that seemingly irrevocable conclusion. Out of the cenotaph of the monstrous diked island city there rose a fiery plumed rocket aimed at us. We let it approach for a space, then mastered it with repulsor and tractor beams and, when its fuel burned out, placed it in the same orbit as *Quester* at a safe distance. Robot examination -but that's the field of my friend across the table."

"—showed it to be a fission-fusion missile of some potency," the Robotist took up. "It was the *delay* in the firing of the missile that seemed to argue *against* a merely automatic defense system triggered by the approach of *Quester* and *for* the presence of living intelligence. If it were merely a robot system like the sun-powered broadcasters, with the decision arrived at by computers, why the delay? Of course there were alternative explanations, such as a cumulative stimulus being required to work the trigger. Still, as I sent down the probes that would engage in detailed explorations, inside structures as well as out, far underground if need be, I felt more than usual excitement, even an uneasy anticipation, as to exactly what they would discover.

"As you know, the probes are of several different sorts, ranging from spheroidal floaters to true robots with eight legs, about my size, able to walk and climb, open or cut through doors, and also fire grapnel lines to bridge gaps, et cetera.

"Such probes were sent not only into the diked city, but also to other localities: on the two serpent-linked continents, on a larger cluster of continents on Three's other side, and on one lonely land mass at his southern pole.

"The same quite interesting general finding soon came back from many localities. The larger structures everywhere were quite devoid of the remains of Three's intelligent life form, which later turned out to be a biped bibrach with an internal mineral skeleton. Its sensorium and organs of mentation were carried precariously in an external braincase, instead of within a sturdy cephalothorax, such as ours, or a single streamlined body, such as yours, my dears."

"How very odd," his Fond Companion said.

"A mineral endoskeleton instead of pliant cartilage," the Planetographer's Sweet Love observed with some distaste. "Bones on the inside, ugh!"

"And how much nicer to be born with tentacles, like ours, or a neat and protective leathery exoskeleton, like yours," the Astrogator's Dear Friend said to him.

"The biped bibrachs had tentacles of a sort," he told her. "Five on each limb, with little bones inside."

"Sounds much too stiff. They must have moved about like rheumatic demi-octopuses. Or paraplegic arachnoids, for that matter."

"As I was saying," the Robotist cut short the digression, "although we found numerous bibrach skeletons, there were none within the larger structures—no, these were empty except for large stores of video and audio records—which did not clash with the notion that these places were for the celebration of rare and arcane religious rites, holy and occult buildings. Why, several of them near the center of the cluster of continents on Three's other side were shaped like huge pyramids and almost solid—just a few tiny rooms and passageways deep inside. Another, which stood on a peninsula one-fifth of our swing down the diked city's meridian, was a hollow cube so vast that several of the bibrach's smaller winged vehicles could have been flown about inside.

"But as you'd expect, the structures in the diked island city were the most monstrous, though one at the drowned foot of the fourth western lake was taller. A large number of our probes were busy there—many of them exploring underground, for the island was formed entirely of fine-grained rock, which the bibrachs had honeycombed with tunnels and basements under basements, like inverted buildings—towers and downward-pointing pinnacles of space inside solidity.

"And then from the probe that had gone deepest—as deep below the surface as the tallest tower extended above—a message was relayed back: it had found life."

There was an uneasy stirring around the round table. It almost communicated itself to the water in which the six friends floated.

"We asked our probes for details and to a degree we got them, although the distance was too great, the angles too sharp, and the relays too many for the accurate transmission back of pictures. There was *one* source of life-indications only, *one* being, and it was strangely wedded to the inorganic."

"Horrors! But how?" his Fond Companion demanded.

"That is the thing our robots could not tell us. We were consumed with wonder and with dread, but above all with a burning curiosity. We decided to go down and see for ourselves—all three, since none of us would consent to be left behind."

"But that was fantastically dangerous," she protested, "and quite against all sound exploratory practice."

"When we are out in the wild worlds of the Rim," the Astrogator put in, "we are not always so particular. I'm afraid we take chances."

"Especially when we are also out of telepathic range," the Planetographer added.

"Besides, there was this *drive*, this burning urge," the Robotist continued. "As soon as the *Quester* had swung farthest north, we suited up and took the landing craft down.

"The skies were brownish gray when at last we saw them from below. So were the seas storming around the island. We landed in a narrow gorge—slit, rather—at the base of two vast rectilinear pylons, from deep below which the signs of life were coming.

"We disembarked, feeling claustrophobic and unclean, despite the sure protection afforded by our suits. The pavement was less littered than I'd expected, though I did note the braincase of a bibrach, brown as the ribbon of sky overhead. The structures hemming us in, their windowed walls staring shortsightedly at each other, were indescribably oppressive.

"The cramping gorge ended at the great dike, and even as I looked up, up, up at its top, I saw a cloud of brown spray thrown high above it as a great wave broke against its other side. The thought of all that poisoned water pressing in on us from all sides, and we already far below its surface, added to the dark weight upon my feelings.

"Our robots were waiting for us, and with them we began the subterranean stage of our journey. We descended chiefly by a series of narrow, vertical, square-sectioned shafts bored in the rock. These carried boxlike vehicles, but we preferred to drop by our own lines. I will not dwell on my ever increasing feeling of oppression. Suffice it that the rocks' vast mass was added in my thoughts to that of the waters.

"We entered at last a dim world of computers, the inorganic remnant, mindlessly functioning, of the core of the bibrach's culture. At its nadir we found our robots clustered around a deep-set window. Here, we knew, was the life they'd found. We ordered them aside and looked through ourselves and say a life-support system automatically maintaining a single bibrach brain that was cyborged to the computer around it."

"Cyborged—how very dreadful," his Fond Companion breathed. "The marriage of flesh to metal—abomination."

"For a long while we stood staring at that poor pinkish thing. The same thoughts and feelings were building up in all three of our minds: the loneliness and agony and desolation of that captive mind, last of its race, sundered by light-years (at least until our arrival) from any other known mentality— the mind that at some pinnacle of hate or terror had sent the rocket at us, the mind that might die the next moment, or perhaps live for eons. In the end I found myself thinking just this one thought: that if Death has a brain anywhere in the universe, it is there on Hope (that circles Lonely way out in the Arm), deep in the rock of the diked island city.

"Perhaps (you'll say) we should have tried to communicate with it, even to disentangle it at any risk from its environs. I only know we didn't. Instead we returned (fled would be more honest), up the skinny shafts into the brown day of the monstrous city, and embarked to chase the *Quester* down its meridian without a thought of waiting its return. Once aboard, we picked up all our probes and left (fled!) Hope and all of Lonely's planetary system and didn't feel really safe until we were in hyperspace again."

"Think of the loneliness of that last brain..." the Planetographer murmured.

"That was the eeriest ruined dawn world—just as I told you at the start," the Astrogator said with conviction. "Don't you agree, my love?"

"I think all three of you behaved like a pack of lunatics," his Dear Friend answered. "You're not to be trusted, any of you, outside the range of our telepathy."

"Why didn't you stay and at least try to talk to that buried brain?" the Planetographer's Sweet Love demanded.

"We had this feeling—" he began, then shrugged.

"We were *scared*," the Robotist said.

"Well, it's been nice to get together," his Fond Companion said briskly, "but now it's time we broke up. You and I, my dear, have to check out that terrarium we're buying at Deep Six."

And without further ceremony the three arachnoids, about as large as gorillas but with brains larger than man's and hands even more manipulative, scrambled into the shoulder niches of their ichthyoid partners. The latter, who were the size of long, sinuous whales with brains one-fifth their mass, supported by ocean and great webs of cartilage, arched upward and then dove down with ponderous grace. Now the ocean was empty again except for the abandoned table bobbing and rocking in the wake of that great treble sounding.

RICHMOND LATE SEPTEMBER, 1849

GASLIGHT FLARED ON white washed brick filmed with soot. Skirts swished against gritty slate sidewalks. There was the small *skip-skop* of heels, the occasional rap of a cane's ferrule, and the large *klep-klep* on cobbles of the iron-shod hooves of horses dragging creaking carriages. Everyone was hurrying a little. There was a hint of autumn chill in the air. And a feeling of aggressive pride and self-confidence. Bracing. Quickening.

The woman looked younger than she was, though queenly. At first sight you might have taken her for a tall slim schoolgirl, no older than the Carlotta of Belgium who would marry the ill-starred Maximilian of Austria, lose her Mexican empire and husband and sanity all at once and live on for 60 more years. But then you would have noticed the woman's slender maturity. She was dressed in gleaming black rep from neck to wrists and toes, yet she showed a gray silk ankle as she walked. She wore gloves of black lace. Her face was very pale, but gay, yet her large dark eyes had a strange dispassionate distance in them. Her glistening black hair was centrally parted in the style of the times, but flared out into the suggestion of a raven's wings.

The man looked older than he was, at least as years are reckoned by an insurance agent. He too was pale and darkly clad, wearing a black alpaca coat. His sunken eyes looked permanently but rather beautifully blacked by the invisible punches of life. Yet there was a jauntiness to him, a power of romance, however desperate. He wore a white shirt and black string tie, and across his upper lip a modest straight mustache.

As they hastened along, not with but near each other, the man sighed very softly yet shudderingly and gently grasped the woman's elbow and said, "Mademoiselle, may I have the honor of buying you a drink?"

She jerked, but chiefly with her chin as she turned her face toward him. With a marked French accent she said, "Sir! You startled me! I did not hear your footsteps."

"Nor I yours. At first I thought you were a spirit."

"And you dared accost me! But see, sir, it is only that I wear caoutchouc over-slippers, as I now perceive you do yourself."

"Mademoiselle has answered one question brilliantly. Now the other. My invitation."

"Sir! You are very forward."

He stared at her with a gloomy smile, not quite apologetic, and answered, "I don't believe I've ever been forward in my life, not even with my late wife. You remind me of her— Virginia was very young—and also the heroine of my story 'Ligeia,' where a beloved wife returns from the dead."

Her nostrils flared, but her expression was still merry. "You Americans are all very forward. And you cry your own wares."

"I'm a mere hack, a pen-pusher," he replied with a slight shrug. "A scribbler of stories which my critics tell me are too strained and trifling, too fantastical, to bear rereading or warrant imitation. But it's true we Americans are supposed to be forward -great hustlers and good at diddling."

"What is that, pray?"

"The art of out-sharping the other man when money is at stake. I once wrote an article on the topic."

"Then I suppose you are very expert at the practice yourself."

He shook his head, the barest swing of his gaunt cheeks.

"My parents were actors and so presumably fakers and good diddlers. Yet I don't recall that I ever did a successful diddle myself in my whole life. I work for such pittances as magazines and lecture-goers disburse."

Hard French practicality showed for a moment in the woman's gaze. She said, "As for making money, I see no harm in that, but merit."

The other smiled, showing dark teeth a little, and lifted a sardonic left eyebrow. "Ah, but suppose a whole nation were bitten by a gold bug. There might be danger then, a sort of fever, a dancing madness."

"You are referring, sir, to the recent gold discoveries in California?"

"No, mademoiselle, only to another story I wrote."

"Pen-pusher! Scribbler!"

"As you say, and as I said before you. But I perceive across the street the lamps of the family entrance of what is a reputable tavern. Not Sadler's, but sufficient."

As they crossed, there came ponderously dashing around the corner ahead, through the gas-fumey murk, a great dray drawn by two huge black horses. Its wheels creaked thunderously on the cobbles, the heavy empty barrels added their gloomy note, while from the whip of the dark, big-shouldered drayman there came a series of loud cracks.

The last crack came quite close to them as they gained the opposite curb, and the woman lifted a hand protectively, though since she did not flinch, the gesture had the appearance of a command.

She said, as soon as the great noise had passed, "What is it, sir? You are shaking, you have grown pale as death. Yet the dray missed us by several yards. Did it perhaps remind you of some dreadful experience in battle? The sounds were indeed somewhat like distant cannonading and nearby musketry."

"No, mademoiselle," he began shudderingly, speaking on the indrawn breath. "True, I was once enrolled at the U.S. Military Academy, but expelled because I deliberately absented myself from call. But ever since, beginning faintly even at West Point," and here his white face took on an agonized look, "I have heard that sound of incessant cannonading. Now faint, now thundering close, I have heard it with the inner ear in Baltimore, Washington, Fredericksburg, New York, Providence, Philadelphia, this Richmond and once, very loudly in Gettysburg. I have seen faces red-lit and blood-stained by broad daylight on peaceful-seeming streets. I have seen them grinning with hate where others perceived only smiles. I have flinched from the imagined, dreadfully real flash of bayonets and rifle-fire. I have heard the screams of the wounded, the jeers of the conquerors, the snarls of the vanquished, the groaning of caissons, the roaring of fires consuming cities. And always, faint and far though near in nightmares by day and night, that endless cannonading."

Now sweat dripped down his face, his cheeks twitched, his eyes blinked incessantly, while the palsied trembling of his hands if anything increased, as if he were about to have an epileptic seizure. The woman moved to soothe and restrain him, but was held paralyzed by his hypnotic glare. Without pause he continued, "Oh and I have written stories about it, I have pushed my pen on many dreadful journeys. 'Metzengerstein,' the apotheosis of a great cavalry charge into a flaming hell. 'The Masque of the Red Death,' where a dire sickness of blood, of streaming wounds, stalks a nation and resistlessly enters the highest homes and stills the most riotous gaiety. 'The Tell-Tale Heart,' where the cannonading becomes the ticking of a tortured heart that will not die in the body of a floored-up murdered man. 'William Wilson,' in which brother pursues with relentless secret hate and stabs down one closer than brother. 'The Cask of Amontillado,' wherein a supposed friend walls up friend alive and the cannonading sinks to the soft thud of brick into mortar. 'The Murders in the Rue Morgue,' where an undiscoverable giant anthropoid wreaks horrid and senseless destruction on the innocent. And 'The Pit and the Pendulum,' all fiery iron and flashing, hissing inescapable steel."

His speech broke off into gasps which swiftly diminished

in volume. His trembling gradually moderated, his cheeks and eyelids grew still, and his eyes lost most of their glare.

"Oh, alas, sir," the woman said with feeling, "you are cursed with a sensitivity like my poor brother's. Perhaps you have the dreadful gift of premonition. These horrible phantasms of war which haunt you may refer to an impending conflict. Is it possible that the Mexicans, though beaten last year, may attack your land and this time successfully?"

"No, something closer." He shivered slightly and blinked his eyes, now as one who returns somewhat wondering to reality. Then he frowned. "But I fear you are correct that it is premonition. There are preternatural sensitivities which we wish were madness, but are not."

"But what nation, if not Mexico?" the woman pressed. "Surely you do not suggest that the British would attempt to reconquer their great colony more than a quarter century since they burnt Washington?"

"Something closer," I said. The glare increased again in his eyes and he struck his stiffly white-fronted bosom. He whispered. "As close as my heart. Look deeply as I have into the gas-lit faces in the streets around us, in the streets of any American city, and you will see a carefully dissembled maniacal hatred, a hooded yet furnace-red glare—"

He broke off. As if in obedience to a mesmerist's command, the woman had begun to look with blank eyes into the various shadowed and high-lit faces of the throng eddying around the island-of-two which they constituted. This grotesque and theatrical action seemed to recall him fully to reality. The visionary glare ebbed entirely from his dark-circled eyes, a comic light momentarily flooded them, his gaunt features assumed a courtly and attentive demeanor, he pressed the woman's elbow, and said, "Your pardon. In pursuing my wild and witless fantasies, I churlishly allowed hospitality to be chased from my mind. It is time and more that we partook of the refreshment which I suggested." And he steered them toward the doubly lamp-lit white doorway decorated with faint arabesques of gilt.

"But sir, will your strength permit it?" the girl protested

anxiously. "Your pallor. Your shivering. I had begun to fear you were suffering with some fever or other malady requiring the attention of a physician."

"No disease which a drink will not cure," he assured her with a quirking smile and ushered her through the doorway which had meanwhile been opened by a bobbing and upward-grinning Negro dressed in red jacket and dark trousers that came to mid-calf. "While life itself is a fever."

"My brother champions the same theory," she murmured somewhat puzzeledly as other drab faces preceded them with obsequious and fawning smiles to two chairs upholstered with red plush and facing each other across a small round table draped with snowy linen.

The man looked around at walls papered in dark red, trimmed with gilt, topped with a red fringe, and mellowly candle-lit.

"No mirrors. Good," he said with a sharp nod, then explained, "I detest looking at my own face, especially when I have a companion with features as fair as yours to gaze upon." Then, as the woman bent her raven-tressed head and demurely lowered her long-lashed, faintly blue-veined eyelids, his voice became very businesslike. "And now may I suggest a sherry flip? I have discovered that an egg mixed with liquor or wine moderates its intoxicating fire while adding desirable nutriment."

"Yes, you may, sir," she said, looking up with a pleased smile. "Oh, you are most wise, sir. My poor brother, though no older than I has already a frightening affinity for one of the most maddening of liquors. You will yourself partake of a sherry flip?"

Changing neither expression nor tone of voice, he said, "No. Blackberry brandy," then added somewhat more loudly but without looking toward the departing waiter, "in a claret glass."

Then for a while he gazed quizzically, almost teasingly at her saddened features. He asked, "You find me something of a paradox?—a Sphinx, an Angel of the Odd, an Imp of the Perverse?"

"A little perhaps, sir," she confessed gravely. "But what are those last two?"

"Titles I have scribbled above stories," he replied, brushing his mustache with a thumbnail. "Last three."

She smiled as if against her will, shaking her head slightly and raising for a moment her hands clad in black lace, as if to say, "You are too much for me, sir." But then her features grew grave again. She leaned forward. Her eyes moved from his toward the doorway by which they had entered, then back again, and she said softly, "What you said about the people in the streets. To me they seemed sane, alert, amiable, even if—your pardon, sir—somewhat uncouth by Gallic standards."

He did not seem to hear her. He was frowning at the doorway by which the waiter had departed and now he drummed the table impatiently with his thin knuckles.

"Oh sir, do you even remember what you said?" she asked concernedly.

"Alert is the significant word," he pronounced. "Alert for any morbid sensation. Sniffing for accidents, altercations, murder, horror. Some of them, I assure you, do nothing else, night and day. Consult my 'The Man of the Crowd,' though that in part describes London."

"But what you said of brother battling brother and friend betraying friend. It is hard for me to believe that could ever happen here, where even bloody revolution took a more moderate, prudent course than in my fierce-minded motherland. During the three quarters of century of its existence, your new nation has increasingly demonstrated its solidarity, the indissoluble union of its states."

"There is another story I have written," he replied, his eyes still on the doorway, his knuckles still lightly drumming. 'The Fall of the House of Usher,' wherein a vast, seemingly eternal structure—a veritable stone nation—cracks asunder. Note that Usher begins with the letters U.S. and ends with the feminine pronoun accusative. Alas, mademoiselle, and all appearance to the contrary, this country is moribund, like the man kept alive after death by hypnotism and instantly collapsing into loathsome putrescence when wakened. My story 'Valdemar.' And none of us will escape the terror when it comes—no, not even if we could fly to the moon with my 'Hans Pfaall.' For the madmen run this particular lunatic asylum—my benign 'Doctor Tarr' and kindly 'Professor Fether.'"

"Oh sir, you have written a story for everything," she told him with laughing resignation lightly touched by mockery.

The waiter had meanwhile trotted prancingly in and placed their drinks before them. Once the man's fingertips grasped the stem of his darkly-filled wineglass, his impatience left him.

"Not a story for the secret of the universe," he said with a jocularly rueful smile. "Once, after inhaling ether, I thought I glimpsed even that. 'Eureka!' I cried out. 'I have found it!' And I did make a lecture of it," he admitted. "But now I doubt the vision. Oh, mademoiselle, I am bombarded or bewhirlwinded by scraps and rags and threads of visions, come from I know not where. I weave them into my flimsy word-tapestries. Rarely I know their meanings. Chiefly I conjecture. And I am certain they have millions of meanings I have never dreamt. That poppinjay of a darky who served us this refreshment, it occurs to me now I may have written about him and all his race."

"That Negro, sir?"

"Yes, that Negro. In another walled-up dead-and-alive story, 'The Black Cat.' And the cat has his ultimate revenge, though it may take a hundred years and more. But away with gloom!" He lifted his glass and said to her over it, gazing at her with admiring, inquiring eyes, "To—?"

She said evenly, "My name is Berenice."

He lowered his glass an inch. "Truly the Angel of the Odd is amongst us tonight. I have written a story 'Berenice' about—But I promised you no more gloom."

"Oh do tell me, sir, you must. You have ignited my curiosity. And one always desires to hear about one's self."

"Namesake only, it had better be—about a girl who is

visited in her flower-fresh tomb by her lover, who pulls out all her teeth."

"Faugh! You have an odious mind, sir. Were I that Berenice, I would buy me sharp false teeth and come back from the grave to bite you. I respectfully suggest that your tales are dark and perverse because you attribute your own morbid thoughts to the persons and scenes around you."

"You have solved my riddle. But recollect, I warned you not to look into that closet, Madam Bluebeard. Once more, away with gloom! To Berenice! To the Berenice across the table!"

She modestly lowered her countenance and then merrily raised her eyes. They took a moderate sip of their drinks, he his dark purple, she her dark yellow one. He had almost returned his wineglass to the table when the muscles of his wrist stiffened, his face grew stern, he returned the glass to his lips and drained it, set it down, rapped out an imperious tattoo, and instantly began to talk animatedly to his companion, his face rapidly flushing and the words rushing out as if he knew he had only a limited time in which to speak them.

"Enchantment rules Richmond tonight. This chamber is the Red Palace and you its queen. Mysterious mademoiselle, saintly Berenice, you are the most beautiful woman I have ever known. The Marchesa Aphrodite Mentoni of my tale 'The Assignation.' Sipping not poison, but sherry flip. And I am the most blessed of men, privileged to share your divine company, rather than sip my poison in some lonely red-litten palace of my own. Another blackberry brandy, boy! Wineglass! On the run! Your features are finer than classic, Berenice. Your hair like a raven's wings. I once wrote a poem called 'The Raven.' Popular success. But the critics saw only an exercise in intricate stanzas and far-fetched rhymes. Like my 'Ulalume,' or my 'Bells.' Emerson calls me the Jingle Man. But I diddled them. I said what my critics said before they did! Took the wind out of their sails. But tonight it comes to me—Thank you, boy. Fetch another, straight off. Oh blessed, grape-dark anodyne! It nourishes the nerves,

Berenice. Makes sensitivity endurable. Blackberry for the black moods. But tonight it comes to me that my Raven is Sam Houston. They call him that, you know. Literal translation of his Cherokee name of Colonneh. He had a young bride. As I did. Ran away from her, no one knows why, to live with the Cherokees again. Resigned the governorship of Tennessee to do it. Made Texas a nation. Freed her from the Mexicans. Licked Santa Anna when no one else could. President Lone Star Republic. Fought corruption, fought the Gold Bug. Helped join Texas to the Union three years ago. Believes in Union. Sees what's coming to the South and'll do his best to stop it. Watching, watching, watching. Pallid bust of Pallas—some state capital building. Houston's shadow on me, demon eyes too, beak in my heart so I won't forget my guilt—I'm America in that poem. Tell Emerson that! Bet he can't work out a compensation. Tell Lowell, too! Put some brandy in his skim milk. Thinks my Raven's a diddle-bird, the ranting abolitionist! Thanks, boy. Just a sip now, to hold my level. What's coming to the South? What I told you when we met, beloved Berenice. Wrote a poem about it too. 'The City in the Sea' and *down* in the West too. Death enthroned on high. The South is building that city. Own universities, own factories, own everything. But the city'll sink in the iron-and-fire Maelstrom and it'll all end in death, Berenice. Death! Death fascinates me, you know."

"Oh sir, sir, sir!" the woman interrupted excitedly. Ever since he had mentioned 'The Raven' she had been trying to break into his monologue, unmindful of his rapid potations and threatening incoherence. "You must be the poet Edgar Poe whom my twin brother Charles admires, nay, adores, ever since he first encountered your writings two years ago. How he envied me my voyage from our native France to this land—he is madly desirous of meeting you. He never showed me your stories. He said they might offend me. But your verse I knew at once. That Raven—his emblem, his obsession. Oh sir, my brother has vowed to devote his life to widening and perpetuating your fame by translating your works and by writing in your manner, so that it will forever be. Edgar Poe, the Master, and the Acolyte, Charles Baudelaire!"

The effect of that last name on the man was extraordinary. He started, he winced as if struck across the face by a whip, then he took control of himself and his speech, so that the three-quarters-filled wineglass stood steady in his forcibly relaxed fingers and his babbling became once more connected discourse. It appeared to require an almost superhuman effort, but he triumphed.

"Yes, I am Edgar Poe, Mademoiselle Berenice. And I am deeply moved that someone of poetic sensitivity in France should find some merit in my poor writings. You are this Charles Baudelaire's sister, you say?" He watched her narrowly.

A rapid nod. "His twin."

"You sailed here from France?"

"Yes, and am shortly to return, taking ship in New York City."

He nodded slowly and started the wineglass toward his lips, became aware of what he was doing, and returned it until it was once more poised an inch or so above the table. Forming his words with care, he said, "You mentioned a liquor for which your brother has a predilection. May I ask its name?"

"Absinthe, sir. It contains oil of wormwood."

"Yes. The Conqueror Worm."

"Also, sir, he is, alas, a devotee—he would wish me to tell you this—of laudanum and morphine and their parent, opium."

Another slow nod. "So true poets and fantasists in France as well as America and England must seek the patronage and protection of that wondrous and terrible family. I should have known." An almost cunning look came into his still watchful eyes. "Tell your brother they are not reliable overlords in adversity." His countenance, grown pale again, filled with misery. "The princely opium genii whirl the rag-tag visions to us from the ends of the universe, but after a while they whirl them past us so fast we cannot quite glimpse them to remember, and in the end they whirl them away."

"Oh sir, I too admire you deeply and your unhappiness tears at my heart," the woman said softly yet urgently, leaning forward and gliding her narrow hand a short way across the table. "Can I not help you?"

He lifted his dark eyes as if seeing her for the first time. His countenance became radiant. "Oh, Berenice, the opiates are sorry, tattered phantoms when matched against the face and form of a supremely beautiful woman and the blessed touch of her fingers." He laid his free hand on hers. She started gently to withdraw it, he increased the pressure of his, gulped the three-quarters-full wineglass of dark brandy, set down the glass so rapidly it fell over, captured her hand in both of his, and drew it across the table to his lips. "Oh, Berenice."

The wineglass slowly rolled in a curve across the white linen to the edge of the small table and stopped there.

The man's face had flushed again and when he spoke his voice was almost maudlin. "Beloved Berenice," he crooned, fondling her hand close to his lips. "Ber'nice with the raven's hair and the little white teeth. Little Ber'nice."

With a strong movement which nevertheless revealed nothing of a jerk, she withdrew her hand from his and quietly stood up. He started to snatch at her departing fingers, broke off that movement almost at once, and tried to stand up himself. He was not equal to it. His ankles twisted together. He started to whirl and fall. He caught hold of the edge of the table and the back of his chair, turning the latter sideways. He managed to get a knee on the seat of the chair and half crouched there, still holding on with both hands and swaying slightly.

The wineglass fell to the floor and shattered, but neither he nor the woman appeared to notice it. The few people at the other tables looked at them. The darkies peered from the doorways.

"Ber'nice, I'm no good tonight," he said hoarsely, drawing rapid breaths. "Can't take you home. Disgraceful. Wretch.

Profound apologies. But I *must* see you again. Tomorrow. Most wonderful woman in the world. Beauty, wit, laughter, *youth, understanding.* Come when all hope gone. Tomorrow. I *must.*"

"Alas, sir, I depart from Richmond tonight on the first stage of my journey back to my brother." Glass crunched faintly under her black caoutchouc over-slippers as she walked around the table toward the doorway. Her face was very grave. "I thank you, sir, for your entertainment."

He reached out to catch her elbow as she passed him and he almost fell again. "Wait. Wait," he called after her, and when she did not, he cried out with a note of spite, "I know one thing about you. You're not Berenice Baudelaire. That's a lie. Profound apologies. But you're a diddler. Charles Baudelaire hasn't got a full sister or brother. Let alone a twin."

She turned slowly and faced him. "How can you know that, sir?"

He winced again as he had when she had first spoken the name Baudelaire. Finally he said in a husky, ashamed voice, "Because I got three letters from Charles Baudelaire about a year ago and never answered them. Told me all about his life. Only child. Praised my works. Understood better than anybody. But I never answered them." A tear ran down his cheek. "Lunatic vanity or resentment. Imp of the Perverse. I kept them in my coat pocket for months. Got all creased and dirty. Lost them in some tavern. Probably reading them aloud to somebody." His voice became accusing. "*That's* how I know you're not Berenice Baudelaire."

She returned a few steps. She said to him, "Nevertheless, Charles Baudelaire did have a twin sister, whose existence was kept a strict secret for reasons which I may not divulge, but which concern the Duc de Choiseul Praslin, patron of Charles' father."

He turned completely toward her, both hands gripping the back of his chair now and his knee still on it, with the effect of a stump. Whenever he tried to put down that foot, he'd start to fall, and he was swaying more now despite his support.

"Lies. All lies," he said, but when she started to turn away again, he quickly added, "but I don't care. I forgive you, Ber'nice. Makes you more mysterious and wonderful. Ber'nice, I *must* see you tomorrow."

She said without smiling, without frowning, "Alas, sir, I must tonight begin my return to France."

He stumped forward a step like a cripple, sliding his chair and once more almost falling, swaying worse than ever, and said, "But you're sailing from New York. Couple days *I'm* going to New York City myself. By way of Baltimore and Philadelphia. Going to New York to close my cottage and bring back Muddie, who's my aunt and poor Virginia's mother, Mrs. Clemm, so she can—" He hesitated, his eyes blearing, and then poured out, "Tell you everything—so she can be here at my wedding with Myra. Myra Royster. Mrs. Shelton. Childhood sweetheart. *Old* woman, old as I am. Doesn't mean anything. Only you, Ber'nice. We can meet in New York. What hotel are you staying at?"

She said to him gravely, "But sir, you do not know me. We met less than an hour ago. How can you be certain that on another day and perhaps in another mood, you will desire my closer acquaintance? Or that you will care for me at all when you know me better?"

"I *know* I will. Only you." His eyes were glazing as he implored, "Tell me who you really are, where you'll be. Or don't tell me, I'll forget. Write it down, then I'll remember. Write down your real name, the hotel you'll be staying at in New York."

She looked at him compassionately, a lovely figure in her black rep that glinted in the candlelight, which also glistened on her swellingly-parted raven's wing hair and made mysterious her more slim than classical pale face and her great dark eyes with the forbidding yet alluring, distance in them, those eyes that while giving absolute attention to the man, still seemed to look at all the world.

Then she turned, saying, "Alas, sir, I cannot meet you in

New York City," and walked glidingly and silently toward the outer door.

Slipping to his knees on the floor, but still clinging to the chair, the man cried piteously after her, "Tell me your name and where. Who really are you, Ber'nice? Virginia come back? Sarah Whitman lost your curls? Mrs. Osgood in your Violet Vane dress? Annabel Lee? Madeline Usher? Aphrodite Mentoni? Ligeia? Eleanora? Lenore? *My* Ber'nice? Really Ber'nice Baud'larie? Don't leave me. Plea' don' lea' me—"

She turned again, and as she faded back through the doorway, which the bobbing darkie opened and closed, her lips shaped themselves in an infinitely tender, utterly infatuated, truly loving smile and she called out clearly, "Never fear, my dear. I will meet you once again, sir. In Baltimore."

THE HOUSE OF MRS. DELGATO

THE HOUSE OF Mrs. Delgato was a sour stench, quite truly, in the nostrils of the respectable citizenry of Felicidad, New Mexico—which in this instance included all the other inhabitants of that lazy border town. They had a name for her house—a name that most people wouldn't consider nice and certainly not respectable.

Yet they delayed in taking decisive action, legal or otherwise, against Mrs. Delgato and "her girls," as she openly referred to them.

There were several reasons for this. The City Fathers were traditionalists: they respected Mrs. Delgato's one-time international reputation—it lent an oblique glamor to Felicidad.

And Mrs. Delgato was a good, even a righteous citizen in most respects. She paid her taxes on the dot, she frowned on noise and drunkenness, she always drew her shades, and she kept her girls within strict bounds. Never were they permitted out on the streets of Felicidad. Seldom were they even allowed to take the air in the high-walled, deep-shaded garden.

Mostly Mrs. Delgato's girls were confined to the imposing dark stucco house proper. Summer and winter, naked and in furs, they lolled in its shadowy bedrooms, or paced restlessly along its corridors behind the drawn blinds, or gathered of an evening in the large parlor with the upright piano, the horsehair sofas, the bead curtain and the peacock plumes.

Naturally enough a shade sometimes failed to be drawn, or rolled up impulsively on some whirringly wicked whim of its own. Even more naturally the more adventurous boys of Felicidad would climb the surrounding trees, or egg one another on to mount the vine-covered wall, in hopes of catching a revealing glimpse of one or more of Mrs. Delgato's girls.

Many of the grown men of Felicidad showed an interest in the house of Mrs. Delgato quite equal to that of the boys, though it was a more covert interest. Not so, however, in the case of Les Grimes, one of Felicidad's mental "unfortunates," who was always either loitering at the railway station, where the trains were a noisy excitement and an occasional quarter could be picked up for toting a stranger's bags, or prowling outside Mrs. Delgato's place, a slack-jawed Peeping Tom. Les liked to mouth over the rude name the Felicidados had given the dark stucco house—he seemed to take an endless pleasure in the terse phrase.

Mrs. Delgato was aware of Les's interest in her girls and when they met on the street she would threaten him jovially with the silver-handled whip it was her habit to carry.

"I saw you luring Lolita, shameless one!" she would cry. "Have a care, man." Or words to that effect.

Lolita was typical of Mrs. Delgato's girls and probably the pick of them for sheer beauty—a luxurious, youthful creature with the striking combination of green eyes and naturally yellow hair. Lazily graceful, forever yawning and stretching, Lolita loved to sunbathe in the garden when Mrs. Delgato permitted. At such times Lolita would croon a little song to herself in a way that was strangely seductive. Small wonder that Les—like others who could be named—was drawn back again and again to the vine-covered wall! Arrogant and seductive, Lolita was the general sort of female Leopold von Sacher-Masoch had in mind when he wrote the celebrated novel *Venus in Furs* that added the word masochism to our vocabulary—and Mrs.

Delgato reinforced this identification of Lolita as the cruel and beautiful *femme fatale* by sometimes referring to her affectionately as *La Muerte Amarilla*, the Yellow Death.

Most Felicidados accepted Mrs. Delgato's odd harsh language and silver-handled whip along with the other eccentricities of this iron-haired dark-skinned little woman, straight-backed and muscular despite her years, who along with her rudely-named and, truth to tell, odorous establishment was one of the prominent features of the town.

Some long-faced citizens, to be sure, enjoyed shaking their heads and predicting that, if action were not taken to make Mrs. Delgato dispose of her girls, there would some day be a scandal, a great tragedy even, and the fair name of Felicidad would be forever smirched. It was unnatural, these argued, for girls like Mrs. Delgato's to behave with unfailing propriety and permit themselves to be cooped up forever. A disgraceful outbreak of some sort was inevitable, these pessimists would dolorously maintain.

But, as we have noted before, Felicidad was a lazy town and things might have gone on without catastrophe for many years, or even until Mrs. Delgato and her girls had withered into moth-eaten scarecrows and been quietly laid away—if Andy Henderson had not arrived in town one evening just as the shadows were darkening from rose to charcoal.

ANDY HENDERSON WAS a person who knew a great deal (which he would tell you loudly on the slightest provocation) about houses where the girls gathered of an evening in a large parlor with an upright piano, horsehair sofas, a beaded curtain and peacock plumes—girls naked and in furs, or otherwise temptingly set forth. Andy gave Les Grimes two bits for carrying his sample case and Gladstone bag to the hotel and there he asked him a blunt and rudely worded question and later he gave Les a larger silver disk for conducting him to the house of Mrs. Delgato.

At the front gate Andy dismissed Les, believing that the companionship of a mature moron would not increase his

stature in the eyes of Madam Delgato—for he was prepared
to address her either as that or as Señora Delgato, he had
not yet decided which. Les for his part was well satisfied
to retreat to his favorite observation post behind the vine-
covered wall.

Moonlight showered excitement on the old dark manse
and on the overgrown jungle-like garden heavy with the
perfume of honeysuckle. The drawn blinds didn't bother
Andy—he had expected those, though it is true that he had
also expected a little light and noise to be filtering through
them. The complete silence and darkness—except for the
silver-scattering moonlight—were a trifle unnerving. A
more wildly imaginative man might have thought of ghost
girls, silver splashed, haunting an abandoned bordello.

But Andy Henderson's imagination, though vigorous,
abided within narrow limits. He rapped in a brash rhythm
on the thick green door and waited, balancing in his mind
the phrases "the girls" and las muchachas." A place like this
might be all Mexican, he reminded himself.

The door did not open and there were no footsteps—at
least not of anyone wearing heels; he *did* fancy he heard a
soft thump and a brief clicking noise, as if a barefoot girl
with a bone or horn anklet worn loosely had taken a quick
step.

Andy frowned and knocked again, more heavily and in
a more solemn rhythm. The door moved inward a fraction
of an inch.

He pushed it open wide and peered inside. There was
only darkness ... a soft crooning that in its strange way
was infinitely seductive ... and, striking through the heavy
sweetness of the honeysuckle, a gaggingly sour stench that
was for the moment quite inexplicable though somehow
most frightening ...

Andy had taken an automatic step forward and a board
creaked loudly under his foot ...

It was his screams—loud though not long—rather
than the incoherent cries of Les Grimes that brought the
Felicidados running. They came with their guns, knowing

that the day of the pessimists had come and they would at last have to take the decisive action they had anticipated but evaded for so long.

Mrs. Delgato's girls were effectively disposed of after considerable excitement and a few days later Mrs. Delgato was conducted to the nearest hospital that the state maintained for the mentally aberrated—conducted with considerable dignity and respect, such as it was only proper to accord to one who carried with her magnificently and to the end the aura of a great professional reputation.

Who could blame her if she had become a shade eccentric with the years and had chosen to live in retirement with "her girls" (as she called them to the end) on a surprisingly democratic footing? Had she not once been Lupe Delgato, known from Tijuana to Trinidad as the Queen of Tiger Tamers?

And who could blame Les Grimes for his infatuation with the rude name given to Mrs. Delgato's establishment—even though it caused the death of a salesman? Not one Felicidado doubted Les's veracity when he explained that Andy Henderson had clearly asked to be taken to the Cat House.

THE BLACK EWE

VERY WELL, I'LL tell you why I broke off my engagement to Lavinia Simes—though I'm not the sort of person who likes to go around broadcasting the facts of his private life. There's altogether too much broadcasting going on these days, by wave, newsprint and heaven knows what subtler avenues of approach to the human mind.

I could sum it all up in one word *horror*. But that doesn't mean much by itself. Besides, it would let you explain it away as a neurotic delusion, aftermath of the near nervous breakdown I had in 1946, when I quit my desk job with OSS. Though why anyone shouldn't have a nervous breakdown these days, with the whole world rushing hypnotized into the mouth of doom, is more than I can see.

At any rate "ridiculous neurotic delusion" is the explanation favored by most of the friends of the Simes— one syllable, you know, rhymes with limes. They delight in telling each other how without any word of warning I walked away from Lavinia in the midst of a sight-seeing tour of Chicago and refused ever to see her again. Which is completely accurate incidentally.

They all think I behaved outrageously.

All of them, that is, except Mrs. Grotius. When I met her afterwards she said, "Well, Ken, at least you won't go the way of Conners Maytal and Fritz Nordenfelt and Clive Maybrick and René Coulet and the other nice young men Lavinia was engaged to."

I didn't want to go into it with Mrs. Grotius, so I merely said, "Oh those were all accidents. And even the coincidence of so many fatal accidents isn't particularly striking when you remember that Lavinia and her father have always managed to be in the danger spots of the world."

"Yes, accidents do seem to cluster around Lavinia," Mrs. Grotius agreed in that dry voice of hers. "I wonder if that's why she always wears black, Ken?"

She always does, you know. It's a regular fetish with her. Lavinia once explained it, with a stab at psychoanalysis, as being an unconscious guilt-reaction to the fact that her mother had died bringing her into the world.

The mothers of monsters generally die giving them birth, so perhaps it's fair enough that the monsters should wear mourning.

Then another time Lavinia suggested, with hush-voiced Midwestern idealism, that perhaps she wore black because she was so conscious of the miserable state of the world. Which may be a lot more to the point.

Now I have a third explanation that's much more convincing to explaining why I left Lavinia on that sight-seeing tour.

I think Mrs. Grotius saw pretty deeply into Lavinia. Underneath her faddish interest in the occult Mrs. Grotius is quite an acute old lady. Come to think of it, it was she who first pointed out to me, in an earlier and idler conversation, another oddity in Lavinia's dress.

"Ever notice anything else queer about the way Lavinia dresses?" she asked me a little teasingly because I had just fallen in love with Lavinia.

"I don't think so," I replied, "except maybe that her clothes are a bit out of fashion."

"Behind the fashions, you mean?"

"I suppose so."

Mrs. Grotius shook her head. "That's what any man would say and most women. And they'd be wrong. Actually Lavinia is always about a year *ahead* of the fashions. But since next year's clothes always look more like *last* year's clothes, most people would explain it the other way. But I notice details and Lavinia is always ahead, not behind."

"Really?" I said, hardly listening.

"Oh yes. Understand, there's nothing particularly clever or striking about her dresses—ugh, that awful black! In fact, they're what you'd call conservative models. Still, they're six months to a year ahead."

"How do you explain it?" I asked, still not much interested.

Mrs. Grotius shrugged lightly. "Perhaps she picks it up when she's off with her father in foreign parts. Though I never knew that Casablanca and Teheran were nerve-centers for the world of *haute couture*. Or perhaps," she added, with a whimsical smile, "Lavinia peeks into the future."

That remark of Mrs. Grotius may not have been pure whimsy. She may have been remembering the thing that happened at a still earlier date. And that takes me back to 1937 and the real beginning of the story of Lavinia and myself. She was about seventeen then and engaged to my friend Conners Maytal.

I didn't have a flicker of conscious interest in Lavinia at the time. I just thought of her as another of those precocious but proper Midwestern girls, brought up in a world of politically-active, internationally-minded adults but never losing that trace of Bible-belt coldness and gaucherie, that "fresh from the prairie" look. Slim, tall, dark-haired, dreamy-eyed, not at all sexy, at least not in any exciting way. I wasn't aware of the excitement of coldness in those days.

We were all gathered in Mrs. Grotius' apartment with its restful pearl-gray furnishings and mildly arty feel. Conners Maytal, a curly-haired, dashing young man with some hush-hush, vaguely dangerous government job. The nubile Lavinia. Theodore her father, a thin-cheeked, beaming man with manners that a lifetime in the Foreign Service had made the easiest and jolliest, most unimpeachable you could imagine.

He's just got back from a legation job in Spain and would soon be off to some other corner of the world. Lavinia, of course, always went with him. He'd raised her from a baby, despite his world-wide jaunts. I imagine it was on her account that he always tried to get back to Chicago between assignments, though Mrs. Grotius claimed it was to stock up on some sensible Midwestern isolationism, after those foreigners drained it out of him.

Besides those three there was myself, Mrs. Grotius, of course, and four or five others. Mrs. Grotius had just heard about Professor Rhine's telepathy experiments at Duke and insisted that we try our luck at them.

She had the stuff you need—a deck of cards with the different symbols—square, circle, star and so on. The way we did it was that one person went slowly through the deck, concentrating on each symbol as it came up, while the other person, who of course couldn't look at the cards, drew a picture of whatever symbol he thought was up at the time.

It turned out to be pretty boring. None of us had anything unusual in the way of scores until it came to Lavinia's turn. She was a whiz at it. Her score was well beyond anything you could reasonably expect—and that in spite of the fact that she drew two or three symbols that weren't on the original cards.

One was just a circle with a jagged line through it—a little like a cartoonist's diagram of the world cracking in two. The other was a bit more complicated. It consisted of two ellipses over-lapping each other crosswise with a dot in the very center.

We puzzled over that latter diagram a good while without recognizing it. The fact is that no one would have recognized it then except a chemist or physicist. Now everyone knows what it means. It's been blazoned all over magazine covers and advertisements -the simplest symbol for the atom.

Maybe that's not beyond the bounds of chance—a girl back in 1937 and repeatedly drawing the symbol of the thing that eight years later was to disrupt the whole course of history. Still, especially with the world of today striding blindly toward some atomic doom like a somnambulist under the control of an evil magician, I don't know.

I like even less to think about that other symbol—the

circle split by a jagged line. You see, we don't know yet what that symbol is going to mean. That is, if it's going to mean anything. Still, I don't like to think about it.

As soon as Lavinia found out that she had drawn some symbols that weren't on the original cards she became very upset and insisted on tearing up all her drawings. I think most of us put it down to some sophomoric passion for conformity on her part. As I said, she seemed a most proper girl, very easily embarrassed.

The next day I received a puzzling visit from Conners Maytal. He wouldn't tell me exactly what was on his mind but he kept pacing up and down and peering out of the window, every now and then letting drop something about a "great danger" over-shadowing him.

"I've got on to something, Ken," he said, impressively. "A piece of information has dropped into my hands. It's big, Ken. So big I'm frightened—so big I don't know where to take it or what to do with it. And the worst thing is that I think certain people know I have this information."

Of course I was curious and very much concerned. Conners was a hero of mine and I tried my best to get him to tell me about it. But the most he would say was, "It's something that would never occur to you in your wildest fancies, Ken. Something utterly strange."

It never entered my mind that there might be any connection with his engagement to Lavinia. Though I did get the impression that someone at Mrs. Grotius' party might be concerned. But the world situation being what it was at the time, my guesses ran almost entirely in the direction of foreign agents and American fascists. Perhaps, I thought, Conners had uncovered evidence of serious disloyalty in high government circles.

He left me without telling me any more.

The next day Conners was knocked down by a hit-and-run driver and his brains bashed out on the curb.

Naturally I didn't rest until I was able to secure a private interview with Conners' supervisor. He listened rather skeptically to my story, and as I told it I became painfully aware that it didn't contain an ounce of concrete fact. Then too, I found that Conners' job hadn't been nearly as undercover or dangerous as some people—not Conners— had made it out to be.

When I finished my story Conners' superior promised me there'd be a thorough investigation. However, he strongly implied that he didn't think anything would be turned up. He was inclined to write the whole business off as nerves on poor Conners' part.

As time passed I was inclined to agree with him. The more so, since I have myself at times experienced some of those same nerves. Often, when you wake up with a start to the terrifying predicament of the world, you wonder for a moment if there isn't something you can do about it.

Something that will avert the horrible dangers mankind is brewing for itself with all the compulsiveness of a drugged savage responding to the tom-tom beat. And you find you can't or that no one will listen. It is enough to drive a man into neurosis.

Back in the years just before the war such feelings were pretty common. We have become a little less sensitive since then, a little tougher-skinned—though that isn't going to help us when the atom bombs start to fall.

Meanwhile the Simes were off to Austria. There was talk of Theodore having hurried their departure on Lavinia's account. She was pictured as a tragic figure—young love cut short and all that.

However, as it happened the Simes were in for an unguessably exciting junket. It was more than five years before they got back to the States. In rapid succession came assignments in Czechoslovakia, Poland, France, London, Leningrad and London again, where they spent a good deal of the war.

From what I've heard of Theodore it was as much his social as his diplomatic abilities that made him valuable to our government and there must have been endless parties and functions, even in war's shadow, that both he and Lavinia attended.

I get frightened now, when I think of the *number* of people, the world's most prominent folk among them, who must have met that colorless-seeming Midwestern girl and listened idly to her chatter and then, later on—But I mustn't get ahead of my story.

Doubtless you noticed something striking about that list of assignments, coming in the order they did—it was like a road map of catastrophe for World War II. Oddly enough, that sort of thing had already given Theodore a peculiar reputation in the Service.

He'd been in Barcelona in '35, just before the Spanish Civil War, and again in '36. In Naples in '33 and '34, the year before the invasion of Ethiopia. As you'll remember, Hitler came to power in Germany early in '32.

Well, a year or so previously Theodore had a post in Nuremberg. He always seemed to keep ahead of the big events, as Lavinia did with her fashions. In some cases, as with Casablanca and Teheran and Shanghai, several years intervened.

Among his colleagues Theodore was jokingly referred to as a black bird of disaster. As soon as he arrived at a legation or consulate, superstitious tongues would start to wag—something would happen there in a year or two. Of course such talk was trifling stuff. Still, there was that feeling. Where Theodore Simes went, there went destiny.

Of course they might just as well have said—where Lavinia Simes went, there went destiny. But people didn't think of Lavinia that way. They just accepted her as "that delightful man's daughter."

However, with their arrival in Vienna late in '37, Lavinia ceased to play quite such a passive part. She began to get her share of the spotlight in a most unhappy way -her singular series of ill-starred courtships, tragically reproducing the pattern of the Conners Maytal episode.

First, it seems, there was Fritz Nordenfelt, a young Austrian official. They had not announced a formal engagement but there was no doubt of the degree to which he was enchanted by his Corn Belt siren. He disappeared shortly after the Anschlusz.

Then there was Elliot Davies, an American attaché at Prague. He died unromantically of a blood infection.

Next came a young Englishman named Clive Maybrick, a Londoner. He fell into an unguarded bomb crater during the blackout, cut his throat on some torn ironwork and bled to death.

Then there was René Coulet, Vichy, killed in a train wreck. And then—oh, there were a couple of others, both of them Americans. One of them, serving in the army in Italy, was run over by a truck miles behind the lines.

Accidents, all. No, hints of a "mysterious danger" as with Conners Maytal—at least none that I heard about.

Except perhaps in the case of Davies. I spoke with someone who visited him before he died. Tossing on his Prague hospital bed, he kept talking about something "weird and horrible" that had come into his life, something that made the world seem like a "madhouse at the mercy of an insane doctor." But with Hitler striding up and down the boundaries of the Sudetenland, snarling and lashing his arms, that wasn't an unreasonable remark.

So much I got from Mrs. Grotius and my other gossips. The Simes eventually came home and I bumped into Lavinia in the Loop in October, '47, and five days later we were engaged to be married.

Sudden? Of course. But there were reasons for that. I'd just quit my government job. I was sick to death for a breath of old times, when we had been dreamy and fresh-spirited, and at least thought ourselves honorable.

I felt that there wasn't a solitary person whose feelings hadn't been shriveled and coarsened by the enlightening horrors of war. I agree, we're probably more honest today and maybe even a bit more considerate in a rough and ready way—but we have lost something.

Well, Lavinia was a breath of the old times and a lot more besides. It sounds silly when you say a person hasn't changed

a bit, because of course they always have. But applied to
Lavinia it really meant something.

In the hustling, stop-light-ignoring Boul Miche crowd, a
black sleeve brushed my elbow and a clear voice said, "Why,
hello, Ken!" and I turned and got that fresh-from-the-prairie
smile and was looking into those misty eyes.

A moment later we were talking about the last thing we'd
discussed at the Grotius party in '37, which was Elizabethan
music, and moments after that were walking arm in arm,
with Lavinia taking those long strides that are faintly
ungainly but graceful—you see what I mean?

Not that ten years of globe-circling hadn't left their mark
on Lavinia. You felt that she had become a very wise person
with all sorts of unknown mystical depths. You felt, possibly
because you'd heard of those ill-starred courtships, an aura
of romantic melancholy around her. You felt, almost, a
touch of something dark and frightening.

But the important thing was that her inmost self seemed
unchanged. Her experiences were like some gorgeous
garment she wore, enhancing her glamour, some beautifully
embroidered and be-diamonded black cloak that she could
wrap around her or throw off at will. Inside she would still
be fresh, innocent, untouched.

I believe that's true in a very literal sense. I mean, I think
that Lavinia was and still is a virgin, though it hasn't made
her sharp or antagonistic or given her a peaked look and
a host of vague ailments or had any other common side
effects.

I don't say that solely because of the touch of Midwestern
puritanism clinging to her or because she always put a
stop to our petting before it had advanced beyond a mild
stage. No, there was more t it than that. I think she stayed a
virgin, not only because it was the safe and proper thing but
because she *needed* to be a virgin.

You know, there were pagan priestesses who stayed
virgins, not because of any notion that sex is sinful but
solely because they believed that sex weakens the special

spiritual powers needed by anyone in communication with those awful influences beyond the world.

To be frank I think a lot more than that. I think that underneath Lavinia liked to tease men. I think she fed on their unsatisfied desire. I think she *got something* out of Conners Maytal and Fritz Nordenfelt and then after she had fed—But I mustn't let my emotions get out of hand.

Well, as I said, after five days we became engaged. And right away the incidents began—the slips—leading up to the frightening affair of the spiked punch at the Grotius party and its horrifying aftermath the next day.

The early slips didn't amount to much. I think the first occurred about two days after we became engaged.

We were alone in the living room of the Simes apartment. We'd been talking about our own future but the conversation had drifted around to politics—Lavinia is a liberal and she was going on at a great rate. I was a darn sight more interested in Lavinia than in any political theory ever conceived and there came a point where I stopped listening very hard to what those desirable lips were saying.

Suddenly the words, "March 1952," hit my ear.

I must have reacted visibly for she broke off at once. She looked at me frightenedly. Then, "Oh, Ken, I shouldn't have said that."

"Said what?" I asked.

"Didn't you hear?"

"I heard you say, 'March 1952.' What did you mean?"

"Yes, but what I said right before that—you heard, didn't you?"

"I'm afraid I didn't," I admitted a little embarrassedly. "I was looking at you and thinking how nice it would be to kiss you and—What was it anyhow?"

"Oh, I'm so glad," she said, putting her hands on my shoulders and granting my desire.

I forgot all about March 1952.

But now I remember it. When that month rolls around I'll be watching the headlines and the undercurrents. Though I don't know how I'll be able to be certain it was her doing. Still, there may be a sign.

The other slips were mostly like that one. None of them made much conscious impression on me. Not even enough to make me think back to the telepathy test and the atom symbol and the other one. But just the same the slips were getting in their subconscious work. Deep in my mind an uneasiness was building, building—toward the night of the Grotius party.

How Lavinia and I were spending our time those days has an important bearing on what happened. I was carrying out a long-postponed project of mine—to really see Chicago. Not the nightclubs and theatres, not even especially the parks and museums, but the solider stuff.

I have a positive passion for the inner workings of cities. I like to see with my own eyes how the vast supplies of food and fuel come in, where the work comes from, where the brain is, how things are moved around—the railroad yards, the warehouses, the wholesale markets, the grubby side-tentacles of the transportation systems, the courts and jails, things like that.

I like to be able to picture a city as a huge steel and stone creature, with people for blood, a creature that breathes and feeds, digests the useful, rejects the useless, builds up protections against foreign bodies.

Lavinia took to my project enthusiastically and of course having her along made it a delightful adventure.

This particular afternoon we'd spent doing Maxwell Street, where the hawkers' stands fill the space normally reserved for parked automobiles. For the next morning we had a somewhat different expedition planned, a little farther south. In between them came the Grotius party.

Let me say at the beginning that it was never discovered who spiked the punch and I don't think it matters. Except that they did an expert job, probably with vodka and orange curacao and extra fruit juice. What matters is that it was the first time in her life Lavinia got drunk.

It was a big party.

Everyone of consequence in Mrs. Grotius' circle was there except Lavinia's father. The arts, journalism and bureaucracy were particularly well represented. You could find all shades and degrees of political opinion, for Mrs. Grotius's contacts cut across ordinary lines of demarcation.

For instance, there were the prominent fellow-traveler Harry Parks and also Howard Fitch, editorial writer for our well-known isolationist paper. There were Bella McCluskey, the sculptress with the "live by the instincts" theories and also Leslie Vail Packard, whose novels are among the more artistic bulwarks of capitalism and propriety.

At first it was a very good party. The unchanging but ever-renewed pearl-gray of the furnishings brought me memories of less nervous years. The inevitable political discussions got underway but due to the unsuspected effects of the punch, they were more exciting than usual and, at first, very good-tempered. For instance Fitch and Parks staged a genial and heart-to-heart talk which everyone appreciated hugely.

Lavinia was her usual well-poised unobtrusive self—I suppose a diplomat's daughter learns early to act that way. She wore a black satin evening gown that was attractive but, as always, subtly "wrong." And that rarity—black silk stockings.

But gradually I became aware of a change in her behavior. She was talking a lot more, to a lot more people than usual, and in an oddly confidential way. She'd link onto someone and draw him aside.

You'd see her eager, intent face and the bobbing head of her companion as they nodded agreement.

I'd give a good deal to know what she said at those times. I asked Leslie Packard about it afterwards. I can't ask most of the others because I don't know them well enough or else they've cut me on account of my behavior toward Lavinia.

Leslie was puzzled at first but then he said, "By George, I believe you're right. I seem to remember that she did say something to me, something that exploded in my brain and left me with the nasty feeling of having been cut loose from my moorings. But I can't remember what it was. I just can't recall." And for a moment he looked at me with an expression of genuine fear.

I wish he *could* recall because it might give me the clue to things Lavinia said to me that night, things that I too have forgotten. But it's probably safer as it is.

Whatever the things were they had their effect. For the party suddenly turned nasty. Of course it was the political arguments, become personal and carried to unwise lengths, that were responsible. But it was more than that, for *they weren't the political arguments of 1949.*

You've read stories of time-travel? Well, this was as if our minds and emotions were time-traveling into the future, living over in one night all the strife and turmoil and suffering of the next ten years. We were adjusting ourselves in instants to new ideas and loyalties that ordinarily we'd have spent months assimilating.

It was as if there were a "wine of life" that is doled out to mankind drop by drop and we had somehow broken open the barrels and were swilling down great bumpers of it.

We acted as if we were choosing sides for some bitter social conflict that is to come. I'll have to call the two sides "reactionary" and "radical" but they weren't reactionary or radical in exactly the sense of those terms today. Because, you see, we were reacting to events that haven't happened yet, to ideas unborn.

This was frighteningly apparent in the way we lined up, for few of us picked the side you'd have expected. I, for instance, found myself among the "reactionaries." Bella McCluskey, looking blank and frightened, joined us.

Leslie Packard, his face suddenly losing its bland expression and setting in sardonic lines, was against us. So, amazingly, was Mrs. Grotius. Red-faced and shouting, her gray silk dress flapping, she looked like an enraged lovebird.

We were only vaguely aware of where we were heading. Actually, and incredible as it may seem, we were preparing, then and there in that pearl-cool apartment, to fight the great war or revolution or counter-revolution or whatever it is that is to come in -Lord, if I could name the year!

I hate to think of that conflict because it isn't going to be nice. Yet I can't tell you a solitary thing about the grounds on which it's going to be fought except—yes—I think it will have something to do with that split-earth symbol.

Of course we were all of us getting drunk without knowing it, but that isn't enough to explain what was happening, not nearly enough.

We were no longer arguing, we were spitting personalities and accusations and threats. Harry Parks' face was grim, his eyes were glassy. Howard Fitch's underlip jutted out with sulky viciousness. Along with the incessant shouldering and back-turning and snatching of drinks, there was an ominous feeling of gathering forces.

It seems to me that the lights grew dim and there was a reddish glow from somewhere but that must have been an illusion. And everywhere went Lavinia, slipping from one person to another, whispering, hinting, inciting—I think.

At last the fighting started—yes, actual fighting, though it was hushed up afterwards. The punchbowl was overset and smashed, the strangely dimmed chandelier was swinging—something must have hit it—and Parks had his fingers around Fitch's throat and Fitch was beating at Parks' face with ineffectual fists. A minute more —

But then, in an instant, the atmosphere broke. Rage fled. The cloud of the future vanished as if it had never been. We were left staring at each other, dumbfounded.

And then, before Fitch's giggle broke the silence, I became aware of another noise, a muffled gasping that came in gargling rushes of sound. I ran down the hall. Lavinia was on her knees in the bathroom, being sick. Mrs. Grotius had her by the shoulders and was shaking her and saying in a low, intense voice, "You little—*witch!* You little—*witch!*"

I think that Mrs. Grotius, who could never possibly lose the last shreds of her propriety, was using the word as a substitute for another stronger word. Involuntarily she probably used the right one.

I pulled Mrs. Grotius away and held Lavinia's head. As

soon as she realized who it was she began to gasp, "Oh Ken, take me home, take me home!'"

Before the others had begun to recover from their stupefaction we were outside. I still have a vivid picture of those little broken groups, eyeing each other incredulously, trying to talk.

Driving home, Lavinia leaned on my shoulder and kept babbling, "Oh Ken, what happened? Oh Ken, I was drunk. What did I say, Ken? What did I do? Oh, I'm frightened. I mustn't ever let that happen again, Ken, I mustn't.

"I let myself go and I'm frightened. I said things I shouldn't have said. What did I say, Ken, what did I say? Whom did I talk to? What did I tell them? What did they say I'd said? What did I say, Ken, what did I say?"

About that time it occurred to me what must have been done to the punch. When I got Lavinia home and Theodore answered the door I explained to him what had happened and how he could check my story. He seemed startled but his usual poise asserted itself as he took charge of the business of getting Lavinia to bed.

Next morning I drove around reluctantly to their apartment, very doubtful as to whether Lavinia and I would go on any expedition at all, certainly not the inappropriate one we had scheduled. But to my surprise Lavinia was dressed and waiting when I came. She looked hardly the worse for the night before and wouldn't hear of any change in our plans. I yielded to her, though I didn't have much stomach for the business myself.

Of course, as you'll understand, it was a great deal more than a hangover I was feeling. A lot of things had been fitting themselves together in my subconscious mind and last night had provided the keystone. I was aware of a mounting feeling of distaste and fear, was almost aware that the distaste and fear were directed at Lavinia.

My war nerves had come back and with them my gloomiest ideas about mankind's mindless stampede toward doom. Last night's scene had been such a terrifying hope-shattering allegory. And below the surface of my conscious

mind was a black theory or rather a dark philosophy of
life that deals an almost permanently crushing blow to any
notion of freedom or joy or good in the universe.

As if to provide the sharpest possible contrast to my mood
the weather was wonderful. It was one of those matchless
balmy days that come once or twice a year in Chicago.
Despite her black linen dress Lavinia managed to look very
cool and airy. Her skin was creamy, her hair was sleek, her
eyes were bright.

We arrived at our destination. I parked the car and
soon we had joined a small group making the tour. With
my queasy stomach I found it rough going, particularly the
omnipresent sweetish odor. I would have liked very much to
turn back.

But not Lavinia. She looked in the best sort of humor,
fairly blooming, as if what we were seeing were giving
her the finest sort of appetite for lunch. I'd never seen her
drink in everything with such eager schoolgirlish eyes. Her
fresh-from-the-prairie look was particularly noticeable this
morning, which in a way was highly appropriate.

We finally halted on a raised platform and the guide
started an explanation. I felt a wave of nausea and gripped
the rail, looking down.

Some distance below and beyond us a narrow, wooden-
walled runway led up toward a dark door. The guide's voice
droned in my ear. Then a low thundering sound began, like
a lot of people crossing a wooden bridge.

The guide was saying, "...and then they're struck on the
head. It's painless. They drop through a trap door onto a
moving belt. Before they regain consciousness, the spinal
cord has been pierced. Then the belt takes them..."

I swayed dizzily, gripping the railing. But now, instead
of physical sickness it was a spiritual nausea that gripped
me. It seemed to me, as I stared down unwillingly, that
the wooden-walled runway was life and that the creatures
pressing up it were mankind, that the dark door was war,
destruction and death. They were all white, those creatures,

but my swimming eyes seemed to make out a black shadow ahead of them.

I couldn't get things straight. I kept looking beside me at Lavinia as she peered down with interest, so fresh in her black linen dress, her skin so creamy-cool, just the tiniest beads of perspiration dewing the powder on her upper lip.

And as I looked at her an unbearable horror would seize me and I would look down at the runway again and another kind of horror would catch hold of me. In my confused mental state it seemed to me unendurable that such a thing as I was witnessing should be—that mankind should go crowding up to the dark door and no man sane enough to call a halt, but everyone mindlessly following, following.

And because of this feeling I asked the guide a question. And because of his answer I turned and walked away from Lavinia Simes without any explanation and have refused to see her ever again.

They say she's gone away with her father once more. The Simes are always on the move, you know. Maybe to Buenos Aires, maybe to Moscow, to Calcutta, Tel Aviv, or some less likely place. I don't know nor do I want to know. It would just give me one more thing to worry about.

I don't really think I'm safe, you see.

I broke off the engagement but still I know too much. No one is safe, who suspects as much as I do.

I wonder how it will come to me when it comes. Will it be the earth rushing up through the fog to crush me—I travel quite a bit by plane—or will it just be a slip on the stairs—and will I see it before I see what's waiting in the dark for all mankind?

As I said, I'd just mumbled a question to the guide and his reply came to my buzzing ears indistinctly, as if from a great distance.

"Oh no, sir, they wouldn't go so easily if we just herded 'em along. In fact, there'd be quite a to-do. Sheep have more brains than most people think and I bet some of them would guess pretty well what was coming.

"But we have a little trick that makes 'em trot along as

nice as pie. We have one animal that we've trained to walk up that runway. It's taken out of line at the last second and given a reward, so there's never any doubt of *it* going up the runway. And then, of course, all the rest follow.

"There, you can see it there, sir, just going through the door.

"We have it a different color so there won't be any chance of it getting destroyed by mistake. Most other slaughter houses do the same. They use a black ewe."

REPLACEMENT FOR WILMER: A GHOST STORY

A S THE HOLES on the tape stopped jumping up and down and took long solemn, longitudinally rectilinear paces, and as the carillon over the bank three blocks away consequently finished its melodious jangling and tolled four o'clock, a cab stopped in front of the Amity Liquor Store and three men, conspicuous in this neighborhood by their coats and neckties, silently crossed the sidewalk. The fourth, who also wore a hat, paused to pay the driver with a handful of half dollars and quarters he had collected from his comrades a block back. He tipped a big four quarters, which made the cabbie shake his head at his sanity.

Once inside the store the four men, after a look at each other, simultaneously removed their neckties and carried them to a hatrack in the carton-crammed rear of the store next to the toilet. One of the men exchanged his coat for a bulky sweater that buttoned up the front, while the man with the hat replaced it with a faded blue cap that covered all of his thinning, mouse-colored hair but made his butterfly ears even more prominent.

Still not saying anything, they trooped back to the front of the store, collecting on the way from the short length of dinted counter denominated as bar the four drinks the store owner, acting as barman and clerk, had uncapped or poured for them.

The man in the sweater, a grizzled-topped hulk with misanthropic, watchful pale eyes, raised his brown beer bottle for a toast.

"Wilmer," he said.

They drank.

As he lowered his gin and lemon soda, the second man quirked his full lips in a satyrlike smile.

"You know, Cappy," he said reflectively to the man in the sweater, "I believe that was the cleanest I ever saw Wilmer's face."

There was a tentative general snort of laughter, followed by a somewhat uncomfortable pause.

Then the third man slowly nodded his big head. "That's only the truth, George," he assured the second man. "It was also the best shave Wilmer ever had in his life. Those guys at the mortuary sure put a gloss on him."

"Bet they had quite a job, though," George shot back, "probably had to sand-blast."

At the same time the man with the butterfly ears reminded the third man, "Hey, Driscoll, Wilmer's dead. We ought to show more respect, at least the first day, or don't you think?" The objection was even more tentative than the snort of laughter had been. Then Butterfly Ears continued, getting onto firmer ground, at least for a butterfly, "You made me wear a hat to the funeral. You said this cap wouldn't look right."

"Now, you're being stupid, Skeeter," Cappy informed him, pointing a grey-sweatered arm. "I hate a stupid man." Then Cappy proceeded to lay down the law. "Look here, we paid our respects to the dead when we went to the funeral. A hat's part of being respectful. But that's over. Now we pay our respects to truth. Even Wilmer had some respect for truth, you know. He'd have never let himself be argued into wearing a hat. Well, I say Wilmer was just about the dirtiest man who ever lived. I don't believe he ever took a genuine bath in his whole life. Anyone care to dispute me?"

There was a chorus of relieved "No's." A happy recollective light came into George's eyes and he said, "Remember the time Wilmer tried to come in here after cleaning catchbasins without even changing to his drinking coat? Ed told him to stay out." (The owner of the Amity Liquor Store, who was leaning forward with spread elbows on the bar, nodded confirmation.) "Wilmer offered to stay in the back room and do his drinking there, but Ed wouldn't agree even to that. Said it would stink up the can. It ended with Wilmer in the alley and Otto taking his shots and beers back to him."

"I remember!" Skeeter put in eagerly. His wide smile seemed almost to link his ears. "I took turns with Otto rushing them. We'd just open the door a crack and stretch out two long arms. Wilmer got stinking too."

"Stinking both ways," Ed said, walking forward behind the counter to wait on a package customer.

George said, "If we had an absolutely clean world—I mean if science had conquered crapping and there were just one turd to be found once a year in one place, Wilmer would buy a ticket a sufficient time ahead and go get it."

"My wife would never let Wilmer set foot in our apartment," Driscoll put in with another of his deliberate nods. "Not even when he'd bring me home drunk. I think she could smell Wilmer in her sleep, and it would wake her up when I couldn't even when I'd fall down."

The happy light was really sparkling now in George's eyes and his satyr grin was at its wickedest as he launched out in the dreamy chant suitable for a big-city pastoral. "Wilmer would come to me and he'd say, 'How do I get a woman, George?' and I'd inhale and make a disgusted face—no, the face of a connoisseur—and say to him, 'First off, take a bath, Wilmer. Take a long, long bath with lots of hot water and soap,' and he'd listen to me and then he'd give me the hurtest look..."

"Maybe Wilmer finally did take a bath," Skeeter burst in excitedly. "Maybe that's what gave him the pneumonia." And he laughed alone in thin high peals.

"Wilmer once did shack up with a woman," Driscoll

stated soberly. "It happened a long while ago. She was as dirty as he was. I know it's hard to believe, but it's true."

George was frowning thoughtfully now. "I get a funny feeling," he said, "thinking of Wilmer standing back there in the alley, covered with sewage, having his drinks, refusing to make even the smallest concession to popular opinion. It's as if he'd created his own little world and were being true to it. I think the key to his character's there, if I could just put it into words."

"You have," Driscoll said heavily.

"Enough of that now," Cappy said with the air of an orchestra leader dropping his baton to bring a movement to a close. "We're agreed Wilmer was the dirtiest man going. I often told him so myself. Now I want to say—"

"I've got it!" George interrupted. "The key to Wilmer's character was ambition. He knew he could never reach the top in any other line, so he decided to become the dirtiest man in the world."

"We've closed that topic," Cappy said impatiently, collecting his brown bottle of beer from the new round of drinks Ed was preparing. "Now I want to make the statement that Wilmer was also the most disgusting drunk I ever knew. We all get a little glassy-eyed from time to time, but Wilmer would get as polluted as a pig day after day. He really craved his liquor."

"That's right, Cappy, that's right," George agreed, easily taking fire again. "Remember how every day at four-thirty, regular as clockwork, we'd watch him come through that back door in his green drinking coat with that oh-so-eager look in his eyes?"

The bank carillon jangled out the quarter hour and for a bit no one said anything. The floor creaked as Driscoll reached for his second bourbon and water.

"Otto would generally be with him," George went on, "because he quit work at the same time. But we'd hardly notice Otto. All we could see would be Wilmer's face as he stuck it ahead of him through the door—Wilmer's face and that longing in it."

"Otto wasn't at the funeral," Driscoll remarked.

"He's having to janitor Wilmer's buildings along with his own until they get a replacement," Ed explained. The owner of the Amity had drawn himself a small glass of beer along with Skeeter's large one and was temporarily part of the group.

"I noticed Otto's drinking coat back on the hatrack," Skeeter put in. "Not Wilmer's green one, though. I wonder what became of it?"

"Stop all that useless chatter," Cappy commanded. "George was describing something I want to hear."

With a quick smile and nod to Cappy, George continued, "That look of longing on Wilmer's face would be so powerful and so touching that time and again we'd all offer to buy him a drink."

"Yes, and he's take them, too," Cappy said curtly. "Wilmer cadged more drinks than most men. He'd accept them and he'd drink them, sometimes two or three at a time, and pretty soon he'd be so polluted I'd get disgusted with him."

"I bet Wilmer left a pretty big tab behind," George said with an inquiring look at Ed. The latter shook his head. "Just eighty-five," he said. "His mother came in and paid it this morning."

"It's strange to think of a big dirty souse like Wilmer still having a mother," George said, puckering his forehead. "I know he roomed with Otto and the old lady would hardly let him in her house, but he depended on her a lot just the same. You could tell."

"You're out of order," Cappy reproved him. "We haven't got to Wilmer's psychology yet. We're still on his drinking."

"Wilmer cadged drinks, all right," Skeeter said. "I bought him a glass of muscatel not two weeks ago. Maybe it was the last drink he ever had. No, I guess not."

"Wilmer was getting to be a wino the last two years," Driscoll said. "He was shifting over. I suppose it was the easiest thing to drink on the job."

"Oh, but there was nothing in the world like Wilmer polluted," George launched out again, the faraway twinkle back in his eyes. "He'd grow a bigger moon face, he'd get stupid-sillier, and he'd even fall on his face with more finality than another man. Remember how he'd always want to pass out and sleep in the back room here and you wouldn't let him, Ed? You'd say, 'No' and chase him out front and ten minutes later he'd be back there and we'd hear empty cartons crunch as he flopped on them."

"I couldn't let him sleep in here by himself," Ed said with a grin. "Imagine what would have happened if he'd waked up alone at four a.m."

Skeeter chortled. "Many's the time," he said, "I helped drag Wilmer out in the alley on a summer night when you'd closed up and we'd leave him snoozing there. Or help Otto get him home, though that didn't happen so often."

"Wilmer's drinking always heavied up in the summer," Driscoll observed, "which isn't the way of a normal man who shifts from whisky to beer then. I suppose he knew he didn't have to worry about freezing to death."

George said, "Right now I can hear Wilmer's snores. I can visualize the dirty green glow of his drinking coat when he was sleeping in the alley with the moon coming over the water tower."

"That's enough about Wilmer's drinking," Cappy said decisively. "I've got one more thing to say about him and then we'll quit. Wilmer was undoubtedly the stupidest man I ever knew in my life."

"Oh, but that's right," George said swiftly. "'How do I get a woman, George?' 'George, how do I get a white-collar job?' 'Why do they hold elections, George, on the days when the bars are closed?' 'George, how do people know if their kids are left-handed?'"

Skeeter boasted, "Once I actually got Wilmer to ask for a left-handed monkey-wrench at Tanner's hardware."

"Wilmer couldn't even do simple arithmetic," Driscoll asserted. "I don't believe he could count on his fingers."

Ed nodded at that. "Sometimes he'd question his tab," he said, "and I'd add it over for him very slowly. It was pitiful how he'd pretend to follow me."

George said, "Remember how for two whole months he thought I was a Communist, because I came in here carrying a book? He even got Otto believing it."

"Yes," Skeeter pressed, "and remember the day you brought a girl in here who was a model—a dress model—and Wilmer asked her how much she'd charge to undress in the back room?"

"That wasn't stupidity," George contradicted, "that was tactlessness. Wilmer never knew how to go about anything."

"All right, all right, we've talked enough about Wilmer now," Cappy commanded loudly, getting his next bottle of beer.

"I guess you're right, Cappy," Skeeter said in a hushed voice. "I forgot we'd just been to his funeral."

"That's not the point," Cappy told him disgustedly, "you're being stupid again, Skeeter. We haven't said anything but the truth and Wilmer can't hear us anyhow. It's just that we've heard enough about him for today. I'm sick of the subject. Somebody talk about something else. Go ahead."

There was a long silence.

George was the first to look around at the others. An odd smile began to switch at his lips.

"You know," he said, "we're going to have a hard time finding something to talk about, now that Wilmer's gone. Something real juicy we can all get together on, I mean."

Driscoll nodded slowly and said, "I guess we talked about him more than we realized."

"Oh, we can keep coming back to Wilmer for a while," George went on, "but there'll be nothing new to add and after a bit the whole topic will be so dead we won't want to touch it at all. You know what? We're going to have to find a replacement for Wilmer."

"How do you mean, a replacement?" Driscoll asked.

"You know," George said, "somebody to talk about, somebody to be the stupidest and dirtiest and drunkenest. If we don't find a replacement, Wilmer will ... well, haunt us, you might say."

"Now you're talking like a superstitious lunkhead,

George," Cappy said sharply. "Wilmer's dead and a dead man can't affect anybody."

George looked at him quizzically.

Cappy continued, "But you may have something in that replacement idea." The gray-sweatered man began to look thoughtfully at Skeeter.

"Hey, quit that, Cappy," Skeeter said uneasily, almost knocking his glass off the shelf as he reached for it. "I'm not going to be any replacement for Wilmer."

Cappy frowned. "I wouldn't be too sure of that, Skeeter," he said. "You're stupid enough sometimes—I've told you twice today—and I've seen you rubber-legged drunk pretty often and I know you don't wash behind those ears more than once a month."

"Better watch out, Skeeter," Ed warned with a chuckle.

"Hey, quit it, you guys," Skeeter protested. "Quit looking at me, Cappy."

Skeeter was watching Cappy apprehensively. All the others were grinning at Skeeter delightedly except George, who was smiling at the ceiling abstractedly and saying, "You know, it's a very funny thing how we really need Wilmer. Here we've been talking for half an hour as if we were glad to be rid of him, when actually nothing would please us more than if he'd push through the door right now."

A sudden gust of wind in the street outside raised thin swirls of dust, momentarily plastered a sheet of newspaper against the water-marked display window, and since it blew from the direction of the bank, it swelled the volume of the computerized carillon jangling out four-thirty.

A man with his head ducked low against the dust and wearing a dirty green coat with stains down the front pushed in through the door.

The five men in the Amity saw him and turned pale. Skeeter's beer glass crashed on the floor. Then the newcomer looked up.

George was the first to recover.

"Otto, you old son-of-a-gun!" he cried. "What are you doing wearing Wilmer's drinking coat?"

"Mein Gott, I didn't know it," the newcomer protested, looking down again and then raising his eyes guiltily. "The two coats always hung each other beside. I thought I was putting on mine. Here, I take it off."

"That's all right, Otto, forget it," George said heartily, stopping him with an arm around the shoulders. "Here, have a shot of gin."

"Have a drink on me, too, you crazy Dutchman," Cappy bellowed, getting two of his brown bottles and uncapping them.

"And on me," Skeeter squeaked, darting behind the counter to get a washed glass and draw the beer himself.

"A drink on each one of us," Driscoll put in, reaching for the whisky bottle. "Finish that gin, I'll pour you a snort of real liquor."

"And when you're ready for it, a peppermint brandy on the house," Ed finished, smiling broadly.

"Shee, fellows, thanks," Otto said a little wonderingly, "but first I better—"

Cappy thrust a hairy finger at him, "You forget that coat for now," he commanded, "and drink your drinks."

"Okay, Cappity, you win," Otto surrendered. "Shee, fellows, I'm sorry not to be at the funeral, but it went against my heart. That Wilmer, I liked him. Nobody's ever going to take his place."

"Forget funerals," George directed. "How's life been treating you, Otto?"

"Shee, Gay-org, I wouldn't know. Say, not too many drinks, fellow."

About ten minutes later they let Otto go back to exchange the green coat for his own. The loud boil of conversation simmered down.

Cappy said in a gruff undertone, wrinkling his big nose, "You know, that Otto stinks. I never noticed it before because he was always with Wilmer."

"He sure snatched at those drinks when he got going," Skeeter put in, a little ruefully.

"And he's stupid," Cappy said decisively. "Only a very stupid man would accidentally put on a dead man's coat."

"What do you think is happening, Driscoll?" George asked lightly.

"How do you mean?" Driscoll asked, frowning. Then his brow cleared and he nodded. "I get you."

At that moment Otto came in from the back wearing his own coat and they all fell silent. The off-duty janitor was staggering a little, but as he surveyed them a momentary flicker of distrust crossed his eyes.

"Say, fellows, what were you all talking about?" he asked.

Cappy answered for them.

"Why, Otto," he said innocently, "we were just all wondering who would ever take the place of poor old Wilmer."

MS. FOUND IN A MAELSTROM

O N JUNE 4, two large boxes without return addresses were delivered at the Manhattan offices of the American Psychological Congress. On examination, they were found to be filled with sheets and scraps of paper tied in packets and covered with a roughly-estimated automatic writing, a veritable maelstrom of verbiage sometimes rhyming and occasionally forming phrases but otherwise incoherent, as far as a sampling showed.

The boxes were turned over to the Creighton Wagram Study of the Psychopathology of Creativity, where their contents were eventually used by Helen Crumly Barnes, graduate student, as raw material for a statistical investigation of rhythm and patterns of word-choice in schizophrenic thought. During the third week of her tabulations Miss Barnes discovered the following narrative in the welter of words. It appeared abruptly, like a deadly rock in a dubious sea. At the time Miss Barnes was being recompensed at the rate of ninety-three cents an hour from a grant made by the General Motors Foundation.

...WRONG WRONG *RIGHT* *right* write write write without sight without light in the night it'll bite and I write in the grave like a slave but I'm brave as a knave from the grave I arose and I pose without clothes but with prose just suppose suppose suppose Suppose someone very close to you whom you had every reason to trust and even love -wife, husband, mother, brother, childhood chum—really hated you insanely and always had hated you far too keenly to grant you the kindness of a quick death.

Suppose this person—apparently normal, having no obvious motive for wishing you ill, at least as clever as yourself, and infinitely more patient and with a medieval taste for long-drawn revenges and a matchless talent for creating alibis and diverting suspicion—suppose this person were plotting spider-like every free instant of his or her life to achieve your ultimate destruction after exquisite torture.

A nightmarish fancy? I agree.

But do not be sure there is not such a person for you. I am such a person for Richard Slade.

I am certain that the seeds of my hatred for Slade were sowed before the beginning of conscious memory. I sometimes think I simply was born hating the type. However, the first incident that comes to my mind when I recall my lifelong persecution of Richard Slade happened in middle boyhood. We were aimlessly loitering through a small town's summer dusk, sucking in the lovely odors of rotted leaves and damp wood.

That morning Dickie Slade had received from a mail-order house a small telescope for which he had saved allowance and errand money for months. He had been showing it off to me all day, dragging it out of his pocket and its case at every opportunity and brandishing it like a royal scepter.

I pretended to admire it, but actually I loathed Dickie's infatuation with the cheap thing and his intention to use it equally for observing the stars, the squirrels in the trees, and the bedroom window of young Mrs. Cloudsley across the street—just as I generally loathed his cowardice, his stupidity, his sneakiness, his gullibility, the intolerable dullness of his spirit.

But my time would come. In fact, it had. We had just reached a weed-walled path—now, in the evening, a dark trench—treading to Dickie's house across an empty lot and past a big hunk of concrete and a dead dwarfed tree that took on eerie shapes when the light failed.

Without warning I said in an anxious voice, "Better hurry, Dickie. You'll be late for supper."

This simple remark, as I had known it would, instantly switched Dickie's mood from dreamy ecstasy to formless dread. He took off down the path like a scared rabbit. At exactly the point where I'd known it would happen, he caught sight of the crouching evil tree. It lent wings to his feet and blinkers to his eyes, though considering the darkness of the path the blinkers were merely one of my artistic touches.

Hardly a second later he tripped over the dead branch I had that morning kicked casually but with infinite precision across the path, so that it was lying just two yards this side of the block of concrete.

The wind was knocked out of him. Far more important, the concrete smashed the object lens of the telescope and drove the other end against his cheek just beside his eye. He would soon have a fine shiner. Of course I would have liked to see him lose the eye eye eye aye aye ai ai ai I I I die and I sigh and I cry by and by but don't lie never lie yet I lie in the rye and my eye sees an eye in the sky why why why in the sky there's an eye there's an eye eye eye but I and the eye could wait. There'd always be another chance at the eye.

As I listened to his retching gasps turn to sobs, as I enjoyed his anguish over the damage to the telescope—his dawning realization that the stars would remain unmagnified and Mrs. Cloudsley cloaked with distance even when she forgot the bedroom shade—I realized for the first time with absolute certainty that this was what I wanted to do all my life. I had found my vocation.

I also knew I had been far too clever for Dickie ever to realize I had engineered the whole thing. He would always think it had been an accident.

However, even then I didn't make the mistake of underestimating my enemy. As Dickie finally got his wind back and limped home, I remember deciding that in the future I would avoid such direct attacks. A wonderful idea came to me. Karswell.

He was a venomous old teacher who was outrageously unfair to us boys. After a particularly nasty session, I egged on Dick to persuade the other boys to neglect their homework for the following day and refuse to recite when called on. I knew Dick had already completed the next assignment.

So the act of revolt was agreed upon, in the far corner of the cindered schoolyard, with all the tribal solemnity of boyhood. The group broke up and Dick and I started home. The walk led us past the police station and the yellow brick courthouse. Casually, as if it meant nothing to my young life, I reminded Dick that what we were going to do was a serious thing. After all, behind the teacher stood the principal, and behind the principal the policeman. Dick tucked his head when genial Officer Mason said hello to him. By the time we got to his house he was very unhappy.

I prudently waited while he went in to his mother—she never did like my looks and I detested her. She had a bad headache and was lying in the darkened parlor. She said something like, "...and always be a good boy." When he tiptoed out I said to him, as if impulsively, "Gee, Dick, I didn't know your mother was as sick as that. I bet if you got in any trouble she'd be awful worried and maybe something would happen to her."

In the dark hallway he twisted as if he had a stomachache.

Next morning Karswell called on Dick as soon as class started. Perhaps he smelled rebellion and was smart enough to attack at the weakest point, Dick, his seat to the rear and well-shielded by the fat boy in front of him, was doodling abstractedly and very rapidly—a habit of his. I saw that this time it was words, not pictures, that his pencil was spawning, with apparent aimlessness, and I noted with approval "police," "jail," and "mother."

Karswell creased his pulpy face and roughened his voice. Dick's pencil fluttered and stopped and like someone talking in his sleep he gave the correct answer.

The revolt fizzled out. None of the other boys had nerve

enough to stand up to Karswell alone, though they had been only too glad of an excuse to skip their homework. Naturally they called Dick a double-crosser and a couple of them picked fights with him which he lost because he knew he was in the wrong. He never did live the blow to his pride down.

By the time we went to college I had my methods for tormenting Slade in smooth working order. I went first to his instructors. To each I said in effect, "Richard Slade is intensely interested in your subject. He will probably make it his life work. He is a very promising student, worthy of special attention."

Naturally they were flattered and modified their behavior toward Slade accordingly. A few months later I paid each of them a second visit. I said, "I can see now that I was mistaken. Richard Slade is not really interested in your subject. He has confused transient mental excitement with enduring intellectual dedication. Just where his actual interests lie it's difficult to say. Perhaps he is incapable of any." Dick, poor fool, could not understand the reason for their sudden cooling, though to my delight he was considerably hurt by it.

With an irony very amusing to me, he ended up by majoring in psychology, which netted him no real knowledge except such oddments of information as "automatic writing is on some respects the equivalent of word-doodling."

His habit of doodling had grown with the years. His compulsion aroused brief interest in a class in experimental psychology and was superficially investigated. He learned nothing about it, but he acquired the practice of storing away all the automatic writing he did—generally without looking at it, for in later years he came to hate his "wild talent," which sometimes operated even when he was asleep.

I wasn't being too rough on Slade at the time. It was a definite part of my plan to cushion him during those early years. Premature jolts must be avoided, I kept telling myself. He must be given the illusion of floating in a dreamy, easy current until I had my fish securely hooked crooked booked rooked cooked what a dish that poor fish ragged lipped

belly ripped wet with blood and with mud in the boat and I
gloat and I hate and I wait for my fate for it's late and I hate
and I love hand in glove yes I love to make love and make
hate with the girls with the girls with the girls With the girls.

I pursued the policy that had succeeded so well with the
instructors, playing "Slade loves you" against "Slade does
not really love you, perhaps he is incapable of love" until
I worked some of them into pitiably neurotic states where
they were as ready to wound themselves as to wound Slade.
That pleased me, since I knew he would suffer in either
case—more in the first.

During his last year at college Slade was deeply attracted
to a girl somewhat more sophisticated than himself. She
liked him and for a time I let matters develop unhindered.

Then I went to a brilliant young instructor who was quite
friendly with Slade because of kindred intellectual interests
and who had a secret reputation for amusing himself with
such girls as were adult enough to be safe.

"Look, Satterlee," I said in effect, "why don't you
sometimes go out with Slade and Beatrice? They both like
you. They're your kind and I'm sure you would have some
good times together. Besides, there's a special reason. Slade's
often afraid he's boring Beatrice. A witty companion would
take care of the dull moments and Slade would be flattered
to have Beatrice know that you are his friend."

Satterlee balked at this somewhat unrealistic suggestion.
So, very guardedly, I introduced an argument that I knew
would eventually get him; namely, that Beatrice was not
much in love with Slade and that Slade, appearances to the
contrary, was even less in love with her and might be glad
of an opportunity to shake loose. Needless to say, the latter
suggestion was a flat lie.

After a few days, the three of them began to be seen
together. There were wondering comments, also sardonic
ones, quite baseless at the time. It was an interesting triangle.
Beatrice was flattered, but a little uneasy. Satterlee, finding
the situation somewhat different from the false one I had
described to him, held his hand but did not withdraw. Slade

kept me awake every night yapping about how happy he was.

Then in the late afternoon of a Saturday when the three of them had a date for dinner and a concert, I lured Slade into a game of chess with an opponent of just the right caliber to test his powers fully. I had selected him for precisely that reason.

It was an intensely exciting struggle, but prolonged. The dusty windows of the café annex grew dark. Lights were turned on. The small hand of the ugly wall-clock began its upward climb. Slade, I noted with approval, was nervously doodling in a notebook where he had started to keep the score of the game, filling page after page with words his eyes would never see.

He was tempted to break off the game by offering a draw, although he was in a winning position. But I pointed out he could forego the dinner and still be in time for the concert. (He held the three tickets.) Twice he tried to call Beatrice or Satterlee, but the lines were busy and he had to hurry back to the board.

Finally he rushed off with barely time to make the concert, having lost the game by an oversight. He was very nervous now and stood on the front platform of the rocking street car, although there were plenty of seats inside. Making good connections, he arrived at the auditorium with ten minutes to spare. But no Beatrice, and no Satterlee.

He paced the lobby until the concert had begun, then risked a dash to the restaurant on the off-chance that they might have waited for him there. Of course they hadn't. He hurried back. Still no Beatrice and Satterlee, although the man in the box office thought a couple answering to Slade's description of them had looked around the lobby and walked out.

Slade tried again to call them. The girl who answered the dormitory phone told him Beatrice had gone out before supper, while the phone in Satterlee's apartment rang unanswered. Eventually he went into the auditorium, leaving the other two tickets at the box office. He spent most of the evening darting back and forth between the lobby and the three empty seats.

Next day Beatrice and Satterlee had their excuses. Indeed at first Slade thought of himself as the guilty party. But I saw to it that he was informed that Beatrice had been seen leaving Satterlee's apartment early Sunday morning lorning warning horning suborning adorning scorning warning stop look listen listen look stop stop stop red red bed bed bred wed dead slain pain pain pain pain pain The pain this discovery caused Slade provided me with rare pleasure for the whole two months before his graduation.

I next turned my attention to the matter of Slade's marriage. From his girl friends I selected one who was rather idealistic, timid, and sympathetic, though by no means lacking in narrow-mindedness. I went straight to her and said, "Slade needs you. Potentially he's a man of creative genius but he's like a child. Will you devote your life to cherishing his dreams, soothing his hurts, shielding him so far as you are able from the harsher aspects of reality?"

The moment sticks in my mind. It was winter and the girl was alone with me. (Slade's best friend, up to a best friend's usual tricks). We were sitting in front of a log fire. Its flames struck mysterious gleams from her dark eyes and lent a false flush to her cheeks as she answered in a whisper, almost reverently, "Yes."

Once outside, I grinned with satisfaction. This was the final triumph. I had procured for Slade a lifelong companion who would reflect all his moods, bringing them to an almost unendurable focus. Little remained for me to do except await the inevitable developments.

The worst frustrations are yet to come. I, who have laid and lit the fuses, know.

At present Slade is working in an insurance office. Outwardly he hasn't done too badly for the past ten years, but two drawers of his desk and a large cardboard box are filled with his hated word-doodlings. He keeps the stuff at his office ever since his wife found out about his accumulated automatic writing, worshipfully decided there might be creative material—"even stories, Dick!"—buried in it, and insisted on reading it.

Slade is very confused. His futile idealisms ache like hard sores, and his wife cherishes him very, very much. I am toying with the idea of infatuating him with the pleasures of the senses. Slade with a mistress—it would be a wonderful comedy. And I may sting him—via the mistress?—into a desperate attempt to make big money. He couldn't succeed in that either, but he could spend several very painful years trying. Oh, the possibilities are endless.

Some day those possibilities, fruitful as they seem now, may be exhausted. In that case I shall kill Slade. But probably that will not be for years. My capacity for devising new and ever more grotesque torments for Slade seems infinite.

I wonder why that is. Why of all the people in the world, I should hate and abominate Richard Slade.

Did Slade originally harm me in some secret, despicable way my memory cannot retain? Or am I simply suffering from a monomania? Is the world my hell and Slade my punishment?

Or ... yes, that might be it ... I may have missed it all these years because of its very obviousness—Perhaps I hate Slade simply because he hates me, because he has sought to trick and persecute me for as long as I can remember, because he has done his best to wreck my life ... and because he placed a dead branch so it would trip me in the dark and make me break my telescope.

For of course I am also Richard Slade slayed made laid grayed grave slave but I'm brave like a slave in the grave and I write in the night without light without sight and I write write right wrong ...

Although Miss Barnes made a careful search, no other connected narratives whatever were discovered in the two boxes, nor any light thrown on their origin. They have since become the property of the Krothering-Kingsley Art Conference.

THE WINTER FLIES

AFTER THE SUPPER dishes were done there was a
general movement from the Adler kitchen to the Adler
living room.

It was led by Gottfried Helmuth Adler, commonly known
as Gott. He was thinking how they should be coming from
a dining room, yes, with coloured maids, not from a kitchen.
In a large brandy snifter he was carrying what had been
left in the shaker from the martinis, a colourless elixir
weakened by melted ice yet somewhat stronger than his wife
was supposed to know. This monster drink was a regular
part of Gott's carefully-thought-out programmer for getting
safely through the end of the day.

"After the seventeenth hour of creation God got sneaky,"
Gott once put it to himself.

He sat down in his leather-upholstered easy chair, flipped
open Plutarch's *Lives* left-handed, glanced down through
the lower halves of his executive bifocals at the paragraph
in the biography of Caesar he'd been reading before dinner,
then without moving his head looked through the upper
halves back toward the kitchen.

After Gott came Jane Adler, his wife. She sat down at her
drawing table, where pad, pencils, knife, art gum, distemper
paints, water, brushes, and rags were laid out neatly.

Then came little Heinie Adler, wearing a spaceman's
transparent helmet with a large hole in the top for ventilation.
He went and stood beside this arrangement of objects: first

a long wooden box about knee-length with a smaller box on top and propped against the latter a toy control panel of blue and silver plastic, on which only one lever moved at all; next, facing the panel, a child's wooden chair; then back of the chair another long wooden box lined up with the first.

"Good-bye Mama, good-bye Papa," Heinie called. "I'm going to take a trip in my spaceship."

"Be back in time for bed," his mother said.

"Hot jets!" murmured his father.

Heinie got in, touched the control panel twice, and then sat motionless in the little wooden chair, looking straight ahead.

A fourth person came into the living-room from the kitchen—the Man in the Black Flannel Suit. He moved with the sick jerkiness and he had the slack putty-grey features of a figure of the imagination that hasn't been fully developed. (There was a fifth person in the house, but even Gott didn't know about him yet.)

The Man in the Black Flannel Suit made a stiff gesture at Gott and gaped his mouth to talk to him, but the latter silently writhed his lips in a 'Not yet, you fool!' and nodded curtly towards the sofa opposite his easy chair.

"Gott," Jane said, hovering a pencil over the pad, "you've lately taken to acting as if you were talking to someone who isn't there."

"I have, my dear?" her husband replied with a smile as he turned a page, but not lifting his face from his book. "Well, talking to oneself is the sovereign guard against madness."

"I thought it worked the other way," Jane said.

"No," Gott informed her.

Jane wondered what she should draw and saw she had very faintly sketched on a small scale the outlines of a child, done in sticks-and-blobs like Paul Klee or kindergarten art. She could do another 'Children's Clubhouse,' she supposed, but where should she put it this time?

The old electric clock with brass fittings that stood on the mantel began to wheeze shrilly. 'Mystery, mystery, mystery,

mystery.' It struck Jane as a good omen for her picture. She smiled.

Gott took a slow pull from his goblet and felt the scentless vodka bite just enough and his skin shiver and the room waver pleasantly for a moment with shadows chasing across it. Then he swung the pupils of his eyes upward and looked across at the Man in the Black Flannel Suit, noting with approval that he was sitting rigidly on the sofa. Gott conducted his side of the following conversation without making a sound or parting his lips more than a quarter of an inch, just flaring his nostrils from time to time.

BLACK FLANNEL: Now if I may have your attention for a space, Mr. Adler —

GOTT: Speak when you're spoken to! Remember, I created you.

BLACK FLANNEL: I respect your belief. Have you been getting any messages?

GOTT: The number 6669 turned up three times today in orders and estimates. I received an airmail advertisement beginning 'Are you ready for big success?' though the rest of the ad didn't signify. As I opened the envelope the minute hand of my desk clock was pointing at the faceless statue of Mercury on the Commerce Building. When I was leaving the office my secretary droned at me, 'A representative of the Inner Circle will call on you tonight,' though when I questioned her she claimed that she'd said, 'Was the letter to Innes-Burkle and Company all right?' Because she is aware of my deafness I could hardly challenge her. In any case she sounded sincere. If those were messages from the Inner Circle, I received them. But seriously I doubt the existence of that clandestine organization. Other explanations seem to me more likely—for instance, that I am developing a psychosis. I do not believe in the Inner Circle.

BLACK FLANNEL (*smiling shrewdly—his features have grown tightly handsome though his complexion is still putty grey*): Psychosis is for weak minds. Look, Mr. Adler, you believe in the Mafia, the FBI, and the Communist Underground. You believe in upper-echelon control groups

in unions and business and fraternal organizations. You
know the workings of big companies. You are familiar
with industrial and political espionage. You are not wholly
unacquainted with the secret fellowships of munitions
manufacturers, financiers, dope addicts and procurers
and pornography connoisseurs and the brotherhoods and
sisterhoods of sexual deviates and enthusiasts. Why do you
boggle at the Inner Circle?

GOTT (*cooly*): I do not wholly believe in all of those
other organizations. And the Inner Circle still seems to me
more of a wish-dream than the rest. Besides, you may want
me to believe in the Inner Circle in order at a later date to
convict me of insanity.

BLACK FLANNEL (*drawing a black brief-case from
behind his legs and unzipping it on his knees*): Then you do
not wish to hear about the Inner Circle?

GOTT (*inscrutably*): I will listen for the present. Hush!

Heinie was calling out excitedly, "I'm in the stars, Papa!
They're so close they burn!" He said nothing more and
continued to stare straight ahead, his eyes diamond bright.

"Don't touch them," Jane warned without looking
around. Her pencil made a few faint five-pointed stars. The
Children's Clubhouse would be on a boundary of space,
she decided—put it in a tree on the edge of the Old Ravine.
She said, "Gott, what do you suppose Heinie sees out there
besides stars?"

"Bug-eyed angels, probably," her husband answered,
smiling again but still not taking his head out of his book.

BLACK FLANNEL (*consulting a sheet of crackling
black paper he has slipped from his brief-case, though as
far as Gott can see there is no printing, typing, writing, or
symbols of any sort in any colour ink on the black bond*):
The Inner Circle is the world's secret élite, operating behind
and above all figureheads, workhorses, wealthy dolts, and
those talented exhibitionists we name genius. The Inner
Circle has existed *sub rosa niger* for thousands of years. It
controls human life. It is the repository of all great abilities
and the key to all ultimate delights.

GOTT (*tolerantly*): You make it sound plausible enough. Everyone half believes in such a cryptic power gang, going back to Sumeria.

BLACK FLANNEL: The membership is small and very select. As you are aware, I am a kind of talent scout for the group. Qualifications for admission (*he slips a second sheet of black bond from his briefcase*) include a proven great skill in achieving and wielding power over men and women, and amoral zest for all of life, a seasoned blend of ruthlessness and reliability, plus wide knowledge and lightning wit.

GOTT (*contemptuously*): Is that all?

BLACK FLANNEL (*flatly*): Yes. Initiation is binding for life—and for the afterlife: one of our mottoes is Ferdinand's dying cry in *The Duchess of Malfi*. 'I will vault credit and affect high pleasures after death.' The penalty for revealing organizational secrets is not death alone but extinction—all memory of the person is erased from public and private history; his name is removed from records; all knowledge of and feeling for him is deleted from the minds of his wives, mistresses, and children; it is as if he had never existed. That, by the by, is a good example of the powers of the Inner Circle. It may interest you to know, Mr. Adler, that as a result of the retaliatory activities of the Inner Circle, the names of three British kings have been expunged from history. Those who have suffered a like fate include two popes, seven movie stars, a brilliant Flemish artist superior to Rembrandt ... (*As he spins out an apparently interminable listing, the Fifth Person creeps in on hands and knees from the kitchen. Gott cannot see him at first, as the sofa is between Gott's chair and the kitchen door. The Fifth Person is the Black Jester, who looks rather like a caricature of Gott but has the same putty complexion as the Man in the Black Flannel Suit. The Black Jester wears skin-tight clothing of that colour, silver-embroidered boots and gloves, and a black hood edged with silver bells that do not tinkle. He carries a scepter topped with a small death's-head that wears a black hood like his own edged with tinier silver bells, soundless as the larger ones.*)

THE BLACK JESTER (*suddenly rearing up like a cobra from behind the sofa and speaking to the Man in the Black Flannel Suit over the latter's shoulder*): Ho! So you're still teasing his rickety hopes with that shit about the Inner Circle? Good sport, brother!—you play your fish skillfully.

GOTT (*immensely startled, but controlling himself with some courage*): Who are you? How dare you bring your babble into my court?

THE BLACK JESTER: Listen to the old cock crow innocent! As if he didn't know he'd himself created both of us, time and again, to stave off boredom, madness, or suicide.

GOTT (*firmly*): I never created *you*.

THE BLACK JESTER: Oh, yes you did, old cock. Truly your mind has never birthed anything but twins—for every good a bad, for every breath a fart, and for every white, a black.

GOTT (*flares his nostrils and glares a death-spell which hums toward the newcomer like a lazy invisible bee*).

THE BLACK JESTER (*pales and staggers backward as the death-spell strikes, but shakes it off with an effort and glares back murderously at Gott*): Old cock-father, I'm beginning to hate you at last.

Just then the refrigerator motor went on in the kitchen and its loud rapid rocking sound seemed to Jane to be a voice saying, "Watch your children, they're in danger. Watch your children, they're in danger."

"I'm no ladybug," Jane retorted tartly in her thoughts, irked at the worrisome interruption now that her pencil was rapidly developing the outlines of the Clubhouse in the Tree with the moon risen across the ravine between clouds in the late afternoon sky. Nevertheless she looked at Heinie. He hadn't moved. She could see how the plastic helmet was open at neck and top, but it made her think of suffocation just the same.

"Heinie, are you still in the stars?" she asked.

"No, now I'm landing on a moon," he called back. "Don't talk to me, Mama, I've got to watch the road."

Jane at once wanted to imagine what roads in space might look like, but the refrigerator motor had said 'children,' not 'child,' and she knew that the language of machinery is studded with tropes. She looked at Gott. He was curled comfortably over his book and as she watched he turned a page and touched his lips to the martini water. Nevertheless, she decided to test him.

"Gott, do you think this family is getting too ingrown?" she said. "We used to have more people around."

"Oh, I think we have quite a few as it is," he replied, looking up at the empty sofa, beyond it, and then around at her expectantly, as if ready to join in any conversation she cared to start. But she simply smiled at him and returned relieved to her thoughts and her picture. He smiled back and bowed his head again to his book.

BLACK FLANNEL (*ignoring the Black Jester*): My chief purpose in coming here tonight, Mr. Adler, is to inform you that the Inner Circle has begun a serious study of your qualifications for membership.

THE BLACK JESTER: At *his* age? After *his* failures? Now we are curtsying forward toward the Big Lie!

BLACK FLANNEL (*in a pained voice*): Really! (*Then once more to Gott*) Point one: you have gained for yourself the reputation of a man of strong patriotism, deep company loyalty, and realistic self-interest, sternly contemptuous of all youthful idealism and rebelliousness. Point two: you have cultivated constructive hatreds in your business life, deliberately knifing colleagues when you could, but allying yourself to those on the rise. Point three and most important: you have gone some distance toward creating the master illusion of a man who has secret sources of information, secret new techniques for thinking more swiftly and acting more decisively than others, secret superior connections and contacts—in short, a dark new strength which all others envy even as they cringe from it.

THE BLACK JESTER (*in a kind of counterpoint as he advances around the sofa*): But he's come down in the world since he lost his big job. National Motors was at least a step in the right direction, but Hagbolt-Vincent has no company planes, no company apartments, no company shooting lodges, no company call girls! Besides, he drinks too much. The Inner Circle is not for drunks on the down-grade.

BLACK FLANNEL: Please! You're spoiling things.

THE BLACK JESTER: *He's* spoiled. (*Closing in on Gott*) Just look at him now. Eyes that need crutches for near and far. Ears that mishear the simplest remark.

GOTT: Keep off me, I tell you.

THE BLACK JESTER (*ignoring the warning*): Fat belly, flaccid sex, swollen ankles. And a mouthful of stinking cavities!—did you know he hasn't dared visit his dentist for five years? Here, open up and show them! (*Thrusts black-gloved hand toward Gott's face.*)

Gott, provoked beyond endurance, snarled aloud, "Keep off, damn you!" and shot out the heavy book in his left hand and snapped it shut on the Black Jester's nose. Both black figures collapsed instantly.

Jane lifted her pencil a foot from the pad, turned quickly, and demanded, "My God, Gott, what was that?"

"Only a winter fly, my dear," he told her soothingly. "One of the fat ones that hide in December and breed all the black clouds of spring." He found his place in Plutarch and dipped his face close to study both pages and the trough between them. He looked around slyly at Jane and said, "I didn't squash her."

The chair in the spaceship rutched. Jane asked, "What is it, Heinie?"

"A meteor exploded, Mama. I'm all right. I'm out in space again, in the middle of the road."

Jane was impressed by the time it had taken the sound of Gott's book clapping shut to reach the spaceship. She began lightly to sketch blob-children in swings hanging from high limbs in the Tree, swinging far out over the ravine into the stars.

Gott took a pull of martini water, but he felt lonely and impotent. He peeped over the edge of his Plutarch at the dankness below the sofa and grinned with new hope as he saw the huge flat blob of black putty the Jester and Flannel had collapsed into. *I'm on a black kick,* he thought, *why black?*—choosing to forget that he had first started to sculpt figures of the imagination from the star-specked blackness that pulsed under his eyelids while he lay in the dark abed: tiny black heads like wrinkled peas on which any three points of light made two eyes and a mouth. He'd come a long way since then. Now with strong rays from his eyes he rolled all the black putty he could see into a woman-long bolster and hoisted it onto the sofa. The bolster helped with blind sensuous hitching movements, especially where it bent at the middle. When it was lying full length on the sofa he began with cruel strength to sculpt it into the figure of a high-breasted exaggeratedly sexual girl.

Jane found she'd sketched some flies into the picture, buzzing around the swingers. She rubbed them out and put in more stars instead. But there would be flies in the ravine, she told herself, because people dumped garbage down the other side, so she drew one large fly in the lower left-hand corner of the picture. He could be the observer. She said to herself firmly, *No black clouds of spring in this picture* and changed them to hints of Roads in Space.

Gott finished the Black Girl with two twisting tweaks to point her nipples. Her waist was barely thick enough not to suggest an actual wasp or a giant amazon ant. Then he gulped martini water and leaned forward just a little and silently but very strongly blew the breath of life into her across the eight feet of living-room air between them.

The phrase 'black clouds of spring' made Jane think of dead hopes and drowned talents. She said out loud, "I wish you'd start writing in the evenings again, Gott. Then I wouldn't feel so guilty."

"These days, my dear, I'm just a dull businessman, happy to relax in the heart of his family. There's not an atom of art in me," Gott informed her with quiet conviction, watching the Black Girl quiver and writhe as the creativity-wind from his lips hit her. With a sharp twinge of fear it occurred to him that the edges of the wind might leak over to Jane and

Heinie, distorting them like heat shimmers, changing them nastily. Heinie especially was sitting so still in his little chair light-years away. Gott wanted to call to him, but he couldn't think of the right bit of spaceman's lingo.

THE BLACK GIRL (*sitting up and dropping her hand coquettishly to her crotch*): He-he! Now ain't this something, Mr. Adler! First time you've ever had me in your home.

GOTT (*eyeing her savagely over Plutarch*): Shut up!

THE BLACK GIRL (*unperturbed*): Before this it was only when you were away on trips or, once or twice lately, at the office.

GOTT (*flaring his nostrils*): Shut up, I say! You're less than dirt.

THE BLACK GIRL (*smirking*): But I'm interesting dirt, ain't I? You want we should do it in front of her? I could come over and flow inside your clothes and —

GOTT: One more word and I uncreate you! I'll tear you apart like a boiled crow. I'll squunch you back to putty.

THE BLACK GIRL (*still serene, preening her nakedness*): Yes, and you'll enjoy every red-hot second of it, won't you?

Affronted beyond bearing, Gott sent chopping rays at her over the Plutarch parapet, but at that instant a black figure thin as a spider shot up behind the sofa and reaching over the Black Girl's shoulder brushed aside the chopping rays with one flick of a whiplike arm. Grown from the black putty Gott had overlooked under the sofa, the figure was that of an old conjure woman, stick-thin with limbs like wire and breasts like dangling ropes, face that was a pack of spearheads with black plumes a-quiver above it.

THE BLACK CRONE (*in a whistling voice like a hungry wind*): Injure one of the girls, Mister Adler, and I'll castrate you, I'll shrivel you with spells. You'll never be able to call them up again, no matter how far a trip you go on, or even pleasure your wife.

GOTT (*frightened, but not showing it*): Keep your arms and legs on, Mother. Flossie and I were only teasing each other. Vicious play is a specialty of your house, isn't it?

With a deep groaning cry the furnace fan switched on in

the basement and began to say over and over again in a low rapid rumble, 'Oh, my God, my God, my God. Demons, demons, demons, demons.' Jane heard the warning very clearly, but she didn't want to lose the glow of her feelings. She asked, "Are you all right out there in space, Heinie?" and thought he nodded 'Yes.' She began to colour the Clubhouse in the Tree -blue roof, red walls, a little like Chagall.

THE BLACK CRONE (*continuing a tirade*): Understand this, Mr. Adler, you don't own us, we own you. Because you gotta have the girls to live, you're the girls' slave.

THE BLACK GIRL: He-he! Shall I call Susie and Belle? They've never been here either and they'd enjoy this.

THE BLACK CRONE: Later, if he's humble. You understand me, Slave? If I tell you have your wife cook dinner for the girls or wash their feet or watch you snuggle with them, then you gotta do it. And your boy gotta run our errands. Come over here now and sit by Flossie while I brand you with dry ice.

Gott quaked, for the Crone's arms were lengthening toward him like snakes, and he began to sweat and he murmured, "God in Heaven," and the smell of fear went out of him to the walls—millions of stinking molecules.

A cold wind blew over the fence of Heinie's space road and the stars wavered and then fled before it like diamond leaves.

Jane caught the murmur and the fear-whiff too, but she was colouring the Clubhouse windows a warm rich yellow; so what she said in a rather loud, rapt, happy voice was: "I think Heaven is like a children's clubhouse. The only people there are the ones you remember from childhood—either because you were in childhood with them or they told you about their childhood honestly. The *real* people."

At the word *real* the Black Crone and the Black Girl strangled and began to bend and melt like a thin candle and a thicker one over a roaring fire.

Heinie turned his spaceship around and began to drive it bravely homeward through the unspeckled dark, following the ghostly white line that marked the centre of the road.

He thought of himself as the cat they'd had. Papa had told him stories of the cat coming back—from downtown, from Pittsburgh, from Los Angeles, from the moon. Cats could do that. He was the cat coming back.

Jane put down her brush and took up her pencil once more. She'd noticed that the two children swinging out farthest weren't attached yet to their swings. She started to hook them up, then hesitated. Wasn't it all right for some of the children to go sailing out to the stars? Wouldn't it be nice for some evening world—maybe the late-afternoon moon—to have a shower of babies? She wised a plane would crawl over the roof of the house and drone out an answer to her question. She didn't like to have to do all the wondering by herself. It made her feel guilty.

"Gott," she said, "why don't you at least finish the last story you were writing? The one about the Elephants' Graveyard." Then she wished she hadn't mentioned it, because it was an idea that had scared Heinie.

"Some day," her husband murmured, Jane thought.

Gott felt weak with relief, though he was forgetting why. Balancing his head carefully over his book he drained the next to the last of the martini water. It always got stronger toward the bottom. He looked at the page through the lower halves of his executive bifocals and for a moment the word 'Caesar' came up in letters an inch high, each jet serif showing its tatters and the white paper its ridgy fibers. Then, still never moving his head, he looked through the upper halves and saw the long thick blob of dull black putty on the wavering blue couch and automatically gathered the putty together and with thumb-and-palm rays swiftly shaped the Old Philosopher in the Black Toga, always an easy figure to sculpt since he was never finished except rough-hewnly, in the style of Rodin or Daumier. It was always good to finish up an evening with the Old Philosopher.

The white line in space tried to fade. Heinie steered his ship closer to it. He remembered that in spite of Papa's stories the cat had never come back.

Jane held her pencil poised over the detached children

swinging out from the Clubhouse. One of them had a leg kicked over the moon.

THE PHILOSOPHER (*adjusting his craggy toga and yawning*): The topic for tonight's symposium is that vast container of all, the Void.

GOTT (*condescendingly*): The Void? That's interesting. Lately I've wished to merge with it. Life wearies me.

A smiling dull black skull, as crudely shaped as the Philosopher, looked over the latter's shoulder and then rose higher on a rickety black bone framework.

DEATH (*quietly, to Gott*): Really?

GOTT (*greatly shaken, but keeping up a front*): I *am* on a black kick tonight. Can't even do a white skeleton. Disintegrate, you two. You bore me almost as much as life.

DEATH: Really? If you did not cling to life like a limpet you would have crashed your car, to give your wife and son the insurance, when National Motors fired you. You planned to do that. Remember?

GOTT (*with hysterical coolness*): Maybe I should have cast you in brass or aluminum. Then you'd at least have brightened things up. But it's too late now. Disintegrate quickly and don't leave any scraps around.

DEATH: Much too late. Yes, you planned to crash your car and doubly indemnify your dear ones. You had the spot picked, but your courage failed you.

GOTT (*blustering*): I'll have you know I am not only Gottfried but also Helmuth—Hell's Courage Adler!

THE PHILOSOPHER (*confused but trying to keep in the conversation*): A most swashbuckling sobriquet.

DEATH: Hell's courage failed you on the edge of the ravine. (*Pointing at Gott a three-fingered thumbless hand like a black winter branch*). Do you wish to die now?

GOTT (*blacking out visually*): Cowards die many times. (*Draining the last of the martini water in absolute darkness*). The valiant taste death once. Caesar.

DEATH (*a voice in darkness*): Coward. Yet you summoned me—and even though you fashioned me poorly,

I am indeed Death—and there are others besides yourself who take long trips. Even longer ones. Trips in the Void.

THE PHILOSOPHER (*another voice*): Ah, yes, the Void. Imprimis —

DEATH: Silence.

In the great obedient silence Gott heard the unhurried click of Death's feet as he stepped from behind the sofa across the bare floor toward Heinie's spaceship. Gott reached up in the dark and clung to his mind.

Jane heard the slow clicks, too. They were the kitchen clock ticking out, "Now. Now. Now. Now. Now."

Suddenly Heinie called out, "The line's gone. Papa, Mama, I'm lost."

Jane said sharply, "No, you're not, Heinie. Come out of space at once."

"I'm not in space now. I'm in the Cats' Graveyard."

Jane told herself that it was insane to feel suddenly so frightened. "Come back from wherever you are, Heinie," she said calmly. "It's time for bed."

"I'm lost, Papa," Heinie cried. "I can't hear Mama any more."

"Listen to your mother, Son," Gott said thickly, groping in the blackness for other words.

"All the Mamas and Papas in the world are dying," Heinie wailed.

Then the words came to Gott and when he spoke his voice flowed. "Are your atomic generators turning over, Heinie? Is your space-warp lever free?"

"Yes, Papa, but the line's gone."

"Forget it. I've got a fix on you through subspace and I'll coach you home. Swing her two units to the right and three up. Fire when I give the signal. Are you ready?"

"Yes, Papa."

"Roger. Three, two, one, fire and away! Dodge that comet! Swing left around that planet! Never mind the big dust cloud! Home on the third beacon. Now! Now! Now!"

Gott had dropped his Plutarch and come lurching blindly across the room and as he uttered the last *Now!* the darkness cleared and he caught Heinie up from his space-chair and staggered with him against Jane and steadied himself there without upsetting her paints and she accused him laughingly, "You beefed up the martini water again," and Heinie pulled off his helmet and crowed, "Make a big hug," and they clung to each other and looked down at the half-coloured picture where a Children's Clubhouse sat in a tree over a deep ravine and blob children swung out from it against the cool pearly moon and the winding roads in space and the next to the last child hooked onto his swing with one hand and with the other caught the last child of all, while from the picture's lower lefthand corner a fat black fly looked on enviously.

Searching with his eyes as the room swung toward equilibrium, Gottfried Helmuth Adler saw Death peering at him through the crack between the hinges of the open kitchen door.

Laboriously, half passing out again, Gott sneered his face at him.

THE BUTTON MOLDER

I DON'T RIGHTLY KNOW if I can call this figure I saw for a devastating ten seconds a ghost. And *heard* for about ten seconds just before that. These durations are of course to a degree subjective judgments. At the time they seemed to be lasting forever. Ten seconds can be long or short. A man can light a cigarette. A sprinter can travel a hundred yards, sound two miles, and light two million. A rocket can launch, or burn up inside. A city can fall down. It depends on what's happening.

The word "ghost," like "shade" or "wraith" or even "phantom," suggests human personality and identity, and what this figure had was in a way the antithesis of that. Perhaps "apparition" is better, because it ties it in with astronomy, which may conceivably be the case in a far-fetched way. Astronomers speak of apparitions of the planet Mercury, just as they talk of spurious stars (novas) and occultations by Venus and the moon. Astronomy talk can sound pretty eerie, even without the help of any of the witching and romantic lingo of astrology.

But I rather like "ghost," for it lets me bring in the theory of the Victorian scholar and folklorist Andrew Lang that a ghost is simply a short waking dream in the mind of the person who thinks he sees one. He tells about it in his book *Dreams and Ghosts*, published in 1897. It's a praiseworthy simple and sober notion (also a very polite one, typically English!—"I'd never suggest you were lying about that ghost, old boy. But perhaps you dreamed it, not knowing you were dreaming?") and a theory easy to believe, especially if the person who sees the ghost is fatigued and under stress and the ghost something seen in the shadows of a dark doorway or a storm-lashed window at night or in the flickering flames of a dying fire or in the gloom of a dim room with faded tapestries or obscurely patterned wallpaper. Not so easy to credit for a figure seen fully illuminated for a double handful of long seconds by someone untired and under no physical strain, yet I find it a reassuring theory in my case. In fact, there are times when it strikes me as vastly preferable to certain other possibilities.

The happening occurred rather soon after I moved from one six-story apartment building to another in downtown San Francisco. There were a remarkable number of those put up in the decades following the quake and fire of 1906. A lot of them started as small hotels but transformed to apartments as the supply of cheap menial labor shrank. You can usually tell those by their queer second floors, which began as mezzanines. The apartment I was moving from had an obvious one of those, lobby-balcony to the front, manager's apartment and some other tiny ones to the rear.

I'd been thinking about moving for a long time, because my one-room-and-bath was really too small for me and getting crammed to the ceiling with my files and books, yet I'd shrunk from the bother involved. But then an efficient, "savvy" manager was replaced by an ineffectual one, who had little English, or so pretended to save himself work, and the place rather rapidly got much too noisy. Hi-fi's thudded and thumped unrebuked until morning. Drunken parties overflowed into the halls and took to wandering about. Early on in the course of deterioration the unwritten slum rule seemed to come into effect of "If you won't call the owner (or the cops) on me, I won't call him on you." (Why did I comply with this rule? I hate rows and asserting myself.) There was a flurry of mailbox thefts and of stoned folk setting off the building's fire alarm out of curiosity, and of nodding acquaintances whose names you didn't know hitting you for small loans. Pets and stray animals multiplied—and left evidence of themselves, as did the drunks. There were more than the usual quota of overdosings and attempted suicides and incidents of breaking down doors (mostly by drunks who'd lost their keys) and series of fights that were, perhaps unfortunately, mostly racket, and at least one rape. In the end the halls came to be preferred for every sort of socializing. And if the police were at last summoned, it was generally just in time to start things up again when they'd almost quieted down.

I don't mind a certain amount of stupid noise and even hubbub. After all, it's my business to observe the human condition and report on it imaginatively. But when it comes to spending my midnight hours listening to two elderly male lovers shouting horrendous threats at each other in prison argot, repeatedly slamming doors on each other and maddeningly whining for them to be reopened, and stumbling up and down stairs menacing each other with a dull breadknife which is periodically wrested in slow-motion from hand to hand, I draw the line. More important, I am even able to summon up the energy to get myself away from the offensive scene forever.

My new apartment building, which I found much more easily than I'd expected to once I started to hunt, was an earthly paradise by comparison. *The occupants stayed out of the halls* and when forced to venture into them traveled as swiftly as was compatible with maximum quiet. The walls were thick enough so that I hadn't the faintest idea of what they did at home. The manager was a tower of resourceful efficiency, yet unobtrusive and totally uninquisitive. Instead of the clanking and groaning monster I'd been used to, the small elevator (I lived on six in both places) was a wonder of silent reliability. Twice a week the halls roared softly and briefly with a large vacuum cleaner wielded by a small man with bowed shoulders who never seemed to speak.

Here the queer second-floor feature hinting at hotel-origins took the form of three private offices (an architect's, a doctor's and a CPA's), instead of front apartments, with stairway of their own shut off from the rest of the building, while the entire first floor except for the main entrance and its hall was occupied by a large fabrics or yard-goods store, which had in its display window an item that intrigued me mightily. It was a trim lay figure, life-size, made of a ribbed white cotton material and stuffed. It had mitts instead of hands (no separate fingers or toes) and an absolutely blank face. Its position and attitude were altered rather frequently, as were the attractive materials displayed with it—it might be standing or reclining, sitting, or kneeling. Sometimes it seemed to be pulling fabrics from a roller, or otherwise arranging them, things like that. I always thought of it as female, I can't say why; although there were the discreet suggestions of a bosom and a pubic bump, its hips were narrow; perhaps a woman would have thought of it as male. Or perhaps my reasons for thinking of it as feminine were as simple as its small life-size (about five feet tall) or (most obvious) its lack of any external sex organ. At any rate, it rather fascinated as well as amused me, and at first I fancied it as standing for the delightfully quiet, unobtrusive folk who were my new fellow tenants as opposed to the noisy and obstreperous quaints I had endured before. I even thought of it for a bit as the "faceless" and unindividualized proto-human being to which the Button Molder threatens to melt down Peer Gynt. (I'd just reread that classic of Ibsen's— really, Peer stands with Faust and Hamlet and Don Quixote and Don Juan as one of the great fundamental figures of western culture.) But then I became aware of its extreme mute expressiveness. If a face is left blank, the imagination of the viewer always supplies an expression for it—an expression which may be more intense and "living" because there are no lifeless features for it to clash with.

(If I seem to be getting off on sidetracks, please bear with me. They really have a bearing. I haven't forgotten my ghost, or apparition, or those agonizing ten seconds I want to tell you about. No indeed.)

My own apartment in the new building was almost too good to be true. Although advertised as only a studio, it contained four rooms in line, each with a window facing east. They were, in order from north to south (which would be left to right as you entered the hall): bathroom, small bedroom (its door faced you as you entered from the outside hall), large living room, and (beyond a low arched doorway) dinette-kitchen. The bathroom window was frosted; the other three had venetian blinds. And besides two closets (one half the bedroom long) there were seventeen built-in cupboards with a total of thirty-one shelves—a treasure trove of ordered emptiness, and all, all, mine alone! To complete the pleasant picture, I had easy access to the roof— the manager assured me that a few of the tenants regularly used it for sunbathing. But I wasn't interested in the roof by day.

The time came soon enough when I eagerly supervised the transfer to my new place of my luggage, boxes, clothes, the few articles of furniture I owned (chiefly bookcases and filing cabinets), and the rather more extensive materials of my trade of fiction-writing and chief avocation of roof-top astronomy. That last is more important to me than one might guess. I like big cities, but I'd hate to have to live in one without having easy access to a flat roof. I'd had that at my old apartment, and it was one of the features that kept me there so long—I'd anticipated difficulties getting the same privilege elsewhere.

I have the theory, you see, that in this age of mechanized hive-dwelling and of getting so much input from necessarily conformist artificial media such as TV and newspapers, it's very important for a person to keep himself more directly oriented, in daily touch with the heavens or at least the sky, the yearly march of the sun across the starts, the changing daily revolution of the stars as the world turns, the crawl of the planets, the swift phases of the moon, things like that. After all, it's one of the great healing rhythms of nature like the seas and the winds, perhaps the greatest. Stars are a pattern of points upon infinity, elegant geometric art, with almost an erotic poignancy, but all, all nature. Some psychologists say that people stop dreaming if they don't look out over great distances each day, "see the horizon," as it were, and that dreams are the means by which the mind keeps its conscious and unconscious halves in balance, and I certainly agree with them. At any rate I'd deliberately built up the habit of rooftop observing, first by the unaided eye, then with the help of binoculars, and, finally a small refracting telescope on an equatorial mounting.

Moreover—and especially in a foggy city like San Francisco!—if you get interested in the stars, you inevitably get interested in the weather if only because it so often thwarts you with its infinitely varied clouds and winds (which can make a telescope useless by setting it trembling), its freaks and whims and its own great all-over rhythms. And then it gives you a new slant on the city itself. You become absorbed into the fascinating world of roofs, a secret world above the city world, one mostly uninhabited and unknown. Even the blocky, slablike high-rises cease to be anonymous disfigurements, targets of protest. They become the markers whence certain stars appear or whither they trend, or which they grace with twinkling caress, and which the sun or moon touch or pass behind at certain times of the year or month, exactly like the menhirs at Stonehenge which primitive man used similarly. And through the gaps and narrow chinks between the great high-rises, you can almost always glimpse bits and pieces of the far horizon. And always once in a while there will be some freakish sky or sky-related event that will completely mystify you and really challenge your imagination.

Of course, roof-watching, like writing itself, is a lonely occupation, but at least it tends to move outward from self, to involve more and more of otherness. And in any case, after having felt the world and its swarming people much too much with me for the past couple of years (and in an extremely noisy, sweaty way!) I was very much looking forward to living alone by myself for a good long while in a supremely quiet environment.

In view of that last, it was highly ironic that the first thing to startle me about my new place should have been *the noise*—noise of a very special sort, the swinish grunting and chomping of the huge garbage trucks that came rooting for refuse every morning (except Sunday) at 4 a.m. or a little earlier. My old apartment had looked out on a rear inner court in an alleyless block, and so their chuffing, grinding sound had been one I'd been mostly spared. While the east windows of my new place looked sidewise down on the street in front and also into a rather busy alley—there wasn't a building nearly as high as mine in that direction for a third of a block. Moreover, in moving the three blocks between the two apartments, I'd moved into a more closely supervised and protected district—that of the big hotels and theaters and expensive stores—with more police protection and enforced tidiness—which meant more garbage trucks. There were the yellow municipal ones and the green and gray ones of more than one private collection company, and once at three-thirty I saw a tiny white one draw up on the sidewalk beside an outdoor phone booth and the driver get out and spend ten minutes rendering it pristine with vacuum, sponge, and squeegee.

The first few nights when they waked me, I'd get up and move from window to window, and even go down the outside hall to the front fire escape with its beckoning red light, the better to observe the rackety monsters and their hurrying attendants—the wide maws into which the refuse was shaken from clattering cans, the great revolving steel drums that chewed it up, the huge beds that would groaningly tilt to empty the drums and shake down the shards. (My God, they were ponderous and cacophonous vehicles!)

But nothing could be wrong with my new place—even these sleep-shattering mechanical giant hogs fascinated me. It was an eerie and mysterious sight to see one of them draw up, say, at the big hotel across the street from me and an iron door in the sidewalk open upward without visible human agency and four great dully gleaming garbage cans slowly arise there as if from some dark hell. I found myself comparing them also (the trucks) to the Button Molder in *Peer Gynt*. Surely, I told myself, they each must have a special small compartment for discarded human souls that had failed to achieve significant individuality and were due to be melted down! Or perhaps they just mixed in the worn-out souls with all the other junk.

At one point I even thought of charting and timing the trucks' exact routes and schedules, just as I did with the planets and the moon, so that I'd be better able to keep tabs on them.

That was another reason I didn't mind being waked at four—it let me get in a little rooftop astronomy before the morning twilight began. At such times I'd usually just take my binoculars, though once I lugged up my telescope for an apparition of Mercury when he was at his greatest western elongation.

Once, peering down from the front fire escape into the dawn-dark street below, I thought I saw a coveralled attendant rudely toss my fabric-store manikin into the rear-end mouth of a dark green truck, and I almost shouted down a protesting inquiry ... and ten minutes later felt sorry that I hadn't—sorry and somehow guilty. It bothered me so much that I got dressed and went down to check out the display window. For a moment I didn't see her, and I felt a crazy grief rising, but then I spotted her peeping up at me coyly from under a pile of yardage arranged so that she appeared to have pulled the colorful materials down on herself.

And once at four in the warm morning of a holiday I was for variety wakened by the shrill, argumentative cries of four slender hookers, two black, two white, arrayed in their uniform of high heels, hotpants, and long-sleeved lacy blouses, clustered beneath a streetlight on the far corner of the next intersection west and across from an all-hours nightclub named the Windjammer. They were preening and scouting about at intervals, but mostly they appeared to be discoursing, somewhat less raucously now, with the unseen drivers and passengers of a dashing red convertible and a slim white hardtop long as a yacht, which were drawn up near the curb at nonchalant angles across the corner. Their customers? Pimps more likely, from the glory of their equipages. After a bit the cars drifted away and the four lovebirds wandered off east in a loose formation, warbling together querulously.

After about ten days I stopped hearing the garbage trucks, just as the manager had told me would happen, though most mornings I continued to wake early enough for a little astronomy.

My first weeks in the new apartment were very happy ones. (No, I hadn't encountered my ghost yet, or even got hints of its approach, but I think the stage was setting itself and perhaps the materials were gathering.) My writing, which had been almost stalled at the old place, began to go well, and I finished three short stories. I spent my afternoons pleasantly setting out the stuff of my life to best advantage, being particularly careful to leave most surfaces clear and not to hang too many pictures, and in expeditions to make thoughtful purchases. I acquired a dark blue celestial globe I'd long wanted and several maps to fill the space above my filing cabinets; one of the world, a chart of the stars on the same Mercator projection, a big one of the moon, and two of San Francisco, the city and its downtown done in great detail. I didn't go to many shows during this time or see much of any of my friends—I didn't need them. But I got caught up on stacks of unanswered correspondence. And I remember expending considerable effort in removing the few blemishes I discovered on my new place: a couple of inconspicuous but unsightly stains, a slow drain that turned out to have been choked by a stopper chain, a venetian blind made cranky by twisted cords, and the usual business of replacing low-wattage globes with brighter ones, particularly in the case of the entry light just inside the hall door. There the ceiling had been lowered a couple of feet, which gave the rest of the apartment a charmingly spacious appearance, as did the arched dinette doorway, but it meant that any illumination there had to come down from a fixture in the true ceiling through a frosted plate in the lowered one. I put in a 200-watter, reminding myself to use it sparingly. I even remember planning to get a thick rubber mat to put under my filing cabinets so they wouldn't indent and perhaps even cut the heavy carpeting too deeply, but I never got around to that.

Perhaps those first weeks were simply too happy, perhaps I just got to spinning along too blissfully, for after finishing the third short story, I suddenly found myself tempted by the idea of writing something that would be more than fiction and also more than a communication addressed to just one person, but rather a general statement of what I thought about life and other people and history and the universe and all, the roots of it, something like Descartes began when he wrote down, "I think, therefore I am." Oh, it wouldn't be formally and certainly not stuffily philosophical, but it would contain a lot of insights just the same, the fruits of one man's lifetime experience. It would be critical yet autobiographical, honestly rooted in me. At the very least it would be a testimonial to the smooth running of my life at a new place, a way of honoring my move here.

I'm ordinarily not much of a nonfiction writer. I've done a few articles about writing and about other writers I particularly admire, a lot of short book reviews, and for a dozen or so years before I took up full-time fiction, I edited a popular science magazine. And before that I'd worked on encyclopedias and books of knowledge.

But everything was so clear to me at the new place, my sensations were so exact, my universe was spread out around me so orderly, that I knew that now was the time to write such a piece if ever, so I decided to take a chance on the new idea, give it a whirl.

At the same time at a deeper level in my mind and feelings, I believe I was making a parallel decision running something like this: *Follow this lead. Let all the other stuff go, ease up, and see what happens.* Somewhere down there a control was being loosened.

An hour or so before dawn the next day I had a little

experience that proved to be the pattern for several subsequent ones, including the final unexpected event. (You see, I haven't forgotten those ten seconds I mentioned. I'm keeping them in mind.)

I'd been on the roof in the cool predawn to observe a rather close conjunction (half a degree apart) of Mars and Jupiter in the east (they didn't rise until well after midnight), and while I was watching the reddish and golden planets without instrument (except for my glasses, of course) I twice thought I saw a shooting star out of the corner of my eye but didn't get my head around in time to be sure. I was intrigued because I hadn't noted in the handbook any particular meteor showers due at this time and also because most shooting stars are rather faint and the city's lights tend to dim down everything in the sky. The third time it happened I managed to catch the flash and for a long instant was astounded by the sight of what appeared to be three shooting stars traveling fast in triangular formation like three fighter planes before they whisked out of sight behind a building. Then I heard a faint bird-cry and realized they had been three gulls winging quite close and fast overhead, their white under-feathers illumined by the upward streaming streetlights. It was really a remarkable illusion, of the sort that has to be seen to be fully believed. You'd think your eye wouldn't make that sort of misidentification—three seabirds for three stars—but from the corner of your eye you don't see shape or color or even brightness much, only pale movement whipping past. And then you wouldn't think three birds would keep such a tight and exact triangular formation, very much like three planes performing at an air show.

I walked quietly back to my apartment in my bathrobe and slippers. The stairway from the roof was carpeted. My mind was full of the strange triple apparition I'd just seen. I thought of how another mind with other anticipation might have seen three UFOs. I silently opened the door to my apartment, which I'd left on the latch, and stepped inside.

I should explain here that I always switch off the lights when I leave my apartment and am careful about how I turn

them on when I come back. It's partly thrift and citizenly
thoughts about energy, the sort of thing you do to get gold
stars at grown-ups' Sunday school. But it's also a care not
to leave an outward-glaring light to disturb some sleeper
who perhaps must keep his window open and unshuttered
for the sake of air and coolth; there's a ten-story apartment
building a quarter block away overlooking my east windows,
and I've had my own sleep troubled by such unnecessary
abominable beacons. On the other hand, I like to look out
open windows myself; I hate to keep them wholly shaded,
draped, or shuttered, but at the same time I don't want
to become a target for a sniper—a simply realistic fear to
many these days. As a result of all this I make it a rule never
to turn on a light at night until I'm sure the windows of
the room I'm in are fully obscured. I take a certain pride,
I must admit, in being able to move around my place in
the dark without bumping things—it's a test of courage too,
going back to childhood, and also a proof that your sensory
faculties haven't been dimmed by age. And I guess I just like
the feeling of mysteriousness it gives me.

So when I stepped inside I did *not* turn on the 200-watt
light above the lowered ceiling of the entry. My intention was
to move directly forward into the bedroom, assure myself
that the venetian blinds were tilted shut, and then switch
on the bedside lamp. But as I started to do that, I heard the
beginning of a noise to my right and I glanced toward the
living room, where the street lights striking upward through
the open venetian blinds made pale stripes on the ceiling
and wall and slightly curving ones on the celestial globe
atop a bookcase, and into the dinette beyond, and I saw a
thin dark figure slip along the wall. But then, just as a feeling
of surprise and fear began, almost at the same moment but
actually a moment later, there came the realization that the
figure was the black frame of my glasses, either moving as
I turned my head or becoming more distinct as I switched
my eyes that way, more likely a little of both. It was an
odd mixture of sensation and thought, especially coming
right on top of the star-birds (or bird-stars), as if I were

getting almost simultaneously the messages, *My God, it's an intruder, or ghost, or whatever* and, *It isn't any of those, as you know very well from a lifetime's experience. You've just been had again by appearances.*

I'm pretty much a thorough-going skeptic, you see, when it comes to the paranormal, or the religious supernatural, or even such a today-commonplace as telepathy. My mental attitudes were formed in the period during and just after the first world war, when science was still a right thing, almost noble, and technology was forward-looking and labor-saving and progressive, and before folk wisdom became so big and was still pretty much equated with ignorance and superstition, no matter how picturesque. I've never seen or heard of a really convincing scrap of evidence for ancient or present-day astronauts from other worlds, for comets or moons that bumped the earth and changed history, or for the power of pyramids to prolong life or sharpen razor blades. As for immortality, it's my impression that most people do (or don't do) what's in them and then live out their lives in monotonous blind alleys, and what would be the point in cluttering up another world with all that worn-out junk? And as for God, it seems to me that the existence of one being who knew everything, future as well as past, would simply rob the universe of drama, excuse us all from doing anything. I'll admit that with telepathy the case is somewhat different, if only because so many sensible, well-educated, brilliant people seem to believe in some form of it. I only know I haven't experienced any as far as I can tell; it's almost made me jealous—I've sometimes thought I must be wrapped in some very special insulation against thought waves, if there be such. I *will* allow that the mind (and also mental suggestions from outside) can affect the body, even affect it greatly—the psychosomatic thing. But that's just about all I will allow.

So much for that first little experience—no, wait, what did I mean when I wrote, "I heard the beginning of a noise?" Well, there are sounds so short and broken-off that you can't tell what they were going to be, or even for sure just how loud they were, so that you ask yourself if you imagined them. It was like that—a tick without a tock, a ding without the dong, a creak that went only halfway, never reaching that final *kuh* sound. Or like a single footstep that started rather loud and ended muted down to nothing—very much like the whole little experience itself, beginning with a gust of shock and terror and almost instantly reducing to the commonplace. Well, so much for that.

The next few days were pleasant and exciting ones, as I got together materials for my new project, assembling the favorite books I knew I'd want to quote (Shakespeare and the King James Bible, *Moby Dick* and *Wuthering Heights*, Ibsen and Bertrand Russell, Stapledon and Heinlein), looking through the daybooks I've kept for literary and what I like to call metaphysical matters, and telling my mind (programming it, really) to look for similar insights whenever they happened to turn up during the course of the day—and then happily noting down those new insights in turn. There was only one little fly in the ointment: I knew I'd embarked on projects somewhat like this before—autobiographical and critical things—and failed to bring them to conclusions. But then I've had the same thing happen to me on stories. With everything, one needs a bit of luck.

My next little experience began up on the roof. (They all did, for that matter.) It was a very clear evening without a moon, and I'd been memorizing the stars in Capricorn and faint Aquarius and the little constellations that lie between those and the Northern Cross: Sagitta, Delphinus, and dim Equuleus. You learn the stars rather like you learn countries and cities on a map, getting the big names first (the brightest stars and star groups) and then patiently filling in the areas between—and always on the watch for striking forms. At such times I almost forget the general dimming effect of San Francisco's lights since what I'm working on is so far above them.

And then, as I was resting my eyes from the binoculars, shut off by the roof's walls and the boxlike structure housing the elevator's motor from the city's most dazzling glares (the big, whitely fluorescent streetlights are the worst, the ones that are supposed to keep late walkers safe), I saw a beam of bright silver light strike straight upward for about a second from the roof of a small hotel three blocks away. And after about a dozen seconds more it came again, equally brief. It really looked like a sort of laser-thing: a beam of definite length (about two stories) and solid-looking. It happened twice more, not at regular intervals, but always as far as I could judge in exactly the same place (and I'd had time to spin a fantasy about a secret enclave of extraterrestrials signaling to confederates poised just outside the stratosphere) when it occurred to me to use my binoculars on it. They solved the mystery almost at once: It wasn't a light beam at all, but a tall flagpole painted silver (no wonder it looked solid!) and at intervals washed by the roving beam of a big arc light shooting upward from the street beyond and swinging in slow circles—the sort of thing they use to signalize the opening of movie houses and new restaurants, even quite tiny ones.

What had made the incident out of the ordinary was that most flagpoles are painted dull white, not silver, and that the clearness of the night had made the arc light's wide beam almost invisible. If there'd been just a few wisps of cloud or fog in the air above, I'd have spotted it at once for what it was. It was rather strange to think of all that light streaming invisibly up from the depths of the city's reticulated canyons and gorges.

I wondered why I'd never noted that flagpole before. Probably they never flew a flag on it.

It all didn't happen to make me recall my three star-birds, and so when after working over once more this night's chosen heavenly territory, including a veering aside to scan the rich starfields of Aquila and the diamond of Altair, one of Earth's closest stellar neighbors, I was completely taken by surprise again when on entering my apartment, the half noise was repeated and the same skinny dark shape glided along the wall across the narrow flaglike bands of light and dark. Only this time the skeptical, deflating reaction came a tiny bit sooner, followed at once by the almost peevish inner remark, *Oh, yes, that again!* And then as I turned on the bedside light, I wondered, as one will, how I would have reacted if the half step had been completed and if the footsteps had gone on, getting louder as they made their swift short trip and there peered around the side of the doorway at me ... what? It occurred to me that the nastiest and most frightening thing in the world must differ widely from person to person, and I smiled. Surely in man's inward lexicon, the phobias outnumber the philias a thousand to one!

Oh, I'll admit that when I wandered into the living room and kitchen a bit later, shutting the blinds and turning on some lights, I did inspect things in a kind of perfunctory way, but noted nothing at all out of order. I told myself that all buildings make a variety of little noises at night, waterpipes especially can get downright loquacious, and then there are refrigerator motors sighing on and off and the faint little clicks and whines that come from electric clocks, all manner of babble—that half noise might be anything. At least I knew the identity of the black glider—the vaguely seen black frame always at the corner of my eye when I had on my glasses and most certainly there now.

I went on assembling the primary materials for my new project and a week later I was able to set down, word by mulled-over word, the unembroidered, unexemplified, unproven gist of what I felt about life, or at least a first version of it. I still have it as I typed it from a penciled draft with many erasures, crossings out, and interlineations:

> There is this awareness that is I, this mind
> that's me, a little mortal world of space and
> time, which glows and aches, which purrs
> and darkens, haunted and quickened by
> the ghosts that are memory, imagination,
> and thought, forever changing under
> urgings from within and proddings from
> without, yet able to hold still by fits and
> starts (and now and then refreshed by sleep

and dreams), forever seeking to extend its bounds, forever hunting for the mixture of reality and fantasy—the formula, the script, the scenario, the story to tell itself or others-which will enable it to do its work, savor its thrills, and keep on going. A baby tells itself the simplest story: that it is all that matters, it is God, commanding and constraining all the rest, all otherness. But then the script becomes more complicated. Stories take many forms: a scientific theory or a fairy tale, a world history or an anecdote, a call to action or a cry for help—all, all are stories. Sometimes they tell of our love for another, or they embody our illusioned and illusioning vision of the one we love—they are courtship. But every story must be interesting or it will not work, will not be heard, even the stories that we tell ourselves. And so it must contain illusion, fantasy. No matter how grim its facts, it must contain that saving note, be it only a surpassingly interesting bitter, dry taste. And then there are the other mortal minds I know are there, fellow awarenesses, companion consciousnesses, some close, a very few almost in touching space (but never quite), most farther off in almost unimaginable multitudes, each one like mine a little world of space and time moment by moment seeking its story, the combination of illusion and hard fact, of widest waking and of deepest dreaming, which will allow it to create, enjoy, survive. A company of loving, warring minds, a tender, rough companioning of tiny cosmoses forever telling stories to each other and themselves—that's what there is.

And I know that I must stay aware of all the others, listening to their stories, trying to understand them, their sufferings, their joys, and their imaginings, respecting the thorny facts of both their inner and their outer lives, and nourishing the needful illusions at least of those who are closest to me, if I am to make progress in my quest. Finally there is the world, stranger than any mind or any story, the unknown universe, the shadowy scaffolding holding these minds together, the grid on which they are mysteriously arrayed, their container and their field, perhaps (but is there any question of it?) all-powerful yet quite unseen, it's form unsensed, known only to the companion minds by the sensations it showers upon them and pelts them with, by its cruel and delicious proddings and graspings, by its agonizing and ecstatic messages (but never a story), and by its curt summonses and sentences, including death. Yes, that is how it is, those are the fundamentals: There is the dark, eternally silent, unknown universe; there are the friend-enemy minds shouting and whispering their tales and always seeking the three miracles—that minds should really touch, or that the silent universe should speak, tell minds a story, or (perhaps the same thing) that there should be a story that works that is all hard facts, all reality, with no illusions and no fantasy; and lastly there is lonely, story-telling, wonder-questing, mortal me.

As I reread that short statement after typing it out clean, I found it a little more philosophical than I'd intended and also perhaps a little more overly glamorized with words like "ecstatic" and "agonizing," "mysteriously" and "stranger." But on the whole I was satisfied with it. Now to analyze it more deeply and flesh it out with insights and examples from my own life and from my own reflections on the work of others!

But as the working days went on and became weeks (remember, I'd pretty much given up all other work for the duration of this project) I found it increasingly difficult to make any real progress. For one thing, I gradually became aware that in order to analyze that little statement much more deeply and describe my findings, I'd need to use one or more of the vocabularies of professional philosophy and psychology—which would mean months at least of reading and reviewing and of assimilating new advances, and I certainly didn't have the time for that. (The vocabularies of philosophies can be *very* special—Whitehead's, for instance, makes much use of the archaic verb "prehend," which for him means something very different from "comprehend" or "perceive.") Moreover, the whole idea had been to skim accumulated insights and wisdom (if any!) off my mind, not become a student again and start from the beginning.

And I found it was pretty much the same when I tried to say something about other writers, past and contemporary, beyond a few obvious remarks and memorable quotations. I'd need to read their works again and study their lives in a lot more detail than I had ever done, before I'd be able to shape statements of any significance, things I really believed about them.

And when I tried to write about my own life, I kept discovering that for the most part it was much like anyone else's. I didn't want to set down a lot of dreary dates and places, only the interesting things, but how tell about those honestly without bringing in the rest? Moreover, it began to seem to me that all the really interesting subjects, like sex and money, feelings of guilt, worries about one's courage, and concern about one's selfishness were things one wasn't supposed to write about, either because they were too personal, involving others, or because they were common to all men and women and so quite unexceptional.

This state of frustration didn't grip me all the time, of course. It came in waves and gradually accumulated. I'd generally manage to start off each day feeling excited about the project (though it began to take more and more morning time to get my head into that place, I will admit), perhaps some part of my short statement would come alive for me again, like that bit about the universe being a grid on which minds are mysteriously arrayed, but by the end of the day I would have worried all the life out of it and my mind would be as blank as the face of my manikin in the fabric shop window downstairs. I remember once or twice in the course of one of our daily encounters shaking my head ruefully at her, almost as if seeking for sympathy. She seemed to have a lot more patience and poise than I had.

I was beginning to spend more time on the roof, too, not only for the sake of the stars and astronomy, but just to get away from my desk with all its problems. In fact, my next little experience leading up to the ghostly one began shortly before sunset one day when I'd been working long, though fruitlessly. The sky, which was cloudless from my east window, began to glow with an unusual violet color and I hurried up to get a wider view.

All day long a steady west wind had been streaming out the flags on the hotels and driving away east what smog there was, so that the sky was unusually clear. But the sun had sunk behind the great fog bank that generally rests on the Pacific just outside the Golden Gate. However, he had not yet set, for to the south, where there were no tall buildings to obstruct my vision, his beams were turning a few scattered clouds over San Jose (some thirty miles away) a delicate shade of lemon yellow that seemed to be the exact compliment of the violet in the sky (just as orange sunset clouds tend to go with a deep blue sky).

And then as I watched, there suddenly appeared in the midst of that sunset, very close to the horizon in a cloudless stretch, a single yellow cloud like a tiny dash. It seemed to appear from nowhere, just like that. And then as I continued to watch, another cloud appeared close beside the first at the same altitude, beginning as a bright yellow point and then swiftly growing until it was as long as the first, very much as if a giant invisible hand had drawn another short dash.

During the course of the next few minutes, as I watched with a growing sense of wonder and a feeling of giant release from the day's frustrations, eight more such mini-clouds (or whatever) appeared at fairly regular intervals, until there were ten of them glowing in line there, fluorescent yellow stitches in the sky.

My mind raced, clutching at explanations. Kenneth Arnold's original flying saucers thirty years ago, which he'd glimpsed from his light plane over the American northwest, had been just such shining shapes in a row. True, his had been moving, while mine were hovering over a city, having appeared from nowhere. Could they conceivably have come from hyperspace? my fancy asked.

And then, just as the lemon sunset began to fade from the higher clouds, an explanation struck me irresistibly. What I was seeing was skywriting (which usually we see above our heads) from way off to one side, viewed edgewise. My ten mystery clouds (or giant ships!) were the nine letters—and the hyphen—of Pepsi-Cola. (Next day I confirmed this by a telephone call to San Jose; there had been just such an advertising display.)

At the time, and as the giant yellow stitches faded to gray unsewn sky-cloth, I remember feeling very exhilarated and also slightly hysterical at the comic aspect of the event. I paced about the roof chortling, telling myself that the vision I'd just witnessed outdid even that of the Goodyear blimp acrawl with colored lights in abstract patterns that had welcomed me to this new roof the first night I'd climbed up here after moving in. I spent quite a while quieting myself, so that the streetlights had just come on when I went downstairs. But somehow I hadn't thought of it being very dark yet in my apartment, so that was perhaps why it wasn't until I was actually unlocking the door that, remembering

the Star-birds and the Silver Laser (and now the Mystery of
the Ten Yellow Stitches!), I also remembered the events that
had followed them. I had only time to think, *Here we go
again,* as I pushed inside.

Well, it *was* dark in there and the pale horizontal bands
were on the wall and the skeleton black figure slipped
along them and I felt almost instantly the choked-off gust
of terror riding atop the remnants of my exhilaration, all
of this instantly after hearing that indefinable sound which
seemed to finish almost before it began. That was one thing
characteristic of all these preliminary incidents—they ended
so swiftly and so abruptly that it was hard to think about
them afterwards, the mind had nothing to work with.

And I know that in trying to describe them I must make
them sound patterned, almost prearranged, yet at the time
they just happened and somehow there was always an
element of surprise.

Unfortunately the exhilaration I'd feel on the roof never
carried over to the next morning's work on my new project.
This time, after sweating and straining for almost a week
without any progress at all, I resolutely decided to shelve it,
at least for a while, and get back to stories.

But I found I couldn't do that. I'd committed myself too
deeply to the new thing. Oh, I didn't find that out right away,
of course. No, I spent more than a week before I came to
that hateful and panic-making conclusion. I tried every trick
I knew of to get myself going: long walks, fasting, starting
to write immediately after waking up when my mind was
hypnogogic and blurred with dream, listening to music which
I'd always found suggestive, such as Holst's *The Planets*,
especially the "Saturn" section, which seems to capture the
essence of time—you hear the giant footsteps of time itself
crashing to a halt -or Vaughan Williams' *Sinfonia antartica*
with its lonely wind-machine finish, which does the same
for space, or Berlioz's *Funeral March for the Last Scene
of Hamlet,* which reaches similarly toward chaos. Nothing
helped. The more I'd try to work up the notes for some story
I had already three quarters planned, the less interesting it

would become to me, until it seemed (and probably was) cliché. Some story ideas are as faint and as unsubstantial as ghosts. Well, all of *those* I had just got fainter as I worked on them.

I hate to write about writer's block; it's such a terribly childish, yes, frivolous-seeming affliction. You'd think that anyone who was half a human being could shake it off or just slither away from it. But I couldn't. Morning after morning I'd wake with an instant pang of desperation at the thought of my predicament, so that I'd have to get up right away and pace, or rush out and walk the dawn-empty streets, or play through chess endings or count windows in big buildings to fill my mind with useless calculations -anything until I grew calm enough to read a newspaper or make a phone call and somehow get the day started. Sometimes my desk would get to jumping in the same way my mind did and I'd find myself compulsively straightening the objects on it over and over until I'd spring up from it in disgust. Now when the garbage trucks woke me at four (as they began to do again) I'd get up and follow their thunderous mechanical movements from one window or other vantage point to another, anxiously tracing the course of each can-lugging attendant—anything to occupy my mind.

Just to be doing something, I turned to my correspondence, which had begun to pile up again, but after answering three or four notes (somehow I'd pick the least important ones) I'd feel worn out. You see, I didn't want to write my friends about the block I was having. It was such a bore (whining always is) and, besides, I was *ashamed*. At the same time I couldn't seem to write honestly about anything without bringing my damn block in.

I felt the same thing about calling up or visiting my friends around me in the city. I'd have nothing to show them, nothing to talk about. I didn't want to see anyone. It was a very bad time for me.

Of course I kept on going up to the roof, more than ever now, though even my binoculars were a burden to me and I couldn't bear to lug up my telescope—the weary business of setting it up and all the fussy adjustments I'd have to make made that unthinkable. I even had to *make* myself study the patterns of the lesser stars when the clear nights came which had formerly been such a joy to me.

But then one evening just after dark I went topside and immediately noticed near Cygnus, the Northern Cross, a star that shouldn't have been there. It was a big one, third magnitude at least. It made a slightly crooked extension of the top of the cross as it points toward Cassiopeia. At first I was sure it had to be an earth satellite (I've spotted a few of those)—a big one, like the orbiting silvered balloon they called Echo. Or else it was a light on some weird sort of plane that was hovering high up. But when I held my binoculars on it, I couldn't see it move at all—as a satellite would have done, of course. Then I got really excited, enough to make me bring up my telescope (and *Norton's Star Atlas* too) and set it up.

In the much smaller and more magnified field of that instrument, it didn't move either, but glared there steadily among the lesser points of light, holding position as it inched with the other stars across the field. From the atlas I estimated and noted down its approximate coordinates (right ascension 21 hours and 10 minutes, north declination 48 degrees) and hurried downstairs to call up an astronomer friend of mine and tell him I'd spotted a nova.

Naturally I wasn't thinking at all about the previous ghostly (or whatever) incidents, so perhaps this time the strange thing was that, yes, it did happen again, just as before though with even more brevity, and I sort of went through all the motions of reacting to it, but very unconcernedly, as if it had become a habit, part of the routine of existence, like a step in a stairway that always creaks when your foot hits it but nothing more ever comes of it. I recall saying to myself with a sort of absentminded lightheartedness *Let's give the ghost E for effort; he keeps on trying.*

I got my astronomer friend and, yes, it was a real nova; it had been spotted in Asia and Europe hours earlier and all the astronomers were very busy, oh my, yes.

The nova was a four days' wonder, taking that long to fade down to naked-eye invisibility. Unfortunately, my own excitement at it didn't last nearly that long. Next morning I was confronting my block again. Very much in the spirit of desperation, I decided to go back to my new project and make myself finish it off somehow, force myself to write no matter how bad the stuff seemed to be that I turned out, beginning with an expansion of my original short statement.

But the more I tried to do that, the more I reread those two pages, the thinner and more dubious all the ideas in it seemed to me, the junkier and more hypocritical it got. Instead of adding to it, I wanted to take stuff away, trim it down to a nice big nothing.

To begin with, it was so much a writer's view of things, reducing everything to stories. Of course! What could be more obvious!—or more banal? A military man would explain life in terms of battles, advances and retreats, defeats and victories, and all their metaphorical analogues, presumably with strong emphasis on courage and discipline. Just as a doctor might view history as the product of great men's ailments, whether they were constipated or indigestive, had syphilis or TB—or of subtle diseases that swept nations; the fall of Rome?—lead poisoning from the pipes they used to distribute their aqueducted water! Or a salesman see everything as buying and selling, literally or by analogy. I recalled a 1920s' book about Shakespeare by a salesman. The secret of the Bard's unequaled dramatic power? He was the world's greatest salesman! No, all that stuff about stories was just a figure of speech and not a very clever one.

And then that business about illusion coming in everywhere—what were illusions and illusioning but euphemisms for lies and lying? We had to nourish the illusions of others, didn't we? That meant, in plain language, that we had to flatter them, tell them white lies, go along with all their ignorances and prejudices—very convenient rationalizations for a person who was afraid to speak the truth! Or for someone who was eager to fantasize everything. And granting all that, how had I ever hoped to write about

it honestly in any detail?—strip away from myself and
others, those at all close to me at least, all our pretenses
and boasts, the roles we played, the ways we romanticized
ourselves, the lies we agreed to agree on, the little unspoken
deals we made ("You build me up, I'll build you up"), yes,
strip away all that and show exactly what lay underneath:
the infantile conceits, the suffocating selfishness, the utter
unwillingness to look squarely at the facts of death, torture,
disease, jealousy, hatred, and pain—how had I ever hoped
to speak out about all that, I, an illusioner?

Yes, how to speak out the truth of my real desires? that
were so miserably small, so modest. No vast soul-shaking
passions and heaven-daunting ambitions at all, only the little
joy of watching a shadow's revealing creep along an old brick
wall or the infinitely blue sky of evening, the excitement of
little discoveries in big dictionaries, the small thrill of seeing
and saying, "That's not the dark underside of a distant low
narrow cloudbank between those two buildings, it's a TV
antenna," or "That's not a nova, you wishful thinker, it's
Procyon," the fondling and fondlings of slender, friendly,
cool fingers, the hues and textures of an iris seen up close—
how to admit to such minuscule longings and delights?

And getting still deeper into this stories business, what
was it all but a justification for always *talking* about things
and never *doing* anything? It's been said, "Those who
can, do; those who can't, teach." Yes, and those who can't
even teach, what do they do? Why, they tell stories! Yes,
always talking, never acting, never being willing to dirty
your fingers with the world. Why, at times you had to drive
yourself to pursue even the little pleasures, were satisfied
with fictional or with imagined proxies.

And while we were on that subject, what was all this
business about minds never touching, never being quite able
to? What was it but an indirect, mealy-mouthed way of
confessing my own invariable impulse to flinch away from
life, to avoid contact at any cost—the reason I lived alone
with fantasies, never made a friend (though occasionally
letting others, if they were forceful enough, make friends

with me), preferred a typewriter to a wife, talked, talked, and never did? Yes, for minds, read bodies, and then the truth was out, the secret of the watcher from the sidelines.

I tell you, it got so I wanted to take those thumbed-over two grandiose pages of my "original short statement" and crumple them together in a ball and put that in a brown paper sack along with a lot of coffee grounds and grapefruit rinds and grease, and then repeat the process with larger and larger sacks until I had a Chinese-boxes set of them big around as a large garbage can and lug that downstairs at four o'clock in the morning and when the dark truck stopped in front personally hurl it into that truck's big ass-end mouth and *hear* it all being chewed up and ground to filthy scraps, the whole thing ten times louder than it ever sounded from the sixth floor, knowing that my "wisdom"— acorn or crumpled paper with all its idiot notions was in the very midst and getting more masticated and befouled, more thoroughly destroyed than anything else (while my manikin watched from her window, inscrutable but, I felt sure, approving)—only in that way, I told myself would I be able to tear myself loose from this whole damn minuscule humiliating project, kill it inside my head.

I remember the day my mind generated that rather pitiful grotesque vision (which, incidentally, I half seriously contemplated carrying into reality the next morning). The garbage trucks had wakened me before dawn and I'd been flitting in and out most of the day, unable to get down to anything or even to sit still, and once I'd paused on the sidewalk outside my apartment building, visualizing the truck drawing up in the dark next morning and myself hurling my great brown wad at it, and I'd shot to my manikin in the window the thought, *Well, what do you think of it? Isn't it a good idea?* They had her seated cross-legged in a sort of Lotus position on a great sweep of violet sheeting that wound up behind her to a high shelf holding the bolt. She seemed to receive my suggestion and brood upon it enigmatically.

Predictably, I gravitated to the roof soon after dark, but

without my binoculars and not to study the stars above (although it was a cold evening) or peer with weary curiosity at the window-worlds beyond that so rarely held human figures, or even to hold still and let the lonely roof-calm take hold of me. No, I moved about restlessly from one of my observation stations to another, rather mechanically scanning along the jagged and crenellated skyline, between the upper skyline areas and the lower building-bound ones, that passed for a horizon in the city (though there actually were a couple of narrow gaps to the east through which I could glimpse, from the right places on my roof, very short stretches of the hills behind smoky transbay Oakland). In fact, my mind was so little on what I was doing and so much on my writing troubles that I tripped over a TV-antenna cable I'd known was there and should have avoided. I didn't fall, but it took me three plunging steps to recover my balance, and I realized that if I'd been going in the opposite direction I might well have pitched over the edge, the roof being rather low at that point.

The roof world can be quite treacherous at night, you see. Our roofs especially are apt to be cluttered with little low standpipes and kitchen chimneys and ventilators, things very easy to miss and trip over. It's the worst on clear moonless nights, for then there are no clouds to reflect the city's lights back down, and as a result it's dark as pitch around your feet. (Paradoxically, it's better when it's raining or just been raining for then there's streetlight reflected by the rainclouds and the roof has a wet glisten so that obstructions stand out.) Of course, I generally carry a small flashlight and use it from time to time but, more important, I memorize down to the last detail the layout of any roof visit by night. Only this time that latter precaution had failed me.

It brought me up short to think of how my encounter with the TV cable could have had fatal consequences. It made me see just how very upset I was getting from my writer's block and wonder about unconscious suicidal impulses and accidentally-on-purpose things. Certainly my stalled project was getting to the point where I'd have to do something drastic about it, like seeing a psychiatrist or getting drunk ... or something.

But the physical fear I felt didn't last long, and soon I was prowling about again, though a little less carelessly. I didn't feel comfortable except when I was moving. When I held still, I felt choked with failure (my writing project). And yet at the same time I felt I was on the verge of an important insight, one that would solve all my problems if I could get it to come clear. It seemed to begin with, "If you could sum up all you felt about life and crystallize it in one master insight...", but where it went from there I didn't know. But I knew I wasn't going to get an answer sitting still.

Perhaps, I thought, this whole roof-thing with me expresses an unconscious atavistic faith in astrology, that I will somehow find the answer to any problem in the stars. How quaint of skeptical me!

On the roof at my old place, one of my favorite sights had been the Sutro TV Tower with its score or so of winking red lights. Standing almost a thousand feet high on a hill that is a thousand already, that colorful tripod tower dominates San Francisco from its geographical center and is a measuring rod for the altitude of fogs and cloudbanks, their ceilings and floors. One of my small regrets about moving had been that it couldn't be seen from this new roof. But then only a couple of weeks ago I'd discovered that if you climb the short stairway to the locked door of the boxlike structure hiding the elevator's motor, you see the tops of the Tower's three radio masts poking up over and two miles beyond the top of the glassy Federal Building. Binoculars show the myriad feathery white wires guying them that look like sails— they're nylon so as not to interfere with the TV signals.

This night when I got around to checking the three masts out by their red flashes, I lingered a bit at the top of the skeleton stairs watching them, and as I lingered I saw in the black sky near them a tremorous violet star wink on and then after a long second wink off. I wouldn't have thought of it twice except for the color. Violet is an uncommon color for a light on a building or plane, and it's certainly an uncommon color for a star. All star colors are very faint tinges, for that matter. I've looked at stars there that were supposed to be green and never been able to see it.

But down near the horizon where the air is thicker, anything can happen, I reminded myself. Stars that are white near the zenith begin to flash red and blue, almost any color at all, when they're setting. And suddenly grow dim, even wink out unexpectedly. Still, violet, that was a new one.

And then as I was walking away from the stairs and away from Sutro Tower too, diagonally across the roof toward the other end of it, I looked toward the narrow, window-spangled slim triangle of the Trans-American Pyramid Building, a half mile or so away and I saw for a moment, just grazing its pinnacle, what looked like the same mysterious pulsing violet star. Then it went off or vanished—or went behind the pinnacle, but I couldn't walk it into view again, either way.

What got me the most, perhaps, about that violet dot was the way the light had seemed to *graze* the Pyramid, coming (it was my impression) from a great distance. It reminded me of the last time I'd looked at the planet Mercury through my telescope. I'd followed it for quite a while as it moved down the paling dawn sky, flaring and pulsing (it was getting near the horizon), and then it had reached the top of the Hilton Tower where they have a room whose walls are almost all window, and for almost half a minute I'd continued my observation of it through the glassy corner of the Hilton Hotel. Really, it had seemed most strange to me, that rare planetary light linking me to another building that way, and being tainted by that building's glass, and in a way confounding all my ideas as to what is close and what is far, what clean and what unclean ...

While I was musing, my feet had carried me to another observation place, where in a narrow slot between two close-by buildings I can see the gray open belfry towers of Grace Cathedral on Nob Hill five blocks off. And there, through or *in* one of the belfry's arched openings, I saw the violet star again resting or floating.

A star leaping about the sky that way?—absurd! No, this was something in my eye or eyes. But even as I squeezed my eyes shut and fluttered the lids and shook my head in short tight arcs, my neck muscles taut, to drive the illusion away, that throbbing violet star peered hungrily at me from the embrasure wherein it rested in the gray church's tower.

I've stared at many a star, but never before with the feeling that it was glaring back at me.

But then (something told me) you've never seen a star that came to earth, sliding down that unimaginable distance in a trice and finding itself a niche or hiding hole in the dark world of roofs. The star went out, drew back, was doused.

Do you know that right after that I was afraid to lift my head? or look up at anything? for fear of seeing that flashing violet diamond somewhere it shouldn't be? And that as I turned to move toward the door at the head of the stairs that led down from the roof, my gaze inadvertently encountered the Hilton Tower and I ducked my head so fast that I can't tell you now whether or not I saw a violet gleam in one of that building's windows?

In many ways the world of roofs is like a vast, not too irregular games board, each roof a square, and I thought of the violet light as a sort of super-chess piece making great leaps like a queen (after an initial vast one) and crookedly sidewise moves like a knight, advancing by rushings and edgings to checkmate me.

And I knew that I wanted to get off this roof before I saw a violet glow coming from behind the parapet of one of the airshafts or through the cracks around the locked door to the elevator's motor.

Yet as I moved toward the doorway of escape, the door down, I felt my face irresistibly lifted from between my hunched shoulders and against my neck's flinching opposition until I was peering through painfully winced eye-slits at the cornice of the next building east, the one that overlooked the windows of my apartment.

At first it seemed all dark, but then I caught the faintest violet glint or glimmer, as of something spying down most warily.

From that point until the moment I found myself facing the door to my apartment, I don't remember much at all except the tightness with which my hands gripped the stair-rails going down ... and continued to grip railings tightly as I went along the sixth-story hall, although of course there are no railings there.

I got the door unlocked, then hesitated.

But then my gaze wavered back the way I'd come, toward the stair from the roof, and something in my head began to recite in a little shrill voice, *I met a star upon the stair, A violet star that wasn't there...*

I'd pressed on inside and had the door shut and double-locked and was in the bedroom and reaching for the bedside light before I realized that this time it *hadn't* happened, that at least I'd been spared the half sound and the fugitive dark ghost on this last disastrous night.

But then as I pressed the switch and the light came on with a tiny fizzing crackle and a momentary greenish glint and then shone more brightly and whitely than it should (as old bulbs will when they're about to go—they arc) something else in my head said in a lower voice, *But of course when the right night came it wouldn't make its move until you were safely locked inside and unable to retreat ...*

And then as I stared at the bright doorway and the double-locked door beyond, there came from the direction of the dinette-kitchen a great creaking sound like a giant footstep, no halfsound but something finished off completely, very controlled, very *deliberate*, neither a stamp nor a tramp, and then another and a third, coming at intervals of just about a second, each one a little closer and a little louder, inexorably advancing very much like the footsteps of time in the "Saturn" section of *The Planets*, with more instruments coming in—horns, drums, cymbals, huge gongs and bells— at each mounting repetition of the beat.

I went rigid. In fact, I'm sure my first thought was, *I must hold absolutely still and watch the doorway,* with perhaps the ghost comment riding on it, *Of course! the panic reaction of any animal trapped in its hole.*

And then a fourth footstep and a fifth and sixth, each one closer and louder, so that I'm sure my second real thought was, *The noise I'm hearing must be more than sound, else it would wake the city.* Could it be a physical vibration? Something was resounding deeply through my flesh, but the doorway wasn't shaking visibly and I watched it. Was it the reverberation of something mounting upward from the depths of the earth or my subconscious mind, taking giant strides, smashing upward through the multiple thick floors that protect surface life and daytime consciousness? Or could it be the crashing around me in ruins of my world of certainties, in particular the ideas of that miserable haunting project that had been tormenting me, all of them overset and trodden down together?

And then a seventh, eighth, ninth footstep, almost unbearably intense and daunting, followed by a great grinding pause, a monstrous hesitation. Surely something must appear now, I told myself. My every muscle was tight as terror could make it, especially those of my face and, torus-like, about my eyes (I was especially and rather fearfully conscious of their involuntary blinking). I must have been grimacing fearfully. I remember a fleeting fear of heart attack, every part of me was straining so, putting on effort.

And then there thrust silently, rather rapidly, yet gracefully into the doorway a slender, blunt-ended, sinuous leaden-gray, silver-glistening arm (or other member, I wondered briefly), followed immediately and similarly by the remainder of the figure.

I held still and observed, somehow overcoming the instant urge to flinch, to not-see. More than ever now, I told myself, my survival depended on that, my very life.

How describe the figure? If I say it looked like (and so perhaps was) the manikin in the fabrics shop, you will get completely the wrong impression; you will think of that stuffed and stitched form moving out of its window through the dark and empty store, climbing upstairs, etc., and I knew from the start that that was certainly not the case. In fact, my first thought was, *It is not the manikin, although it has its general form.*

Why? How did I know that? Because I was certain from the first glimpse that it was *alive*, though not in quite the way I was alive, or any other living creatures with which I am familiar. But just the same, that leaden-gray, silver-misted integument was skin, not sewn fabric—there *were* no sewn seams, and I knew where the seams were on the manikin.

How different *its* kind of life from mine? I can only say that heretofore such expressions as "dead-alive," "living dead," and "life in death," were horror-story clichés to me; but now no longer so. (Did the leaden hue of its skin suggest to me a drowned person? I don't think so—there was no suggestion of bloat and all its movements were very graceful.)

Or take its face. The manikin's face had been a blank, a single oval piece of cloth sewn to the sides and top of the head and to the neck. Here there was no edge-stitching and the face was not altogether blank but was crossed by two very faint, fine furrows, one vertical, the other horizontal, dividing the face into four approximately equal quarters, rather like a mandala or the symbol of planet Earth. And now, as I forced myself to scan the horizontal furrow, I saw that it in turn was not altogether featureless. There were two points of violet light three inches apart, very faint but growing brighter the longer I watched them and that moved from side to side a little without alteration in the distance between them, as though scanning me. *That* discovery cost me a pang not to flinch away from, let me tell you!

The vertical furrow in the face seemed otherwise featureless, as did the similar one between the legs with its mute suggestion of femininity. (I had to keep scanning the entire figure over and over, you see, because I felt that if I looked at the violet eye-points too long at any one time they would grow bright enough to blind me, as surely as if I were looking at the midday sun; and yet to look away entirely would be equally, though not necessarily similarly disastrous.)

Or take the matter of height. The window manikin was slenderly short. Yet I was never conscious of looking down at this figure which I faced, but rather a little up.

What else did I glean as this long nightmarish moment prolonged itself almost unendurably, going on and on and on, as though I were trapped in eternity?

Any other distinguishing and different feature? Yes. The sides and the top of the head sprouted thick and glistening black "hair" that went down her back in one straight fall.

(There, I have used the feminine pronoun on the figure, and I will stick with that from now on, although it is a judgment entirely from remembered feeling, or instinct, or whatever, and I can no more point to objective evidence for it than I can in the case of the manikin's imagined gender. And it is a further point of similarity between the two figures although I've said I *knew* they were different.)

What else, then, did I feel about her? That she had come to destroy me in some way, to wipe me out, erase me—I felt a calmer and a colder thing than "kill," there was almost no heat to it at all. That she was weighing me in a very cool fashion, like that Egyptian god which weighs the soul, that she was, yes (And had her leaden-hued skin given me a clue here?), the Button Molder, come to reduce my individuality to its possibly useful raw materials, extinguish my personality and melt me down, recycle me cosmically, one might express it.

And with that thought there came (most incidentally, you might say—a trifling detail) the answer I'd been straining for all evening. It went this way: *If you could sum up all you felt about life and crystallize it in one master insight, you would have said it all and you'd be dead.*

As that truism (?) recited itself in my mind, she seemed to come to a decision and she lithely advanced toward me two silent steps so she was barely a foot away in the arcing light's unnatural white glare, and her slender mitten-hands reached wide to embrace me, while her long black "hair" rose rustlingly and arched forward over her head, in the manner of a scorpion's sting, as though to enshroud us both, and I remember thinking, *However fell or fatal, she has style.* (I also recall wondering why, if she were able to move silently, the nine footsteps had been so loud? Had those great crashes been entirely of mind-stuff, a subjective earthquake? Mind's walls and constructs falling?) In any case her figure had a look of finality about it, as though she were the final form, the ultimate model.

That was the time, if ever (when she came close, I mean), for me to have flinched away or to have shut tight my eyes, but I did not, although my eyes were blurred—they had spurted hot tears at her advance. I felt that if I touched her, or she me, it would be death, the extinguishment of memory and myself (if they be different), but I still clung to the faith (it had worked thus far) that if I didn't move away from and continued to observe her, I might survive. I tried, in fact, to tighten myself still further, to make myself into a man of brass with brazen head and eyes (the latter had cleared now) like Roger Bacon's robot. I was becoming, I thought, a frenzy of immobility and observation.

But even as I thought "immobility" and "touching is death," I found myself leaning a little closer to her (although it made her violet eye-points stingingly bright) the better to observe her lead-colored skin. I saw that it was poreless but also that it was covered by a network of very fine pale lines, like crazed or crackled pottery, as they call it, and that it was this network that gave her skin its silvery gloss ...

As I leaned toward her, she moved back as much, her blunt arms paused in their encirclement, and her arching "hair" spread up and back from us.

At that moment the filament of the arcing bulb fizzled again and the light went out.

Now more than ever I must hold still, I told myself.

For a while I seemed to see her form outlined in faintest ghostly yellow (violet's complement) on the dark and hear the faint rustle of "hair," possibly falling into its original position down her back. There was a still fainter sound like teeth grating. Two ghost-yellow points twinkled a while at eye-height and then faded back through the doorway.

After a long while (the time it took my eyes to accommodate, I suppose) I realized that white fluorescent streetlight was flooding the ceiling through the upward-tilted slats of the blind and filling the whole room with a soft glow. And by that glow I saw I was alone. Slender evidence, perhaps, considering how treacherous my new apartment had proved itself. But during that time of waiting in the dark my feelings had worn out.

Well, I said I was going to tell you about those ten endless seconds and now I have. The whole experience had fewer consequences and less aftermath than you might expect. Most important for me, of course, my whole great nonfiction writing project was dead and buried, I had no inclination whatever to dig it up and inspect it (all my feelings about it were worn out too), and within a few days I was writing stories as if there were no such thing as writer's block. (But if, in future, I show little inclination to philosophize dogmatically, and if I busy myself with trivial and rather childish activities such as haunting games stores and amusement parks and other seedy and picturesque localities, if I write exceedingly fanciful, even frivolous fiction, if I pursue all sorts of quaint and curious people restlessly, if there is at times something frantic in my desire for human closeness, and if I seem occasionally to head out toward the universe, anywhere at all in it, and dive in—well, I imagine you'll understand.)

What do I think about the figure? How do I explain it? (or her)? Well, at the time of her appearance I was absolutely sure that she was real, solid, material, and I think the intentness with which I observed her up to the end (the utterly unexpected silvery skin-crackle I saw at the last instant!) argues for that. In fact, the courage to hold still and fully observe was certainly the only sort of courage I displayed during the whole incident. Throughout, I don't believe I ever quite lost my desire to *know*, to look into mystery. (But why was I so absolutely certain that my life depended on *watching* her? I don't know.)

Was she perhaps an archetype of the unconscious mind somehow made real? the Anima or the Kore or the Hag who lays men out (if those be distinct archetypes)? Possibly, I guess.

And what about that science fiction suggestiveness about her? that she was some sort of extraterrestrial being? That would fit with her linkage with a very peculiar violet star, which (the star) I do *not* undertake to explain in any way! Your guess is as good as mine.

Was she, *vide* Lang, a waking dream?—nightmare, rather? Frankly, I find that hard to believe.

Or was she really the Button Molder? (who in Ibsen's play, incidentally, is an old man with pot, ladle, and mold for melting down and casting lead buttons). That seems just my fancy, though I take it rather seriously.

Any other explanations? Truthfully, I haven't looked very far. Perhaps I should put myself into the hands of the psychics or psychologists or even the occultists, but I don't want to. I'm inclined to be satisfied with what I got out of it. (One of my author friends says it's a small price to pay for overcoming writer's block.)

Oh, there was one little investigation that I did carry out, with a puzzling and totally unexpected result which may be suggestive to some, or merely baffling.

Well, when the light went out in my bedroom, as I've said, the figure seemed to fade back through the doorway into the small hallway with lowered ceiling I've told you about and there fade away completely. So I decided to have another look at the ceilinged-off space. I stood on a chair and pushed aside the rather large square of frosted glass and (somewhat hesitantly) thrust up through the opening my right arm and my head. The space wasn't altogether empty, as it had seemed when I changed the bulb originally. Now the 200-watt glare revealed a small figure lying close behind one of the two-by-four beams of the false ceiling. It was a dust-filmed doll made (I later discovered) of a material called Fabrikoid and stuffed with kapok—it was, in fact, one of the Oz dolls from the 1920's; no, not the Scarecrow, which would surely be the first Oz character you'd think of as a stuffed doll, but the Patchwork Girl.

What do you make of that? I remember saying to myself, as I gazed down at it in my hand, somewhat bemused, *Is this all fantasy ever amounts to? Scraps? Rag dolls?*

Oh, and what about the lay figure in the store window? Yes, she was still there the next morning same as ever. Only they'd changed her position again. She was standing between two straight falls of sheeting, one black, one white, with her mitten hands touching them lightly to either side. And she was bowing her head a trifle, as if she were taking a curtain call.

DO YOU KNOW DAVE WENZEL?

WHEN DON SENIOR said, "There's the bell," and pushed back his chair, Wendy had just upset her bowl, John's hand was creeping across the edge of his plate to join forces with his spoon, and Don Junior had begun to kick the table leg as he gazed into space at an invisible adventure comic.

Katherine spared Don Senior a glance from the exacting task of getting the top layer of mashed carrots back into the bowl while holding off Wendy's jumpy little paws. "I didn't even hear it," she said.

"I'll answer it," Don Senior told her.

Three minutes later Wendy's trancelike spoon-to-mouth routine was operating satisfactorily, John's hand had made a strategic withdrawal, and the rest of the carrots had been wiped up. Don Junior had quietly gone to the window and was standing with his head poked between the heavy rose drapes looking out across the dark lawn—perhaps at more of the invisible adventure, Katherine thought. She watched him fondly. *Little boys are so at the mercy of their dreams. When the "call" comes, they have to answer it. Girls are different.*

Don seemed rather thoughtful when he came back to the table. Suddenly like Don Junior, it occurred to Katherine.

"Who was it, dear?"

He looked at her for a moment, oddly, before replying.

"An old college friend."

"Didn't you invite him in?"

He shook his head, glancing at the children. "He's gone down in the world a long way," he said softly. "Really pretty disreputable."

Katherine leaned forward on her elbows. "Still, if he was once a friend—"

"I'm afraid you wouldn't like him," he said decisively, yet it seemed to Katherine with a shade of wistfulness.

"Did I ever meet him?" she asked.

"No. His name's Dave Wenzel."

"Did he want to borrow money?"

Don seemed not to hear that question. Then, "Money? Oh, no!"

"But what did he want to see you about?"

Don didn't answer. He sat frowning.

The children had stopped eating. Don Junior turned from the window. The drapes dropped together behind him.

"Did he go away, Dad?" Don Junior asked.

"Of course."

It was quiet for several moments. Then Don Senior said, "He must have cut around the other side of the house."

"How strange," Katherine said. Then, smiling quickly at the children, she asked, "Have you ever seen him since college, Don?"

"Not since the day I graduated."

"Let's see, how long is that?" She made a face of dismay, mockingly. "Oh Lord, it's getting to be a long time. Fourteen, fifteen years. And this is the same month."

Again her husband looked at her intently. "As it happens," he said, "it's exactly the same day."

* * * *

When Katherine dropped in at her husband's office the next morning, she was thinking about the mysterious Mr. Wenzel. Not because the incident had stuck in her mind particularly, but because it had been recalled by a chance meeting on the train coming up to town, with another college friend of her husband.

Katherine felt good. It is pleasant to meet an old beau and find that you still attract him and yet have the reassuring knowledge that all the painful and exciting uncertainties of youth are done with.

How lucky I am to have Don, she thought. *Other wives have to worry about women (I wonder how Carleton Hare's wife makes out?) and failure (Is Mr. Wenzel married?) and moods and restlessness and a kind of little-boy rebelliousness against the business of living. But Don is different. So handsome, yet so true. So romantic, yet so regular. He has a quiet heart.*

She greeted the secretary. "Is Mr. McKenzie busy?"

"He has someone with him now. A Mr. Wenzel, I think."

Katherine did not try to conceal her curiosity. "Oh, tell me about him, would you? What does he look like?"

"I really don't know," Miss Korshak said, smiling. "Mr. McKenzie told me there would be a Mr. Wenzel to see him, and I think he came in a few minutes ago, while I was away from the desk. I know Mr. McKenzie has a visitor now, because I heard him talking to someone. Shall I ring your husband, Mrs. McKenzie?"

"No, I'll wait a while," Katherine sat down and pulled off her gloves.

A few minutes later Miss Korshak picked up some papers and went off. Katherine wandered to the door of her husband's office. She could hear his voice every now and then, but she couldn't make out what he was saying. The panel of frosted glass showed only vague masses of light and shadow. She felt a sudden touch of uneasiness. She lifted her hand, which was dusted with freckles almost the same shade as her hair, and knocked.

All sound from beyond the door ceased. Then there were footsteps and the door opened.

Don looked at her blankly for a moment. Then he kissed her.

She went ahead of him into the gray-carpeted office.

"But where is Mr. Wenzel?" she asked, turning to him with a gesture of half-playful amazement.

"He just happened to be finished," Don said lightly, "so he left by the hall door."

"He must be an unusually shy person—and very quiet," Katherine said. "Don, did you arrange with him last night to come and see you here?"

"In a way."

"What is he after, Don?"

Her husband hesitated. "I suppose you could describe him as a kind of crank."

"Does he want to publish some impossible article in your magazine?"

"No, not exactly." Don grimaced and waved a hand as if in mild exasperation. "Oh, you know the type, dear. The old college friend who's a failure and who wants to talk over old times. The sort of chap who gets a morbid pleasure out of dwelling on old ideas and reviving old feelings. Just a born botherer." And he quickly went on to ask her about her shopping and she mentioned running into Carleton Hare, and there was no more talk of Dave Wenzel.

* * * *

But when Katherine got home later that afternoon after picking up the children at Aunt Martha's, she found that Don had called to say not to wait dinner. When he finally did get in he looked worried. As soon as the children were asleep, Don and Katherine settled themselves in the living room in front of the fireplace. Don made a fire, and the sharp odor of burning hardwood mingled with the scent of freesias set in a dull blue bowl on the mantelpiece under the Monet.

As soon as the flames were leaping, Katherine asked seriously, "Don, what is this thing about Dave Wenzel?"

He started to make light of the question, but she interrupted, "No, really, Don. Ever since you came back from the door last night, you've had something on your mind. And it isn't at all like you to turn away old friends or shoo them out of your office, even if they have become a bit seedy. What is it, Don?"

"It's nothing to worry about, really."

"I'm not worried, Don. I'm just curious." She hesitated. "And maybe a bit shuddery."

"Shuddery?"

"I have an eerie feeling about Wenzel, perhaps because of the way he disappeared so quietly both times, and then—oh, I don't know, but I do want to know about him, Don."

He looked at the fire for a while and its flames brought orange tints to his skin. Then he turned to her with a shamefaced smile and said, "Oh, I don't mind telling you about it. Only it's pretty silly. And it makes me look silly, too."

"Good," she said with a laugh, turning toward him on the couch and drawing her feet under her. "I've always wanted to hear something silly about you, Don."

"I don't know," he said. "You might even find it a little disgusting. And very small-boy. You know, swearing oaths and all that."

She had a flash of inspiration. "You mean the business of it being fifteen years, to the exact day?"

He nodded. "Yes, that was part of it. There was some sort of agreement between us. A compact."

"Oh good, a mystery," she said with lightly mocked childishness, not feeling as secure as she pretended.

He paused. He reached along the couch and took her hand. "You must remember," he said, squeezing it, "that the Don McKenzie I'm going to tell you about is not the Don McKenzie you know now, not even the one you married. He's a different Don, younger, much less experienced, rather shy and gauche, lonely, a great dreamer, with a lot of mistaken ideas about life and a lot of crazy notions ... of all sorts."

"I'll remember," she said, returning the pressure of his fingers. "And Dave Wenzel, how am I to picture him?"

"About my age, of course. But with a thinner face and deep-sunk eyes. He was my special friend." He frowned. "You know, you have your ordinary friends in college, the ones you room with, play tennis, go on dates. They're generally solid and reliable, your kind. But then there's a special friend, and oddly enough he's not so apt to be solid and reliable."

Again he frowned. "I don't know why, but he's apt to be a rather disreputable character, someone you're a bit ashamed of and wouldn't want your parents to meet.

"But he's more important to you than anyone, because he shares your crazier dreams and impulses. In fact, you're probably attracted to him in the first place because you feel he possesses those dreams and impulses even more strongly than you do."

"I think I understand," Katherine said wisely, not altogether certain that she did. She heard Don Junior call in his sleep and she listened a moment and looked attentively at her husband. *How extraordinarily bright his eyes are*, she thought.

"Dave and I would have long bull sessions in my room and we'd go for long walks at night, all over the campus, down by the lake front, and through the slum districts. And always the idea between us was to keep alive a wonderful, glamorous dream. Sometimes we'd talk about the books we liked and the weirder things we'd seen. Sometimes we'd make up crazy experiences and tell them to each other as if they were true. But mostly we'd talk about our ambitions, the amazing, outrageous things we were going to do someday."

"And they were—?"

He got up and began to pace restlessly. "That's where it begins to get so silly," he said. "We were going to be great scholars and at the same time we were going to tramp all over the world and have all sorts of adventures."

How like Don Junior, she thought. *But Don Junior's so much younger. When he goes to college, will he still ... ?*

"We were going to experience danger and excitement in every form. I guess we were going to be a couple of Casanovas, too."

Her humorous "Hmf!" was lost as he hurried on, and despite herself, his words began to stir her imagination.

"We were going to do miraculous things with our minds, like a mystic does. Telepathy. Clairvoyance. We were going to take drugs. We were going to find out some great secret that's been hidden ever since the world began. I think if Dave said, 'We'll go to the moon, Don,' I'd have believed him."

He came to a stop in front of the fire. Slitting his eyes, he said slowly, as if summing up, "We were like knights preparing to search for some modern, unknown, and rather dubious grail. And someday in the course of our adventuring we were going to come face to face with the reality behind life and death and time and those other big ideas."

For a moment, for just a moment, Katherine seemed to feel the spinning world under her, as if the walls and ceiling had faded, to see her husband's big-shouldered body jutting up against a background of black space and stars.

She thought, *Never before has he seemed so wonderful. And never so frightening.*

He shook his finger at her, almost angrily, she felt. "And then one night, one terrible night before I graduated, we suddenly saw just how miserably weak we were, how utterly impossible of realizing the tiniest of our ambitions. There we were, quite floored by all the minor problems of money and jobs and independence and sex, and dreaming of the sky! We realized that we'd have to establish ourselves in the world, learn how to deal with people, become seasoned men of action, solve all the minor problems, before we could ever tackle the big quest. We gave ourselves fifteen years to bring all those small things under control. Then we were to meet and get going."

Katherine didn't know it was going to happen, but she suddenly started to laugh, almost hysterically. "Excuse me, dear," she managed to say after a moment, noting Don's puzzled expression, "but you and your friend did so get the cart before the horse! But you had a chance for some adventure, at least you were free. But you had to go and pick on the time when you'd be most tied down." And she started to laugh again.

For an instant Don looked hurt, then he began to laugh with her. "Of course, dear, I understand all that now, and it seems the most ridiculous thing in the world to me. When I opened the door last night and saw Dave standing there expectantly in a sleazy coat, with a lot less hair than I remembered, I was completely dumbfounded. Of course I'd forgotten about our compact years ago, long before you and I were married."

She started to laugh again. "And so I was one of your minor problems, Don?" she asked teasingly.

"Of course not, dear!" He pulled her up from the couch and hugged her boisterously. Katherine quickly closer her mind to the thought, *He's changed since I laughed—he's shut something up inside him,* and welcomed the sense of security that flooded back into her at his embrace.

When they were settled again, she said, "Your friend must have been joking when he came around last night. There are people who will wait years for a laugh."

"No, he was actually quite serious."

"I can't believe it. Incidentally, just how well has he done at fulfilling his end of the bargain—I mean, establishing himself in the world?"

"Not well at all. In fact, so badly that, as I say, I didn't want him in the house last night."

"Then I'll bet it's the financial backing for his quest that he's thinking about."

"No, I honestly don't think he's looking for money."

Katherine leaned toward him. She was suddenly moved by the old impulse to measure every danger, however slight. "Tell you what, Don. You get your friend to spruce up a bit and we'll invite him to dinner. Maybe arrange a couple of parties. I'll bet that if he met some women it would make all the difference."

"Oh no, that's out of the question," Don said sharply. "He isn't that sort of person at all. It wouldn't work."

"Very well," Katherine said, shrugging. "But in that case how are you going to get rid of him?"

"Oh, that'll be easy," Don said.

"How did he take it when you refused?"

"Rather hard," Don admitted.

"I still can't believe he was serious."

Don shook his head. "You don't know Dave."

Katherine caught hold of his hand. "Tell me one thing," she said. "How seriously, how really seriously, did you take this ... compact, when you made it?"

He looked at the fire before he said, "I told you I was a different Don McKenzie then."

"Don," she said, and her voice dropped a little, "is there anything dangerous about this? Is Dave altogether honorable—or sane? Are you going to have any trouble getting rid of him?"

"Of course not, dear! I tell you it's all done with." He caught her in his arms. But for a moment Katherine felt that his voice, though hearty, lacked the note of complete certainty.

* * * *

And during the next few days she had reason to think that her momentary feeling had been right. Don stayed late at the office a little more often than usual, and twice when she called him during the day, he was out and Miss Korshak didn't know where to locate him. His explanations, given casually, were always very convincing, but he didn't look well and he'd acquired a nervous manner. At home he began to answer the phone ahead of her, and one or two of the conversations he held over it were cryptic.

Even the children, Katherine felt, had caught something of the uneasiness.

She found herself studying Don Junior rather closely, looking for traits that might increase her understanding of his father. She went over in her mind what she knew of Don Senior's childhood and was bothered at how little there was. (*But isn't that true of many city childhood's?* she asked herself.) Just a good, conscientious boy, brought up mostly by two rather stuffy yet emotional aunts. The only escapade she remembered hearing about was once when he'd stayed at a movie all afternoon and half the night.

She was up against the realization that a whole section of her husband's thoughts were locked off from her. And since this had never happened before she was frightened. Don loved her as much as ever, she was sure of that. But something was eating at him.

Weren't success and a loving wife and children, she wondered, enough for a man? Enough in a serious way, that is, for anyone might have his frivolities, his trivial weaknesses (though actually Don had neither). Or was there something more, something beyond that? Not religion, not power, not fame, but ...

* * * *

She badly needed more people around, so when Carleton Hare called up she impulsively invited him to dinner. His wife, Carleton said, was out of town.

It was one of those evenings when Don called up at the last minute to say he wouldn't be able to get home for dinner. (No, he couldn't make it even for Carleton -something had come up at the printer's. Awfully glad Carleton had come, though. Hoped very much to see him later in the evening, but might be very late—don't wait up.)

After the children were shepherded off and Katherine and Carleton had paraded rather formally into the living room, she asked, "Did you know a college friend of Don's named Dave Wenzel?"

Katherine got the impression that her question had thrown Carleton off some very different line of conversation he had been plotting in his mind. "No, I didn't," he said a little huffily. "Name's a bit familiar, but I don't think I ever met the man."

But then he seemed to reconsider. He turned toward Katherine, so that the knees of his knife-creased gray trousers were a few inches closer to hers along the couch.

"Wait a minute," he said, "Don did have an odd friend

of some sort. I think his name may have been Wenzel. Don sometimes bragged about him—how brilliant this man was, what wild exciting experiences he'd had. But somehow, none of us fellows ever met him."

"I hope you won't mind my saying this," he continued with a boyish chuckle that startled Katherine a bit, it was so perfect. "But Don was rather shy and moody at college, not very successful and inclined to be put out about it. Some of us even thought this friend of his—yes, I'm sure the name was Wenzel—was just an imaginary person he'd cooked up in his mind to impress us with."

"You did?" Katherine asked.

"Oh yes. Once we insisted on his bringing this Wenzel around to a party. He agreed, but then it turned out that Wenzel had left town on some mysterious and important jaunt."

"Mightn't it have been that he was ashamed of Wenzel for some reason?" Katherine asked.

"Yes, I suppose it might," Carleton agreed doubtfully. "Tell me, Kat," he went on, "how do you get along with a moody, introspective person like Don?"

"Very well."

"Are you happy?" Carleton asked, his voice a little deeper.

Katherine smiled. "I think so."

Carleton's hand, moving along the couch, covered hers. "Of course you are," he said. "An intelligent, well-balanced person like yourself wouldn't be anything else but happy. But how vivid is that happiness? How often, for instance, do you realize what a completely charming woman you are? Aren't there times—not all the time, of course -when, with a simpler, more vital sort of person, you could..."

She shook her head, looking into his eyes with a childlike solemnity. "No, Carleton, there aren't," she said, gently withdrawing her hand from under his.

Carleton blinked, and his head, which had been moving imperceptibly toward hers, stopped with a jerk. Katherine's lips twitched and she started to talk about the children.

During the rest of the evening Carleton didn't by

any means give up the attack. But he carried it on in an uninspired fashion, as if merely to comply with the tenets of male behavior. Katherine wanted to burst out laughing, he was so solemn and dogged about it, and once he caught her smiling at him rather hysterically, and he put on an injured look. She tried to pump him, rather cruelly, she felt, about Dave Wenzel and Don, but he apparently knew nothing beyond what he had told her. He left rather early. Katherine couldn't help suspecting that he was relieved to go.

She went to bed. Her somewhat amusement at Carleton Hare faded. The minutes dragged on, as she waited for Don.

A voice woke her. A mumbling distant voice. She was hot with sleep and the dark walls of the bedroom pulsated painfully, as if they were inside her eyes.

At first she thought it was Don Junior. She felt her way into the hall. Then she realized that the voice was coming from downstairs. It would go on for a while, rising a bit, then it would break off several seconds before starting again. It seemed to pulsate with the darkness.

She crept downstairs barefooted. The house was dark. Dimly she could see the white rectangle of the door to Don's study. It was closed and no light showed through the cracks. Yet it was from there that the voice seemed to be coming.

"For the last time I tell you, Dave, I won't. Yes, I've gone back on my word, but I don't care. The whole thing is off."

Katherine's hand trembled on the smooth round of the stair post. It was Don's voice, but tortured, frantic, and yet terribly controlled, like she had never heard it before.

"What's a promise made by a child? Besides, the whole thing's ridiculous, impossible."

She tiptoed toward the door, step by step.'

"All right then, Dave, I believe you. We could do everything you say. But I don't want to. I'm going to hold fast to my own."

Now she was crouching by the door and she still couldn't hear the answering voice in the silence. But her imagination supplied it: a whisper that had strength in it, and richness, and mockery, and a certain oily persuasiveness.

"What do I care if my life is drab and monotonous?" Her husband's voice was growing louder. "I tell you I don't want the far cities, and dark streets shimmering with danger. I don't want the gleaming nights and the burning days. I don't want space. I don't want the stars!"

Again silence, and again that suggestion of a resonant whisper, adrip with beauty and evil.

Then, "All right, so the people I know are miserable little worms, men of cardboard and dusty, dry-mouthed puppets. I don't mind. Do you understand, I don't mind! I don't want to meet the people whose emotions are jewels, whose actions are sculptured art. I don't want to know the men like gods. I don't want my mind to meet their minds with a crash like music or the sea."

Katherine was trembling again. Her hand went up and down the door like a moth, hovering, not quite touching it.

"So my mind's small, is it? Well, let it be. Let someone else's consciousness swell and send out tentacles. I don't want the opium dreams. I don't want the more-than-opium dream. I don't care if I never glimpse the great secrets of far shores. I don't care if I die with blinders over my eyes. I don't care, you hear, I don't care!"

Katherine swayed, as if a great wind were blowing through the door. She writhed as if each word scalded her.

"But I tell you I don't want any woman but Kat!" Her husband's voice was filled with agony. "I don't care how young and beautiful they are. I don't care if they're only twenty. Kat's enough for me. Do you hear that, Dave? Kat's enough. Dave! Stop it, Dave! Stop it!"

There was pounding. Katherine realized she had thrown herself against the door and was beating on it. She grabbed the knob, snatched it open, and darted inside.

There was a whirling of shadows, a gasping exclamation, three pounding footsteps, a great crash of glass, a whish of leaves. Something struck her shoulder and she staggered sideways, found the wall, groped along it, pushed the light switch.

The light hurt. In it, Don's face looked peeled. He was

turning back from the big picture window, now a jagged hole of darkness through which the cool night was pouring and a green twig intruded. In it, only a few daggers and corners of glass remained. A chair lay on the floor, overturned. Don stared at her as if she were a stranger.

"Did he ... jump out?" she asked shakily, wetting her lips.

Don nodded blindly. Then a look of rage grew on his face. He started toward her, taking deliberate steps, swaying a little.

"Don!"

He stopped. Slowly recognition replaced rage. Then he suddenly grimaced with what might have been shame or agony, or both, and turned away.

She moved to him quickly, putting her arms around him. "Oh, what is it, Don?" she asked. "Please, Don, let me help you."

He shrank away from her.

"Don," she said hollowly after a moment, forcing the words, "if you really want to go off with this man..."

His back, turned to her, writhed. "No! No!"

"But then what is it, Don? How can he make you act this way? What sort of hold does he have on you?"

He shook his head hopelessly.

"Tell me, Don, please, how can he torment you so? Of please, Don!"

Silence.

"But what are we going to do, Don? He ... oh he must be insane," she said, looking uneasily at the window, "to do a thing like that. Will he come back? Will he lurk around? Will he ... oh, don't you see, Don, we can't have it like that. There are the children. Don, I think we should call the police."

He looked around quickly, his face quite calm. "Oh no, we can't do that," he said quietly. "Under no circumstances."

"But if he keeps on..."

"No," Don said, looking at her intently. "I'll settle the whole matter, myself, Kat. I don't want to talk about it now, but I promise you that it will be settled. And there will be no more incidents like tonight. You have my word on it." He paused. "Well, Kat?"

For a moment she met his eyes. Then, unwillingly—she had the queer feeling that it was the pressure of his stare that made her do it—she dipped her head.

* * * *

During the next two weeks there were many times when she desperately wished she had insisted on bringing things to a head that night, for it marked the beginning of a reign of terror that was all the more unnerving because it could not be laid to any very definite incidents. Shadows on the lawn, small noises at the windows, the suggestion of a lurking figure, doors open that should be closed—there is nothing conclusive about such things. But they nibble at courage.

The children felt it, of that Katherine was sure. Don Junior started asking questions about witches and horrors, and he wasn't quite so brave about going upstairs at night. Sometimes she caught him looking at her or at his father in a way that made her wish she didn't have to be so untroubled and cheerful in his presence and could talk to him more freely. John came to share their bed more often in the middle of the night, and Wendy would wake whimpering.

Don's behavior was very reassuring for the first few days. He was brisk and businesslike, not moody at all, and had an unusually large supply of jokes for the children and of complimentary remarks for her—though Katherine couldn't shake the feeling that these were all carefully prepared and cost him considerable effort. But she couldn't get near him. He showed an artfulness quite unlike his ordinary self at avoiding serious discussions. The two or three times she finally blurted out some question about Dave Wenzel or his feelings, he would only frown and say quickly, "Please don't let's talk about it now. It only makes it harder for me."

She tried to think herself close to him, but when a contact between you and the man you love is broken, thoughts aren't as much help. And when you feel that the love is still there, that only makes it the more baffling, for it leaves you nothing to bite against. Don was slipping away from her. He was growing dim. And there was nothing she could do to stop it.

And always the long brittle train of her thoughts would be snapped by some small but ominous incident that set her nerves quivering.

Then the reassuring aspects of Don's behavior began to fade. He became silent and preoccupied, both with her and with the children. His emotions began to show in his face—gloomy, despairing ones, they seemed. The children noticed that, too. At dinner Katherine's heart would sink when she saw Don Junior's glance lift surreptitiously from his plate to his father. And Don didn't look at all well, either. He got thinner and there were dark circles under his eyes, and his movements became fretful and nervous.

He had a habit, too, of staying near the hall when he was at home, so that it was always he who answered the door as well as the telephone.

Sometimes he'd go out late at night, saying he was restless and needed a walk. He might be home in fifteen minutes—or four hours.

Still Katherine made efforts to get through to him. But he seemed to sense what she was going to say, and the look of pain and misery on his face would choke off her question.

Finally she could stand her fear and uncertainty no longer. It was something Don Junior told her that gave her courage to act. He came home from school with a story of a man who had been standing outside the playground at recess and who had walked behind him on the way home.

That evening before dinner, she went to Don and said simply, "I am going to call the police."

He looked at her closely for several seconds and then replied in as calm a voice as hers, "Very well; I only ask you to wait until tomorrow morning."

"It's no use, Don," she said. "I've got to do it. Since you won't tell me what this cloud is that's hanging over you, I must take my own precautions. I don't know what you'll tell the police when they talk to you, but..."

"I'll tell them everything," he said, "tomorrow morning."

"Oh, Don," she said, stiffening her face to hold back emotion. "I don't want to hurt you, but you leave me nothing else to do. I gave in to you before; I gave you time to settle the matter in your own way. I was willing to let whatever it is be a closed door, so long as it was closed, but things have only got worse. If I give in to you now, you'll ask me to give in to you again tomorrow morning. And I can't stand any more of it."

"That's not fair," he said judiciously. "I never set a date before. I am setting one now. It's a very small thing I'm asking of you, Kat. Just a few more hours in which to" -suddenly his face grew very hard—"settle this matter for once and all. Please give me those hours, Kat."

After a moment she sighed and her shoulders slumped. "Very well," she said. "Except I won't have the children in the house tonight. I'll take them to Aunt Martha's."

"That's quite all right," he said. He bowed his head to her and walked up the stairs.

* * * *

Calling Aunt Martha, spinning an explanation for her, convincing the children that this was the jolliest of impromptu expeditions—these were tasks that Katherine welcomed for the momentary relief they gave. And there were a couple of moments, driving over to Martha's with the children all piled in the front seat beside her, when she felt almost carefree.

She drove home immediately, after repeating to Aunt Martha her story of a sudden invitation she and Don had gotten to a city party given by a publisher whose favor Don particularly courted. When she arrived, Don was gone.

The house had never seemed so empty, so like a trap. But as she crossed the threshold, she gave over the control of herself to that same cold willpower she had depended on earlier that evening in talking to Don. She didn't wander through the house; she didn't let herself stand aimlessly for a moment. She picked up a book and sat down with it in the living room, reading the meaningless words carefully. She did not let her gaze stray occasionally toward the dark windows and doorways, though she knew that would have been normal. That was all.

At ten-thirty she put down her book, went upstairs, bathed, went down to the kitchen, heated some milk, drank it, and went up to bed.

She lay on her back, wide-eyed, motionless, almost without thoughts. Occasionally the lights of a car would sweep across the ceiling. Very rarely, for it was a still night, the leaves outside the window would whisper. She felt that for the rest of her life this sort of trance would substitute for sleep.

It must have been at least three when she heard the key grate in the lock of the front door. She did not move. She heard the door open and close, then cautious steps coming up the stairs and along the hall. A dark shape paused outside the half-open bedroom door, then went on. There was the snick of a light switch and the hall glowed dimly. A little later came the sound of running water.

Katherine got up quietly and looked into the hall. The bathroom door was open and the light was on. Don was standing in front of the wash basin, holding something wrapped in newspapers. She watched him unwrap something that flashed—a long hunting knife.

He inspected it minutely, then laid it down on the newspapers.

He took off his coat and looked it all over, particularly the sleeves. He frowned, soaped a washrag, and rubbed one of the cuffs. Likewise he inspected his trousers and shirt.

He took off his shoes and carefully rubbed them all over, including the soles, with the washrag.

He looked over his hands, and bare arms inch by inch. Then he critically studied his face in the mirror, twisting it this way and that.

Katherine swayed. Her wrist knocked the wall. He jerked around, tense, on guard. She went toward him, taking short unsteady steps. "Don," she gasped out, "what have you done?"

There came over his face a look of utter tiredness and apathy. He blinked his eyes flickeringly.

"I did what you wanted me to," he said dully, not looking at her. "I got rid of Wenzel. He'll never trouble you again."

Her gasps formed the words. "No. No."

He lifted his hand toward her. "Dave Wenzel is dead, Katherine," he said very distinctly. "I have finished off Dave Wenzel forever. Do you understand me, Katherine?"

As he spoke the words, the wild tiredness seemed to drain from his eyes, to be replaced (as if he had spoken words of exorcism) by a clear steadiness that she hadn't seen in them for weeks.

But Katherine was no longer just looking into his eyes. The clarity between them had seeped into her mind and she was thinking. *Who was Dave Wenzel? I never heard the doorbell the first time. It never rang. Don Junior didn't see him go, Miss Korshak didn't see him come, Carleton Hare never saw him. I never saw his shadow, I never heard his voice. Don broke the window with the chair, and—the knife is unstained.*

There never was a Dave Wenzel! My husband was hounded by an imaginary man—and now he had exorcized him by an imaginary murder.

"Dave Wenzel is dead," Don repeated. "He had to die—there was no other way. Do you want to call the police?"

She slowly shook her head.

"Good," he said. "That leaves just one more thing, Katherine. You must never ask me about him: who he was or how he died. We must never talk about him again."

Again she slowly nodded.

"And now," he said, "I'd like to go to bed. I'm really quite tired." He started toward the bedroom.

"Wait, Don," she said uncertainly. "The children—"

He turned in the bedroom door. "—are at Aunt Martha's,"

he finished for her, smiling sleepily. "Did you think I'd forgotten that, Kat?"

She shook her head and came toward him smiling, glad in the present, choking down the first of the thousand questions she would never be able to ask him.

A VISITOR FROM BACK EAST

*D*EAR JOE ... *How is sunny Cal? You got the laugh on us here in snowy Chi. Your new canyon home as they called it looked very sharp in the Sports Gazette picture. Give my regards to the sucker gamblers and slots addicts who paid for it. It will sure impress your new girl friends and you will have fun with them there, won't you, Joe?*

The Jag in the picture looked sharp too. But don't drive it too fast on those switchback canyon roads. You never were as hot a driver as you thought you were Joe and we are all getting older. Yours truly has given up stock car racing. Getting much too rough for this old girl.

And you looked sharp too Joe. Only thinner and a little older like I said. Take care of your nerves Joe. As you know better than anybody some people have weaker nerves and brains than others but even the strongest crack if they're not careful. Hey Joe you're getting a lot darker like all old guys like you. I'm just kidding Joe I know it's the sun bathing. And you're not ole Joe just mature.

That's enough chatter for this letter. I'm writing to tell you Eleanore died yesterday. The funeral will be from the mental hospital tomorrow. She would want it that way having been four years in the place. Also by her wish she'll be buried in that white leather coat you gave her. That was the only money you ever spent on her wasn't it Joe? She even had to pay for her abortion.

It was nephritis. My little sister passed away in great pain but she talked about you to the end in her cuckoo way. She said to me Marge don't let Joe past the door I haven't my face on. As if you'd come anywhere near her. She did look a slob poor Nore. Even if loonies try to dress nice it looks wrong on them and she never cared except for always wanting to wear your white leather coat even to meals and bed when they'd let her. You remember how much time she spent on her lovely blonde hair Joe? Well it got to look like a big rat's nest. And she'd got very fat these last months and the nephritis didn't help. Who'd expect it too?

I was with her all the time at the end. She always would mind me when I was around. Too bad I was away on the racing circuit when you got at her but that's the way things happen.

Once she reached her hand out of bed and said Give this diamond to Joe to remember me by. It was just a hunk of coal and I told her so. I don't know how she got it. She said It's a diamond that didn't get squeezed enough. Makes sense when you think of it. Funny. I took it out with me when I went back to the motel at Cargo that night and I threw it in a ditch because I know you're not sentimental Joe.

Just before she went she said When I get to heaven I'm going to hit the first beauty parlor and stay there till Joe comes. For his sake I'll have them fix me up just like I was.

I don't know about heaven but I don't think the makeup man at Cargo will be able to do much for her before they plant her.

I stayed with her all last night after she went. They tried to put me out but you know me Joe stubborn. Just before morning she belched and tried to sit up like she had remembered some unfinished business or maybe just wanted to go to the bathroom. The guard said they all do it rigor mortis. It would make some people wonder but we aren't superstitious are we Joe?

Yours truly,
MARGE DOVGARD

P.S. There's one thing about your new canyon home Joe it looks lonely. I'm not thinking of you Joe you never did want people around unless you had a use for them business or pleasure but I'm thinking of the new girls especially the flippy ones.

I know your tastes Joe you've always had a weakness for the ones with weak minds because they're easier to get into bed and then boot out the door. Don't scare them Joe go easy on them and at least help them

with their abortions. Remember Nore and
try to be halfway decent Joe you've got the
money now. Well I'll quit preaching.

JOE GRIMALDI grinned as he crumpled the three closely
written pages into a ball and pitched it across the black slate
flagstones into the crackling fire. It tipped the top of the
chain-net curtain but still went in, like what he'd learned at
the tennis club to call a let service.

He was glad now that he hadn't scaled the envelope into
the flames unopened, as he'd been tempted to do when
he saw the return address. Marge had been writing him
for three years to give him the latest disgusting dope on
Eleanore, trying to rub his nose in it because she'd got the
crazy idea he was responsible, but this time Marge had
really had something to report.

It sure set him up to know that Nore had finally popped
off. No man with any feelings likes to think of a girl he's
actually made love to drooling around some asylum, a big
fat slob. Why, there had been times when some hot little
sexpot's squeal had reminded him of Nore and taken away
half the pleasure for him. Now that wouldn't happen any
more. And of course it was better this way for Nore too.

A funny gal, Marge—a little toughie when she was under
the roll-bar of a stock car and with an eye for the boys too
then, but a sanctimonious resentful old battleaxe where her
little sister had been concerned. Not that Marge had been
any bigger than Nore or more than a couple of years older,
but she'd always been the boss—when she'd been around.

Sharp too. That crack about his tastes hadn't been so
far off, though not for the reasons she gave. He always had
gone for the babes with sketchily furnished top stories -it
somehow made them cuter; you itched to rough them up
and make those baby eyes widen.

But Marge had a hell of a nerve saying he hadn't helped
on Nore's abortion. Why, he'd given Nore the phone number
and the password! And gin on the rocks had had more to do
with Nore going batty than any part of her love life.

Nore had been a sweet kid, though, before she'd gone off her rocker. And to think that she'd stayed nuts about him to the very end. It sure bucked a man up to hear something like that. Joe Grimaldi smiled and for a moment his eyes grew dreamy.

Nore was no more good to anyone now, though. He checked the postmark on the envelope—yep, she'd been under the ground a whole day already. He rolled the torn envelope into a smaller ball and pitched it after the letter. It cleared the net and fell in the backhand corner of the blaze—a service ace.

That evening Joe got a long-distance call. From Springfield Missouri the operator said, but the connection was bad and he heard nothing but a sort of wailing, like a wind in the wires. Before he could get the operator to fix it the party making the call hung up. Joe often got long distance calls, not all of them completed. He thought nothing of it.

But the next night, as he was having himself a lonely highball in front of the fire, he got another. It was unusual for Joe to spend two consecutive evenings alone, but the babe he'd been all set to push over—a lovely little dimwit with lots of money and a taste for Benzedrine—had called him at the last minute to tell him that her father and mother had unexpectedly descended on her from San Francisco and she simply had to spend one evening with them to pamper their parental anxieties, and would Joe wait until tomorrow night please?

Joe had said yes grudgingly and then after mature consideration had decided he didn't want to bother ringing Agnes and having her send a girl to fill in.

This long distance call was from Amarillo, Texas, and it was exactly like the other one—just a lot of wailing and sobbing on the wire, followed by the party hanging up. And maybe—only maybe—in the middle of the sobbing a girl crying, "Joe! Joe!" in a voice like Nore's—not that every other fading sexpot Nore's age didn't have the same voice from imitating the same movie queen.

Hell, he wouldn't even have thought of Nore except for

the letter that had come from Chicago that morning—right
next to the classy heartwarming invite to become a senior
lifetime member of the tennis club. There hadn't been
anything in the Chicago envelope but a torn-out column of
death notices with one circled with black grease pencil. The
fine print had read:

> DOVGARD, Eleanore, beloved
> sister of Marge. Cargo Mortuary,
> Cargo, Ill. Private

That bitch Marge was still trying to rub it in.

He got out a road map. Yep, Springfield and Amarillo
were both on Route 66 and at about the right distances for
stops one and two in a four-day drive from Chicago to L.A.
Let's see, stop three would be Flagstaff, Arizona, most likely.
But what the hell, it was only in corny horror films that
crazy women walked out of mortuaries or clawed their way
out of graves with the dirt cascading off their prize white
leather coats and got into the nearest unlocked empty car
and headed west.

Joe Grimaldi displayed both his fair-mindedness and his
complete lack of superstitious fear by laughing at himself.
The laughter was quite loud, bouncing back and forth
hollowly between the black fireplace and the view window
that opened on a dark downward slope studded with pale
gray rocks that loomed like ghosts when the moon was
shining.

He started to crumple up the roadmap and pitch it in
the fire, but decided that would be attaching too much
importance to the coincidence.

The next evening he was alone and seething a bit. His
lovely little dimwit had called him up to say that her folks
were still on her neck, acting like they'd got the wind up
about something. But she'd ditch them tomorrow for sure
and be very nice to Joe if he'd just forgive her for standing
him up again and if he'd have some bennies for her. Joe
had grumbled at that and made her crawl and promise a

bit more before finally agreeing. Once more he stubbornly decided against a call girl, telling himself it sometimes did a man good to wait a night or two.

The phone rang as he seethed. It was Flagstaff, Arizona. This time there wasn't any wailing on the wires, just the dial tone. Apparently the other party had hung up immediately.

It was more than Joe could take. He talked to the operators and put in a long distance call to the pay station from which the broken-off call had originated. He got tavern sounds and the voice of a hard-boiled babe.

"Look, mister, I don't know about no phone calls. It's not my job to watch this booth. Mister, there's been fifty guys in and out of here just in the last ten minutes. I'm being paid to wait on them, I got no time to watch them.

"Mister, there hasn't been a woman in here all night— except for one fat old bag in a dirty white leather coat. You wouldn't be interested in her—nobody would. She looked terrible. I asked her if she was sick and she said yes, and ordered gin on the rocks—"

Joe poured himself four fingers of aquavit and then threw it in the fireplace and laughed loudly at himself and his moment of panic as the flames blazed up wildly.

As the next evening closed down, Joe Grimaldi was alone again at his new canyon home. A man less able to laugh at himself would probably have been somewhere else.

The evening had not started pleasantly. The dimwit had called to say that her parents had her locked in a hotel room and they were going to have her committed for her drug habit and would Joe break in and rescue her and remember to bring some bennies along for the love of God.

She knew Joe could get away with it she had said, because her parents were so scared of him they were thinking of going to the police about him. Joe had told her to go to hell and suggested that the quickest route out was out of the window.

Then he'd rung Agnes and after she'd told him that the first three girls he mentioned weren't available tonight for home calls, he'd bawled the hell out of her too, and told her to get at least one of the trio to him if she valued the reputation of her service. Then he'd slammed down the phone before she could say anything.

At that point he almost decided to drive into town. He stepped out into the car port and stood by his pale yellow Jag, weighing his desire against his stubbornness. The brief California twilight was almost over, and the rock-studded hills around him stood out spectrally in a faint yellow light.

With the faintest sigh of rubber on asphalt or perhaps with no sound at all, a big car came gliding down the dark gray two-lane road that circled downward in a seaward direction from the nearby crests past Joe's narrow terrace. It was one of those black, seven-passenger cars that Joe had been recently told were smart second-hand buys if you could stand their looks, because they'd never been driven at more than twenty miles an hour, ferrying relatives of the deceased from some mortuary to some cemetery and back again.

The funeral car seemed to be coasting, out of gear, motor off, but swiftly gathering speed as it approached the jutting shoulder of rock and the low fence of stout white posts and white-painted steel cable that marked the first of a half dozen hairpin turns.

Joe could see no one behind the wheel—no one in the car at all—as it disappeared behind the shoulder. He waited for the *thud-scrape* of it hitting the cables and maybe for a series of diminishing crashes as it went over the cliff. But there was no sound at all. He dug a finger in his ear and shook his head.

As if by some instantaneous chemical reaction the faint yellow drained out of the air. Joe got in his Jag and sat there for ten seconds, his finger over the starter button, and then he got out again and went back in the house. He expressed his reaction with harsh peals of laughter, but they changed to a choking fit. This time he didn't throw the aquavit in the fire.

He went to bed rather early that night and blacked out almost at once, remembering before that, however, to pull the curtain across the one tiny window and double-lock the door that opened on the side patio.

A series of dark wind-filled nightmares were finally succeeded by an extremely satisfying dream in which Joe sat wagging a pointer behind a teacher's desk in front of a classroom of big girls, including the dimwit and Agnes' trio, who were wearing little girl dresses. He had set six of them the task of writing on the blackboard a hundred times, "I Will Do Everything Joe Grimaldi Tells Me." He studied their six cute behinds as they laboriously copied and re-copied the letters.

Joe woke up. The dream lingered while in the dark bedroom, then faded. The squeak and scrape of chalk changed to the dragging of fingernails across the screen of the little window.

In the mood in which the dream had left him Joe was sure it must be one of Agnes' trio or maybe even the dimwit. He grabbed the flashlight, stepped quietly across the room, jerked aside the curtain and shot the light through the 18-inch opening into the face of Eleanore Dovgard.

She looked as beautiful as he ever remembered her, just a trace thinner and with the faintest of dark smudges under her wide gray eyes. Her lovely hair, beautifully dressed, was like a turban of spun silk, ghostly in its fineness. The upturned leather collar brushing her chin glistened whitely.

She showed no surprise at the light but pleaded softly, "Joe, oh Joe, let me in. I've made myself beautiful for you, Joe, but I don't know how long I can hold it. Quick, Joe."

Joe Grimaldi was above all else a practical man, even in his reactions to the supernatural—which up to this point in his life had been a meaningless term. The girl outside the window was a beautiful dish and he was still very close to his dream. Analyzing was for dopes who didn't know how to grab opportunity.

"Just a second, Nore, I'll have the door open," he said as he moved to it.

He was slow on the double lock and as it yielded she

pushed her way through. He ran the flashlight up her body—
and writhed backward from her.

The stinking thing that had pushed through the door was
so grossly fat the soiled leather coat covered only the back of
its shapeless dress. The face was puffy and yellow white and
streaked with dirt. The hair was a rat's nest.

"I couldn't hold it, Joe," the thing croaked, pawing at him
frantically. "Love me, Joe, so I can come back."

Joe tore himself away, plunged into the living room,
clawed open the door to the car port, jumped in the Jag,
punched the starter button, and took off down the hill,
nursing the motor as it alternately choked and whined. The
cold air whipped his green silk pajamas but he didn't feel it.

He was rounding the third hairpin turn when he saw
the big black funeral car moving up behind him, still
without lights. He risked a look back and it came round
the turn after him. The beam of his backing light struck its
windshield and behind the steering wheel he saw Nore, slim
and golden-haired as she'd been outside the window.

On the fourth turn he skidded and scraped the fence. He
knew he shouldn't be in the third gear. But the black car was
coming up.

Approaching the fifth turn he tried to double-clutch back
to second. The back of the car seemed to lift sideways as he
braked. His backing searchlight again struck just over the
hood of the black car, spotlighting behind the wheel Nore
as she'd been inside the door.

The white-painted cable twanged as the Jag went over
the fence. The car turned over in the air so that it was like a
pale yellow canopy over Joe Grimaldi as he fell in his green
pajamas. Then a pale gray rock came out of the dark below
and smashed him.

With a long squeal of brakes like a tuba's bray the black
car came to a stop fifty yards ahead. The bloated thing in
the filthy leather coat craned her neck out of the right-hand
window and frowned. Little flames started fifty yards back
and about the same distance below. They swiftly grew bright

enough to show the red blood on the pale rock. The frown on the face of the bloated thing vanished.

"You can sit up now, Nore," she said.

The slim golden-haired girl in the spotless white leather coat unfolded herself from the left-hand corner of the front seat. "It's about time, Marge," she said. "I don't want to double up like that any more and I don't want you to drive doubled up and just peeking, even if it's part of the game. It's too scary."

"The game's over, Nore," Marge Dovgard said, taking out a handkerchief and beginning to rub her fat cheeks. She sighed. "Now maybe I'll be able to take off some of this weight."

"Aren't you going to play any more with Joe?" Eleanore Dovgard asked. "It's his turn to scare us now. Joe! Oh, Joe!"

"Shut up, Nore! The game's over."

"Well, if the game's over, I want my coat back," Eleanore complained. "They're going to be mad at you, Marge, stealing me out of the hospital and saying I was dead in the papers."

Marge shrugged. "Come on, slip across me," she said. "We've got to change seats right now. You and me."

The fire behind and below them flared. Marge looked straight ahead as she switched on the headlights.

"Cheer up, kid," she said, as the car eased forward, "we're going home."

DARK WINGS

R OSE LOCKED THE stout screen door of heavy mesh behind them, then closed and double locked the solid door, put on the chain, shot the three bolts (high, medium, and low) and squatting somewhat precariously on her high heels, tugged at the door's hinged buttress-bar to free it from its clamp.

Vi said mischievously, "Now we're locked in for the night," but when Rose looked up startledly, explained , "just the tag line of one of the standard ghost stories," and remarked, "you really do things thoroughly."

"A girl can't be too careful," Rose stated, tugging some more. "There have been three burglaries since I moved here a year ago, two muggings just outside the lobby, and one attempted rape. Oh blast!—this always sticks. I won't let a strange man inside my apartment unless the manager's with him—she's a woman. Ow!—now I've pinched my finger." She winced and sucked it.

"Par for the Village," Vi said. "Here, let me."

She knelt effortlessly, one leg stretched out behind, her back straight, freed the buttress-bar with a controlled jerk, and forced its end into the socket in the floor-plate. There was a harsh, grating, rather high-pitched scrape and click. Rose winced again.

Vi said, "That sort of sound sets my teeth on edge too. But why do you shut your eyes?"

Rose replied, "I've got synesthesia—I see sounds, hear

colors, that sort of thing. My psychiatrist says I'm a classic case. She says most people only imagine the colors, but I actually see them. The bar was a lilac flash, my pinched finger a bright red one. It didn't break the skin, though," she announced after studying it closely. "Come on, Vi, let's compare some more. There really wasn't a proper mirror in Nathan's," and rather shyly taking the other young woman's hand, she led her to a large mirror that made up one third of the inner wall of the pleasantly furnished, medium-size one-room apartment.

"It really is remarkable," she said softly after a bit.

"As we already decided at Nathan's," Vi reminded her, but her voice was a shade awe-struck too.

Anyone studying the two faces side by side, as they were now, would have concluded that beyond the shadow of a doubt these two were identical twins. Their figures were alike—slender, petite. Vi was two inches shorter—her flats—but Rose toed off her shoes and that difference vanished. Rose wore a knee-length blue dress that buttoned down the front and her blonde hair in a page-boy bob that brushed her shoulders. Vi, a trim blue slack suit, a shirt of paler blue, and her blonde hair cut short, almost *en brosse*. They looked like one of those delightful, genetically impossible sets of boy-girl identical twins from Shakespeare, only in this case Violet was Sebastian and Rose, Viola.

Rose said, "Blue is my favorite color."

Vi said, "So is mine."

Rose said, "I had my appendix out a year ago."

Vi responded, "They took mine too—year and a half."

Rose said, "My first pet was a kitten named Blackie."

Vi echoed, "And so was mine, believe it or not, Little Black."

Their eyes were getting wider all the time.

Rose continued, almost chanting, "I have a mole on my left breast."

Vi grinned, held up a palm, and swiftly unbuttoned her shirt. Rose gave a start, drew off a little, and watched uneasily in the mirror. Vi, studying her sidewise, pulled down her paler blue singlet of ribbed lightweight cotton, exposing her small, attractive breasts, a dark brown mole on the inner curve of her right one.

She said insistently with an odd undercurrent of amusement, "For a moment you were scared I was a man after all, got in past your locks. Well, weren't you?"

"Well, yes," Rose admitted uncomfortably, blushing, then said eagerly, "but you do have a mole, and on your left breast too."

"Wrong, right," Vi corrected. "You're looking in the mirror which reverses. We're mirror-image twins, like all identicals. Now, how about you?" She smiled.

"Oh, yes," Rose said apologetically, quickly beginning to fumble at the neck of her dress. "There's a tiny hook and eye here. I can never—"

"Let me," Vi said cooly, still smiling, and undid it, then went on efficiently to unbutton the top of the blue dress. Rose was wearing a dark blue brassiere. Vi's eyebrows lifted.

Rose explained hurriedly, "Mother—I mean my foster mother got me to always wearing one. I still don't ever wear pantyhose," as she took over, saying, "this hooks in front. With my all-thumbs fingers I never can work the ones that hook behind. There. See the mole?"

The touch of awe briefly returned to Vi's voice as she said, "And to think that two hours ago neither of us knew we had a sister, let alone an identical twin."

Rose said, "Vi, why do you suppose our foster mothers never told us about each other?"

Vi chuckled harshly. "Mine would never have told me anything nice. She hated me, because foster papa liked me— and more and more the more I grew. Dig?"

"Oh," Rose said feebly, hooking her brassiere again. "My foster father was sort of weak and timid. Mother—my foster mother, I mean, ran everything, especially me. She smothered me with love, very possessive and jealous, and wanted me to be like her exactly. I guess that's why she never told me about you. You'd have been a rival. You might have taken me away from her."

Vi's chuckle was bitter, though the undercurrent of distant amusement was still there. "The wonder is they told us our right birthdays."

"So we could find out tonight they were the same," Rose took up. "Just think, Vi, in three weeks we can have a birthday party together—two Children of the Moon."

"That's right, dear sister, two Cancers, the dark sign," Vi agreed, giving Rose's waist a brief squeeze with one arm as she moved away from the mirror towards the day bed with its light paisley spread and scatter of gay pillows.

"Gee, it's so strange to have someone calling me sister," Rose said, smiling in wonder.

"Not just someone," Vi reminded her, grinning mischievously back over her shoulder.

"That's what I mean," Rose protested, "a sister calling me sister ... sister darling," she added, getting a lump in her throat as she said the two words.

Vi nodded as she looked the bookcase over and then studied more closely the dozen volumes between collie-dog book ends on the low table in front of the day bed, as she sat down on it.

"You have a lot of books," she observed.

"I'm in the publishing business," Rose explained. "That is, I make indexes for a man who is. Say, would you like some more coffee? I'm going to make some," she continued, opening some light folding shutters in the nook that also held the bathroom door and revealing a small refrigerator top, electric stove, and sink all in line with cupboards above and below.

"That would be fine," Vi said. "I dance for a man who does TV toothpaste commercials. I'm the third vampire. We dance slow motion in filmy negligees that float out very artistically all over a huge bathroom, baring our teeth. Then Dracula comes in, flashing *his* teeth, in a black dressing gown, a head taller than any of us and very thin, and we make love to him with our large dark liquid eyes, flashing our teeth some more, and he holds up the toothpaste we all four use as (in the newest version) we come together for a group tooth-baring, facing camera. Actually he's gay. And then four evenings a week I have my ballet classes."

"Why, I've seen that commercial," Rose said, filling and putting on the stove the silvery hemisphere of the teakettle. "But you don't look like you. Your hair—"

"—is a long black wig," Vi interrupted. "And then those three-quarter-inch eyelashes do something to my face. Not to mention all that blood-red lipstick, which they varnish on so it won't smudge our teeth. It takes us fifteen minutes to get it all off afterwards. But not Dracula—the make-up boy is his very special friend. Say, these books are interesting— more twin identicalities." And she read off, "*The Plays of Shakespeare, Newman on Twins, Fear of Flying, Women and Madness* by Phyllis Chesler, *The Wind in the Willows,* Jung's *The Archetypes, Animus and Anima,* by Joan S. Rosenbloom, M.D.—that's one I don't have—"

"She's my psychiatrist. My firm published it. I did the index," Rose said proudly, sitting down on the day bed two feet from Vi, between her and the casement windows, which were open a third of the way and locked in that position. Traffic sounds floated in irregularly and the faint steady thud of a hi-fi's woofer. "You know the animus, of course, if you've read Jung—the male self that haunts and inspires and sometimes terrifies each of us women, overshadowing the shadow. The equivalent of the anima in a man." An intense look came into Rose's face, contracting her soft brow. She looked a little like a blonde Barbie doll being very fierce. "I'd like to be some man's anima, some young stud's," she said with surprising venom. "I'd terrorize him. I'd make him suffer."

"Think you'd be up to it?" Vi asked her playfully, but with the distance again, her chuckle throaty. "Like your foster mother terrorized her husband, eh? But worse than that, of course."

"I'm not sure," Rose confessed flusteredly, her face relaxing. "All the archetypes can be pretty frightening sometimes, just to think about. But to actually be one..." She hesitated, then blurted out, "You know, Vi, I've sometimes imagined they really existed. The archetypes, I mean. Not just in my mind, but somehow outside where I might see and touch them."

"Why not?" Vi asked lazily yet soothingly, apparently still playful. "That's how everything exists—outside. Nothing's just in the mind and nowhere else. Witches are real people, aren't they? Then why not demons and other so-called spirits? Jesus was a real person, wasn't he?—but also God. Then why not a real Jungian shadow moving around, a real anima? And a real animus."

There was a sudden rushing, whirring sound and something struck one of the black casement windows with a jar and rattled the pane sharply. Rose started to clutch at Vi, then checked herself, her face twisted towards the night.

"Relax," Vi said with a gentle chuckle. "That was just a bird. A lost and mixed-up pigeon, probably."

"If it had been a pigeon, we'd have seen a flash of white. Did you?" Rose said rapidly, breathily. "Or a dove. They're white too. Some of them nest here, under the eaves."

"There are black pigeons—and black doves too, I suppose," Vi said. "Relax."

"Yes, and black hawks and eagles ... and other things. Besides, that was too heavy for a dove or pigeon."

Vi sat up a little, smiling with a mixture of amusement and tenderness, and slowly reached out a hand, saying, "A black eagle in Manhattan! What would it do, Rose? Fly in ominous circles over Wall Street?" but before her fingers quite touched Rose there came a sudden fluttering whistle which swiftly grew louder and shriller. Rose got up hurriedly and crossed to the kitchenette, her hands ahead of her and her eyes closed or rather almost closed, like a person walking into a dusty wind.

"What's the matter, Sis? Are you getting more lilac flashes?" Vi asked solicitously, watching her.

Rose lifted the steam-jetting kettle off the heating element. The whistling quickly died.

"Yes, I was—bright ones that hurt," she answered sharply and a shade defiantly, reaching down a brown jar of coffee crystals out of the cupboard. "They started green, then went through blue to violet as the pitch rose. With streaks of red—the pain."

"I'm truly sorry," Vi said. "That must be very strange and frightening, what you have—and also very painful, your?..."

"Synesthesia," Rose supplied. "How big a teaspoon do you take? Level, mounded, or heaping?"

"It doesn't matter—" Vi began. Then, "No—heaping."

Rose brought the two steaming mugs over and set them on the table. "Watch out," she said rather huffily, "they're hot." Suddenly her eyes flashed and she grinned like a naughty girl. "Suppose I put a little brandy in them," she whispered loudly to Vi. "There's some left from a bottle I bought for Christmas."

"I think that would be fun," Vi told her.

Rose's eyes got bigger still with the mischief of it as she fetched and added the brandy, a pony apiece and then a little more at Vi's suggestion. They took a burning, aromatic, eye-moistening swallow together, looking at each other, and Rose confessed, "I got a little mad when I got scared and you just told me to relax. But now I'm feeling wonderful."

"And so am I," Vi assured her. "What is that mournful night sound?" she asked, eyeing the windows.

"Oh, that's the doves," Rose said. "Whatever it was must have waked them up. They nest under the eaves, as I told you, and this apartment is right under them."

"I'd think you'd be afraid of someone getting in that way," Vi suggested, serious eyed. "You know, down off the road, around the eaves, and in through the windows. Though he'd have to have a good head for climbing."

"Don't think I'm not," Rose assured her aggressively. "But they've each got a hook and also a bolt bar which can't either be unfastened from the outside when I leave them partly open in warm weather like this."

"That sounds completely safe," Vi said neutrally, drinking her coffee royale.

Rose took a big swallow of hers and said, "I know you think I'm silly, Vi, for being so scared and fussing so about my locks and bolts. But really, Vi, if anyone ever got in and raped me, I know I'd die, or else go crazy."

"You think so now," Vi said softly and bitterly, eyeing the floor. "Your locks and bolts—I think they're sensible."

"What do you mean?" Rose demanded. Then her eyebrows went up. "You mean that you?..."

Vi nodded.

"Oh, you poor thing," Rose gasped. "Oh my God, how horrible, how terribly horrible. How did it happen, Vi? Did someone con his way into your place, get you to take off the chain? Or were you out alone late at night on some dark street? Or—"

Vi shook her head. "I was home in my own bed, being a good girl," she said with a sour smile and wrinkled nostrils. "I told you that my foster father had a lech for me—"

"Oh, my God," Rose breathed.

"Well, one night when he was drunk—and after getting my foster mother dead drunk, of course—he just came into my bedroom and satisfied it. Afterwards—"

"Didn't you try to fight him off, Vi? Were you so terrified that—?"

"Of course I did and in every dirty way I knew," Vi said harshly, "but they weren't dirty enough and he was stronger."

"Oh my God, Vi, did it hurt?"

"It hurt like hell," Vi said savagely. "But even that wasn't as bad as the way he slobbered over me afterwards, telling me how sorry he was. There wasn't even much blood. No, the worst thing was being touched—and not only touched, but invaded—where only you have ever touched yourself before, and then only very gently, very tentatively, almost reverently, a special thing, just like (I suppose) a man touches his—"

"I know, I know," Rose groaned, rocking back and forth. "I've dreamed of it."

"Anywhere else, almost, they have to cut you with a knife to get inside you," Vi said viciously. "But there—"

"I know, I know," Rose echoed herself agonizedly. "I *hate* to be touched there, even by cloth."

Vi caught her breath, drank the last of her brandy and

coffee, and said in another voice, a more open and even roughly humorous one, "I'll give the gays this. At least they know what it's like to be raped."

"How do you mean?" Rose asked, gulping the last of hers.

"Oh, come on, Rose," Vi said impatiently, but with a little grin, "you've got the books right out there, dear identical: the Masters and Johnson, *The Joys of Sex*, even *Anomalies and Curiosities of Medicine*—you know, that's the only other copy I've ever seen of that oldy besides my own."

"Yes, I do know how you mean," Rose admitted, looking away, "but really, it's all so horrible and disgusting and frightening. Oh, I don't see how you managed to stand it, Vi."

"I wasn't asked whether I wanted to," the other said shortly.

Rose said, "At least you got back at that horrible beast a little by telling your foster mother?"

Vi replied cynically, "She'd have been the last one to believe he would ever have had to rape me. She had her own evaluation of Sweet Fourteen.

"Now, come on, Rose, it's not so terrible," Vi continued, "or rather, yes, it was just that terrible, but it's all over now. It happened long—well, fairly long ago. As for the gays, they're mostly quite charming, or at least funny. The make-up boy I mentioned has breasts, for instance—cute little silicone ones. Of course the nipples are a little small."

"I don't believe that," Rose protested, clapping her fingers to her mouth to smother a nervous giggle.

"True, just the same," Vi settled back and her face got a tight little smile. "Besides," she said, breathing deeply, "I got my own back at my loving father, let me tell you, in my own sweet time and way. After—"

She broke off because there was a repetition of the whirring, rushing sound and again the black pane was jarred and rattled with no flash of white, as if a ragged portion of the night had launched itself down at it, only this time the sounds kept up—there was a frantic beating and loud rapid brushing at the pane and then a series of higher and higher pitched, skirling, inhuman cries.

And this time Rose clutched at once at Vi through the bright magenta flashes that had invaded her eyes.

Her twin clasped her protectively, saying, "There, there, Rose, it's all right. It's just a bird again, only this time it's somehow caught itself. My God, your heart is pounding. I'm looking over your shoulder straight at the windows and I can't see anything through them or in the space between them, except maybe a sort of black flashing. There, there, I'd better go and try to release the thing. No, let me go, Rose, it's the only way we can make the noise stop."

Terrified, palms pressed to her ears, Rose watched through slitted, lash-blurred eyes and purple floods as Vi went to the windows and stood before them, a slender blue figure against the big black square they made, turning sideways to thrust a shoulder through the narrow space between them and all that arm and her cropped blonde head and her other arm to the elbow. Between the torturing, skirling cries, which rose in volume, and the beating, which became still more frantic, she heard Vi give a sharp exclamation, then both cries and beatings were receding rapidly, the pitch of the former dropping, and then the sounds were cut off completely, almost abruptly.

In the shocking though very welcome silence that followed, Vi withdrew her upper body from the night and turned around and said, returning towards Rose, "It was a large black bird I didn't know, some kind of predatory hawk, I'd think, a *raptor*, though certainly not an eagle, perhaps a crow or raven. Its wing was caught under one of the bolt bars. While I was loosing it, it struck me twice with its beak, but—" (She lifted her hand towards her eyes and rotated it) "—it didn't break the skin."

All this while Rose was staring at her as if hypnotized and without moving a muscle except that her hands dropped slowly away from her ears.

Vi seated herself on the day bed close beside her, between her and the window, and put her arms around the frozen form and pressed her chest against hers firmly and, turning her face sideways so their noses missed, kissed her upon the lips.

A distant foghorn sounded, a car turned a corner far below, a dove mourned, and then time began to move again.

Vi reached for the brandy bottle and the miniature goblet of the pony glass, saying, "After that fright you need another drink."

Rose said, as if still half in a dream, "That was the first time that we ever kissed. Identical twin sisters. Imagine that."

Vi said companionably, but with her voice a shade brisk, like that of a nurse, "Here, drink this down. You need it straight. No, all at once."

Rose complied, shuddering.

"That's a good girl," Vi said and kissed her quickly on the corner of the mouth.

After a moment Rose returned the kiss in the same way.

Vi left one arm lightly beside her twin's waist. Her other hand lay against Rose's knee. She asked, "During that ruckus did you have your synesthesia?"

"Yes, very badly," Rose replied, wincing in recollection. "I never had it quite as bad, in fact."

"What color were the lights this time?"

"Violet. I never had so much violet before."

"Perhaps I am responsible for that," Vi joked with a chuckle. "My name, you know."

"Silly," Rose said indulgently, giving the hand that lay against her knee an affectionate squeeze. Then, more seriously, though still a shade dreamily, "I wonder if those were our real names from the start. Could be, you know. They're both flower names."

"Maybe," Vi said, "or maybe not. Maybe our real mother never had time to give us any."

"Do you suppose we're illegitimate?" Rose asked solemnly.

"I'd think so," Vi replied. "That's where most foster children come from."

"But maybe they were married," Rose said happily, her

elbow pressing Vi's hand against her waist. "Maybe our father died early in the Vietnam War."

Vi said, frowning a little, "There's one thing bothers me about your synesthesia."

"What's that?"

"That I don't have a trace of it. Which is strange, seeing we have so many other twin identicalities."

Rose said consolingly, "You probably have some other equally distinguishing peculiarity or ability or trait to match my colored sounds thing. There's your ballet dancing—how about that? You're terribly graceful and strong and competent-fingered ... and brave too," she added, looking over Vi's shoulder at the black windows and remembering the slim blue fingers fearlessly thrust between them. "By comparison, I'm clumsy as a cow."

"No, a big floppy dog," Vi decided, running her fingers lazily into the pageboy bob and twice pushing the side of Rose's head—who sketched a bowwow comically and said, "That's right. And you're a kitty cat."

"But dancing and finger dexterity and all that are things that are learned," Vi said more seriously. "You could develop them too if you practiced and exercised instead of sitting inside all day making your indexes—and reading all night." She nodded towards the bookcase. "They're not like your synesthesia," she finished regretfully.

"You think that's so great?" Rose challenged lightly. "You should try it some time. But maybe you've got a mix-up on some other senses." She pulled away a moment to gesture at the thickest book on the table between the collie book ends—*Anomalies and Curiosities of Medicine*. "I remember the case of a girl there who heard odors as sounds. Or was it sounds as odors? I forget. Or maybe you've got absolute pitch or are double jointed or—"

"Oh, if you're using *that* book, anything goes," Vi asserted happily. "Maybe I've got supernumerary nipples, or a little hairless tail, like that noble European family—I haven't looked today. Or six fingers on each hand—no, five, I just counted. And then there was that woman who had a clitoris four inches long when stimulated."

"Vi, you're making that one up," Rose protested, seeming to flush, and looking aside.

"Oh, no, I'm not, as you know very well," Vi laughed, bringing her head around to look her twin straight in the eyes. "I thought so. Somehow that's the first thing everyone reads."

Rose squirmed.

Vi grew thoughtful, the distance coming back into her eyes. She mumbled, "I wonder if that would be the animus—a female with a penis? The grand hermaphrodite. Or would that be the anima? Or neither?" She looked behind her towards the night outside and said more clearly, "You know, Rose, when I was at that window with that bird, I had the strongest feeling of the presence of one of the archetypes."

"So did I too!" Rose blurted out tensely. "It was very scary, something beyond the flashing lights and pain."

Vi embraced Rose reassuringly, one hand upon her shoulder, the other on her cheek, pressing her other cheek against her own. "There, there," she breathed and Rose was comforted.

Vi gave them both a little more brandy and said, "Remember how you said you'd like to be some man's anima and torture him?"

Rose nodded. "Though I don't think any more that I'd be up to it."

"So? Well, I was once my foster father's anima. After he raped me I knew I was going to leave home for good, but I wanted to get my own back at him first—or should I say our own? I got ready to leave—money and clothes, an address in New York—and all the while I watched him like a hawk. For a while he held off from me. He was afraid, of course, he might have got me pregnant. He hadn't—I had my period a week later, though I took care not to let either of them know. A few nights after that he tried the same trick again—getting my foster mother dead drunk and all—but I was ready for him and I kicked him in the balls (I'd kept my shoes on) so that he squealed and fainted."

Rose breathed, "My God."

Vi continued, "The next couple of days my foster mother kept asking him why he was walking bowlegged and bent over. He said it must be rheumatism inherited from his great grandfather, who'd fought in the Civil War.

"You'd have thought he'd have had enough by then, of course, but he kept trying—men are such fools, or rather they have an endless blind persistence when it comes to *that*. This time he changed his tactics. After he'd put my foster mother to sleep again, he presented me with a dozen red roses and a real diamond ring and the *cutest* black silk peekaboo panties and half-cup brassiere—he even had the right size.

"And this time he'd decided he had to get me drunk too because I was such a smart and worldly little bitch. I played along with it, pretending to get soused with him and promising him that just in a little while longer I'd model the brassiere and panties for him. He kept stumbling around after me in circles. The music throbbed, the lights were low, and every little while I'd dump a little whisky down my neck to make me smell as if I had been drinking.

"Eventually he passed out blotto flat on his face on the floor. I took what cash he had and what more he and his wife had around the house and brought down my bag—it was already packed—and then I hauled down his pants and greased my old toothbrush and rammed it up his ass, bristles first, all the way in."

Rose gasped, "My God. *My God*!"

"And then," Vi finished, "I scattered the dozen red roses over him and departed that place."

She took a deep breath and let it out. Rose sat frozen, as if in thought or shock.

Vi asked, "So how does it feel to have a twin sister who's a criminal, who rips off loose cash and sees that the men she disapproves of get buggered?"

Rose shook herself a little, smiled nervously, and said

quickly, "Oh, no, it feels all right. It's just that my own foster father was so very different. He was very gentle, almost timid with me. I can't remember him ever touching me. He treated me like a little stranger princess. He read me fairy tales and books like *Winnie the Pooh* and *The Borrowers* and *Little Women* and, later on, *Wuthering Heights*. He had poor health and couldn't get good jobs. He would have liked to be a beatnik poet. I thought he was perfect until— but that came later on. No, it was from my foster mother that all the violence came, the things that frightened me and ruled my life."

"That figures," Vi said. "I mean, you said she was possessive and bossy?"

"She was more than that, Vi. She was the power and she was the law. She was almost—My first memory was of her leaning over my bed and smiling down at me fiercely like the sun, bare to the waist and with her arms and breasts thrust out to either side like Theda Bara, as if she were trying to imprint her personality on me. She called her breasts her wings."

"Jesus, how corny," Vi commented. "What a kook."

"I can see that now," Rose said. "She studied Zen and karate and shaved her legs and armpits with a straight-edge razor. She said the books my foster father read me were romantic crap and that he was trying to make me weak like him. She was always bawling him out for not being successful and showing more manhood."

"I'll bet," Vi said, "especially in bed."

"She fussed a lot about my health and keeping clean and not getting infected and not touching myself or letting anyone touch me. But she was always touching me herself for inspection or instruction, especially my private parts (she called them, but they were anything but private to her, you can believe me). She made me do her exercises with her. And she was always quick to give me slaps, which always made my foster father wince, although he never did anything to stop her. She said I needed reminders—it was Zen. But every once in a while she'd snatch me up and hug me fiercely, holding me high as if I were some sacrifice, or as if she were trying to inspire and terrorize me at the same time. I was plain scared to death of her. As soon as she came near, I'd tighten up."

Vi shook her head. "The things they do to us, one way or another."

"For a long while she scared me off other children. I made up an imaginary playmate, a little girl exactly like me except her mother was dead." Rose's eyes widened. "Oh, Vi, do you suppose I somehow knew I had an identical twin? Or that there's been telepathy between us?"

"Could be," Vi said thoughtfully, "but maybe most imaginary playmates are like that."

Rose continued, "But eventually I got to have a real girl for a pal, a black girl who was very slender and had narrow hands and long fingers like ours. I think she must have had Watusi blood. At first it was because she had a kitten. We'd play together on the way home. She loaned me Wonder Woman comics and Vampirella and Pantha."

"I used to read those," Vi said. "Was Pantha the one who'd change into a black panther to destroy her parents and teachers and men who bothered her?"

"That's right. One dark afternoon we dared each other to go into a park we weren't ever supposed to. A storm was coming on but we kept daring each other to stay. It started to rain a little and we took shelter under some trees on a hilltop. Then thunder growled and the wind blew hard, tossing the leaves and branches, a siren started to wail down in the city, and we got this feeling that there were great dark wings over us. We both got very scared and held each other tight. And then it quieted down and we were touching each other.

"Oh God, Vi, to be touched with love! Not like my mother, as if you were something she owned and could handle exactly as she pleased, but something that's respected and understood and cherished."

"I know," Vi said softly, coming closer again, their hands lightly meeting. Rose went on, "For a while we were very happy, but what happened next, as you'd expect, was that my foster mother found out about our friendship. She was too smart to make it a racial thing—my foster father was very leftist in some ways—but that my little pal was light-fingered. She pretended to catch her stealing and called up her parents. There was a row and we were not allowed ever to see each other again. And then I found out that she'd also seen us touching and once kissing because she gave me an awful spanking, to teach me, she said never again to risk getting infected and that, although there was nothing wrong with black girls, they could never help me to be successful.

"And after that she seemed almost to be more worried about girls touching me than boys. Of course it all put me off other kids again and I read a lot and even tried to write poetry and stories myself. That brought my foster father and me quite close for a while. He still read to me and we even talked about writing and things, although my foster mother watched us like a hawk and kept ranting about success and the main chance and how we both would be better off in mental hospitals.

"But she couldn't object to my next girlfriend (who came three years later) because she was from a wealthy Northshore political Irish family (her father was a state senator) and wore very expensive clothes and was white of course. My foster mother even tried to get palsy with her at first. But Siobhan could be very snotty in a ladylike way.

"Siobhan always had lots of spending money. With that and her hauteur she got us into adult X-rated movies. Jane Fonda was our idol. We ate up *Klute* and *Barbarella* too. We romanced about becoming spacewomen and call girls. Under her snotty shell she was in many ways naïve as I and lonely too. One of us would pretend to be Snow White and the other would wake her. It was together that we learned French kissing and to pet to climax. And once we smoked some marijuana she'd snitched from her brother. I was wildly happy, but also very scared too from time to time—I'd get that dark wings feeling. Vi, would you be mad at me if I had some more brandy?"

"Of course not, Rose," the other said. "I'll have some too. To tell the truth, I was more shaken up at the window than I let on."

"Why? What was it?" Rose demanded uneasily.

"At first the thing that was caught there seemed too big and yet somehow too insubstantial for a bird—as if it were a frantic invisible being in a cloak of bright black feathers."

"Oh God! But it *was* a bird?"

"It was a bird," Vi assured her. "Here's our drinks—ah, that's better. Now how did your mother manage to wreck things this time?"

"She went to Siobhan's father at his office (she told me this when she confronted me) and made a big scene there, accusing Siobhan of corrupting me sexually and getting me on drugs and threatening to go to the other political party and their newspaper if he ever let Siobhan see me again. Of course he denied everything, but actually she'd hit on just the right way to throw a scare into him. Siobhan was taken out of school and sent to one in the East, I think. At any rate I never saw or heard from her again.

"And then my foster mother headed home, breathing fire, and confronted me with my foster father there, telling him his Little Miss Innocent and Fairy Princess was nothing but a dirty little lesbian bitch and demanding that he whip me with her razor strap and when he wouldn't, jeering at him and telling him then he could watch her do it.

"Oh God, Vi, it was awful. He pleaded with her, or rather he kept repeating that he didn't think it was wise or right— things like that—but, oh God, Vi, he didn't even try to stop her and he didn't run away, he stayed."

"And you just stood still and let it happen," Vi observed gently.

"No, Vi, I didn't," Rose sobbed, tears spurting from her eyes. "I fought hysterically then but—just as with you and your foster father—*she* was stronger. She twisted my wrist behind my back and forced me over, making it weirdly sexy, and then she whipped me. It hurt like hell, God how it hurt, there was some blood, but the worst thing was that I knew he was getting a thrill out of it. His little princess, and he was getting a thrill!"

"There, there, it's over," Vi said soothingly, drawing Rose's head towards her shoulder.

"But it wasn't, Vi, that wasn't the worst," Rose said, dry-eyed now, pulling away. "After that happened I knew, like you, that I had to get out of there. And I guess my foster father knew that same thing, because two days later he ran away with a young hippy woman it turned out he'd been having an affair with, but oh God, Vi, he didn't take me with him.

"I could have forgiven him being a coward and afraid to stop her—I was scared to death of her myself. I could even forgive him having sexual feelings seeing me whipped—I'd had sexual feelings myself, and not always at the nicest things, but oh God, Vi, he didn't take me with him! He ran away and didn't take me with him."

Vi did not move to comfort her this time. Instead she studied her cooly and thoughtfully, missing nothing, not the track of one tear, as if Rose were an artist's model taking a pose and Vi the painter. Her pale blue eyes were at once sympathetic and merciless, and the distance within them was very great.

She said at last, "Not to be loved, to find yourself betrayed ... it's a very dry pain, isn't it? As if you were being tortured on the rack for witchcraft and then they stop, the instruments relax their poignant grip, the blinding light recedes and the tormenting endless, nagging questions come to an end.

"At first all that you feel is blessed numbness and a great enfolding silence. You think with quiet joy that perhaps you are dead at last.

"And then every last injury they've done you comes to excruciating life. There's the refinement of the cruelty—*they* don't have to do anything to you at that point; your body does it all, remembering. Yes, each hurt they've ever inflicted on you begins to throb unceasingly, the pitch mounting and mounting, until you think the agony can't become greater, but it does.

"And then you pray that they will start torturing you actively again—anything, *anything*, to disturb the embrace (as if it were a second skin) of that dry, fiery shroud."

"You must have been there too," Rose said quite quietly. "Well, after my foster father ran away, my foster mother became quite insane in her hatred of all men ... and of all girls too. She acted as if all the males in the world and every woman younger than herself, but especially the teen and sub-teen girls, the nymphets, were in a vast conspiracy against her. She kept threatening me with reform school and the mental hospital and she whipped me again.

"But then she overreached herself, thank God!—she really was crazy, Vi. She actually petitioned to have me sent to reform school as an uncontrollably wayward girl. I went to my high school English teacher, who'd encouraged me about my writing, and told her about it, and she brought in a social worker who was a friend. I still had the weals and cuts from the whipping and my foster mother went into a sort of fit in court. In the end I was put in a halfway house for girls with family problems like mine—or yours, Vi ... fathers and brothers with incestuous tendencies.

"And for the next couple of years or so I lived a strange sort of half life there and in similar places (and really it's gone on—the limbo life—here in the Village too). They dunned my foster father and mother too for my support and got a little money from each of them from time to time, with difficulty, and they shifted me around between agencies.

"When I say half life, I mean in several ways. I came close to the edge, mentally, more than once. I was still basically a very shy child and my experiences made me shrink away from friendship. And after those whippings my mother gave me I just didn't have any sexual feelings at all for a long while. A doctor once told me that if the mind doesn't trust a sensory message coming from some part of the body, it registers it as pain—the panic reaction. So for that time most sexual feelings were actually painful to me—and frightening. A finger touching me would seem to burn—it's mixed up with synesthesia, I'm sure.

"And then I was very mixed up as to how I felt about girls and sex generally. A couple of young women at the institution where I lived openly boasted about being lesbian, as if it were something very special, which didn't turn me on at all. I also knew that the people on whose good will I depended, even my English teacher, didn't approve of and wouldn't sympathize with that sort of thing at all. So I knew I had to hide any feelings like that and my experiences with my little Watusi and Siobhan.

"And all the while I was still terrified of boys, of course—I mean young men—and still am, you can believe me. Knowing it was my foster mother's strange teachings and my foster father's betrayal didn't change that one bit and never has. And that basic fear of mine was reinforced when a male counselor tried to seduce me. He actually tried to use sleeping pills to help, Vi, can you imagine? And then a girlfriend here in NYC who'd said she was uncertain about which sex she was, fell for a man real hard and got the idea one night it would be real cute and a big favor to me if he introduced me to sex with men—whether under her active supervision or not I never learned. I almost panicked before I managed to get rid of them.

"Well, anyway, my English teacher stuck with me through all this, the darling! And as soon as I was barely old enough, helped me to get the job that I hold now. She thought I needed a change of city and she was right. I even inherited this apartment from an old friend of hers.

"So here I am, Vi, living my halfway life, making indexes, and trying to be a writer. I've just had a story rejected by *Cosmopolitan*, but they wrote a nice letter saying that it came close and asking me to keep submitting."

"I've my ambitions too," Vi said.

"Ballet?" Rose asked.

"In part," Vi answered. "But ultimately solo pantomime—concise, dramatic acts, historical, contemporary, and fantasy. My own costumes, settings, music—everything. There was a dancer and mime named Angna Enters. Something like hers."

"That's wonderful," Rose said. "Maybe I could write acts for you."

"I'm sure you could and maybe I could give you ideas for stories. Will you write one about tonight?"

"I don't know," Rose said thoughtfully. "Long lost twin sisters find each other -where's the conflict? It's all happy ending."

"You'd have to work out a surprise premise for it," Vi said rapidly, sitting up straighter. "Suppose I were a young man who looked exactly like you—maybe identical twins of different sexes are possible this once. I have this overpowering lech for you, but I also know about your locks and bolts and fears. So I have my breasts injected. I even know about your mole and duplicate it—"

"Oh, Vi!" Rose said reprovingly. "That's just too complicated."

"Well if we _were_ identical twins of different sex," Vi argued, "maybe I'd have female breasts too with the mirror-image mole, so I wouldn't need injections. Maybe only the primary sex organs would differ."

"Stop it," Rose said. "I don't like that plot—it's too farfetched. Besides, you're thinking like your foster father." Her hands moved as if she were going to button the top of her dress.

"I do believe I've frightened you again," Vi teased, grinning a little.

"No, you haven't," Rose denied, her hands dropping away. "Remember, along with your breasts I've seen your nipples. It's just that I've gotten depressed. Reaction, I guess, or maybe the brandy. And then you start—" She broke off and impulsively moving closer, her arms hanging limp, her hands with palms upturned, said in a quavering, oddly tragic voice, "Vi, comfort me."

Vi did not move, except that her gaze wandered about Rose's face and shoulders, dropped to the supine hands, then traveled up to the woeful eyes again. She was smiling tenderly, but her own eyes had the distance in them.

There came that skirling cry, muffled this time, and

(muffled too) a high, twanging sound, as of something sharp scraped across metal mesh. Rose started violently, wincing, then twisted around abruptly to look at the door. Vi got up then and moved towards it.

Rose followed her closely, hands trembling, but poised as if about to grab the other's shoulders, crying, "Don't open it!"

Standing on tiptoes, Vi put her right eye to the fish-eye lens set just above the little door-in-a-door masking the grille.

"I can't see anything," she said cooly. "The hall light must be out," and unlatched the little door.

"Don't!" Rose said, clutching her shoulders now, but Vi opened it.

Another skirling cry, unmuffled, came knifing in and with it the brushing and beating of wings and the unnerving scrape of claws (or was it that?) on heavy wire.

"Still can't see anything," Vi reported tersely. "A black flashing—"

The sounds broke off except that of something like a huge but unsubstantial bird blindly brushing and buffeting about in the black hall.

"Please close it," Rose implored. Vi did so.

Unmindful of Rose dragging her back, Vi said, "I really should go out there—"

Rose said, "No, No!" —

"though how that bird managed to get inside—" She looked at Rose and said reasonably, "Well, should we call the apartment manager (there is one?) or the police?"

"The phone's disconnected," Rose said miserably. "I let the bill get too big."

"So—?" Vi said quizzically (they could hear nothing now outside the door) "—well, we could scream."

Rose answered. "The room was soundproofed by an earlier tenant—my English teacher's friend."

Vi smiled. "Well, I suppose we could always open the windows wide and scream together—"

"Don't make fun," Rose protested. "Oh, Vi, I'm so scared

and miserable. You've just got to stay with me tonight. Oh, Vi, comfort me. Take off your clothes and come to bed and comfort me," she pleaded, clutching the other again and pressing her head between the other's neck and shoulder.

After a bit she heard Vi say tenderly but very deliberately, "Very well, I will." Then she felt her hands being gently but firmly disengaged and put to her sides and then she felt the pressure of Vi's palm in the small of her back, guiding her back to the low day bed.

"Sit down," she heard and did so on the edge, looking at her stockinged knees. She heard Vi moving around. The lights went out. There were soft sounds. Then Vi returned and sat down close to her. The soft glow from the bathroom showed her Vi's dimly gleaming knees beside her own and she saw how alike they were. Then with a little sob that surprised her (she thought she'd quieted down) she turned to Vi, who'd left her singlet on, and clutched her, saying, "Oh, Vi."

"Be still," she heard Vi calmly order her. "How can I comfort you properly if you're crawling all over me?"

Again she felt her hands being gently but firmly disengaged, only this time Vi put them behind Rose's back and pinioned the wrists in her left hand.

Rose looked up shyly into Vi's ghostly face, the eyes dark smudges below the close-cropped head, neat as a bird's, and said, "We've both got very long-fingered hands, only yours are stronger."

"Is that bad?" Vi teased and then, nodding towards the books, "You've read about it all in *The Joys of Sex*, I'm sure—bondage and discipline. Do you like it?"

"Unless it gets too scary," Rose confessed, lifting her fact to kiss Vi's chin lightly.

"Well, as to that, one cannot tell ahead of time. We play by ear," Vi said, giving her a soft peck between the eyes. Then her right hand went to Rose's brassiere. Pinching one cup between thumb and forefinger and the other between little finger and palm, she drew them together and used her middle finger to nudge loose the hook. She touched

Rose's breasts in turn and leaned her cheek against them. Vi's eyelashes felt to Rose like a tiny bird fluttering. She felt Vi's hand trail down between her breasts and then finish unbuttoning her dress.

Vi lifted her face, smiling, and drawing Rose's arms a little farther down behind her back to expose her neck, gave her a gentle nip between the hinge of her jaw and her collarbone, and then again on the lobe of her ear, breathing humorously, "Don't struggle—it won't help you. I'm the third vampire, remember?"

Rose felt quite frightened and yet not afraid, as if there were flashes of light on the verge of vision or at its edges, too faint to hurt or even to be seen. She felt adventurous.

Still holding her wrists tight, that arm against Rose's hip and garter belt, Vi slipped around and knelt on the carpet in front of her, very close to Rose (still on the edge of the low day bed) but with back so straight that her face was on a level with Rose's, even a little higher, her eyes flashing in the gloom.

Rose thought, "I'm like Andromeda chained to the rock. Only the monster's friendly."

As if Vi were reading her mind, she heard her say, "It's fun to play with fears, now isn't it? You could safely imagine now that your twin's also a bird-woman, one of the archetypes, even. The animus."

Rose felt the spread fingers of Vi's right hand push into her hair and through it around the sides of her head to the nape of her neck and grip a large lock there (it pulled her scalp) and lift her face, bending it back a little, and then Vi kissed her mouth, her eyes, her cheek, her neck, her breasts. It took her breath away, she gasped, "Oh God, oh Vi," and seemed to hear, but only in her imagination, only playfully, the rush and beat of wings, the skirling cries, Vi's fingers velvet talons and her soft lips a beak.

She felt Vi press her body more closely against her own, front to front. She tried to push away, but Vi's strong left hand pinioning her wrists pressed them into the small of her back, against her coccyx, so that she couldn't move in that direction and the stockinged soles of her feet kept slipping on the carpet as they pushed frantically and finally kicked.

And then she felt (she experienced it as a point of intensely bright white light, shockingly painful) the unknown forcibly and irresistibly entering her between her legs.

She gasped, "Oh no, oh no," Vi whispered fiercely, "There, there," the point of light grew to an almost blinding white-hot moon that suddenly began to flash with scarlet. She squeezed her eyelids but it didn't stop. Vi's shrewd right hand closed alternately on her breasts, now left, now right, lightly pinching her nipples, her wrists and Vi's left hand pinioning them were like an iron knot at the base of her spine against which her body was jolting violently, there was a bitter taste at the base of her tongue and a brimstone stench high inside her nostrils, she heard Vi whisper, "The ego is not inaccessible, you see," and then she was seeing Vi through flashes of black light that made it seem as if her twin's slim dancer's body was covered with bright black feathers and the night itself was like great dark wings beating rhythmically, there was a skirling and deep booming in her ears, and Vi was saying through her devouring kisses in tones that kept gathering force, "There, there; there, there; there, *there*!"

SOME NOTES ON THE TEXTS

John Pelan & Steve Savile
(With thanks to David Read)

SINCE WE FAILED to provide comprehensive data on the stories included in *The Black Gondolier*, our inaugural volume of Fritz Leiber's stories (an oversight that many readers saw fit to call to our attention); and it's somewhat safe to assume that readers of this volume have also purchased the aforementioned, we'll include information on the stories from the first book as well. We have several other Leiber collections in the works due to a discovery of a considerable amount of previously unpublished material. At least two collections will be predominantly SFnal in content and will be published under the Darkside Press imprint. These books will be identical in format to *The Black Gondolier* and *Smoke Ghost,* with the only substantial difference in presentation being the imprint.

There are several reasons for doing this, not the least of which is to avoid an identity crisis here at Midnight House. We are a publisher of weird and horror fiction and realize that many of our readers may not care to include Science Fiction in their collections, conversely, those that do want the entire Leiber set will be able to have a nicely matched set of volumes. I fully realize that Leiber (and several of our other authors, most notably Bob Leman) often blur the boundaries between genres. In the case of these books there may well be some SF in the Midnight House books and some weird or horrific elements in the stories in the SF collections, but by and large we'll attempt to split the tales up in a manner that will seem at least somewhat logical.

THE BLACK GONDOLIER

"The Black Gondolier" 1964, *Over the Edge* (Arkham House)

"The Dreams of Albert Moreland" 1945, *The Acolyte* (Spring)

"Game for Motel Room" 1963, *The Magazine of F & SF* (March)

"The Phantom Slayer" 1942, *Weird Tales* (January)

"Lie Still, Snow White" 1964, *Taboo* (New Classics House)

"Mr. Bauer and the Atoms" 1946, *Weird Tales* (January)

"In the X-Ray" 1949, *Weird Tales* (July)

"Spider Mansion" 1942, *Weird Tales* (September)

"The Secret Songs" 1962, *The Magazine of F & SF* (August)

"The Man Who Made Friends with Electricity" 1962, *The Magazine of F & SF* (March)

"The Dead Man" 1950, *Weird Tales* (November)

"The Thirteenth Step" 1962, *The Fiend in You* (Ballantine Books)

"The Repair People" 1980, *Transmission*

"Black Has Its Charms" 1984, *Whispers 21-22*

"Schizo Jimmie" 1960, *The Saint Mystery Magazine*

"The Creature from Cleveland Depths" 1962, *Galaxy* (December)

"The Casket-Demon" 1963, *Fantastic* (April)

"Dr. Adams' Garden of Evil" 1963, *Fantastic* (February)

SMOKE GHOST &
OTHER APPARITIONS

"Smoke Ghost" 1941, *Unknown* (October)
"The Power of the Puppets" 1942, *Thrilling Mystery* (January)
"Cry Witch!" 1951, *Ten Story Fantasy* (Spring)
"The Hill and the Hole" 1942, *Unknown* (August)
"The Enormous Bedroom" Original to this volume.
"Black Glass" 1978, *Andromeda 3* (Futura)
"I'm Looking for Jeff" 1952, *Fantastic* (Fall)
"The Eeriest Ruined Dawn World" 1976, *The Ides of Tomorrow* (Little & Brown)
"The House of Mrs. Delgato" 1959, *Rogue* (May)
"The Black Ewe" 1950 *Startling Stories* (May)
"Richmond, Late September, 1849" 1969, *Fantastic* (February)
"Replacement for Wilmer: A Ghost Story" 1990 Philcon Program Book
"MS. Found in a Maelstrom" 1959, *Short Stories for Men*
"The Winter Flies" 1967, *The Magazine of F & SF* (October)
"The Button Molder" 1979, *Whispers 13-14* (October)
"Do You Know Dave Wenzel?" 1974, *Fellowship of the Stars* (Simon & Schuster)
"A Visitor from Back East" 1961, *Mike Shayne's Mystery Magazine*
"Dark Wings" 1976, *Superhorror* (W.H. Allen)

ABOUT THE AUTHOR

Fritz Leiber is considered one of science fiction's legends. Author of a prodigious number of stories and novels, many of which were made into films, he is best known as creator of the classic Lankhmar fantasy series. Fritz Leiber has won awards too numerous to count, including the coveted Hugo and Nebula, and was honored as a lifetime Grand Master by the Science Fiction Writers of America. He died in 1992.

OPEN ROAD
INTEGRATED MEDIA

Open Road Integrated Media is a digital publisher and multimedia content company. Open Road creates connections between authors and their audiences by marketing its ebooks through a new proprietary online platform, which uses premium video content and social media.

CPSIA information can be obtained
at www.ICGtesting.com
Printed in the USA
JSHW031212150922
30555JS00001B/18

9 781497 642195